HEATHER GRAHAM
CARLA NEGGERS
SHARON SALA

On the Edge

ISBN 1-55166-711-8

CONTENTS

BOUGAINVILLEA

Heather Graham

Prologue _____

It had been foolish to make threats, Marina knew. Obviously. But, then, she'd been so angry, frustrated and powerless, and in all honesty, her temper had always been her downfall. Well, there was nothing she could do about it now. Her words couldn't be taken back.

She blinked back a sudden onslaught of tears, thinking of the people she had not meant to hurt. Including herself, she reflected wryly. But she had been feeling weepy. Still was. But she shouldn't have been drinking. Drinking always compounded everything. Along with the guilt, anger, and sorrow that were going to haunt her when she turned the world upside down tomorrow, she was going to have a crippling hangover.

She quickened her pace along the walkway that led deeper into the grounds of Bougainvillea, the vast Delaney estate, knowing that she might somewhat calm her state of anguish if she could just reach the beach, feel the soft breeze that came with the late afternoon, and watch the sunset falling over the pond near the docks. This is what she would miss. She loved the property as no one else did. Unless it was...

That despicable man!

Oh, they were all despicable. Seamus, Martin, Lenore, Josh, Kaitlin. Sometimes even David, because he could look at her with such strange eyes...

Then, if the household wasn't enough, there were the

neighbors. Always there. Martin Callahan and his darling little Shelley. And Eli.

The ones she needed to be thinking about were Mark. And Kit.

Not now, she was in such a roil of anger!

She quickened her pace and reached the beach at last. The scene before her was postcard perfect. Lazy palms, drifting in the breeze. Golden sand, stretching out to the surf. The water, with small whitecaps forming that just caught the dying light, and dazzled beneath it like diamonds. A little crane strutted along the beach, at once elegant and gawky. A gull swept down, and the crane took flight.

"Marina!"

She heard her name called, and she knew his voice. As she turned back, she trembled, both with fury and because she wanted what she shouldn't have. Even when she knew better.

"Don't!" she told him as he caught up with her on the beach. "Don't come near me…this is entirely wrong, and I'm going to leave, do you understand?"

But he kept coming anyway, and his features carried the same agonizing torment as her own. He reached out and pulled her into his arms and ended her tirade with a passionate kiss. In those first moments, she would have pulled away. But he was stronger, and proving his force. She stiffened, willing to fight…but for no more than embarrassingly brief seconds. Then a sense of nostalgia seized her. She was leaving…just one last taste of everything that was forbidden, and she would spend her life repenting her sins, repairing the damage she had done…

With that logic and illusion, and of course, a bit of the alcohol coursing through her bloodstream, she began kissing him in return with equal passion. Hot, wet, greedy kisses as they fumbled with each other's clothing. He shoved her skirt up to her hips while she ripped his shirt from his pants, and slipped her hand beneath his belt line, fondling his erection. Half undressed, they tumbled to the damp sand together. They made love desperately, like a pair of maddened animals, natural perhaps, for the lover she had taken. For brief moments in the aftermath of their violent mating, she was sated and satisfied, as if something had come to completion. Yes, she'd needed this once more. A tempestuous and dramatic goodbye. If *nothing* else, we've had this passion, burning too brightly perhaps, so illicitly, but precious nonetheless. Because it's so sweet to have this power, something I can lord over one man...

That would devastate another.

Remorse set in.

But she reminded herself once again, she was leaving. And she would use the years ahead to atone for all that she had done.

Tomorrow, she would become everything that she should have been all along. A good wife. Lord knew, her husband deserved as much. More than that, she would be a good mother. She had always intended to be.

Tomorrow....

Tomorrow she was leaving. Before that, however, she would see to it that she carried out her threats. She meant to tell everything that she knew.

She meant to atone.

And so, by God, would the others.

All of them.

For everything.

But that would be tomorrow! Her resolve was strong; she could and would change. But for now, she needed to cherish these last few precious seconds. She would first finish what she had begun, then she would leave, and never look back.

She had just seconds left.

And then...

Tomorrow.

But for the moment, they lay side by side, both aware that they were going to have to rise, and deal with the fact that they'd mangled each other's clothing and that they did have to go back to the house. But she didn't want to talk yet. She just wanted to feel what it was like to lie beside him as if she belonged there. The sun had now created beautiful crimson streaks across the sky. The ocean was darkening, the whitecaps would soon have to look for moonlight, and the color of the air was dusky and gentle and the breeze was sweetly sensual.

"Marina—"

"Shh. Just close your eyes. Hold me, please. Just for a minute."

He held her. He closed his eyes, as she did. The palms whispered softly as the breeze lifted them.

The parrots were back.

Early every evening, the little buggers escaped their tourist-attraction home and hightailed it across town. They landed in the trees, and they began squawking. Making tea in the little bungalow on the Delaney property that had been her home since 1935, old Mary O'Hara, retired now from her post as head housekeeper, looked out her rear windows.

"Birdies!" she exclaimed with disgust. "Bloody, wretched birdies!" she continued, raising her fist toward them. She shook her head, wondering how any creature that screeched so loudly and annoyingly could entice a paying audience. Ah, well. The parrots hadn't always come here. Maybe they'd find a new place to visit soon.

She made her tea, sat in her rocker and turned on a repeat of *Hollywood Squares*. She just loved game shows. And at her age…well, there were only so many pleasures left. She raised the volume on her television. All right, she was nearly as old as God himself, and maybe she was losing her hearing a bit, but it was those bloody birds forcing her to turn the TV so high, and that was a fact!

She paused for a moment, predicting that sometime to-night Marina would come. Mary's hearing might be bad, but she did still know what was going on around the place. She believed that she had talked the girl into her senses. Marina, for all her madness, was one of those few pleasures Mary had left, along with her reruns. Marina always made her laugh. Mary loved the girl, and knew for her own good, Marina had to leave. But she would come to say goodbye. But until then…

Mary turned up the television again. The birds were so loud! She simply wasn't able to hear any of the punch lines.

Marina had been too sated, and too wrapped up in the drama of her own life, to notice anything else in the world. Lying there, in his arms, on the beach, was, at least, far too perfect an ending.

She had become too comfortable, and she had actually dozed. So much for the great trauma of guilt and proposed redemption.

She awoke slowly, groggily, feeling as if she already had a hangover. She thought at first that it was him tugging at her to awaken her, that he wanted to make love again. *No.* She had said her goodbyes. And there was someone else who mattered more now, someone who mustn't pay for her sins. She opened her eyes. Her head was foggy. She could barely move. *It wasn't him…was it?* She blinked, thinking incredibly briefly that it might be good that they had been caught together half-naked on the sand because that could force everything out into the open. Everything. She could just admit it all, not just this, but the entire truth of every-thing at Bougainvillea, and her fellows in deception and sin would be brought to answer for everything that they had done as well. All the duplicity and the illicit truths. Those who were innocent could choose whether or not to for-give…

She realized that it was not her lover trying to awaken

her. She was being…dragged. And she didn't just have a hangover; it was something else. She could barely twitch. Barely think, function, reason…

Then she knew. The drinks she'd had that night. They'd seemed more potent than usual. She'd thought that it had been her mood, her recklessness, her anger. But there was more. She should have known. She knew it now, because this was no simple hangover she was feeling. She had been drugged.

She tried to move, tried to understand what was happening to her. Who was taking her…

Where.

And *why*.

Then she saw.

She could hardly purse her lips or even breathe deeply, and she couldn't seem to control her limbs at all.

Her throat seemed…locked.

She forced her lips to open. Forced air into her lungs. Prayed for sound. And at last…

She started to scream.

Because although her limbs were like lead, her mind was working. She understood then exactly what was happening. And why.

She kept screaming. High-pitched, terrible. She knew that she had to keep up the desperate summons for help.

Her lips wouldn't really form at all, certainly not into words. And still, noise came from her. Shattering in the foliage. The dense foliage.

Someone must hear. They must.

She felt her body, sliding roughly over sand and little outcrops of vegetation. Felt the roughness, the hold on her body, and still, she hadn't the power to move or fight.

Tomorrow, she realized desperately, *might never come!*

She fought…and screamed louder. And screamed…and screamed.

Until her screams were silenced.

Forever.

Mary leaned forward, trying to catch an answer from the pretty young starlet in the middle square. The birds had started shrieking again, right at the most important moment of the show. Mary missed what was said, but she saw the stars laughing, and the contestant win the prize.

Damned parrots.

Shrieking and shrieking. They sounded just like a woman, screaming in bloody terror.

1

As Kit slowly awoke and opened her eyes, she saw a man standing in the doorway. He was very tall, and in the shadowy, dim light he at first appeared to be dark—and sinister. She had the uneasy feeling that he had been standing there, staring into the room in silence for a long time. Staring as she slept, making her feel oddly vulnerable.

His shoulders were broad beneath a heavy winter coat, and he seemed to stand very straight, with a great deal of confidence and assurance. She sensed that he wasn't watching her. He was watching her father.

Waiting for him to die.

Kit blinked, and awkwardly tried to rise, wanting to demand to know who he was, and what the hell he was doing. But when she blinked, he was gone. There was no man in the doorway.

Frowning, she rose and walked to the door and looked out into the hall. There was no one there, either.

She'd fallen asleep in the hospital chair at her father's side, and apparently dreamed that he was there.

"Katherine Delaney, you're losing it—though exactly what 'it' is I'm not sure, nor am I sure you ever had it," she said aloud to herself, trying to dispel the unease that had settled over her. She looked around her father's darkened hospital room once again. It had been late afternoon when she dozed. It might well be late in the night now. Shadows were everywhere.

Kit watched the IV's clear liquid as it dripped, traveled along the length of tube, and entered into Mark Delaney's vein.

He hadn't moved for a long time, and until she had opened her eyes to see the vision in the doorway, neither had Kit. Of course, it had been longer for him. He had lain in a coma for more than a week now, and it was doubtful that he would ever awaken again. She had accepted that fact. There had been days when she had tried not to cry because she had wanted to encourage him as though he could still hear her. There had been days when she had cried buckets. Now, there was an acceptance in her heart, but she had no intention of leaving him now, not until the very end. And it didn't matter whether he knew that she was there or not.

She knew.

A rueful half smile curved her lips. In her dozing, she had probably had strange snatches of dreams. Her friend Jennifer would say that she was having desperate illusions. Her subliminal mind was *inventing* a tall, dark, mysterious stranger for her, since it had been months now since she had done anything but work or spend time with her dad. Jennifer basically understood, but she shook her head over the fact that Kit hadn't taken so much as a few hours to go out and find a handsome hunk, a suitable dinner companion or—for sanity's sake—a one-night stand on her own.

"Jen, it's just not the time," she said softly, and looked down at her father. His illness had ravaged his features, but he was still handsome. His cheeks were sunken, his eyes were closed. But she would remember them, forever. Bright powder-blue, full of life, laughter and wisdom.

"Kit?"

She started as Sherry, her father's very skinny but wonderfully compassionate and competent nurse, slipped quietly into the room. Had it been Sherry she had seen in the doorway before? Had Kit, in strange, quiet dreams of drifting time, imagined the nurse to be a tall stranger in a winter coat?

"I didn't mean to startle you," Sherry said.

"No, no, it's okay."

"He showing any signs of distress?"

Kit shook her head. She knew that the doctors had told the nurses all they could do at this stage was make their patient comfortable. When he needed more morphine, he was to get it. But he hadn't shown any signs of distress. He hadn't shown any signs of life, either, other than the little blips on the screen, for days now.

"Honey, it's way, way past dinner time. You go on out for a few minutes. Stretch, walk, get yourself something to eat and some coffee."

"I don't want to leave him alone."

"I'm signed out, my paperwork is done and the night shift nurses arrived a long time ago," Sherry informed her. "I'll sit right here with him and read up on the new drug literature."

"Sherry, you've worked all day! I can't impose—"

"Get!" Sherry said firmly, settling into the chair by Mark Delaney's side.

Kit started to protest again, but Sherry had already turned on one of the lights and opened her book. "You're ruining my concentration," Sherry informed her.

"Thanks," Kit said graciously. She did need to get out of the room.

It was late, she realized as she walked down the hallways. Past regular visiting hours, though the fact that the hospital offered all private rooms kept patients' family coming in and out around the clock. No one seemed to be around at the moment. The hallways were entirely deserted as she walked toward the elevators. "Shades of *Halloween II!*" she murmured softly as she punched the down button.

She hadn't seen the slasher movie in years, but she could suddenly recall a limping Jamie Lee Curtis being chased along empty hospital corridors. The homicidal maniac coming after her relentlessly. In the movie, the night nurse couldn't help because she'd been having sex in the hot tub with another hospital employee and the murderer had boiled them both. Kit, however, sincerely doubted, that, should she need help, the hospital staff would all be parboiled in the therapy whirlpool. Sherry would be indignant and furious at such a suggestion.

Scary movie, though. Jen would probably say that it carried a subliminal message warning employees to avoid sex in the workplace.

Strangely, she was actually feeling a little nervous. Sure, people would show up if she screamed, but of course, they would think her a maniac, and have her escorted out of the hospital—and possibly admitted into another kind of institution. She had nothing to be afraid of here, and she knew it. It was strange how the mind played tricks. Especially now, when she was so tired. However, the emptiness of the corridors still seemed a bit eerie.

The cafeteria would definitely be closed, she thought, walking along the ground floor hallway. Maybe *Halloween II* hadn't been quite so silly. She'd changed floors and hallways, and still hadn't encountered another soul.

"Kit, get a grip!" she said, then realized that she'd spoken aloud to herself several times in the last hour, and groaned.

"Coffee, I need coffee!"

She was doing it again. But she spoke aloud often in the hospital room, talking to her father. As long as the graph on his monitor was "blipping," she was going to talk to him.

The cafeteria was closed and locked, but she'd learned through experience that, oddly enough, the vending machine in the snack shop made decent coffee, even going so far as to offer a choice of Colombian, cappuccino, espresso, and French roast. Naturally, however, as she stood in front of the machine, she realized she had no change. Ah. The machine took dollar bills.

Except for *her* dollar bills, she realized with aggravation as the machine spit back her third one-dollar bill.

"Dammit! I *do* have the president facing the right way!" she informed the machine.

She dug through her bag and tried all five ones in her possession, but the coffee machine continued to spit them back. Frustrated, she swore and kicked the machine.

"May I help?"

The deep, slightly amused male voice coming from behind her startled her so badly that she jumped and spun around, her heart in her throat. She almost expected to see the maniac from *Halloween II* standing there.

But of course that murderer hadn't looked anything like the stranger before her.

This man might have stepped out of the pages of *GQ*. Jen would say that he was "devastating, to die for." He wore a business suit, expensively cut, possibly Armani or Versace, she guessed. He was tall, broad-shouldered, and wore the suit well. It was late, and he had loosened his tie; the weariness about him seemed to add to his rugged good looks. She estimated him to be somewhere between thirty and thirty-five years old, with dark-auburn, collar-length hair. His eyes were true brown, without a touch of hazel, so dark that they appeared black as coal. He was bronzed as though he spent a lot of time in the sun. Strange, Kit thought, since snowstorms were currently plaguing the north from Seattle to Maine.

She realized that she was just staring at him. And for the first time in forever, she was wondering about her own appearance. Naturally, she was a disaster. Wearing worn jeans and a Museum of Natural History T-shirt with a large dinosaur that appeared to roar. Her hair was probably clean enough, but not brushed. And she wasn't wearing a speck of makeup, but maybe that would be all right. She was supposed to look a great deal like her mother, and Marina, she had been told, had possessed some of the finest coloring in the world, with hair so dark her father described it as the "ebony of a raven's wing" and eyes "so blue they were like the sky right when dusk began to turn to twilight."

Ah, the human mind! She wanted to explain to the stranger that she was usually halfway decent looking. Then she wondered what difference it made, he was a man visiting a relative, compassionate enough to try to help her get some coffee, and she was here...well, she was here for very serious reasons. How could she even worry about something so superfluous as looks at a time like this?

"May I help?" he repeated politely.

Embarrassed, she felt herself flushing. She wasn't usually dumbstruck at the sight of a man, not even one as imposing as this.

"I'm so sorry. You startled me. The place is so quiet. Like a morgue." *Bad choice of words.* "If you have any more luck with machinery than I do, I'd be grateful for any form of a cup of coffee."

He grinned, stepping by her. "It *is* quiet here tonight," he said. "Sorry, I didn't mean to scare you."

"I wasn't scared."

He looked at her, arching a brow slightly. He clearly didn't believe her. "Good," he said, reaching into his jacket and pulling out a leather wallet. His bills were clean and crisp and hadn't been wadded into a messy purse like her crumpled ones. The machine took his dollar instantly. Kit resented the machine and wondered if an inanimate object could have feminine traits and respond to a man.

"What would you like?" he asked her.

"What would I like?"

"Coffee—espresso?"

"Oh, I'm not just going to get coffee, but the choice the machine promises. French roast, thank you," she said, flushing again as he pressed the right button. Coffee poured into a foam cup. He reached for it, handed it to her, then put another bill into the machine and hit the same button again. She was still just standing there, staring at him.

"I—thank you. Oh! How rude of me, I'm sorry. Here's one of my reject bills—" she began, offering him a dollar.

He shook his head. "It's all right. I needed coffee myself."

"Thanks so much, but I can't let you do that—"

"It was a dollar. Just a dollar. And I got change back, too." He fingered the coin return, and produced several quarters. "See?"

"But really—"

"Are you a raging feminist?" he inquired, a dark brow arched, his smile amused.

"No!" she exclaimed. "Well, of course, I believe in equal rights and equal pay and—"

She broke off, because he was subtly smiling at her. Not in a mean way. She didn't need to explain herself.

"I'm not a raging feminist," she said evenly. "Thank you for the coffee." She could be gracious, and judging by the cut of his clothing, he could certainly afford to squander a few quarters, even on a stranger. What did he do for a living? she wondered. Attorney, she decided. He'd be wicked in court.

"My name is David Moore," he said, offering her his hand.

She smiled, accepting it. "Kit—Katherine, Mr. Moore, and thank you very much for the coffee."

He inclined his head slightly. "You're staring at me strangely, you know."

"Am I? Sorry. I'm tired I guess."

"You were thinking something," he prodded.

She laughed then. "Yes, I was. I was thinking that you look like you should be an attorney."

"Prosecution or defense?"

"Prosecution—or defense, either. I admit, in my mind's eye, I saw you making mincemeat of a witness on the stand. Or…telling a jury with passionate indignation that they can't possibly convict a man for such a horrendous crime on circumstantial evidence."

"Hmm, interesting. Do I look like an ogre?"

"Fierce. Intense—or possibly cool as a cucumber. Are you an attorney?"

"I keep up my credentials in the state of Florida, but I haven't practiced for a while."

"Ah, but you were an attorney!"

"Yep, I worked for the district attorney for several years. And I was with a firm in private practice as well."

"But no more?"

"No more." He didn't explain further. Looking at his suit, she wondered if he'd won a lottery. Florida. That explained the tan. It didn't explain what he was doing in frigid Chicago. "And you?" he asked.

"Pardon?"

"What do you do?"

"Oh. I do a syndicated comic strip."

"Great. Have I read you?"

"Maybe. I'm just beginning to get picked up. I do a little strip called *Annie's Day*. Pitfalls of day-to-day life, dating in the twenty-first century and the like."

"Ah. Nice."

"Have you seen it?"

"Yes, I think I have."

"You're just being polite."

"I'm seldom just polite."

She arched a brow, sipping her coffee, shaking her head. "I can't believe that. You came to my aid with your dollar bills. Oh, and listen, I'm sorry to have kept you. I imagine you're here to visit someone?''

"An old friend, a man I haven't seen in years. In fact, I believe I've made the trip for nothing, so it was delightful to talk with you.''

"Your friend has passed away?''

"I just asked about him at the information booth. They said that if I waited, a nurse would be free to speak with me. I may not even get to see my friend. He's in a coma.''

Suspicion triggered quickly in Kit's mind. "What's his name?'' she asked thickly.

"Delaney. Mark Delaney.''

"My father,'' Kit said softly.

He arched a brow very high, and seemed to reassess her. Carefully. He smiled. "I should have known. Kit. Katherine. Katherine Delaney. You didn't say that.''

She kept staring at him, confused. "How could you have known? Or—should I know you? You're an old friend of my *father's?*''

He nodded, smiling ruefully. "A voice from the past, actually.'' He hesitated. "And I should have known you because you're the spitting image of your mother. I'm not so sure you'd remember me, but, yes, you did know me. You were very young at the time, but once, you lived at a huge estate called Bougainvillea. On the water. Your mother died when you were just six—''

"She drowned.''

He nodded. "Your father was devastated when she passed away. He left Miami—and never returned.''

"I have a very vague memory of Florida,'' Kit said, intrigued. "My father didn't want to remember a lot. We didn't talk about it. I do remember a big beach area, ponds, long grass, lots of flowers, a big old house with arches and gables...partially constructed out of coral rock. I had a wonderful room with a tiled balcony. And I remember a vague assortment of people there—but forgive me, how rude, I don't remember you.''

"You were a child. And I was the adoptee, you see, away a lot of the time,'' he explained, and when she knit her brows in puzzlement, he continued. "Years and years ago, in the late 1930s, my grandfather, your grandfather, and his cousin, Seamus Delaney, started a company called Sea Life Enterprises. They founded it on property bought by the first Delaney to settle there, soon after the turn of the last century. The main business is boats—speedboats and pleasure craft. Anyway, my grandfather was a designer, but he had a falling out with your grandfather and Seamus a few years before I was born, and split from the corporation. After he passed away, my father raced for Sea Life, and raced well—but he was killed one day while out diving. Old Seamus decided he had to take me in, so he did, and then shipped me right off to boarding school at every opportunity. So you probably didn't see much of me. When your mom died, I was away at school. And your father left Bougainvillea quickly after the accident.''

"How strange. I don't remember ever hearing about Sea Life.''

David shrugged. "Your grandfather had passed away, and your father sold his share of the business to Seamus. Your dad truly adored your mother, and I think the only way he could see clear to raise you was to start over completely. So he severed all ties to the past.'' He paused, shrugging. "That's why I don't practice law anymore...I wound up heavily involved in the family business. I'm also an avid amateur photographer, so...but, trust me, in business, that law degree always comes in handy.''

Kit nodded, "Yes, I can well imagine," she agreed, then shook her head, staring at him pointedly. "I'm grateful for the coffee, of course... But I'm not sure I understand why you're here. Now. At—at this late date.''

"I just heard Mark was gravely ill. And I didn't know

if he needed help. I knew, of course, that he had you, but I didn't know if there was anything I could do. Mark was always so damned decent to me. Seamus was a tyrant. He gave me what I needed—the best education money could buy. While your father..." He shrugged, lifting a hand. "He took me fishing. Taught me to dive. He took me to movies, out waterskiing. The fun stuff."

"By chance did you come by my father's room earlier?" Kit asked, remembering her dream.

"No, why? Was someone there?"

"I thought so. I'd fallen asleep...I might have been imagining things. I suppose it was the nurse."

David shrugged, then reached for her hand. "You know, I supplied the coffee, but you might be a godsend to me. I'd truly love to see your father. Could we go to him? If you don't mind me with you?"

"No...of course not. Except that...I'm not sure what good it will do you. The information you've been given is correct...he's been in a coma for days now and it's not likely that he'll come out of it."

He bowed his head. She couldn't see his features, or his reaction to her words.

"I would appreciate any chance to see him."

"Then certainly, come with me."

Sherry rose when they entered the room, her eyes round as she met David. She was impressed to learn that he and Kit shared a strange history, and her look fully conveyed to Kit that she should see what she could do to bring the past up to the present.

"Honey, your dad hasn't moved, he's hanging in. He's due for another shot in a few minutes. And two of your friends called—Jen and Steve. Both just wanted to wish you well and said for you to call them if you needed anything, anything at all."

"Thanks, Sherry." Kit gave the nurse a quick hug. Sherry bid her good-night, leaving her alone with her father and David Moore in the hospital room. David approached the bed. Kit watched his face, but the light in the room was so muted that she couldn't read his expression. He took her father's hand—the one without the IV needle.

He stayed for several minutes without moving or talking, then gently released Mark Delaney's hand and came to Kit. "I'll leave you alone with him," he told her softly. "This is your time, and I am intruding. But, please, when you're up to it, give us a call. Bougainvillea is your heritage as well." He produced a business card and handed it to her. "If you need any help—with arrangements, anything— please call."

"I'll be fine," she said. "But thanks. And some-time…certainly, I will call."

He bid her goodbye, taking her hands. His were strong, powerful, and seemed to offer tremendous encouragement.

"Thanks," she told him.

He left the room. Kit sat beside her father on the bed, taking his free hand in hers.

Hours passed.

She was nearly dozing again when she felt a squeeze against her fingers. She jerked to attention. Her father's eyes remained closed, but his lips were moving.

"It's okay, Dad," she said gently. "I'm here."

She leaned very close, trying to ascertain what his murmurings meant. She didn't want him suffering any pain. But she couldn't understand him.

"I'm here, Dad, I'm here."

To her surprise, her father opened his eyes. Sharp, clear blue, they stared up at her for a fleeting moment.

"Kit," he said fitfully.

"I'm here, Dad."

"I love you."

"I love you, too. So much."

He squeezed her hand again. His eyes closed, then opened again. They met hers.

To her amazement, he whispered one word.

"Bougainvillea."

His eyes closed again.

His last word.

David Moore walked into the penthouse office. Seamus Delaney was seated at his desk, but his swivel chair was turned toward the windows that overlooked the city. The view was spectacular, south-southeastern, encompassing the brilliant, colorful lights of downtown Miami to the immediate east, and Coconut Grove to the south. The panoramic view offered expressways, glittering water, beautiful residential sections—and the slums that came with any big city, but which were nicely concealed by the dark shadows of night. Night helped hide the sins of the city. Darkness was always kind to what was wicked. Still, David loved the city. Seamus Delaney did, too. It was an unspoken but mutual bond between them.

"You asked me to come," David said.

"Kit Delaney has yet to call, or appear." Seamus kept his back to David.

"Mark is barely cold in his grave," David said.

"I can read the papers…I saw his obit. He's been dead almost a week now. What did you do, hang around Chicago?"

"I went to the funeral."

"Was she surprised?"

"She never saw me. I kept my distance."

"You should have asked her right then and there to come home with you."

"This isn't her home."

"It *is* her home," Seamus insisted.

"Seamus, she's been gone nearly twenty years."

"I want to see her. I need to see her." He hesitated, aggravated. He spoke more softly. "This is important to me.... And that's the point. I've waited nearly twenty years. Tell me more about the girl.''

''Woman. She's all grown up. And she's going to need time. Mark was her father. Naturally, she's devastated.''

The man in the swivel chair waved his hand in the air. ''I don't want to know her current emotional state.''

David arched a brow. ''No, you don't, do you? Well, all right. But you want to know more about her now? She's just what you'd expect. You knew her as a child. And you knew Mark. He would have done all the right things, raising a child. His daughter is bright, charming—and incredibly attractive. As charismatic as her comic strip. Independent, capable. Reeling, at the moment. It will take her some time to get back on her feet. She was devoted to her father.'' He leaned against the back of Seamus Delaney's chair. ''Devoted, loyal. She adored Mark. Everything about her seemed admirable.''

Seamus grunted. Then he swung around, his hands folded prayer fashion before him. He tapped his lips thoughtfully with his fingers. ''Go back for her. Bring her here.''

''Bear in mind, Seamus, it's a free country—''

''Go get her. Do whatever you have to do. Just go get her, and bring her back here.''

''She'll come. When she's ready.''

''I don't want to wait any longer. I'm not sure I can wait any longer.''

David walked around the chair to the front of the desk, staring the old man in the eyes. ''And just what the hell am I supposed to tell her?''

''Tell her whatever you want. Do whatever you have to do. Just get her here. I need her *here*. Dammit, you owe me. I don't care at all how you manage it, just get her here.''

David straightened, shaking his head. He was about to

reply angrily. But Seamus issued one soft, seldom spoken word.

"Please."

David threw up his hands.

"I'll bring her here. *After* a few months. You're just going to have to hang on a while. I mean it, Seamus. I won't intrude on her right now."

"Dammit, David—"

"I'll get her here. In a few months. I will do my absolute best," he promised.

"There's a lot at stake. For you as well."

"For me?" David challenged, irritated.

"This is very important to me. I've waited. Now, it's my turn."

"I said that I'd do my best," David repeated.

Seamus nodded. "Time is at a premium. You must bring her back as soon as you can."

"Once again—I'll do my best."

David left the penthouse, angry, frustrated.

But hell, Seamus was right. He owed him. He'd go for Katherine Delaney.

And he would bring her back.

2

"**O**h, my God!"

Jen Harrison whispered the words while kicking Kit Delaney beneath the table. Kit winced, but didn't look up. She was sketching in a Valentine's heart as she autographed a copy of her first book for a young woman with a baby in her arms.

Jen was not about to be ignored.

"Oh, my God, will you look at what's coming next? To die for!" she whispered dramatically.

Despite her dedication to her task, Kit had to smile.

Jen was perfectly comfortable here at the New England Bookseller's convention, a massive trade show for writers and books of all kinds. Jen had been a popular comic strip artist for years; her *Down-Under Girl* strip had been in syndication for over a decade and the book she was signing today was the fourth she had written and illustrated featuring her main character. Kit, on the other hand, had known but a year's success in the syndication field and this was her very first book. Though she was determined not to show it, she could definitely describe herself as a nervous wreck. There were hundreds of publishers represented here, as well as hundreds of writers and illustrators—not to mention movie stars or pro athletes who might have written a book in the last year! Right before the show had opened, she'd felt a moment of pure panic—what if no one wanted a copy of her autographed book? The humiliation would kill—especially since the books were being given away at the trade show that also featured such revered comic artists as Jim Davis.

"And you thought no one would buy your book!" Jen teased, this time elbowing Kit so forcefully she had to look up.

She'd finished her sketch. Smiling, she handed the book to the waiting young woman, who thanked her in turn. The "to die for" man in line stepped up next.

She arched a brow, stunned. It was David Moore.

"Hi!" she exclaimed.

"Hi?" Jen whispered at her side. "Who is he?"

Kit ignored her, as David had apparently not heard her.

"Hey. How's it going? You managing okay?" he asked.

"I'm doing fine, thanks," she said. Then she shook her head, smiling ruefully. "I'm sure you're not at a trade show just to see how I'm doing, so…just what *are* you doing here?"

"I did a photography book—*Birds of South Florida*. Actually, it's a few years old, but winter in New England— the publishers thought a trade reprint might be in order, and this was a good place to get some word-of-mouth going." He lowered his voice, and leaned closer to her. His tone was husky and he smelled subtly of a spicy aftershave.

"Want to autograph a book for me? It will keep the folks in the line behind me from getting dangerously hostile while I talk to you."

"And come on to you?" Jen suggested in an audible whisper.

David didn't bat an eye. His small, rueful smile deepened. "And try damned hard to come on to you."

"A book—sure. Sure, of course." She was almost stuttering. Flustered despite herself, she opened a book and started writing in it.

"Are you free for dinner?" he asked.

"Oh, I don't know—" she began.

Jen kicked her. Hard. She looked at Jen who was staring at her as if she'd completely lost her mind.

She had to smile. She looked back to David. "I think that my colleague is assuring me I've no obligations to my publishers this evening."

"Thanks," he said to Jen, grinning.

"My pleasure," Jen responded, still staring at him. "It's the least I can do for a man honest enough to admit he's coming on to a woman."

"Miss Harrison, would you please do my book?" a fan asked, drawing Jen's attention back to the task at hand.

"Oh, I'm so sorry!" Jen said, and began writing again.

"Which hotel are you in?" he asked.

She shook her head. "My plane was delayed. I don't have a hotel as yet. I think I'm supposed to be at the Copley."

"I'll pick you up here then. Meet me at the coffee cart after the show. I've got a car. What about your bags?"

"All I have is one overnighter, but a car will be great, thanks. We'll meet at the coffee cart."

His dark eyes were on her. Sensual, amused.

"I'm sorry. Is there anything else?"

"My book?" he said.

"Oh!" She handed it to him, glad that her inscription seemed friendly, but not…fawning. *To David, with gratitude to a new friend in the right place at the right time! Kit Delaney.*

He read it in silence, smiled, closed the book.

"Thanks." He stepped quickly out of line.

"You know him!" Jennifer accused her softly, her head lowered as she signed a book.

"Not really."

"What do you mean, not really?" Jen demanded.

"I've met him once. Before. Well, supposedly I knew him a long time ago."

Jen handed the book to a little girl who wanted to grow

up to be an artist. Despite her conversation with Kit, she managed to tell the little girl to stick to her guns.

"Kit, this calls for an explanation," Jen said.

"We're only here another fifteen minutes...I've kind of told you about it before. We'll run out for a few minutes when we're done," Kit told her.

Jen didn't mean to let it slide. When their signing session was finished and the next group of artists came to take their seats, Jen immediately caught Kit's arm. "There's an actual sit-down restaurant with booths below. We're going there and you're going to give me all the dirt! I'm so, *so* pleased that it looks as if you're going to have some excitement in your life."

"I told you, I don't really know him."

"Ah, but I think you're going to," Jen said sagely.

Luckily, it was deep into the afternoon, and they only had to wait a few minutes for a table. Jen was anxious, demanding that they order first.

"We only ate three hours ago, and I'm supposed to be going to dinner," Kit protested.

"Eat lettuce, then. Order, or we won't get to keep the table."

Kit ordered a salad. Jen, stating that she didn't have a hot dinner date that night, ordered a steak. She didn't intend to wait for their food to arrive, even if she did order her meat "mooing."

"Tell me about him."

"I did. I met him at the hospital, actually, the day my dad died. I know I told you that a friend from the truly distant past had come in."

"You certainly didn't describe him," Jen said reproachfully.

Kit shrugged. "It was just so strange. I mean, my dad never, absolutely never, talked about the past. In all the years since we moved to Chicago, it was as if we had never lived anywhere else. He didn't ignore my mother's existence or anything. He kept her picture, and he would tell me how kind and lively she was, and that I looked a great deal like her. Oh, and of course, he would tell me that she looked after me from heaven. But then, on that last day, I ran into David Moore, the guy in line, at the hospital. He told me a little bit about the past, and I remembered snatches of Bougainvillea, but not him. Then—''

"Then," Jen jumped in, "your father's last word is spoken, and it's 'Bougainvillea'! Man, I see shades of *Citizen Kane* all over!"

"Don't be ridiculous. My dad was a scholar, not an entrepreneur, and he didn't have a mean bone in his body. You know as well as I do that there's no way my father hurt anyone in his entire life."

"Okay, okay, skip the *Citizen Kane* reference. Still, isn't it incredibly intriguing? And hey—you said that at the time, this guy, David, said that you should come to Bougainvillea."

"Right. And I intend to, of course."

Jen stared at her.

She shrugged. "I needed a little time."

"Okay, understandable. But here he is—this mysterious giver of machine-accepting dollar bills, a paragon of studly beauty from your past. And you were hesitating about a dinner invitation!"

"I really don't remember the guy."

"Who cares?" Jen said with an outraged sigh. "Any sensible, living, breathing, single woman in the world would jump at a chance to have dinner with him. And you hesitate!"

Kit arched a brow. "I can't help but wonder..."

"What?"

"My mother died at Bougainvillea," Kit said.

"Yes, she drowned when you were a little girl. Very tragic. But a very long time ago, as well."

Kit leaned forward. "My dad left there, and totally

erased the place from his past. Then he dies saying 'Bougainvillea.' It makes me wonder.''

"Wonder what?''

"Why would he leave like that, and never, never speak of the place—except with his dying word?''

Jen stared at her. "You're kidding, right?''

"No!''

"Kit, your mother died there. Your father was desperately, madly, in love with her. He never remarried. She was truly the great passion of his life. He left and never returned because he simply couldn't bear it. Of course he was thinking about her. It's so, so sad, and tragic, and yet really beautiful.''

"Maybe.''

"What's maybe about it?''

"Well, at any rate, I have intended to go there. It didn't really matter that David showed up here today. Actually, it rather caught me off guard,'' Kit said.

"Because you've taken too much time.''

"Hey, I work for a living, remember? I had a lot to catch up on and we were scheduled for this show, remember?''

"We still have such things as airplanes, remember?'' Jen countered.

"I'm going to go see it,'' Kit assured her. "Now that Dad is gone, I'm really anxious to find out about the past. Truthfully, I hadn't even thought about Bougainvillea in years. But since I ran into David at the hospital, I've been remembering more and more.''

"It's an estate, right on the bay, in Miami. Sunshine, sand, warm weather! Hell, I can guarantee you, *I'd* be remembering it,'' Jen said, laughing.

Kit laughed. "Jen, you're thirty years old, and totally independent. You could move to Miami if you wanted.''

"Not on my own! I'd need a friend there. Besides, I'm rather happy with my life, really. I make a good living, and

I'm proud of it. I'd like to see you happy, because you've gone through so much lately."

Their food arrived and they thanked their waitress. When she was gone, Jen said, "I think that everyone else in the entire world has an aunt, an uncle, grandparents, parents, or a sister or brother who has moved to Florida. Not me. But now...I'm going to wait for you to go down to this Eden in the tropics, find out if you move, and then...wow. We could cruise the clubs on South Beach. Dance salsa. I could have a social life," she said, laughing, "as well as a great career."

"Jen, I'm not planning on *moving* down there. I'm just going to go and visit. If I'm actually invited for a real visit."

"If you're invited for a visit!" Jen repeated incredulously. She wagged a finger at Kit. "You've already been invited."

"I was told to call if I needed anything."

"Honey, you can pack your bags tonight. I saw the way that he was looking at you."

"And he may be damned practiced at looking at people that way," Kit said sagely.

"Great. Someone gorgeous is looking at you, and you're going to be skeptical."

"You bet."

"You're impossible."

"No—just wary. But anxious as well, I'll admit."

"So does David own the place now?" Jen asked.

"No," Kit assured her.

"Who does actually own it?"

"A man—I guess an old, distant cousin named Seamus Delaney. It's kind of a confused story, and I probably wasn't paying attention at the time I heard it. I think that my grandfather had an ownership in it, along with David's grandfather, but they both sold out to my grandfather's cousin, another Delaney—Seamus. There are other people living there, too—I don't really know who they were, or their connection to the place because what I remember is more the physical, you know, the little lagoon, the house, stuff like that.''

"I'd better get an invitation down there," Jen said firmly.

"I don't own the place!"

"But you're a long, lost child of Eden!" Jen protested. "So get to work. Learn more from tall, dark, and radiantly studly tonight, get down there, and get me an invitation!"

"I'll do my best," Kit assured her dryly.

Jen glanced at her watch. "Hey, it's getting close to show time."

"We're all right."

"No, let's get the check, and head back up. There's too much confusion when everything closes down. Heck…it's going to take me forever to get back to my hotel. There are going to be long lines for the buses and at the taxi stands. Hmm." She looked at Kit pointedly.

"What?"

"He said he had a car. I'm going to meet him with you— he can drop me off at my hotel, okay? Besides, that way I'll check him out for you really good, though you know you're not supposed to look a gift horse in the mouth."

"David is a gift horse?"

"He would be in my life, honey! Seriously," Jen said, growing serious. "Would you mind asking him to give me a ride? It's so difficult to get out of here on the buses or in a taxi. And seriously, I will give him a good once-over, make sure you're not taking off with a homicidal maniac, or anything."

"I'll be happy to see if he can give you a ride," Kit assured her, smiling. Jen had done a million favors for her. Since they had met at Kit's first comic convention, Jen had shared her knowledge and experience freely. She was truly a best friend. She liked to tease about her own lack of a real social life, but in truth, she was confident in her abilities, and in herself. And Kit knew that Jen was anxious that she get over the loss of her father, and start to live a full life again.

It took them a full thirty minutes to get their check, pay it and make their way through the throng of tired and worn people at the convention center to the coffee stand where they were to meet David.

He wasn't there. Kit was surprised to feel a tremendous sinking in her heart; she hadn't realized she was as anxious as she was to spend time with him. No, she told herself firmly. It wasn't the man who intrigued her so much; it was her own past. She wanted to know more about her mother.

"He isn't coming!" Jen said with dismay, looking around. She glanced at her watch again. "We *are* late," she murmured disgustedly.

"Jen, don't worry, if he doesn't show, I have his card."

Jen grinned at her. "I'm not getting any younger, standing here. I need you to get me to Florida. And when you do, I'm going to meet an incredibly handsome Latin American, marry him and live happily ever after."

Kit laughed. "I'm glad you've got it all planned out."

"There!" Jen said. She lowered her voice. "Here he comes."

Since he was tall, they could see David wending his way through the crowd, stopping to say a hello to someone here or there.

He reached her with an apology. "Sorry—who would have figured? Wildlife photography is big again this year." He noted Jen. "Hello, again."

"David, you said you had a car here—or coming. I was hoping we could drop Jen at her hotel before we went to dinner. It gets so crazy here, when this thing is over."

"Absolutely," he said. "Let's head out, huh? Make our way through the gauntlet."

He started on ahead of them. Jen looped her arm through Kit's. "Oh, Kit, he is a keeper!"

"He's still a stranger!" Kit whispered back.

"All strangers are just friends waiting to happen," Jen said primly. Then she grinned.

Outside the convention hall, David led them away from the bus and taxi lines to a side thruway where a number of limos were waiting. Jen gave her another little approving glance when she saw that they were being led toward one that was a white stretch.

Jen crawled in first, unabashed.

"Champagne!" she said delightedly, noting the ice bucket and glasses arranged in a nook on the limo's inner right side. Then she did look abashed. "Oh, sorry—"

David laughed. "Obviously, it's there to be enjoyed. Please, let me."

As the limo took off, he leaned forward, smoothly popping the cork, and pouring three glasses.

"Is this how they do it in Miami all the time?" Jen asked, leaning back.

"Actually, in Miami, I drive a rather beat-up van most of the time. The Bougainvillea estate is big, and we all find ourselves driving around with new plants or even canvas for the sail shops, or something else that's big and needs transport," he told her. His eyes were on Jen. He smiled slowly. "Is something wrong?" he inquired.

"Wrong?" Jen said. "No, this is great!"

"You keep staring at me," David said, smiling.

"Oh, sorry." She winced. "I just think it's such a great story…that Kit has an extended family she doesn't even know, or doesn't remember. And the place sounds incredible."

"Bougainvillea?" he said. Kit thought there was a tone of real affection in his voice when he said the word, almost as if the property actually had a personality. "It is great. Hang on, you can see it."

Jennifer was sitting on the long seat that ran vertically along the car's length while Kit had found herself next to their host on his left. He leaned past her and Jennifer, pulling a large, coffee-table book from the seat next to Jen.

Kit was startled at the rush of memory that swept over her at the sight of the front cover. There it was, in full-color glory. Bougainvillea. The massive main house, in coral rock, concrete block, and stucco, covered with twisting bougainvillea vines. The photograph on the cover of the book was a shot of the front of the house from the street, with little more than the sweeping lawn before it to show the extent of the estate. But just seeing it, Kit was suddenly reminded of the rear of the house, the cottages and outbuildings that seemed haphazardly and yet somehow aesthetically strewn out behind it, bordering the lagoon and the water. She could see the winding paths, the exotic plants and flowers, the incredible wealth of birds that were forever flying in. As if something were sparked, she could almost hear a dog barking, and if she closed her eyes, she knew that she would see a beach scene, her mother holding her hand, hurrying her along the path that curled so beautifully around the lagoon. She was startled by the sudden urgency to be there again.

And equally, she was disturbed by a strange feeling that swept over her, of suspicion, unease...something not quite right, that filled her heart with a sudden aversion to the place.

Such a strange mixture of emotions, she thought, and all from one photograph.

"How gorgeous!" Jennifer exclaimed, bringing her back to earth.

"Are you all right?" David asked.

Kit realized that although Jennifer had swept up the book, David was looking at her.

She nodded. "Of course. It's just...well, the photograph. I'm suddenly remembering so much. About the place. But it's very strange—I seem to have such a blank about the people there.''

"Ah!'' Jen said, looking up from the book. "Maybe there's someone mean and nasty that you want to forget! Any ogres at the family estate?'' she teased David.

"Just people—with their good points and bad.'' He changed the subject suddenly. "Where are we going, Jennifer? Which hotel?''

"Oh!'' She looked out of the window, unaware that the limo had managed to arrive at the hotel so quickly. "I'm right here.''

"So am I,'' David said. "So is a large part of the convention, I imagine.''

"I'm supposed to be,'' Kit said. She looked at David. "Would you mind if I went ahead and checked in?''

"Not at all. I'll just run up to my own room,'' he said.

"David, I'm in love,'' Jen said, gripping the book. "Mind if I keep it a while?''

"I'm at the convention giving away copies. You're more than welcome to keep it forever.''

"Great, thanks. And thanks so much for the ride!'' Jen leaped out first, rolled her eyes at Kit in a way that warned her she must be charming rather than skeptical, and ran into the hotel.

David spoke to the driver, asking him to wait, then said to Kit, "We'll meet back at reception?''

"Terrific,'' she said, thinking she might have time for a quick shower.

Except that it didn't turn out to be so. She waited in a long line, then gave her name, and then her publisher's name. It took them forever to find her reservation, and she was in the midst of being told that the hotel had overbooked, she was actually past check-in time and something had gone wrong with the guarantee. She didn't know whether to be indignant or furious, or give way to frustration. However, the clerk behind the desk was obviously even more distressed than she was, and she checked her anger, thanking him as he said he'd need a few minutes to find her accommodations—somewhere—and that the hotel would be happy to make it up to her—complimentary, of course—at a later date.

As she stood fuming by the counter, her feet hurting, feeling that she could really, truly use a quick shower, David returned.

"Problem?" he asked.

"They overbooked."

"But you've had reservations?"

"Of course. At first, I was ready to strangle someone at my publisher's house, but they found the reservation. They simply overbooked, and everyone else had the sense to check in early."

The harried desk clerk rushed over to her side. His hair was very short, but it was evident he'd been tearing through it with his fingers. "Thanks so much for your patience. I'm still working on it."

She started to say something but he rushed off to the office to the far left of the desk.

"Looks like I'm staying somewhere else. Hey, you know, we can scratch this dinner thing. I don't mean to keep you waiting."

He hesitated a moment, studying her, and she thought he was planning on backing out.

"I don't have a thing to do this evening, I assure you. And I was really looking forward to spending some time with you."

"Really? You've such a strange look on your face."

"Well, I was thinking I can solve your problem—if you don't think it too…forward, I guess, is the word I'm looking for. I have a huge suite. Two bedrooms."

She wasn't sure what her expression might have been because he gave her that wry amused smile of his and added, "Two bedrooms with locking doors. Living room, kitchen. And a great balcony."

She opened her mouth. "I can't accept, really."

"We shared a house years ago, you know."

She had to laugh.

The clerk came rushing by, his cheeks red as he hesitated briefly, looking at her mournfully. "Still on it!"

Kit stood there, trying to offer no expression at all as she looked at David. She knew she wanted an invitation to Bougainvillea. She was dying to go there, and yet…she still felt that same strange sense of aversion. She didn't understand it, or her father's dying word. *Bougainvillea.* Something that seemed important in life was eluding her, and it was at Bougainvillea.

However…

David really was striking, self-assured and certainly accustomed to the ways of the world. His world. In a stratosphere above her own. She wondered if he considered her woefully naive. She wasn't.

"If you'd rather, I could try pulling some weight with the management here," he said.

Kit glanced at the harried clerk. "Poor fellow. It seems as if he's really having a bad time."

"Well, you did have a guaranteed reservation. I can make him even more miserable."

"I don't want you to do that. He looks as if he might cry already."

"There's my suite," he reminded her. And he was laughing somewhere inside she knew, well aware that he was playing with a very good hand.

She gazed at the clerk. He was sweating bullets.

She looked back at David and shrugged. "I don't want to put you out."

"You won't be putting me out. My accommodations are ridiculous for a single traveler."

"Why so large?"

"I had some meetings up there," he explained briefly.

"Ah." She kept looking at him. He was definitely pursuing her. Why? Was he using her in some way?

She certainly intended to use him. But then again, maybe none of it was so sinister. All she wanted to do was see Bougainvillea, and it didn't seem that was going to be a problem.

"All right, sorry, bad idea. Give me a minute. I'll have them call the manager."

She laughed. "No, please. I was just hoping that your suite had two great rooms and two great showers. If you're sure, I'll accept your offer."

He nodded simply. "Ralph!"

The harried clerk came running over. "It's all right. Ms. Delaney has graciously accepted a part of the suite."

Poor Ralph, she thought. His relief was evident. In fact, he looked as if he were about to leap over the counter and hug David.

"Oh, Mr. Moore! Ms. Delaney, thank you so much. We'll see to it that you're given an all-expense paid voucher for a stay in the future," Ralph said. He was still sweating.

"Great. Thank you," Kit said.

"That your bag?" David asked.

"Yes, thanks."

"Come on. I'll show you the way."

"Thanks," she told him.

Strangely, she felt as if she had just taken the first step back to something she had left long ago.

No...

The step had already been taken. At the time he had come to the hospital.

Or, perhaps, on the day her father had died. And he had whispered the word.

Bougainvillea.

Again, though, she felt the strange hesitance. And an intuition.

Something had gone very wrong at Bougainvillea. What, exactly? She would never know unless...

Unless she let him...show her the way.

3

The suite had to be the hotel's best, Kit thought as she looked around. It was two levels, with a winding staircase rising from the living/dining area to the bedrooms above.

The "guest" bedroom in the suite was larger than any room she'd stayed in before. It opened to a balcony with an incredible view of the city.

"I'll leave you alone," David told her. "Whenever you're ready, I'll be in the parlor."

Kit waited until he was out of the room, then made a beeline for the telephone and dialed the operator, asking for Jen's room. When her friend came on the line, she said, "You're not going to believe this," and proceeded to tell her about the suite.

"The plot thickens!" Jen said delightedly.

"What does that mean?" Kit asked.

"The guy is truly after you."

"Maybe he's just being really nice."

"He may be really nice, but guys are guys. Anyway, I want the details, *all* the details, tomorrow," Jen said.

"There aren't going to be any details," Kit assured her.

"Are you an idiot? He's gorgeous, and, apparently, rich. If you don't come up with some details, you're a fool. I guarantee you, I'd have details in your position! Anyway, I want to see the suite, too."

"That I can arrange. I think," Kit told her.

"Go work on your details," Jen told her.

Kit hung up. Starting the shower, she mused over her friend's words. Jen was right. Everything about this guy seemed to be picture perfect.

There was just *something*....

It all had to do with Bougainvillea.

Seamus Delaney rose from the table, looking at those around him. "Lovely dinner. Nice to see us all together. Martin, Shelley, Eli, great to have you. Thank you, all."

He walked away from the table in the expansive dining room of the main house. At seventy-eight, he was still ram-rod straight, tall and an imposing figure. He had a full head of silver-white hair and piercing blue eyes. He'd been the driving force behind Sea Life since his teens, taking a raw wilderness and molding it into a business, and an estate. The power he had wielded through the years still wrapped around him like a cloak of invincibility.

Michael Delaney watched his father leave the dining room. He noticed with some humor that everyone at the table was doing the same, different expressions in their eyes.

"Lovely dinner," Josh, Michael's son, said, a light of amusement in his eyes. At thirty-six, Josh had come to have a deep appreciation for his family's business and position. Michael could honestly say that he was proud of his son. He'd gone through many of the usual adjustments when going from his teen years into adulthood—dropping out of college, bumming around Europe, taking a job with a sail maker just to stay away from the family—then diving back into hard work at Sea Life. Thanks to the way Bougainvillea had been planned—almost like a little compound for the Mafia, Josh was independent, living on the property but in one of the cottages that surrounded the lagoon. "But! I've got a date. Anyone mind if I take off?"

"We do have company," Lenore, Josh's mother, reminded him.

"We're not really company," Martin Callahan said. "We're just the next door neighbors."

"And we couldn't care in the least if Josh has a hot date!" Shelley, his daughter, teased. "Damn, but, you know, Seamus sure looks great," she added. "He seems so alive again! He seemed really depressed there for a while."

"Uncle Seamus is going to live forever, the tough old bird," Josh said, still grinning.

"Josh," Lenore remonstrated.

"As well he should," Michael said.

"He was so depressed when he heard about Mark dying," Eli, Shelley's brother, said softly.

"But now he's excited again, because he thinks he's going to see Kit Delaney down here soon," Josh told him.

"*I'm* excited!" Shelley said. "Kit and I were in first-grade together—at least part of it. Then her mom died, and…"

"That's what was getting to old Seamus, I think," Josh interrupted her. He leaned low against the table. "Shades of guilt! The deadly siren of Bougainvillea drowns, and only the good Lord knows what was really going on!"

"Marina liked to drink," Martin Callahan reminded them all quietly.

"She liked to do a lot of things," Josh said, his words light, and yet rueful.

"Josh," Michael said softly. He felt a surge of unease. Strange, it was still too easy to remember the days when Marina had been here. A woman so stunning and full of energy that she had set the entire place on edge. He knew for a fact that Seamus himself had been captivated by his cousin's wife, just as he had been himself, Michael was honest enough to reflect. Both Josh and David had been teenagers at the time, and they had idolized her. Even Eli and Martin knew what it had been like to fall beneath her spell. He would never go so far as to say that Marina had actually been evil, but close. She had loved her power, and loved knowing that she'd had them all tripping over themselves because of her, arguing and making power plays. Well, she was dead, God bless her. But now... "That girl shouldn't be coming here," Kaitlin said flatly. Kaitlin wasn't a member of the family. Not exactly, and certainly not in a normal or accepted manner. She had worked for Seamus for over twenty years. Like Seamus, she sometimes reminded Michael of Dorian Grey. Surely, she had an aging picture of herself stashed somewhere. She had to be in her early forties now, and she still had the face and figure of a twenty-year-old. As well she should. As Seamus's personal assistant, she had been extremely well paid for all those many years. She had ample time off, and lots of vacations.

After all these years, Michael thought with some amusement, his wife still hated her. Not that Lenore was wearing so badly. His wife was quite an attractive woman as well. She kept her hair the deep dark auburn it had always been. She was blessed with huge hazel eyes that hypnotically ruled her face. She spent a day every week at the spa, where God alone knew exactly what they did. Hell, yes, the women at Bougainvillea either fared very well...

Or they died.

"Kaitlin! Why on earth would you say that? I'm dying to see Kit," Shelley said.

"If she looks as much like her mother as she used to, I'll be darned excited to see her again, too," Eli said.

"Eli," his father warned edgily.

"Hey, Dad, I'm not a teenager anymore. All right, so we all had silly little crushes on Kit's mother. That was so long ago. But Kit was an adorable little girl."

"And she shouldn't come here," Kaitlin repeated.

Annoyed, Eli stared at her. "Once again, why would you say that?"

"Why would I say that?" Kaitlin arched a perfect, blond brow. "It's going to be miserable. She'll be all wide eyed wanting to know about her mother. And we'll all have to lie and say ridiculous things, because we all know her mother was a wretched little slut.''

"Kaitlin!" Lenore said, horrified.

"Come on, now, she's been dead a very long time," Michael said.

"Let's be honest—she should stay that way," Kaitlin said. She rose, walking to the buffet and drawing a cigarette from an old humidor.

"Don't light that in here—Seamus will go through the roof," Josh warned.

"Whatever, I say that Seamus wants Kit Delaney here, and he'll get her here, and she'll stay, no matter what it takes," Martin said. "Trust me, I know the man. Whether it's guilt or what, he hasn't been his usual self since David brought him the news that Mark was dying."

"Thank God he at least let the man die in peace!" Shelley said softly. The others stared at her. "Well, for good reason, Mark hated the place. He wouldn't have wanted to know that his daughter was going to return."

"We don't know that she will return," Eli said.

Kaitlin let out a long sniff. "If she's anything like her mother? You bet she'll come. She'll sniff out the money in this place in seconds flat."

"And if she's anything like her mother, old Seamus will fall for her, and we might just find ourselves all out on our little rumps in the cold, huh, Kaitlin?" Josh said lightly as he stood up. "Good night, one and all."

He kissed his mother on the forehead, lifted a hand to Michael and the others, and left.

"How on earth do you let him get away with talking like that? Honestly!" Lenore said to Michael.

He couldn't help but smile at his wife. "Because maybe he's speaking the truth, hmm? Martin, Eli, anyone for a brandy?"

"I'd love one," Kaitlin said. "Eli, be a dear, and bring it to me on the porch? I'm dying for a cigarette."

Dying for a cigarette.

Those were the last words Marina Delaney had said in this very room, before she had run out of the house.

Dying...

And she had done just that.

Michael felt a chill sweep through him, and he knew why.

He didn't want Kit Delaney back here. The very idea of it all but caused his limbs to gel. He was afraid.

Very afraid.

And he knew, as well, he wasn't the only one.

"It's not as confusing as it sounds," David said, leaning back on the sofa, sounding somewhat affectionately amused. He and Kit had opted for dinner in the room—quite impressive, since the suite came with a butler and the food was excellent.

"There were the three original partners—Seamus, my grandfather, and your grandfather. Seamus has a son, Michael, there's his wife, Lenore, and their son, Josh. My grandfather had my father, who had me. Your grandfather had your dad, who married your mother, and had you."

"And everyone but me lives at Bougainvillea?"

"That's not as weird as it sounds, either," he assured her. "It's not just one house. There's the main house, Seamus's place, and then all the cottages around the lagoon. Don't you remember?"

"Actually, I do," she murmured. "I remember the lagoon well, and the paths around it that head down to the beach. And there was a darling little bridge that connected the land where the lagoon went on out to the sea. Is it all still there? I was thinking that, after all these years, a storm might have altered it somewhat."

David shook his head. "It's all still there. So, when are you coming down? You could fly home with me after the convention."

She smiled and laughed. "Wow! That would be fast."

"Fast is good."

She sobered somewhat. They'd shared an incredible bottle of Cabernet.

Fast is good.

And it would be.

Ah, well, Jen would be proud of the sensations sweeping through her, if no one else. The mood in the suite was far too relaxed. She was sitting on her own side of the sofa, but she wasn't immune to temptations of simple pleasure. He had changed into a pair of soft, worn blue jeans and a long-sleeved knit shirt. Very casual. She had changed, too, but in the opposite direction. Not knowing he had decided to order in, she had gone for a business dinner staple, a sleeveless black cocktail dress. At least thirty minutes ago, however, she had shed the heels she'd been wearing. Her stocking feet were curled beneath her. They'd talked about art and photography, boats, weather, the construction projects in Boston, the wonders of Chicago, and gone back to Bougainvillea. It had been a long day filled with trepidation for her, at first. She would love to lean back…actually, she would love to lean against his shoulder, or stretch out with her head in his lap.

She sat straighter.

"There's no time like the present, or something like that," David said.

A slow smile curved into her lips. "Actually, there is. I have to go home to Chicago."

"Why is that?"

"I have a cat."

"Where is he—she?—now?"

"He's at a neighbor's who has to leave on a sales trip this weekend."

"Hmm. Maybe we can send for the cat."

"I have to work as well. It's a syndicated strip," Kit reminded him.

"On day-to-day life. Imagine what new fuel you'd have for the machine, coming to Bougainvillea."

"Oh?"

"Well, there's Seamus, who is the real deal. Old South. A ramrod. All courtesy and graciousness—while he's gripping the neck of his competitors. Michael, who works in the business end of the company, but hates it. He wants to take off in a sailboat and write the great American novel. He should, too—he's good. Then there's Lenore, who wants to be the great lady of the South, which is funny, in its way, because the community is so very Latin American, very progressive. Still, you know, she belongs to all the right clubs, hosts charity events, and plays the grande dame. Josh is about my age, and pretty much deep into the business as well. I'm better at money and naturally, any legalities involved, while he's better at design. Kaitlin could fill you in on the what and where of the Miami club and dating scene—she's Seamus's assistant. We've great neighbors, by the way. I think you actually went to school with Shelley Callahan."

"Shelley. Sounds familiar," Kit told him.

He laughed. "Maybe we are a bit of a weird group, because Eli and Shelley still live at home, too. It's an old place on the property, much smaller than Bougainvillea, but it had a carriage house, which is Eli's now, and a garage apartment, which is where Shelley lives. She's your age, and getting her master's degree in literature at the university. Eli became a cop. Their father, Martin, is a retired cop, and just does a lot of fishing now. They're actually more like family than neighbors, since we've shared holidays, dinners, and what have you ever since I can remember. Oh! We've also got one of the most wonderful and fascinating women you'd ever want to meet living on the property. Mary is a hundred and one."

"Mary!" Kit swung her feet down. "She's still living! My, Lord, she seemed ancient when I was a child."

"You remember her?"

Kit nodded. "She was a sweetheart...wow, I remember more and more, actually. Lenore was this glorious, rather imperious beauty who...didn't particularly like me. And..." She paused, frowning. "I don't remember my mom being there in the afternoons. After school, kindergarten, whatever it was. So I would sneak out of the main house as soon as I could, and go to the cottage. And Mary always smelled like gardenias, and she'd make me tea and give me little sugar cookies. I would love to see her again, thank her."

"She's a hundred and one," he warned. "You can't wait too long."

Kit grinned. "I won't. I'm curious as all hell about the place. Except that...hmm." She fell silent. How could she explain to him that there was something in her memory that disturbed her about the place?

"Except that what?"

She shrugged. "I don't know."

"Did your father say something negative about the place?"

"No. He never talked about it at all." She realized that her words were only a minor lie. He had never talked about it at all. Not until he had spoken that final word. Bougainvillea.

"You miss him a great deal, don't you?"

"Of course. I adored him. He was an incredible person. Wise, funny, always helping me, encouraging me. Even when he was in pain, he could make jokes about the hospital, his doctors, and all the little ironies of life—and death. He thanked me for being such a great daughter, and he gave me all the strength and peace I needed to go on. Of course I miss him."

"I am so sorry."

"Thanks," she said lightly, no wanting to grow morbid. Then she stood resolutely. She was going to go to bed before she spent any more time with him. Jen would be disappointed, of course, that there wouldn't be any details. But she wasn't as trusting as Jen. Not that her friend could be called promiscuous, certainly not by current standards, but Jen was a big believer in chemistry. It was there, or it wasn't. You trusted, or you didn't. Knowing someone a great deal of time couldn't change any, either.

"Would you mind if I crashed?" she asked. "It's been a really long day for me."

"Not at all." He stood, not to stop her, but merely in a polite gesture.

"Good night," he told her. "By the way—what time do you need to be back at the convention center in the morning?"

"Nine, nine-thirty, somewhere around there."

"I'll see that the butler has breakfast here by eight."

She couldn't help but grin. "Mind if I invite Jen over? I told her where I was. She wants to see the place."

"Absolutely. Bring her."

He remained standing while she walked to the stairs. As she ascended, she heard him ordering breakfast for three. Before retiring, she tried calling Jen's room, but her friend was out. She left her a message to join them in the suite at eight.

That night, she dreamed of Bougainvillea. Not so much of anything in particular, but just of being there. She could almost feel the breeze, damp sand beneath her feet, and see the riot of color caused by the bougainvillea creeping over the walls of the main house and cottages. The sensation was at first incredible, sweet as the clean sea air. Then, it was as if shadows fell, darkening everything around her.

When she came down in the morning, Jen was already there. She was enthusiastically talking to David about his home, his photography, and her own work. She greeted Kit with her back to David, brows arched with excited curiosity. Kit shook her head.

Later that day, at the convention center, Jen grilled her. "Nothing? You two did nothing?"

"We talked."

Jen let out a disgusted sigh. "It's so obvious, the chemistry between you! It's just so right—I can tell."

"Jen, would you sleep with a guy you'd only seen once before?"

"If it was right—you bet."

"Well, he didn't make any moves."

"*You* make a move!" Jen suggested.

"What, just say, 'excuse me, we've got chemistry going here, let's sleep together'?"

"If all else fails," Jen said seriously. "Are you supposed to fly out tomorrow?"

"Yes."

"Get him tonight, then."

"Jen, I don't want to 'get' anyone."

"Then you've been celibate far too long," Jen said sagely. "What, are you going to turn your comic character into a nun? Get out there, live, give yourself something to work with!"

That night, David took her to dinner at a wonderful, intimate little restaurant in Little Italy. Every time his arm brushed hers, or his hand reached out as he escorted her in or out of the car, into her seat, into her jacket, she felt as if electric jolts ripped through her. The man was undeniably sexy, and sensual, with his dark eyes often seeming to hide a wry amusement with himself, with her, and with the world around them.

He told her more about his education, and how Seamus had insisted he not just slide into the business, but work hard in school and find a serious profession as well. He had liked practicing law, but discovered later that he was equally fond of business, and, when the demands of the company had begun to take more and more of his time, he'd been ready to leave his practice behind, and take all that he learned with him into the family company.

Kit realized that as the meal progressed, they were leaning closer and closer to each other as they talked and laughed and shared the wine. She was aware that she was breathing in his delicious aftershave, a scent that was inextricably linked to him and extremely evocative.

Back at the hotel, they lingered for a few minutes in the parlor, sipping a last brandy. Their conversation turned again to Bougainvillea, and his life there.

Kit could admit to feeling a slight buzz from the wine, but she definitely had not overdone. Still, she found herself smiling ruefully and asking him, "I have to admit it—I don't quite get it."

"What's that?"

"The fact that you're not married. I mean—you're not, right?"

He laughed. "No, not married."

"Not even involved?"

"Certainly, I have been at times over the years. But not now. What about you?"

She grinned. "Well, there was Ray Leone in high school. We were the hot item for a while. At Northwestern, there was Mason Rigg. Law student. But very old-fashioned. I found that out when he became annoyed by the amount of women in his classes. The place for a woman, in his mind, is in the home. Supportive, you know. Taking the kids to school and doctor appointments and arranging business dinners. Not that I wouldn't want to take my kids to doctors' appointments and the like." She fell silent, wondering why she was explaining herself that way. "Sorry. Wow. How embarrassing. I didn't mean to give you a list."

He was smiling, moving across the room to where she sat on the couch. The lights of Boston swept gently into the suite. Muted. He sat down beside her, took her glass, set it on the table, then held both her hands in his. "I like your list. It's wonderfully honest. Like you." On the last, his voice was low, soft, husky. This close, the scent of his aftershave was pure intoxication. When his mouth touched hers, she was immediately aware of a melting sensation. She was equally aware that he was very experienced, a practiced lover, lips moving hers, fingers threading into her hair, tilting her head at a perfect angle for his tongue to do the most incredibly seductive things inside her mouth. Instinct, or maybe it was Jen's chemistry, reigned, and she moved against him, wishing nothing more, it seemed, than to sink right inside him, flesh, bone, heart and soul. Yet he drew back, not too far, dark eyes on hers. "I should slow down," he said gently.

She searched out his eyes. "Why?"

His lips turned in that somewhat knowing grin that seemed to catapult her bloodstream all over again.

"Because I have a confession to make."

"Oh?"

"I came here specifically to find you."

"That's nice," she said dreamily.

Then, he hesitated slightly.

"You see, Seamus wants you at Bougainvillea. I was sent to get you down there, whatever it took."

She withdrew slightly, frowning as she looked into his eyes. "Why?"

He shrugged. "I don't know the details of exactly why. You'd have to ask Seamus. But I imagine I know what he's feeling. Your mother died, and your father left. The place was really as much your heritage as, say, mine, or the others. He's probably always harbored a certain amount of guilt as well that Marina died on the property. He was sorry when your father left—Seamus really liked and admired Mark. He understood, of course. But still…he was nuts about you when you were a little girl. You were Marina—except small, innocent, and completely loving and sincere.

I'm not surprised that he wants to see you so badly. Make amends for all the bad things that happened—maybe atone for some of the recklessness and carelessness of his own youth.'' He lifted his hands as if his explanation was insufficient. ''Only Seamus knows what makes him really tick. But he's sincere in wanting to see you.''

''That's nice…I guess,'' Kit murmured uncertainly.

''So….'' he said slowly.

''So?'' she echoed.

''So, where does that leave us?'' he asked very softly.

She smiled. ''I don't know.''

''I would have come after you myself, no matter what,'' he insisted.

''Say it again.''

''I would have come after you myself, no matter what.''

''Why?''

''Because you're fascinating and beautiful.''

''Such a good reply,'' she teased.

''I mean it. The confession is real, too, though. So tell me, where does that leave us?'' he demanded insistently.

''On the sofa,'' she returned, eyes carefully on his.

''When there are perfectly good bedrooms,'' he mused.

''Perfectly good,'' she agreed.

Kit wasn't quite sure that she believed her own actions, but she pressed him aside, rising.

''I'll be in one,'' she told him.

She walked up the stairs thinking that Jen would be proud. Then she had a moment's panic as she thought she might be a fool. What a line.

And what if he didn't follow? She'd probably remain a burnt crimson called ''mortification'' for the rest of her life.

She stepped into the guest room, her heart thundering. She didn't turn on a light, but for a moment, simply stood against the wall, wondering if he would enter behind her.

He did.

She felt herself ever so gently pinned against the wall.

And then his hands, on her face, and the huskiness of his whisper. "You're sure."

And in that minute, she was.

Chemistry was just right...or it wasn't.

But it was. There was a second's awkwardness for her. She'd been out of touch with the real world, so it seemed, for a long time. Out of dating, speaking, laughing, even *trusting* another person. And yet...there it was, everything just right; *he* was not out of touch. Again, his touch, the feel of his fingers against her face, the warmth of his breath, the molding of his kiss. Everything that should have been awkward...

The pressure of his body dispelled all else. She felt that her body fit against his like a glove. They never left the wall, that first time. His shirt was shed, and she inhaled the richness of the scent of his flesh, felt the vibrant constriction of his muscles, and the warmth of him that quickly seemed to enwrap her in an urgency that throbbed within her mind, her blood, her limbs. One touch of flesh and clothing seemed to melt away, easily, so easily. She felt no shyness, only that drumming need to crawl closer and closer into him, become a part of him. Standing, she felt the molten liquid of his kiss against her lips, her cheeks, her throat, down to her collarbone, between her breasts. His fingers moved with brushes of sensuality, teased and caressed. His touch was elusive and powerful. She hungered, wanted, burned. There was no past and no present, no memory of a different life, or even the current one. She was aware of the texture of his hair, and again of the heady scents, of musky cologne, of the man, skin and muscle beneath her touch, the texture of his face, and even in the dim shadows of moonlight, the dark fascination of his eyes. She stood, and for long moments was all but locked in place, simply feeling the brush of his fingers and the hot sweep of his tongue. Where he touched her she was a mass of pure heat, and when that touch left her, the air returned to caress and arouse anew. He moved against her body, lower, lower.

The tip of his tongue on her flesh.

The stroke of it...

The fullness...

The sensations were excruciating. Honeyed, hot. Abandoned, totally impassioned.

This was the kind of desire one could...

Die for.

Her fingers thread through his hair, kneaded his shoulders, stroked, and dug. No words left her lips, but soft sounds escaped her, ragged gasps. When the liquid heat had all but caused her to melt away, he lifted her against the wall, her arms tight around his shoulders, her hips wedged hard, and he moved, fluid, powerful, until she felt that the world exploded in her, around her, and her head fell against his shoulder. At last, they left the wall, and she was barely aware that she came down gently on the comfort of a bed.

Moments later, even in shadow, she was aware of his eyes on hers, and she smiled. She was tempted to say thank you, just because it seemed that it had been so long since she had even contemplated such an evening, and he was simply so incredible.

"No regrets?" he murmured slightly.

She turned to him, eyes widening. "Should there be? Are you feeling any?"

"I couldn't regret tonight to save my life," he told her.

She curled against him, feeling the dampness of his chest beneath her cheek, the strength of his legs, tangled with her own. Moments later, it was she who initiated intimacy, running her fingers down his rib cage, feeling the muscled ripple of his abdomen, and going lower, fingers brushing, then curling over the length of his sex. He turned to her quickly, hardening within her hold, and the melting began again. The urgency, the desire, the incredulous wonder, and the satiation were so sweet, she felt she soared in another world.

He rose later, as confident and imposing naked as he was in a designer suit, and brought champagne from the kitchen, crackers, bites of different cheeses. And they talked, comfortable in their state. It was the most wonderful night Kit had ever known.

But at last, when they slept, she dreamed. And it wasn't of wonder, fulfillment, or laughter. She dreamed of Bougainvillea.

She walked in the sand. She felt the breeze, the cool dampness of the earth beneath her. There was a scent on the air of night-blooming jasmine. And there was a screeching sound that terrified her.

The parrots, just the parrots, Mary always told her.

But she could see her mother's face, almost hear her speak. She was in her bedroom in the main house, the Delaney house, so big and vast. There were windows that faced the lagoon, and they were open because the dead heat of summer was gone, and the slight, beautiful dip of temperature that heralded the coming of their oh so slight winter had come.

"Tomorrow, baby. Tomorrow. You, Daddy and I are going away. Poor, sweet thing! I promise you, I'll be with you then, I'll be with you, always."

Kit awoke with a jerk; the dream had been so real.

At her side, David stirred, and sat up. "What's wrong?"

"Nothing. I'm so sorry! I didn't mean to wake you."

"What was it?"

She forced an awkward laugh, not wanting to share the strange vision—or memory—that had come as she slept. "I don't know. Something just…woke me. Nightmare, I guess. But I woke you, too. I'm sorry."

He pulled her close. "I'm not."

They made love again. Intimately, as if they had been together forever. As if she had known him for years.

Technically, she supposed, she had.

But in reality, she realized, he was little more than a stranger.

4

"Details!" Jen exclaimed. "Details!"

Kit finished filling Whitney's bowl with cat food, cradling the phone between her head and shoulder.

"I am not giving you details," Kit said firmly. "It was simply far too…well, I'm not talking about any of it."

"Great," Jen said. "I'm trying to live an exciting life through you, and I'm getting nowhere."

Kit grinned and slid a hand down Whitney's black back as he happily scrambled for his bowl. "You're life is exciting enough. You do exactly what you want to do."

"No, what I want to do is meet Mr. Perfect. He's going to have a job that he loves and gives him confidence, and he's going to be proud of me as a cartoonist. We're going to have one boy and one girl, and we're both going to be loving parents. Sometimes, I'll bring him breakfast in bed, and when I'm rushed, he's going to make coffee in the morning and make sure that the dinner we've ordered out has arrived."

"He's out there somewhere."

"Maybe. But in the meantime, I want my invitation to Bougainvillea. Okay, and this is why I'm so confused. Why aren't you there already?"

"Because I came home first. I had to get the cat, you know."

"The cat!"

"I wanted to get ahead a bit, too, on the strip. So that when I go, I can have a real vacation."

"Vacation, huh?" Jen sniffed. "Sounds like you're going to be living there."

Kit was silent for a moment, feeling the little rush of being wildly, ecstatically in love. But then, even the feeling of total euphoria that threatened to overtake her was dampened.

She was still uneasy about the place. Almost as if Bougainvillea was the same as the bogeyman.

"I don't know," Kit murmured.

"He's with you, right?"

"Yes, he's here." Kit glanced toward the bedroom. David had been up most of the night, faxing back and forth to the Sea Life offices in Florida. He'd shown her some of the sketches for a sailboat they were working on, and then gone back to crunch numbers himself.

He hadn't gone home—or back to his office—since the convention.

He'd stayed in Chicago for almost three weeks, despite her suggestion that it would be all right for him to go home, that she'd hop on a plane as soon as she was caught up and ready.

But he had lingered anyway, assuring her that in this age of e-mail and high-tech communications, there was little that he couldn't do while waiting on her. Kit couldn't help but be pleased, because it seemed that he was loathe to leave her, to be away from her for any time at all. It was also heartening to see that he completely understood and supported her career.

"Has he asked you to marry him?" Jen demanded.

"Jen! We've only been together a little over three weeks!"

"But three perfect weeks," Jen reminded her.

Kit was silent.

"Chemistry. It's right, or it's not right. You're too careful, young lady. You don't take risks, and you don't get ahead in life if you don't take risks.''

''Jen! Personal relationships are not about getting ahead in life.''

''Same point,'' Jen said with exasperation. ''Sometimes, when you want something, you have to dive right in.''

''I'll keep that in mind.''

''Marry him!''

''He hasn't asked me.''

''He will.''

''We'll see.''

''It'll be winter soon, Kit. You're in wretchedly cold Chicago and I'm in wretchedly wet Seattle. I need a great place to go for winter.''

''Hmm. I've got it. I'll send you down to Bougainvillea as my scout. Tell them you're my representative or something. Bask in the sun—''

''Why don't you want to go down there?'' Jen demanded flatly.

''I do!'' she protested.

But Jen was right. She was procrastinating. Because…
There was something dark about all that sunlight.

''Gotta go,'' Jen said. ''Keep me posted. And don't let everything slip through your fingers!''

''I'll stay under your wisdom and advisement,'' Kit assured her.

She hung up and walked into her office, and over to her drafting table. She glanced down at the strip she had just finished. She was ahead now—way ahead. She'd been able to practically churn out really good little strips at an incredible rate.

Because she was happy, she thought. And because she actually knew something about a relationship once again.

She was sitting in her chair staring at the last strip when she became aware of David standing in the doorway in his terry-cloth robe. His dark hair was tousled and he had a bit of five-o'clock shadow. He still appeared every bit as arresting as he ever had, if not more so. She reflected that the longer she was with him, the more exciting he became. Familiarity was not breeding contempt, but making her more aware daily of just what she had. She was tempted to rush up and slip her arms through the V of the robe, feel his flesh, bury her face against it.

"Hey," he said softly.

"Hey."

He walked into the room and stared down at her strip. "Very good," he mused.

She looked up at him. "You would say so no matter what."

"Actually, no, I wouldn't. Ask Josh. I tell him when I think a design sucks. Wait—let me think. You can't ask Josh. You don't know him. Or don't remember him."

"I will meet him again, or see him again," she said.

"When?"

"I'm almost ready to go," she said. She hesitated then. "David, is there a reason I shouldn't want to go there? Did something terrible happen?"

He looked away from her, staring at the strip again. "You know something terrible happened," he said. "Your mother died."

"No, of course, but she drowned. That was terribly tragic. But not…dark," she said at last, unable to think of another word.

"Any death is terrible, and Marina's rocked everyone there," he told her.

Then Kit said, "She wasn't liked, was she?"

He looked at her then, and offered her a strange, wry grimace. "There were moments when she could be very cruel, but she was young, you know, when she first met the Delaneys. I think sometimes she was just unsure of herself. She was rash, impetuous—and gorgeous. No, she wasn't always liked. But she was also adored. Mary thought the world of her. I was in awe of her—Josh, too. Seamus adored her. She was human, Kit. She had her bad points, but she had her very good points, too. You must know that. She meant everything in the world to your father.''

Kit nodded.

''You're afraid to go there,'' he said.

''No, I'm not afraid,'' she said. ''Really, I'm anxious.''

''We'll get there then,'' he said lightly. He walked to the door. ''Sorry, hope I didn't disturb your work. I'm going to shower and get on the computer.''

He left her alone in her office.

That night, she dreamed of Bougainvillea again. She was with Mary, who seemed to have been crying, but the old woman was holding her, and trying to reassure her. ''Just the birds, love. They're so loud. You can always hear those wretched creatures.''

Then she was running on the sand, and she was trying to get away from someone. She was terrified, and she didn't know why.

She woke with a start again, then bit her lower lip, trying not to move. She felt David's arm tighten around her. Instinct?

If she had awakened him, he gave no other sign of it, and she fell uneasily back to sleep.

The next evening, as they walked along the lake, he spun her around to face him.

''Marry me,'' he said softly, dark eyes intent.

''Marry…?'' she murmured.

''Yes, you know. Become man and wife.''

''I…''

''I love you, you know. I mean in all honesty, I thought you were the most desirable being ever created from the moment I saw you. And it might not have been the greatest idea, seeing as how my mission was to bring you home, but sleeping with you had been at the top of my mind every moment we were together. But I never realized myself how deeply I could need you every moment, how your scent would linger or haunt me in the midst of all else. So…you see, I am madly, deeply and passionately in love with you. I want to marry you.''

She stared at him, incredulous. The emotion in his dark eyes was so intense, so serious. So very real.

''Oh!'' she whispered.

''Well?''

''Um…ditto.''

He smiled, still the master of composure, always his own man, strong in success, and failure.

If he ever failed.

''So—does that mean you will marry me?''

She nodded, still stunned. ''Um…what were you thinking? Here, Florida? A year, six months…what?''

''Now. Tonight. We can get a plane to Vegas. And fly home from there.''

''Home?''

''Bougainvillea.''

''I still have the cat.''

''He can be best man.''

She finally had to laugh. ''This is crazy. Insane. I mean, my folks are both dead, but really, don't you want to see your family?''

''My folks are both gone as well.''

''But you're part of…of an enterprise, or an extended family, or something.''

''Actually, they're your family,'' he reminded her.

''Tonight?''

''I want to spend the rest of my life with you,'' he said. ''I know it as I've never known anything before in my life. I believe that you feel the same way. So marry me, tonight.''

''We will need a ticket for the cat, you know,'' she told him.

He wrapped her into his arms. And it seemed the most natural thing in the world then, to fly to Las Vegas. To marry, that night.

Lenore let out a cry of rage.

Michael, sipping coffee and reading the paper, nearly jumped out of his chair.

"What?" he demanded.

She was standing next to the phone. She gripped the receiver so tightly the veins were standing out on her hand. Her free palm covered the mouthpiece.

She shook her head at Michael, her face dead-white.

"How lovely," she said into the phone. "We're—well, yes, we're stunned, but…delighted."

Like hell she was delighted, Michael thought, and he didn't even know what she was talking about.

"Naturally, I'll tell Seamus right away."

"My dear, what is it?" Michael demanded as she set the receiver down.

Lenore spent several minutes looking as if she was about to have apoplexy. She was trying to speak. Her mouth was working, but words wouldn't come. Then finally, she said, "He's married her!"

"What?"

"David has gone and—and *married* Kit Delancy."

"Wow. That was fast," Michael said.

"That was fast? That's all you have to say? It was wretched…horrible…that he was bringing the little…the little…"

"Hey, anybody seen my keys?"

Josh chose that moment to walk in. His keys were forever lost on some piece of furniture.

"Mom, who are we talking about? Let's see…wretched and horrible, that little…little—*bitch* would probably be the right word. Who's she talking about?" he asked his father cheerfully.

"Kit Delaney."

"Hey, she was a cute little kid. Mischievous, but hey, you expect that in a kid. Why is she a bitch?"

"Apparently, David has married her," Michael informed his son.

"Married! David went off and married her?"

"That's what your mother says."

"I'll be damned. David. Married. Hmm. That will dampen a few expectations around here, won't it?" he said, and laughed. "So have you seen them?"

"Seen what?" Lenore asked.

"My keys."

"David Moore has gone off and married Kit Delaney, and all you're concerned about is your keys?" Lenore said, incredulous.

"Can't drive without them," Josh said. "Hey, does Seamus know yet?"

"No," Michael told him.

"Well, I tell you, you've got to give it to David. Send him off to retrieve someone, and he sure goes all the way. When are they coming here?"

"I don't know!" his mother said icily.

Kaitlin came breezing in, walking toward the liquor cabinet. "Good evening, all," she said, then paused, studying them. "Did someone's dog die?" she asked.

"Worse," Josh said gravely. He stared at Kaitlin, a wry grin curling his lips. "David has gone off and married Kit Delaney."

It was a good thing Kaitlin hadn't picked up a liquor bottle—she would have dropped it. Her mouth gaped for a moment before she thought to snap it shut.

"You're joking," she said.

"No, we're not." Lenore's voice remained grim.

"But...how? When?" Kaitlin demanded.

"In Las Vegas. Last night," Lenore said.

"But...I don't believe it," Kaitlin said.

"Why not?" Josh asked. "If she looks anything like Marina, which she definitely did as a kid, she must be stunning. And why not keep it all in the family, as they say?"

"She's not our family," Lenore protested.

Michael looked at his wife. "She's a Delaney, my dear. Just the same as I am."

Lenore stared at him, started to speak, and clamped her lips shut.

"I just don't believe it!" Kaitlin said. "It's just David. He's called with this jest to yank our chains. I mean, all right, Seamus wants to see Kit. He's filled with remorse over all the arguments and the fact that Marina died here. But David must be aware that... well, that no one else could possibly want her around!"

"Does anyone matter but Seamus?" Josh asked lightly.

At that moment, the phone rang. Michael strode past his still stiff wife to answer it. "Hello?"

"Michael, it's Shelley. David just called, and told me about Kit, then put me on the phone with her. I'm so excited. I was thinking about planning a party for when they come home—except that I don't want to step on any toes. I thought that you might want to plan the party. Isn't it wonderful? It's just incredible. After everything that happened, Kit will still be coming back here to live. Isn't it just great?"

"Who is it, Michael?" Lenore demanded.

He turned the phone away from his mouth. "Shelley. She's sure we're just ecstatic about David marrying Kit," he told her, his expression totally deadpan. "She wants to plan a party."

"A party?" Lenore all but exhaled fire.

He spoke to Shelley again. "She thinks it's a wonderful idea."

"Please, either let me plan it, or be in on the planning," Shelley said. "Can you imagine! She was my best friend in first grade. But I hardly remember her. She sounded wonderful on the phone. And she's going to be really famous, you know. Her comic strip is in syndication. More and more papers are picking it up.''

''Yes, seems like she must be very talented.'' He thought of his own love of drawing. For him, it was design. For Kit, a comic strip. Mark Delaney, the scholar, had sketched great sailing ships and landscapes. Seamus still doodled constantly.

Kit was, whether she knew it or not herself, definitely one of the family.

''We'll plan a wonderful party for them,'' he said.

''How did Seamus like the news?'' Shelley asked.

''I don't think he knows yet,'' Michael told her, arching a brow to his wife. ''I know that Kaitlin or Lenore will be delighted to bring him the news.''

Her lips pursed, Lenore turned toward the west wing of the main house where Seamus kept his home office. Kaitlin gave him a scathing look and picked up the bottle of Scotch.

''Dad, has anyone seen my keys?'' Josh demanded.

On the other end of the line, Shelley was still talking. ''I can't wait to tell Eli and my dad. Dad always raved so about Marina—and I'm certain that Eli had a schoolboy crush on her. Wait till I tell them that Kit is coming here now as David's wife!''

Michael was still for a moment, pained as he mused over the past.

''I'm sure they'll both be very excited,'' he said dryly. ''Nice to talk to you, Shelley. We'll get going on it as soon as we know if and when they're coming home. I know Lenore will be happy for you to help with the arrangements.''

''Thanks, Michael. Bye.''

He hung up and looked across the room at Kaitlin, shrugging at the glare she gave him. ''What are you going to do?'' he inquired softly. ''Kit is coming here. As David's wife. That's all there is to it. Pour me a Scotch, too, please. Make it a double.''

''Ah-ha!'' Josh cried out.

''What?'' Michael and Kaitlin said in unison, staring at him as if another earth-shattering revelation was forthcoming.

''My keys!'' Josh said happily. ''There they are, right next to the Scotch.'' He scooped up his keys and stared at the other two. ''All right, then, pour me one, too. Make it very small though—just a sip. Gotta drive you know. But we should salute the new lovers.''

Kaitlin didn't move fast enough for him. He smiled, took the bottle from her, and poured out three glasses of fine amber liquor, making his a bare taste. He lifted his own glass, amused. ''To the newlyweds!'' he cried. The others just stared at him. ''What, you're not drinking with me?''

He drained the small amount in his glass, set it down, and grinned. Grabbing his keys, he started for the door. ''Sweet dreams, all,'' he said cheerfully, and was gone.

Kaitlin made a noise and took her Scotch with her, toward the stairs.

Michael mused over the amber color of his drink for a moment. Then he lifted the glass. ''To the newlyweds,'' he said softly. ''May they live long and prosper. Or…well, may they live.''

David leaned against the wall of the hotel, staring out at the brilliant lights of Las Vegas.

In comparison, the room was muted in soft blue shadow. Great honeymoon room—only a bit tacky with the heart-shaped whirlpool bath and feathery cover on the bed. He loved the way the lights played into the room, and loved them even more the moment that Kit stepped back out from her shower.

His wife. She had married him.

He felt as if a fist squeezed around his heart.

She smiled, wrapped in a white towel, shaking her hair free and running her fingers through the midnight-black length of it. She was stunning in every way, compact and perfectly formed, her facial structure incredible, beyond even classic beauty. And yet it was the way that she smiled that tore into his heart and soul.

She walked over to him, sliding her arms around his waist. He tugged at the towel, allowing it to drop to the floor. He drew the length of her body, hot and damp from the shower, against his own, and it felt as if every longing within him erupted cleanly to the surface.

And yet...

As the urgency of passion engulfed him, a warning teased at the back of his mind.

Stay away...

Stay here, take her somewhere else, anywhere.

Don't go back to Bougainvillea.

Later, much later, he was puzzled by his strange sense of panic when he had held her, the sense of fierce protection, and of dread.

Bougainvillea.

He had always loved the place. It was home.

And still...

He awoke the following morning with the knowledge that the past had been bitter.

They might be so much better off if she never knew all that had gone on during those long-ago years.

5

"There, the Everglades," David said, pointing out the window as their plane made its initial descent toward Miami International Airport. "The area is fascinating. I love to go out there. Lots of airboats, alligators, Seminole and Miccosukkee villages, music fests at times—and mosquitos, too. Sawgrass and snakes. But beautiful birds, and incredible photo opportunities." He shrugged. "Some people hate it."

"Shark Valley," Kit said, grinning at him. "I came out on a field trip with my first-grade class!"

"So," he mused, dark eyes curiously on her. "Memories are coming back."

"I remembered Shelley so clearly when I talked to her the other night."

"I imagine more and more will come back to you when you see people—and Bougainvillea itself, of course."

"I'm sure. It's great, really. I'd like to have more of a memory of my mother."

He looked out the window again, not replying. Then he turned to her. "You know, if you find that you're unhappy there—overburdened with family—we can just move."

"Some of the business offices are on the estate, aren't they?" she asked.

He shrugged. "Convenience can be regained. The main facilities are down closer to the marina in the Grove. Trust me, if you wish, we can move. After all, you've already taken the step from one State to another. I can move into a new house.''

''But you love the estate, don't you?''

He was silent for a minute, watching her. ''You'll love it, too, when you see it again. But still....'' He gave her something of a strange, awkward grimace. ''I love you. And if you're unhappy...sand is sand. And buildings are just concrete, nothing more.''

She smiled, wondering if it would be possible to be this much in love, in euphoria, forever. Surely not, and yet she knew that although excitement might wear away somewhat with time, love could grow into something deeper, and even better. However, as she sat by him then, she wondered if even the excitement would ebb away. David had an appeal that came with the fact he was unaware of the way he did something so casual as walk, smile or speak. His confidence seemed ingrained; he was the type who commanded respect without raising his tone. She was still just as hypnotized by the scent of him, the sound of his voice, his slightest touch.

''We're landing. Look, there's the Biltmore—an historic hotel, really beautifully redone. Downtown Miami is off that way. And...you can't see it, but there, in that direction, toward the water, is Bougainvillea.''

They deplaned and exited the gate area, leaving to the right of the security check where outgoing passengers were setting their luggage down to be scanned. By then, Whitney was meowing constantly from his under-the-seat carrier.

They had barely left the area before Kit heard her name being called excitedly. ''Kit! David!''

''It's Shelley,'' David said.

Kit barely got a chance to see the pretty woman who came flying across the concourse to throw her arms around her. Shelley. She'd enjoyed her phone conversation with the girl who had apparently been her best friend in first grade, and seeing her was even better. Shelley hugged her

tightly, then withdrew to hug David as well. Then she stood
arm's distance from Kit, and they stared at one another.
They were nearly the same size. Shelley, however, was a
flaming redhead. Her eyes were hazel and fiery, and she
was deeply tanned. Kit quickly recalled an image of a little
girl with carrot-colored pigtails, braces, and a smattering of
freckles on her nose.

"A cat, huh?" she said.

"Whitney."

"You always loved animals! What a fortune you cost
your folks on getting strays settled. Hey—we both made
five-seven, so it seems. And they claimed that we'd both
be tiny little things all our lives!" Shelley said with a laugh.
"Look at you, though!" She glanced at David, then back
at Kit. "Well, you must know, of course, that you are the
spitting image of your mother. Your hair is almost pitch-
black—do you dye it? Rude question, sorry. Your eyes are
just like hers, too, almost violet. Contacts? No, your Mom's
weren't. Wow, I'm horrible, aren't I? Not really, because
you know, we did use to talk about everything."

"Well, I more or less remember," Kit said with a laugh.

"You don't remember anything. You moved far away
and grew up to become rich and famous."

"Not rich or really famous, I'm afraid. Slightly known,"
Kit told her ruefully.

"You'd be surprised," Shelley told her.

"You know," David said, "we could continue this outside of the airport."

"Right, of course, let's go. Luggage is below," she informed Kit, linking arms with her as she led the way.

Once they were in Shelley's car, she glanced at Kit in
the rearview mirror. "I'm afraid you're going home to a
zoo," she said.

"Oh?" David said, somewhat sharply.

Shelley shrugged. "My idea. I thought we should welcome Kit with a party. I think Lenore might have been

upset that I had the idea first. I'd wanted to plan something small, and well…'' She glanced at Kit in the rearview mirror again. "You're about to meet the mayors of three of the little municipalities, the chairman of a local children's charity, and well, God alone knows who else. They've thrown a major festival.''

"Great,'' David muttered.

"It's all right,'' Kit said quickly. "Might as well jump right into the fire.''

"Into the fire. Right,'' David said. He looked out the window, and didn't seem to pay attention to any of the conversation in the car from that point. It didn't matter; Shelley was talkative, pointing out streets and landmarks as they went along. Driving down Red Road, she pointed out Coral Gables to the left, West Miami to the right, and then South Miami when they came to a certain point. Coconut Grove wasn't actually its own city, just an area. But they were in it, and the foliage along the road grew thicker and thicker and very beautiful. Finally, they came to gates off the side of the road, where Shelley paused to punch in a code, telling Kit the numbers as she did so. Kit wondered if Shelley was aware that she would never remember them.

A long drive through dense and colorful bushes and trees brought them to the front of the house.

Bougainvillea.

And she remembered it.

The house was a combination of old Southern and medieval Spanish architecture, the huge porch with its thick pillars covered in coral rock. The length and breadth of it was tiled; heavy planters flanked the large doorway and a number of the windows. The second floor, rising above the covered porch, gave way to a number of trellised balconies. The whole of the front of the house gave off an odd sense of perfectly balanced art and architecture, the bottom story being sturdy, the second level far lighter, and together, they appeared postcard perfect.

Cars were parked everywhere on either side of the drive. Faint music could be heard.

"They hired a band?" David said, staring at Shelley.

She shrugged. "There's at least a hundred people here."

"She couldn't give us a chance to unpack and shower, huh?" David muttered.

"You know Lenore. I guess she decided that she had to look like the grand society dame, welcoming you and your new wife." Shelley shrugged, looking at Kit. "I'm a schoolteacher and my brother is a cop, but such is this area that we can be neighbors. Actually, I personally like Lenore's forays into keeping up with the Joneses. Best chance I ever get to meet mayors."

"That's not the point, Shelley," David said softly.

"Right. I know."

"See why I mentioned moving?" David said to Kit.

"Don't move...please don't move! You won't be next to me, and we won't be able to run over at any time," Shelley said.

Kit didn't have to answer. They were getting out of the car. David looked at Kit. "We can grab my car and escape, you know."

She smiled. "Actually, I've never met a mayor before myself."

"We can go straight in, then," David said.

"But the cat!" Kit said.

"I'll leave the door unlocked and send someone to see that he makes it to David's place," Shelley assured her.

They left the luggage in the car and walked around the porch to the back of the estate. And there was the area Kit really remembered. The lagoon, like a tiny finger inlet, drove deep into the center of the property. It was surrounded by beach—man-made, she was fairly sure. A tiled path meandered around the lagoon on either side, and the cottages lay at pleasant but haphazard angles behind the paths. At the end of the western side, a dock gave berth to a number of boats. On the east, a wooden jetty streaked out over the water, a place to walk out to see the sunsets. At the moment, canopied tents lay over the grounds. Near the rear of the main house, on the rear side of the porch where a coral rock slab stood a few feet off the ground, a four-piece band was playing oldies, and barbecues were working full-time.

"David, you're back!"

The woman who sauntered with long strides toward David instantly struck a chord of memory in Kit's mind—but not a very pleasant one. It was Lenore Delaney, she knew. Michael's wife, Josh's mother. She was slim to the point of gaunt, beautifully made-up and coiffured, elegant in every way, her features made almost excessively sharp with her slimness. She was platinum-blond, and appeared much younger than Kit knew she had to be.

She greeted David with apparent warmth, hugging him, and offering him a kiss to each cheek. He responded politely, but, Kit thought, stiffly. He was angry, and hadn't wanted this kind of a commotion when they returned.

"Honestly, David, you've got to talk with Mayor Solquist—he thinks that you must run for public office, that you're perfect. Ah hah! And there she is. Kit Delaney. You little tomboy, all grown up, and back home. Married!" She punched David on the shoulder and gave him a coy, reproachful look. "What a surprise. I know Seamus told you to find our girl and bring her home, but did he tell you to marry her?"

"Marriage was my idea, Lenore," David said dryly. "Where is Seamus?"

"Let me say hello to your wife. Kit, dear, welcome home."

Lenore kissed Kit on both cheeks, her smile welcoming, her eyes cold. Kit murmured a thank you, withdrawing from the woman's hold as quickly as she could. She was startled to feel a mixture of warmth and wariness as she met Lenore. She hoped she didn't betray her unease, but even as she drew away from Lenore, a man approached them, grinning from ear to ear. She immediately knew that he was a Delaney, his sandy hair showing a few signs of coming gray, his eyes a steady hazel. His eyes bore a twinkle of merriment, and his smile was generous. "Kit! I'm Michael, remember me?"

He gave her a simple, warm hug.

He seemed honestly glad to see her. She was grateful.

"I admit," she told him, "most of my memories are pretty vague. But thank you, the party seems wonderful."

"My wife's idea, of course."

"Quite a bit for a first night here, don't you think?" David asked Michael.

Michael shrugged. "My thought exactly, when I saw the tents arriving. But, you know Lenore. She likes things done up larger-than-life."

"Come dear, you must meet some people!" Lenore said, sweeping over for Kit like a stalking vulture.

Kit found herself whirled from group to group. She was introduced over and over again: the Tylers—a wonderful political family; the Herrerras, owners of a local business featuring the finest Cuban cigars made in Miami; Nadia Jamison—simply born rich, a philanthropist in the area, Lenore informed her on the side. There were the mayors, their wives, sons, daughters, lawyers, doctors, historians, architects, sailboat makers, racers, divers, documentary producers and more.

Somewhere in it all, she met Josh, who was very much like his father, warm, definitely a Delaney, a handsome fellow with a continual dry grin that seemed to take in all life. Josh seemed amused and pleased to see her, and once she had spoken with him, she thought that she remembered him—vaguely. Kaitlin came purposely to find her, introducing herself, though reminding Kit they knew one another. "Actually, I was your baby-sitter now and then,"

Kaitlin said. "I was in my teens when I started working here, then on my way through college for a business degree. Seamus helped me out a great deal."

Kit assured her that she remembered her, and she did, but very vaguely. She wondered what the woman might have been like then, because she was quite incredible now—a platinum blond with immense, seductive dark eyes and a way about her that was sheerly elegant and sensual, almost as if she were a cat, toying with most people, sleek and ready to pounce when the right moment came. Though Kaitlin's words to her were pleasant enough, and she smiled a lot, as if truly welcoming Kit, there was an edge about her. As if beneath it all, she resented Kit and her marriage.

Shelley rescued her from hearing the entire history of how the flamingo came to be in Florida, introducing her to her brother, Eli. He was a tall guy with dark auburn hair as well, a smattering of freckles, and a pleasant smile, and her father, Martin, from whom the red hair, hazel eyes, and freckles apparently came. Both seemed far more laid-back and real than most of the people at the party. Martin, especially, was funny, and took the time to tell her how sorry he was about her father, just how much she looked like her mother, and how beautiful Marina had been.

Talking to him, she again felt a faint stir of memory and nostalgia. He seemed exceptionally nice, a great father figure.

It was as she was standing with them that she heard her name called in a deep, husky voice, filled with a trembling emotion.

She turned. She knew instantly that she was coming face-to-face with Seamus Delaney, after her many, many years away.

"Kit…Katherine Delaney. You've come home."

She knew that he was in his late seventies. He moved with the ramrod assurance of a much younger and very powerful man. He was tall and lithe, but his shoulders still showed an imposing breadth. His eyes were light green, his head was still well covered with thick white hair.

He resembled her father so much, before the illness had set in, that for a moment, her breath was caught.

But only a moment. He strode through the crowd toward her, paused a moment, his smile deep, and then said, "Welcome." He wrapped her in his arms as if he were indeed welcoming back a long cherished and deeply loved child. Still holding her, his eyes alight with a smile, he said, "I cannot tell you how good it is to see you, how wonderful it is to have you here."

"Thank you," she said. And she smiled ruefully. "You gave me a bit of a start. You look so much like my father."

He shook his head. "I was the older—your father looked like me," he informed her. He studied her for another long moment. "And you, my dear, are the exact image of your mother."

"So I've heard."

"It's a compliment, you know," he said. "Marina was probably the most gorgeous creature to walk the earth."

As Kit thanked him again, she saw that Lenore had been within hearing distance. She seemed to let out something of a snort, quickly concealed, before she turned away.

Seamus might have noticed because he excused himself to Shelley and her family and set his arm around Kit's shoulders. "Let's escape for a minute, shall we? Are you too tired? I think that Shelley's plan had been an intimate dinner, just her family and ours. Lenore likes everything a bit outrageous, you know. None of us had any idea she had planned…this."

"It's fine," Kit said. "Might as well plunge right in."

He looked at her sharply. She arched a brow to him.

"Sorry, but you just sounded exactly like your mother, too. So rash, impetuous—and ready to rush in. Do you remember?"

"Well, of course, I remember her. Just not very well," Kit admitted. "But I didn't remember a great deal, until I arrived."

"I'm afraid you'll remember more and more," he said with a sigh.

"I already realize that she wasn't particularly liked by everyone," Kit told him honestly.

"Let's go to my library. We'll talk there."

They entered the main house through one of the oversize sets of French doors that led out to the patio. They came through a massive family entertainment area with a mammoth television screen set amid a cabinet filled with electronic devices. The back room crossed through to a hallway. Kit saw a formal dining room and kitchen and breakfast nook to the left, and a living room to the right, just to the side of the stairway. They mounted the stairway to the second level.

"My suite is this way," he said, directing her to the right.

His door opened into a masculine office with a fine desk made of what he told her was Dade County pine. Windows opened to the rear; they could see the party going on below. Upholstered leather chairs sat in front of a fireplace—lots of the old places had them, even in Florida, he told her. It could go into the thirties—if only for a few days—in winter, and once, just like in the rest of the country, a fireplace had provided heat.

They sat in the chairs that faced the unlit hearth. "Jealous!" Seamus told her.

"Pardon?"

"If any of the old bats hated your mother, it's because they were jealous," he said.

She had to smile. "Oh."

He shook his head, somehow lost in memory himself. "She was too impetuous, I'll tell you that." A deep sigh trembled through him. "Confident and reckless. The night she died…she was angry with everyone, I think, and so she walked out to the lagoon, and plunged into the water."

"You don't think that she—that she tried to kill herself?" Kit said.

Seamus shook his head emphatically. "Marina Delaney? Never! She could swim like a fish, and she was prone to popping out into the water at any hour of the day or night." He arched a brow. "You still swim, don't you? When your father left here, he was heartsick, hated the ocean, the water, even the sun and the moon, I think."

"My Dad was the most incredible man on earth," Kit said, her pride and affection mingling with the pain of loss. "He taught me everything he thought important. I was on my high school swim team. I never saw him in the water, but he never stopped me."

"Good, good. The water is part of life down here. Of our lives, anyway. We build boats, you know. Some of the best in the country. Sea Life racers enter almost every important event across the country."

"So I understand. And Michael, your son, designs them?"

"Some. I still design myself. And Josh…Josh is showing a real talent. Michael doesn't want to do anything but live out his dream—taking off on one of the sailing vessels and cruising the Caribbean endlessly. Your husband is the one with the real nose for business, you know. There were times when, I admit, in the last years, we might have lost the whole shebang. Your fellow kept us afloat. But there must be something about the place—maybe in the water!" he said with a wink. "David has his camera out all the time. He has a real artistry with it. And you—I've seen your strips, of course. I've followed them since you started."

"Why didn't you ever…why did I go all these years without hearing from anyone here? I know that the pain of my mother's loss sent my father away, but…"

"When Mark left here, he was running, yes. And he

didn't want to be reminded of Marina or anyone or anything here. I understood that. And later, when I thought he might relent, I wrote to him. He said that he could never bear to come back here, and that life was good in Chicago.''

Kit nodded. She was startled to feel a bit of resentment. She understood her father's pain. After all, she had been a child suddenly bereft of a mother. But still, her heritage was here…and he had kept her from it.

''You're here now!'' Seamus said, still eyeing her as if the most incredible treasure had been set before him. It was a pleasant feeling.

''Come, I'll show you something.''

Seamus rose suddenly. She followed.

They went back into the hallway. He pointed to the door to Kaitlin's office. She had a little bungalow down by the lagoon, but there was a futon, full bath, and even a little kitchenette in her office, just for those nights when business became too hectic. ''Sometimes, we're up all night because we deal with customers all over the world,'' Seamus said.

Then he opened a door to the left.

There was a scent of jasmine on the air. Subtle, below the surface, but there. A silvery white negligee was lying over the bed. Along with the scent of jasmine, there was something a little musty. Windows opened to the rear of the house, and the curtains drifted inward on the breeze, which carried with it the faint sound of conversation and music below.

''This was your folks' room. I never changed it. I never allowed anyone in it. I've spent all these years thinking that one day Mark would come back, and I'd have everything just as it was. Then he could go through your mother's belongings, and his own. Find some sweet nostalgia, and maybe even ease his heart.'' He paused for a moment, and in that time, he suddenly looked very old. ''Feel free to come here, whenever you like. Actually, the house is yours, the run of it, anytime. I wish that your husband liked the main house, but he doesn't. Your luggage has already been taken to his place. It's the cottage closest to the water on the dock side of the lagoon.'' He looked at her, studying her again. ''I hope, however, that to humor an old man, you'll spend a lot of time here, with me. There's a lot of family history here.''

''Of course,'' Kit told him. She hesitated then, and walked into the room, fascinated. This was where they had lived together, her parents. She had a vague memory of running into the room, bouncing onto the foot of the bed, and throwing herself into their arms. For a moment, she remembered her mother clearly. Laughing, scooping Kit up close to her, and hugging her tightly. She felt a sweet elation, certain that, whatever her mother's faults might have been, Marina Delaney had loved her daughter.

Kit tentatively walked to the open doors overlooking the porch, and the party. Lenore had invited at least a hundred people. They milled everywhere.

The view from here was excellent. She could see the lagoon, the dock, the wooden jetty. The pool was off to the left side of the house. The bungalows and cottages dotted the banks of the lagoon. She saw Shelley with a group of young people, eschewing a fancy glass and drinking her beer from the bottle. Eli and Martin Callahan were deep in discussion with Josh.

And David...

She searched the crowd and saw him deep in conversation with Kaitlin. The beautiful blond had her hand on his shoulder in a proprietary manner that brought a little shudder to Kit's heart. What was Kaitlin now? About forty? And David was thirty-seven.

Impulsive...

Marina had been impulsive.

And she was like her mother. Strange, the way that she

had fallen head over heels for David, never questioning his past.

She was suddenly certain that at one time, in some way, David had been involved with Kaitlin.

She was still staring out at the scene below when Lenore found them.

"What on earth are you two doing up here? Seamus, I want Kit to meet Lara Kinney, who sponsors the theater. She's very important, dear."

Seamus nodded, offering Kit a secret smile and widening his eyes slightly with amusement. "You must go meet the very rich and famous," he told her. He winked. "They buy newspapers and sometimes, I believe, even read comic strips."

"Seamus, you're acting as if we're snobby and catty, and we're not, not at all. We like to contribute to the community, and you're the one who taught me that, father-in-law dear!" Lenore said. Her voice was light, filled with affection. Kit thought it sounded false.

But she smiled to herself and accompanied Lenore downstairs, and smiled her way pleasantly through all the introductions. She had just met the head of the opera guild and listened to a long bemoaning of the lack of real supporters for the ultimate art when David slipped his arm around her. "Jean! Great to see you, I'm so glad that you could come. I see that you've met Kit. Will you excuse us? Seamus wants Kit to meet a racing friend."

Kit murmured something appropriate; Jean of the opera sadly watched them move on.

"Who am I meeting?" Kit asked.

"No one—we're escaping," he told her with a grin.

He moved faster and faster, leading her through the crowd, and then down a path that led to some dense foliage.

By then, it was growing dark. Kit laughed. "Where are we going?"

"Back way—to our own home!" he told her.

A few minutes later, they were bursting through pines and crotons to a tiled and pillared porch, then through glass doors to a high-ceilinged rec room, complete with billiards and an entertainment center compatible to that in the main house. Ship models handsomely adorned panelled walls. Collector pieces, old swords, antique guns, African and Caribbean art were displayed on various shelves. Kit stopped dead still for a moment, looking around, realizing that the items actually represented a world she didn't share with her husband.

A meow and a brush of fur against her leg suddenly reminded Kit that she had brought a piece of her own home with her.

"Whitney!" she cried, and scooped him up. He purred happily. "Poor thing. The flight was traumatic, I think."

David took the cat from her. "Believe me, Lenore hires the most efficient help in the state. He's been fed and watered, and I'm sure he's making himself quite happy here. Actually, too bad we don't live in the main house. Both Lenore and Kaitlin hate cats."

"David, that's mean!"

"To the cat or the two witches?"

She laughed. "You don't like them very much, huh?"

He shrugged. "They're like family—I guess. Therefore, I get to call them witches. Or worse."

He set the cat down.

"Question," he said, moving close to her. "Want to see more of my place first—or of me?"

She smiled slowly. "Hmm."

"Well?" he persisted.

"Question."

"Yes?"

"Does that mean you're eager to see more of me, now that we're alone?" she demanded.

"You bet."

She laughed softly, curling her arms around his neck.

He'd carried her over the threshold of their over-the-top hotel room in Vegas. Now he swept her up again, dramatically romantic. Her foot banged against the wall as he walked up the steps.

"Ouch!"

"Well, that kind of ruined the moment, didn't it?" he inquired dryly. "Maybe not…we'll reach my room—*our* room—and start with the foot."

"Kinky."

"The foot is attached to the ankle."

"Ankle fetish. Great."

"Is attached to the calf. Calf to the knee, knee to the thigh…when we get there," he drawled lazily, "I'll explain completely just what's attached to what."

He did just that. Touch, kiss, and caress her, from her feet, to her ankle, calf, knee, and thigh on up. Kit found herself amazed again at the extent of urgent passion he could arouse in her, and the euphoria that followed. Then laughter as well, and talk, and making love all over again.

They never said goodbye to the many guests at the party. It was into the wee hours of the morning when she finally explored her new home, and with it, learned much about her husband, his love for the sea, and his photographs.

They stayed awake to admire the sunrise, an event she could watch every morning from bed.

Her life, it seemed, was too good to be true. Yet for her first several weeks at Bougainvillea, it stayed the same.

David showed her Sea Life's construction facilities in Coconut Grove, and she met his friends and the many people employed by Sea Life. She lunched with him, Josh and Michael, at the little marina café where apparently they went almost daily at noon. Lenore brought her around town, showing her theaters, galleries and a zillion shops where the Delaneys were esteemed clients. Kaitlin gave her lists of the places they used for home services, and showed her some of the local boutiques she thought Kit should know.

On one of those occasions, Kit was startled to realize that Kaitlin definitely bore her own memories of the past, and they certainly weren't all good.

It was a Wednesday afternoon and they had gone down to Cocowalk to shop. Kit was trying on a halter dress in a blue flowered pattern and came out of the dressing room to ask Kaitlin's opinion.

She was startled by the way the woman stared at her.

"What is it?"

Kaitlin shook her head. "I really don't like it. Not at all."

Frowning, Kit turned to look in the mirror. She loved the color. And she loved the dress. It seemed to enhance her figure, and bring out the depths of her eyes. She really believed that David would love it.

Kit turned to Kaitlin. "What's wrong with it?" she asked carefully.

"It's just wrong, all wrong," Kaitlin told her.

"But—"

"If you must know, it makes you look too much like Marina. And that doesn't make us all feel comfortable, I'm sorry to say!"

Angry, Kaitlin walked out of the shop. Kit watched her go, then quickly changed. In spite of Kaitlin, she bought the dress. She'd make sure she wore it when she and David went out, and not around Bougainvillea.

Kaitlin was quiet all the way home. Kit tried to tell herself she was imagining the waves of pure hostility that seemed to roll off of her.

"Kaitlin," Kit told her, as they returned to the compound. "You know, you're definitely not obligated to be in my company."

Kaitlin stared at her, startled that she had been so transparent. Then she looked ahead, over the steering wheel. "Sorry. Honestly." She stared at Kit again. "In truth, there is a lot of resentment going on. Did I want you here? No. But you are here. So...we need to get along.''

"Like I said," Kit told her, getting out of the car, "you're not required to show me around."

She felt uncomfortable when she returned to the main house that afternoon, but as usual Seamus was waiting for them, wanting always to chat with Kit.

Other than her experience with Kaitlin, Kit found that her days were almost idyllic.

Shelley picked her up a few times after work, and they explored malls and saw a few movies. Shelley was great, helping her to remember many little things about the place and her childhood.

Then there were Martin and Eli.

Eli worked long hours as a cop, but he was always fun when he was around.

Martin was often at his own home, rigging his fishing gear. He was always glad to see Kit if she walked over. He'd tell her about some of the parties that used to be held at Bougainvillea, and how other women had hated Marina sometimes just because she had been so darned beautiful.

"Now Lenore, I think that she wanted to be a decent human being, but maybe forgot how. She got too caught up in being the first lady of Bougainvillea. She wasn't terribly fond of Marina, because Marina, of course, was a threat. And Kaitlin. Well, you've noticed, she's pretty darned exotic." He winked. "I think she always thought David would marry her one day. But David never considered her as a love interest, so don't you go worrying. There's a chip on that girl's shoulder." He laughed. "Okay, so she didn't like your mom, either. But you, you just hold your own and thumb your nose at them. Seamus has been pining for you to come back for years. And David—well, he was kind of the cream of the Sea Life crop, you know what I mean? You two will be fine. Just hunker down and bear with the sharks!''

Martin always tried to make her feel better and more welcome, so it seemed. He also seemed to delight in his amusement with the foibles of the Delaney family.

"What did you feel about my mother?" Kit asked him frankly one day.

He hesitated. "Honestly? She was beautiful. And seductive. She could be charming and sweet. She could be hell on wheels, making everyone around her miserable. She was human, and quite a character. But she loved you. And in the end, she loved your father."

"In the end?"

"Well, she liked to flirt," he said uneasily. "But, like I said, she loved your father."

He wouldn't continue. Kit left soon after their conversation, a light feeling of dread threading its way through her heart.

David had come home early that day, eager to see Kit.

He knew that Seamus was in seventh heaven, where he should have been himself.

He was.

Except that he couldn't quite shake an uneasy feeling.

Kit wasn't at the cottage when he first came home. He turned on the stereo and stretched out on the sofa, wondering where she was. Although Kit hadn't said anything, he had the feeling that she was sometimes uncomfortable being there.

So we should get the hell out, he thought.

Marina Delaney had been dead a very long time. And yet, with Kit here, it seemed as if people were remembering her as if she had died only yesterday.

And it was true...

A trick of light, and she might have been her mother, *returned,* in the flesh.

It had all been so long ago, and yet, he knew bits and pieces of what had gone on. Marina knew about all the deep dark Delaney family secrets. Were they really so secret, though? Most of the dirt on the family could be easily uncovered.

Most of the scandals had to do with Seamus and what had once been his philandering days. But who the hell cared anymore?

People only cared when it affected them.

And still…

Why this constant feeling of unease?

Because of what Kit might discover? Because of the cataclysm that might be caused by her return?

The door opened, and he straightened, looking toward it. Kit was home. "David?"

"I'm here."

She rushed over to the sofa, bounding on top of him, grinning beautifully from ear to ear. She had something Marina had never possessed: a natural love of people, and of life. He touched her hair, smoothing it back, amazed that she was his.

"You're early," she whispered.

"I needed to be home. I'm a newlywed, you know."

"And I wasn't here!" she said.

"Chatting away the hours with old Seamus?" he asked gruffly.

She laughed. "No, getting the spin from old Martin next door," she told him.

He watched her carefully for a moment. "You're happy here?"

"You bet."

"Despite the dragon queens up at the big house?" he demanded.

She laughed. "They're not so bad beneath the surface."

He tightened his arms around her. "I was thinking we should leave, find our own place."

She drew away. "Not…not now, David. It would hurt Seamus too deeply, I think. Besides," she said, and a low, sensual quality crept into her tone as she lowered closer to him again, "we *are* alone, all alone…here. Now."

He laughed. It was an invitation if he had ever heard one.

"There is the cat, you know," he reminded her primly.

"Ah, that's why the good Lord invented doors."

He swept her up dramatically, and started for the stairs. In a few moments, it didn't matter where they were.

They had created their own private heaven.

And it wasn't until hours later that he lay at her side, feeling the unease again, and remembering his own relationship with Marina Delaney.

Kit hadn't been there a full two weeks before David had workmen arriving at their cottage, determined to make space in one of the extra bedrooms into a perfect artist's studio for Kit. She became involved in the planning herself, and the days passed quickly.

Jen called frequently, and Kit kept her up to date.

And every night, she lay in David's arms, amazed that her depth of passion and love for him could continue to grow and become ever stronger.

It was the night he wound up not coming home— stranded down in the Keys because of an auto accident on US1, that the perfect tapestry of her new life began to unravel.

It began when she found the cat at the rear door to their cottage, stiff and cold and dead as a doornail.

6

Devastated, Kit cradled Whitney and strode purposely to the main house, entering with her beloved pet. The compound lights gleamed around the lagoon, but they were soft, and shadows from the foliage edging the path and beachfront fell heavily all around her. She took no notice of them.

They were gathered in the family room, where the widescreen television was showing something done by the History Channel. Kaitlin, Lenore, Michael, and Josh were there, all engrossed in the show. But when Kit entered, carrying her dead pet, Michael instantly turned the volume down and sprang to his feet. "Kit! What happened? He didn't wander off the property and get hit, did he?"

She shook her head, tears in her eyes, staring at them all. "There's nothing wrong with him at all," she began.

"Dead does seem to be wrong," Kaitlin told her drolly.

She flashed the woman a furious glance. "He hasn't been hit by anything. There's not a mark on him. He's just dead and stiff. I'd say he'd been poisoned."

"Good heavens, dear! Are you suggesting that one of us would poison your cat?" Lenore said indignantly.

"No, but I'd like to know what did happen," Kit said, wondering if she *had* come ready to accuse one of the "witches" of killing her cat.

"Poor thing," Josh said, stroking Whitney's cold back. "He must have gotten into one of the storage sheds and eaten something. I'm so sorry, Kit."

"There's fertilizer for the plants, all kinds of stuff in the storerooms—rat poison," Michael said. "He might have gotten into anything, I'm afraid."

"We have a little pet burial ground...it's very nice," Josh told her, smiling with sheepish sympathy. "My canary is there, an old one-eyed stray we took in once, and Shelley's Pomeranian. It just died last year."

Bury him. Of course. That was what you did with creatures that died.

She didn't want to bury Whitney. She wanted David to be there, and she wanted to cry her heart out, because suddenly it didn't seem fair that her father *and* her cat had died.

"I should find out how he died," Kit said, her anger taking root with her pain.

"You want to autopsy the cat?" Kaitlin said, and laughed.

"What good will it do you?" Michael reasoned gently. "I'm afraid that I agree with Josh—he got into poison. And as I said, we do have it in the storeroom, down by the docks. We've never had an animal get into it before, but then, we never really had pets here before."

He was right, and she knew it. She could autopsy the cat, and find out that it had died from rat poison. She couldn't find out if Whitney had been given poison *on purpose* or not.

"We'll find you another one," Lenore said impatiently. "There are always stray cats out by that marina shanty where the guys go for lunch every day. We'll just replace him."

She didn't want to discuss the loss of a loved pet with people whom she doubted could really even understand the loss of a human being.

"I don't want another cat," she said angrily and turned on her heel and left.

She was partway down the path when she heard footsteps

behind her. For a moment, she felt a strange rake of fear streak down her spine. Having left the main house, she was suddenly aware of the darkness in the brush surrounding her, and of the many shadows created in the soft, surreal light.

She came to a dead stop and spun around. At first, she saw no one. She turned again.

The sound of footsteps reached her once again. She was being followed. Still frightened, she spun again.

"Kit! Wait up!" It was Josh. She had been followed. And yet, Josh was dead center in the path now, and running. He hadn't been following her slowly—or furtively.

She waited for him to reach her.

"Kit, are you okay?"

She nodded, then felt the tears fall.

"Ah, Kit, I'm so sorry!" He comforted her with an awkward arm around her shoulder. "I'm afraid you've got to ignore my mom and Kaitlin. They're both pet haters." She wondered what he saw in her expression then because he quickly said, "No, no—they would never hurt your cat!"

"This place just doesn't seem to be kind to my branch of the family," she murmured.

Josh hesitated, looking at her. "Please don't feel that way."

"I'm sorry. I don't know what I'm really feeling."

"David will be back tomorrow. Things will look better again."

She nodded.

"Hey, I really adored your mom, you know. I missed her terribly," he said.

"Thanks."

"I'll walk you back to the cottage. You can make me a drink."

"Great. Thanks."

At the cottage, Josh took Whitney and gently wrapped him in a big towel, then secured his body in a garbage bag.

He thanked Kit for the rum and Coke she prepared him, drank it down, and suggested that they go bury the cat right then. Josh shrugged shyly. "We can both say a little prayer, graveside."

"Thanks."

It was dark at the pet cemetery. The compound lights didn't quite make it through the thickness of the foliage that surrounded the inner area of the estate. Josh had found a shovel in the work cabinet on the porch, so he led the way, pushing aside bushes as they walked. Once in the little area, Kit was touched to see that Shelley had ordered bronze markers for all the dead pets—even a goldfish someone had lost along the way.

As Josh dug a hole, Kit mourned her cat, her best friend when times had been the darkest. He was twelve years old, so she could at least assure herself that he'd had something of a life.

Not the life he should have had.

She had killed him by bringing him to Bougainvillea. Where her mother had died.

"He was beautiful, Kit, really," Josh said, tamping down the dirt and then coming to stand beside her and set an arm around her shoulders. "Honestly, I'm so sorry."

As sweet as he was being, she just wanted to be alone. She kissed his check. "I think I'm going to call it a night. Thank you, really."

He wanted to do more, she was certain. But he stayed there, watching as she walked away.

The little pet cemetery had been deep in the brush. Walking back, she felt the darkness all around her again. The bushes began to close behind her, separating her from Josh. She quickened her footsteps. It seemed that she heard the brush rustling, and she was afraid again, so much so that she didn't want to stop and listen for footfalls in her wake.

She hurried to the back door of their cottage, and realized that she had not locked the sliding doors when she had stormed out. She wondered what on earth she could be afraid of—there was a wall with a gated alarm system surrounding the compound.

Still, she grabbed an umbrella from beside the door as she walked through the cottage, going so far as to open every closet door. At length, she was assured she was alone. Only then did she sit down and call David.

His voice was strong over the phone, with the right touch of sympathy and assurance.

She didn't mention her accusation to the family. He told her he could try to get a flight in through a friend that night, but she told him it was too late, and she didn't want him rushing around to get back. She'd see him the next day.

Even when her dad had died, she had never resorted to drugs. But tonight was different. Kit mixed a few beers with mild sleeping aids, hoping to relax as she tried to pay attention to a Pay-Per-View movie. But she lay on the bed, wondering, despite herself, if her poor cat had just wandered in where he shouldn't have been, or if he had been tempted by something, or someone, far more dire.

The next morning, she made herself coffee, then hurried over to the main house. No one was around, but she helped herself to more coffee and walked up the stairs to the room that had been her parents' when they had resided there. She smiled, seeing the nightgown on the bed; Seamus had really ordered that nothing—nothing at all—be changed.

She stood without moving for several minutes, surveying the entire room. Then she idly began going through the drawers. The scent of jasmine rose to her, and she felt an aching sense of nostalgia. Her mother's taste had run toward the truly elegant. At first, Kit found nothing but her clothing.

In the nightstand by the bed, she found a journal. She took it from the drawer and sat on the bed and opened it to the first page. She noted that it began about a month before her mother had died. The first few pages offered nothing but appointments and social engagements, but again, Kit felt that comforting sense of nostalgia, just seeing her mother's handwriting. She had gone no further when she was startled by a voice from the doorway. "What are you doing? What are you looking for?"

Kit looked up to see Kaitlin, knuckles white as she gripped the door frame. Kit surveyed her for a moment before speaking. "I'm not looking for anything in particular. Just exploring my folks' room."

"Maybe you don't want to know more than you do," Kaitlin told her.

Kit stared at her and sighed deeply. "Kaitlin, I get the feeling that we weren't great friends when I was a kid, whether you baby-sat me or not. And I definitely get vibes that you really didn't like my mother. I don't think that I'm going to find anything so bad. Maybe she could be a bitch. Well, if so, she fit right in here, and must have done so well."

She slid the journal into her shoulder bag and rose, walking past a startled Kaitlin.

As she continued down the hallway, Kaitlin called out to her. "You know, we really didn't want you here."

Kit turned around. "Wow. Duh. I think I've picked up on that."

"Seamus sent David to bring you back."

"Really?" she deadpannned. "What a shock."

"Maybe David doesn't even really want you here," Kaitlin suggested. She probably hadn't meant to go quite so far, but since her previous jibes hadn't garnered the response she wanted, she had pushed.

"If David didn't want me here, I wouldn't be here," Kit assured Kaitlin smoothly, and sailed on by her. She was glad that she could portray a far greater confidence than she was feeling that morning.

As she hurried down the stairs to exit the main house,

Kit nearly collided with one of the day maids, a middle-aged, perpetually smiling woman named Rosa. She was carrying a tray.

"Where are you off to?" Kit asked her.

"To see Miss Mary."

"Mary!" Kit repeated, standing dead still. "My God, Mary! I don't believe it—I had forgotten that she was still here, still alive. And no one reminded me! No one has mentioned her since I've been here."

Rosa sighed softly. "She isn't well, Mrs. Moore. She is so old, you know? And she had a flu, so now…her mind wanders and she is very weak. She is in bed."

"I still want to see her, as soon as possible. Now. May I come with you?"

"Of course!"

Rosa chatted happily about the beautiful day as they walked along the trail. Mary's little cottage was on the opposite side of the lagoon from Kit and David's, but like theirs, closest to the water.

Rosa pushed open the door to the cottage, calling out to announce her arrival. A young woman in a nurse's uniform came to greet them. Rosa introduced her as Alicia. She seemed pleased to meet Kit, and assured her that her patient was doing well that day. "Her mind wanders almost continually, but she's as sweet and wonderful as ever," Alicia said. "She'll enjoy seeing you."

Kit thanked her, and stepped toward the bedroom. The windows to the water were wide open. Mary, tiny, thin, was in a hospital bed, and it was levered up so that she could look out on the beauty of the bay.

She heard Kit's arrival though and turned. Her eyes widened with pleasure. She weakly reached out an arm, lips turning into a smile that lit up her entire face. Kit was surprised that she would recognize her, even if she had remembered her.

But then Mary spoke, and Kit understood. "Marina!

They said you were gone. I knew you would never leave without saying goodbye to me."

Little strings pulled around her heart. Walking quickly, she came to Mary's bedside. Mary's fingers curled around hers with surprising strength.

"Come close!" Mary whispered.

Kit leaned closer to her, trying to explain. "I'm not Marina, Mary. I'm Kit, her daughter."

Mary didn't hear her. Or else she heard what she chose to hear, accepted what she wanted. "Marina, you must leave, though. You must leave with Mark. Young lady! I know where your heart lies, but give a good man a chance. I'm not happy, I'm worried. I hear the birds, you know. I hear the birds all the time. They bother me, but they worry me, too. They force me to listen. Because they are warning me, about you."

"Mary, it's okay," she said gently. "It's all right, honestly. I'm Kit, not Marina."

Mary's grip grew impossibly tighter. "Stop seeing him. Never see him again. Ever. Get out. Get out with Mark, quickly. I know that you love me. But you must go. You and Mark...you can send for me, sometime."

Kit didn't think she'd ever convince Mary that she wasn't her mother. She felt uneasy, but first, she had to do something to reassure the old woman so that she wouldn't be so agitated.

She kissed Mary's forehead, tenderly stroking back her silver hair. "It's okay, Mary. Honestly. It's okay. Everything is fine."

Mary looked back out to the water. "You know now. You know, you'll be careful. You'll watch what you say. You won't get angry, speak when you shouldn't. You must be ready to leave with Mark, promise me."

"I promise," Kit said. A feeling of deep unease swept over her. *You know now.* What had her mother known? *That Kaitlin hated her?*

Or someone else?

Hated her enough to…kill her?

Mary's eyes closed.

A gentle hand fell on Kit's shoulder. Alicia spoke quietly, ''She's sleeping again. She wakes, sleeps, wakes, naps. She's just getting better, you know, and she's very, very old.''

''I know,'' Kit said. She rose, smiling at Alicia. ''She was wonderful to me, though, when I was a little girl. I'll be back. When she's too weak to see me, just tell me. But I'll be here. Every day.''

She left Mary's little cottage deeply disturbed, but when she returned to her own home, she allowed her renewed feelings of unease to slip to the back of her mind.

Entering, she saw a large box set right in the midst of the parlor. Frowning, she remembered that once again she had left the doors unlocked.

Naturally. It seemed that no one locked doors in the compound.

She approached the box, and was startled when it wriggled. Carefully, she continued toward it, and saw that it wasn't really a box at all, just a large sheet of brown mailing paper cast loosely around something. Curiously, she pulled at the paper.

It was covering a large crate.

And inside the crate was a bouncing ball of fur that immediately began to whine. A puppy—a *really big* puppy.

''Hey!'' she said softly, bending down to scoop up the creature. The puppy was black with huge feet. His little body wriggled with happiness as he attempted to lick her face. ''What on earth are you?'' she said, laughing.

''Great Dane,'' she heard in reply.

Turning, she saw that David was home, smiling as he watched her from the bottom step of the stairway. ''I know he can't replace Whitney,'' he told her softly. ''And I thought a kitten wouldn't be quite right now. So…he's a

Great Dane puppy. Not a lapdog, of course, but I thought that maybe...?''

Kit smiled slowly. She was delighted to see that he was back from the Keys, and touched that he would be so thoughtful to realize that a kitten could not replace Whitney, but that a puppy might be just what she needed.

"Too big? We can choose something else."

The squirming ball of fur and feet in her arms licked the bottom of her chin, whining softly for attention. She stared at David, hugged the puppy, and set him back in his crate, then hurried to David, throwing herself into his arms.

"Is he a good gift?"

"You being back is a good gift. The puppy is just...wonderful."

"Sure you don't want something smaller."

"I like big."

"Hmm. Do you?" he teased.

"Think the puppy will be okay for a few more minutes?" she queried.

"The puppy will be just fine. He's going to have to learn that there are times...well, times he stays in his crate!"

He kissed her. The kind of kiss that insinuated much more, then he swept her up, laughing, telling her to watch her feet, and she forgot everything else in the world, because he was back. Their clothing was soon strewn along the stairway, and she knew that nothing in the world would ever take her away from the man she loved.

It wasn't until much later that they dressed and came down to play with the puppy. They decided to call him Thor. Kit didn't care that the name might have been overused and not at all imaginative for a Dane.

David had to leave to go to the Coconut Grove office very late in the day. It wasn't until then that Kit took out her mother's journal once again, and began reading it. She read about day after day of lunches, dinners and appointments. As she reached the end, though, a piece of paper fell from the book. She recognized her mother's elegant scrawl and began to read.

Dear, I want you to know that I never meant to hurt you, that in my heart there will be a place where I hurt and sorrow and miss you all my life. But this isn't right. What I've done to a very good man who already forgave far too many sins is terrible, and in the best interest of everyone, including you, I intend to leave immediately. Tonight, I will have the showdown. And tomorrow, I will leave forever, and make a better world for my daughter and my husband. Lord knows, I owe him so much.

The letter wasn't signed, but it was definitely her mother's handwriting. Nor was it addressed to anyone other than *Dear*.

Kit bit into her lower lip, wondering how her father had carried his love for her mother all those years, when here, sadly, was the proof that she had been cheating on him.

But with whom?

Kit felt slightly ill, knowing why Marina Delaney might have been more than disliked by many people. And still…

She remembered the things that Mary had said to her. Mary had thought that she was Marina. Mary was worried about her.

There had been a showdown, the night her mother had died. Marina had planned on leaving Bougainvillea—forever.

If she had planned on leaving, why go swimming straight out into the ocean the night before?

The memory of finding Whitney returned to her, and mingled with the new sense of dread regarding her mother.

Healthy cats didn't just die.

No, there had been poison involved. Naturally, with all the foliage, buildings, possible rat problems, there were poisons on the estate.

But Whitney hadn't been a wanderer. He was well fed, and he was also picky about his food.

The feelings of suspicion and uneasiness that too often filled her in regard to Bougainvillea arose again.

Her husband popped into her mind.

He'd admitted that Seamus had sent him to get her. But she had been so enamored of him, so in love, she had wanted to believe what he had said. That he would have come for her anyway. He had married her. He made love to her as if she was as seductive as pure fire, as if she were truly cherished as well.

No. David would never hurt her, or use her for his own gain.

Still…. She might hedge around her suspicions, but…

Was someone at Bougainvillea capable of murder?

7

"I think it's curious that the cat just died," David said, staring at Michael and Josh over a beer at the frond-shaded restaurant on the bay. "The animal was perfectly healthy when it came here."

"Jeez, David, you're not accusing one of us of killing Kit's cat, are you?" Michael said.

"David, you *are* saying something," Josh told him. "Kit thought it was odd, too. She stormed into the house. And you know Mom and Kaitlin—they were hardly sympathetic. I hope I made her feel somewhat better. We buried the cat in the pet cemetery."

"Hey!"

From a distance, they saw Eli. He was still in his police uniform, but apparently off duty because he took a beer from the bartender before threading his way toward them.

"Hey, Eli. Long day?" David said.

"Hell, it's always a long day around here lately," he told him. "There was a brawl in a bar on Grand Ave, some junkies attacked a little old lady on her way home from the grocery, and what else? Oh, a traffic accident on US1 that tied up the city for four hours. Yeah, it was a long day. What's with you guys?"

"David thinks we poisoned his wife's cat," Josh said dryly.

"I didn't say that," David said with weary irritation. "I

said it was damned strange that a healthy cat came to Bougainvillea and then died.''

"Kit's cat died?'' Eli said, shaking his red head sympathetically. "Poor girl. Her dad not even a year ago, and now her cat.''

"It's all right. David brought her back a puppy,'' Michael said.

"A puppy? A monster,'' Josh supplied.

"Great Dane,'' David explained.

"A dog. Good,'' Eli approved. "Dogs are protective. And a Great Dane? Your wife will be in good shape.''

"Let's ask Eli,'' David said. "Don't you think it's rather strange that Kit's cat gets here and suddenly dies?''

Michael let out a sound of irritation. "David! We all know that there's poison on the estate. Rat poison. Cats get into everything. Kit's cat got into one of the storerooms. It's really sad, and I'm sorry as hell but there's no conspiracy here.''

Eli sipped his beer, looking at them all. He met David's eyes.

"You're a cop, Eli. What do you think? Really sad? Or really odd? It was really sad about Kit's mother, too, wasn't it? She's due to leave the following morning—and she turns up dead instead.''

"David, that was a really long time ago,'' Eli said.

"What the hell are you implying now?'' Michael said angrily.

David leveled his eyes on Michael. "I was only seventeen when she died, Michael. But I think I'm getting at the possibility that we all considered at the time. What the hell, Eli, you remember when Marina washed back up on shore.''

"She drowned, David,'' Josh said softly. "There was an autopsy.''

"She drowned, yes. Water in her lungs.''

"She was also drinking like a damned fish that night," Michael reminded him.

"And she could swim like a fucking fish, knew the water and currents like the back of her hand," David argued.

"That's right, isn't it?" Josh said slowly, staring at David. "You swam with her so often. Come to think of it—you followed her around like a puppy dog, so you would know all about her abilities, what she could do, couldn't do? What she was willing to do—and what she wasn't. Hell, she sure had her affairs. Were you the last one, David?"

He was tense, wary, and he didn't know why. Afraid, something he'd never been before. Not for himself.

He shouldn't have married Kit. Shouldn't have brought her to Bougainvillea.

His temper snapped. He rose, ready to take a swing at Josh that would have decked him.

Eli rose between them. "Hey, guys. Cop here. I'll haul you both in on assault. Settle down. The whole thing with Marina was tragic, and the cat bit is tragic, too, but it's going to be all right."

"David, I'm sorry," Josh told him quietly.

"Yeah." Josh had been his own age when Marina had died. They had both thought she was gorgeous. And she had always shown them every kindness. He wasn't really angry with Josh.

He was just…afraid. Settling back in his chair, he decided that convenience should be damned. He didn't want to live at Bougainvillea any longer. He'd tell Kit when he got home.

But when he returned, Kit met him at the back door, a slightly frazzled look on her face. "We've got company. I hope you don't mind."

Jennifer Harrison came running from behind Kit, giving him a warm hug, and planting a sloppy kiss on his cheek. "I had to be in the area for a cartoonists' conference. I thought I'd surprise you both. I hope you don't mind? I'm just here for a while—I have a hotel room on the beach.''

"Don't be ridiculous. You have to stay at Bougainvillea," David said. He glanced at Kit. She gave him a look of appreciation that was deep and gratifying.

"We're dining up at the main house tonight," Kit said. "You know Jen—she wants to meet everyone. And Lenore actually seems excited to have company—she's invited Eli, Shelley and Martin over as well.''

"I'm flat-out nosy as hell, you know that!" Jen told him.

David smiled. "Well, that's good. I hate to admit it, but we can bring new meaning to the concept of dysfunctional. Hey, how do you like the puppy?''

"He's great. A slobber factory, but he's great!" Jen assured him. "Kit—what a super addition he'd be to your comic strip. Hey, did you set up a studio?''

"Yes, and it's gorgeous, wonderful," Kit said, smiling at David.

"Show me!" Jen insisted.

After the brief tour, they walked together to the main house.

Dinner, David had to admit, went well. They might have been one big, happy family. Seamus was in rare form, regaling Jen with stories about early area pioneers. Both Kaitlin and Lenore were polite, even laughing, seeming to have a good time.

Josh was exceptionally attentive to Jen—as was Eli. Jen was given a bedroom in the main house, though she warned them she'd be taking off for her publisher's sales conference early every morning for the next few days. Lenore assured her that there was coffee on every morning by six—Seamus was often an early riser.

When they returned to their cottage that night, David was relieved. Jen's arrival had seemed to help ease Kit's grief over Whitney, as had his return and, he hoped, the new puppy.

He was glad he had been delayed no longer than a night. Kit was curled in his arms as soon as they returned to their place, totally abandoned, as if she needed to bury herself in him, or in the euphoria of sex. It was difficult to find fault with a lover so sensual, beautiful, and enthused, and yet…he wondered if she hadn't been making love almost desperately.

As if she were running. And learning far too much about the past at Bougainvillea.

The alarm rang at six the next morning. David quickly clamped a hand over it, trying not to wake Kit. He had a lot to catch up on. There was no reason for her to be awake so ridiculously early.

But as he dragged his fingers through his hair, telling himself he had to rise, he saw that she was looking at him, as if she had been awake for a while. He felt a tensing in his limbs and groin; she was extraordinary, even first thing in the morning, midnight hair a tangle over the pillow, eyes deep violet, the length of her barely covered by the white textured sheet. He was about to reach for her, a smile curling into his lips.

But she spoke. "David, do you know who my mother was sleeping with when she died?"

His body went cold. "No," he lied. He kissed her lightly on the lips. "What makes you think your mother was having an affair?" he asked carefully.

"I found a letter she wrote to a lover."

"Well, who was it addressed to?"

"'Dear,' she told him.

He held her for a moment, his eyes intently on hers. "Your father loved her, she loved him. She had some wild times, and yes, I guess, she had affairs. But I really believe she meant to change all that, for your father. And for you."

"I can't believe it's taken me this long to ask you, but

where is my mom buried? I'm such a horrible daughter. I should bring flowers.''

David hesitated. "Look up," he said softly. "Out the window."

"What does that mean?"

"Her ashes were scattered at sea. That's what she wanted."

"Convenient," Kit said.

"What?"

"She could never be dug up for a second autopsy."

"She drowned, Kit. There was an autopsy."

"A long time ago. Medical science has come a long way."

He kissed her again, worried. "I love you," he said softly.

She smiled, cradling his head. "I love you, too."

He rose then, and headed for the shower.

Having Jen around made the world a lot better. Kit had yet to lay out on the beach, so on the fourth day of Jen's stay, when her business was done, they donned suits, grabbed towels, and a little radio/cooler comber and headed down to the lagoon.

Kit told Jen about her mother's letter, and about the things Mary had said as well.

"Wow. Does Mary still think that you're your mother?" Jen asked her, eyes bright.

"I go over every day now. And yes, she keeps calling me Marina."

"Poor thing."

Kit shrugged. She had been able to find out a few details about her family here that she considered very bad—but there were a few that were good as well. Everyone in the household was fiercely protective about Mary—she was to have the best care, never want for anything and never suffer. Kit hadn't realized it at first, but everyone in the house visited her as well. They knew how to take care of their own.

Jen sighed softly again. "I'm so sorry, Kit. I guess your mom was pretty...promiscuous."

Kit stared at the water in front of her. "I think she was killed, Jen."

Jen looked around. "Murdered?"

"Yep."

"By someone here?"

"Who else?"

"Lord, don't say that too loudly!"

"Well, I'm not!" Kit said with exasperation. She waved a hand around them. "Who else is here?"

Jen waved a hand around as well. "Storage shed over there, bushes—lots and lots of bushes!—all around us." She shook her head. "Kit, I'm sorry, I know it hurts. But apparently your mother was sleeping around. She was really, really drunk that night, and she considered herself an Olympic swimmer, so it sounds. She went into the water to cool off...and she died."

Kit shook her head. "I don't think so. She was leaving the next morning. There was probably some kind of a terrible showdown, and she came out here, and..."

"And what?"

"I don't know from there," Kit admitted. "Wish I knew who she'd been sleeping with!"

"You can be a lot more nosy, you know. Except that, well, if someone here killed her, you're going to have to be very careful."

"Why?" Kit asked dryly. "She's been cremated. No one will ever dig her back up again."

"True, but still. If she threatened someone...they might get scared."

Kit stared at the water. "I intend to be careful. But I also intend to get the truth."

Jen spun around suddenly, staring at the brush.

"What?"

"I heard rustling."

"Rustling?"

"Yeah, you know, bushes moving."

"The place is filled with birds, squirrels and possums," Kit said. "Besides, Thor isn't barking."

Just then, the puppy spun around on his gangling legs and stared past the tiled path toward the bushes and started barking.

"There!"

Kit arched a brow to Jen. "He barks at squirrels, birds and possums!" she said.

"I think someone was there," Jen said.

Kit felt a shiver sweep through her. "Maybe it's time to go in, shower and change." She began gathering up their things.

Back at Kit's house, Jen was finishing up her shower when the phone rang. It was Shelley. She had had only a half-day of classes and it had turned out that Eli was off as well. They wanted Kit and Jen to come over and join them and their dad for a barbecue lunch.

Jen liked the prospect. She was enjoying the attention she was receiving from both Eli and Josh.

"Would I really want to marry a cop, though?" Jen mused.

"Is it that serious?" Kit teased.

"You always have to take everything into consideration. Now, Josh. He's a mover. I like that. Are we driving over?"

"No—there's a little path to their place, and then a wooden gate that we jump."

"Pants would be in order then, huh?" Jen said.

As large as the Bougainvillea property was, the Callahan place was small. The lot size was no more than ten thousand square feet, but the house was charming, typically Mediterranean. The large porch boasted a huge barbecue, with a small, kidney-shaped pool stretching out, uncovered, in the yard beyond.

When they were seated and Kit had taken her first bite of hamburger, she nearly choked as Jen said, ''Hey, you guys, you were around all those years ago when Kit's mom died. So sad. And tragic. And strange.''

Silence surrounded the table. Everyone stared at Jen, who shrugged. ''Naturally, Kit is suspicious about it all. What do you think? Especially you, Eli. You're a cop.''

''I'm not homicide,'' Eli said, staring at Kit. ''You really think someone killed her?''

''I didn't say that, exactly,'' Kit told him uncomfortably.

Eli shrugged. ''Might have been foul play. Wow. It was a long time ago. I was just a kid. But if so, why? Dumb question, I guess. Why not? She really could flaunt her assets—and temper.'' Eli spoke calmly, and didn't seem at all shocked or worried.

''Don't get her thinking such a thing, son!'' Martin protested. ''Kit, your mama drowned.''

''But she was sleeping with someone, cheating on my dad, when she died,'' Kit said softly.

''Oh, Kit! Trust me, Mark Delaney loved her no matter what!'' Eli said. ''Your father would have never killed your mother.''

''I never thought my father killed her!'' Kit protested. She realized they were all staring at her sadly. Why not? She had to wonder. Mark Delaney would have been the injured party if his wife was having an affair. They were supposedly leaving, yes. But what if he had just been sick to death of her cheating on him time and again, and truly wanted a break—for his daughter, and himself?

''No!'' she said firmly. ''I knew my father too well. I would bet my life that he would have never hurt her.'' She leaned forward suddenly. ''But I think I understand now why he never wanted to come back—and why he never mentioned it to me, or suggested that I had relatives who might want to see me. My dad might have suspected something, and that could be why he was determined to keep me away from Bougainvillea.''

"Kit, that's kind of speculative and wild," Martin warned her.

She shrugged. "Eli, okay, so you're not homicide. Doesn't the way she died seem a little suspicious to you?"

"Kit, I was a teenager at the time. We were all stunned and brokenhearted, that's all I really remember. But like you said, your dad adored her. He didn't kill her, and he was the affronted party. So who would have done it?" Eli asked her sympathetically.

"I don't know. But I'd like to find out," Kit said evenly.

"Well, let's face it, both Kaitlin and Lenore hated her," Jen pointed out. She shivered. "Even I get vibes from those two!"

Eli set an arm around her shoulder, laughing. "They're a pair of prime bitches, but hardly lethal!" he said.

Kit kept silent. She wasn't so certain.

Seamus signed the contract, then David added his signature, binding them to a deal to design and build two sailing ships for Mario Marius, one of the newest—and richest—Latin singing sensations to have made the crossover to American music.

"Kit's friend is leaving Sunday," Seamus said as they left the office. "I thought we'd get the Callahans and the family and head out for a day on *The Sea Star*."

"Sounds nice. Strange, I haven't had her out sailing yet."

"I haven't been out in a long time myself," Seamus told him. "I miss the water when I'm not right on it for any length of time."

The valet brought their company car, a handsome Cadillac. David slipped into the driver's seat. In a few minutes, they were out of the Brickell area offices, and heading through the winding trails back to the Grove.

"I'm going to tell Kit the truth soon," Seamus said.

"The truth?" David said, frowning.

"That she's my child," Seamus said softly.

David nearly drove off the road. He regained control of the car just in time to avoid massacring a group of palms.

"You didn't know?" Seamus said, nonplussed. "I thought you did." He shrugged. "I was sure everyone knew—or suspected."

David was silent several minutes. "Seamus, if you tell her, it's going to be for yourself—not for her. She loved Mark. Really loved him. Let her keep that memory."

"People have to know the truth," Seamus said.

"Why?"

"Because I intend to leave Bougainvillea to the both of you."

"Seamus, don't do it," David said uneasily.

"Why?"

David took a moment to answer. "What if someone killed Marina?"

"Like my brother?"

"No. We both knew Mark. He was patient beyond endurance. And in the end, Marina knew that. I think she really intended to start a new life with him, far away from here."

"Then, who would have killed her?" Seamus demanded.

"Don't say anything. Don't ruin it all for Kit, please. Let her keep what she has."

Seamus was silent. David prayed that he was seeing the wisdom of his words.

Saturday started out brilliantly. The day was clear and beautiful, the seas were calm. *The Sea Star* was one of the finest sailboats Sea Life had ever produced, and luckily, the family had maintained her.

For the first time in a while, Kit realized, she was feeling exceptionally light, as if her world was completely normal. Kaitlin and Lenore were both in high spirits. Lenore even admitted that she thought Thor was cute and well behaved on the boat. Kit was amused to see that even Seamus acted like a little boy on the boat, allowing David to captain her, but running around to set the sails at the appropriate times, and enjoying the race with the perfect breeze.

They anchored out by one of the islands in the bay, and laughed as they walked the picnic items to shore. Jen began squalling and nearly dropped the six-pack of beer she was carrying when a crab crawled over her bare feet. Kit laughed as both Josh and Eli rushed to her rescue.

"Now this," Michael announced, gnawing on a piece of fried chicken, "is the way to live. Just sailing. Feeling the breeze. Finding an island."

"No cable television, no whirlpool tub for a good soak, no hairdressers, no movie theaters—ugh!" Lenore told her husband.

He laughed, setting an arm around his wife's shoulders and pulling her close. "Once upon a time, you just needed me—not the hairdresser!" he told her.

She flushed, as if slightly embarrassed by his display of emotion, then she smiled. "Maybe we could sail part of the year, and have movies and theaters and hairdressers the other part of the year."

"Hey, maybe," Michael said with surprise and pleasure.

"I don't know what any of you are talking about—living at Bougainvillea is like living in Paradise," Jen said, shaking her head.

"You can always come back down, you know. You're always invited," Josh told her.

"Always," Seamus agreed. "Any friend of my girl is a friend of the family," he added, beaming at Kit.

Kit noticed the mood change then, as if a bolt of lightning had struck.

Kaitlin suddenly rose in all her platinum, regal glory and glared at Seamus. "*Your* girl. Kit, Kit, Kit. It was always Kit—and before that, Marina." She turned and glared at Michael. "Doesn't this all ever infuriate you, as well?"

"Kaitlin, stop!" David warned angrily.

"Stop! Oh, yeah, right. Because you're just the wonder boy. The only one around here who isn't part and parcel of Seamus Delaney's lechery."

"Kaitlin!" David had come to his feet. Kit was startled by the knotted tension in his body. Afraid that he was about to walk around and deck the woman, she grabbed his arm.

"David?" she said softly, not knowing what was going on.

Kaitlin glared at Kit then, pure hatred in her eyes. "Ever since you've come along, he wants to throttle me. It didn't use to be like that." She turned abruptly. "Michael, get some balls up! Hey, you're the legitimate child, right? Someone, tell Kit the truth. See if her friend, Jen, wants to come back to Paradise then!" Kaitlin locked her gaze on Kit once again. "Guess what, Kit? Your precious father wasn't really your father. Seamus Delaney is. Mark married your pregnant mother instead of Seamus because Seamus's wife was still alive at the time. Which is the same reason why, of course, he couldn't marry *my* mother, either. That's right—I'm his daughter, too. The great, proud, Seamus Delany! Responsible for all his deeds! So he supports us all. But Marina was the one who finally spit in his face. He couldn't keep her. He's still in love with her after all these years, and determined that he'll have her back one way or another. David knew that—why the hell do you think he married you, instead of just inviting you down? Hell, you're going to be the next generation of Sea Life. Seamus will leave the whole damned thing you. His precious girl. The rest of his children can go rot!"

She spun around, kicking up sand as she headed down the beach.

Dead silence reigned for an eternity. Kit could only stand there, stunned.

Then David turned to Kit and spoke earnestly. "Mark Delaney loved you with his whole heart. He raised you. He was your father, do you understand? He was your father."

Kit hadn't really grasped the truth of all that had been said until David spoke. Then shock set in. And denial.

And then...

She stood on shaky legs. "I really think the picnic is over," she said softly, and started to turn around, but then stopped. She knew that what Kaitlin had said was the truth—she just knew it instinctively.

She should have walked away as she had intended. But she didn't. She stood her ground, and she looked around the lot of them.

"That's why my mother died, isn't it? Because I was Seamus's child, and she knew too much about all of you. She would have told him the truth about anything he wanted to know." She knew this was crazy. She should never be saying such things, not to this group. But the sudden announcement Kaitlin had made had shocked her to the core.

"One of you killed my mother," she stated flatly.

"Kit! No!" Seamus protested.

David was up and behind her by then, slipping his arms around her. She shook off his touch, squared her shoulders, and headed for the boat.

"I'd say this picnic was definitely over. Thor! Come, *now!*"

The puppy had never really obeyed a command before. But this time, even the dog listened to her.

She strode back toward the water where *The Sea Star* was docked, the Dane right on her heels.

She sat at the front of the boat, stiff and straight, the puppy at her side. She heard the men shouting orders back and forth as they raised the anchor.

They didn't sail back to Bougainvillea.

They used the motor.

Kit had planned to shrug off David's touch if he came near her. But he didn't.

Either he figured the truth was out...

Or he had his pride as well.

Not even Jen tried to speak to her. When they returned to the dock at Bougainvillea, Kit walked straight to the cottage, up the stairs, and locked the door to their bedroom before David could catch up. She showered, changed, and lay on the bed, staring at the ceiling.

She had wanted to know the truth so badly.

And yet...

She should leave. Her mother was dead. Her father— yes! David was right on that point, at the least. Mark Delaney would always be her father. Her father was dead, too.

Even her cat was dead. And her marriage might be dead as well.

She needed to get the hell out of Bougainvillea.

She heard the doorknob twist, and then David's voice.

"Kit!"

"David, I'd really like to be alone for a while."

"Alone is exactly what you don't need to be," he called angrily.

"I don't want to talk right now."

"Kit, we'll leave Bougainvillea."

She surprised herself by catapulting out of the bed and to the door, flinging it open and confronting him.

He was still in the pair of cutoffs he had sailed in. He was muscled, sleek, and brown from his broad shoulders to his feet. His eyes were dark and intent; his hands rested upon his hips.

"You believe all that bullshit?"

"Is it true?"

"That your mother once had an affair with Seamus? I imagine it could be. That Kaitlin is his child—yes, I imagine that could be true, too. But did I have an affair with Kaitlin, was I ever thinking of becoming involved with her—no. It was no before I ever met you. Have I had affairs, yes, tons of them. Did I marry you because I thought you might be Seamus's daughter, heir to it all? No. I married you because I fell in love with you. I thought you felt that way about me.''

"I don't know what the hell I feel right now,'' she responded angrily. It was a lie. She felt the urge to fling herself against him, cry, and pretend that none of this was real. To pretend that Bougainvillea was filled with fine people who had loved her mother, rued her death. That they had all been normal—and good.

But she couldn't allow herself to fall into his arms so easily. She needed time.

"Leave me alone for now, David. I mean it. Leave me alone.''

"Kit, I am not leaving!''

"Then I am!''

She brushed past him. He caught her arm, spinning her back angrily. She landed hard against his chest, and he held her there and tilted her head upward. He kissed her the way that only he could. With liquid fire and insinuation, passion and force. The kind of kiss that seduced, and made everything else disappear except the need to be closer and closer, make love, touch him, inside and out...

"No!'' she exclaimed furiously, pushing away. "I need to be away—away from you!''

She ran down the stairs and out of the house, nearly tripping over Thor.

Once outside, she didn't know where she was going. And then she did. She went running far around the path, heading for Mary's place.

David swore as he stormed down the stairs.

He should never have come home. Never have brought

Kit here. They should have bought a condo on the beach instead.

Hell, he should have quit Sea Life.

He leaned against the mantel in the living room, gritting his teeth, wondering where the hell she had gone. He began to worry.

Kaitlin had spat out a truth they had all suspected.

And so had Kit.

She suspected that her mother had been murdered.

And now, wherever she had gone...

Maybe she was learning too much.

He pushed away from the mantel, intent on finding her.

That night. Before she could discover anything else, and announce what she knew to the world.

Alicia answered the door, startled to see her.

"Didn't think you'd be back so soon. Guess it is dark out there now. I didn't realize how late it had gotten." Alicia yawned. "Mary is sleeping, but you go right on in with her."

"Thanks," Kit told Alicia, and walked into Mary's room.

She took the old woman's hand in her own. Mary opened her eyes and smiled at her.

"You've come. You've come to say goodbye."

Kit was startled to realize it was the truth. She loved David. She didn't want to leave him, and she didn't exactly intend to do so. But she was going to leave, with Jen, tomorrow. David could come to Chicago if he wanted. They could talk there.

He would come, she thought, if he really loved her.

"Mary, I am leaving," she said softly. "But I'll come back. I wish you could help me. Marina was seeing someone. You knew who it was."

Mary squeezed her hand. "Mark loves you. I know that you broke it off with Seamus when he married you. What

I don't know is why you ever cheated on him again. Kaitlin hates you, seriously hates you, you know. She knows the baby is her half sister.''

A lump formed in Kit's throat. "Mary, did Kaitlin kill my mother?''

"Marina, Lenore is dangerous, too. She's afraid that her own boy will be left out.''

"It's all right, Mary.''

"I heard the screaming. I thought it was the parrots. You were crying out for help, and I knew it. David came. He was supposed to be away at school, but he came.''

Her heart froze. A sense of illness swept through her.

Suddenly, Mary's hand curled tightly around hers. "Josh...they were all there. If only...you could have been helped. If I had known. I thought it was the parrots...only later.'' Mary suddenly looked really distressed. "You've got to go! Now. Tonight.''

Kit felt a chill invade her as never before. She tried to remain calm. "I'm going, Mary,'' she said softly. "I'll be safe, I promise.''

She remained calm and easy as she kissed the old woman, and then slipped out, speaking lightly to Alicia in the living room of the cottage before hurrying out the door.

She realized she didn't have a cent on her. There was only one thing to do. Run to the Callahans' house, borrow some money, call the police and get away.

She knew there was nothing she could prove to the police. But it didn't matter. She just needed to get away from Bougainvillea—before she followed her mother's footsteps to a watery grave.

The compound lights were dim, but she realized that she would be well enough illuminated on the tile path around the lagoon. She kept to the bushes, hiding in the shadows.

It seemed to take her forever to get around the little inlet. At last, she reached the foliage.

"Kit!''

David was out on the path, calling her name.

She hunched down into the foliage until he walked by. Then she spurted through the path.

Seconds later, she came to the little pet cemetery. In the dim light here, the markers seemed as eerie as death itself. There was the lump in the ground where poor Whitney had so recently been buried.

She fell dead still suddenly, aware that the bushes were moving to her side.

"Kit!"

Her name was being called. She knew the voice. It was Josh. She was startled by the overwhelming sense of fear that streaked through her like lightning.

What the hell was he doing in the bushes?

Her mind raced. Had he simply called her name? Or whispered it softly? She was afraid for him to find her here. Alone.

She inched slowly toward the farside of the burial area.

"Kit!" It seemed that Josh lunged out of the bushes, rushing for her. Shadows surrounded him. She couldn't see his face, and the terror remained with her. Panicking, she looked around and noted the spade he had so recently used to dig Whitney's grave. She grabbed it and clanged him on the head as he neared her. Regardless of the noise she made, she ran pell-mell down the path toward the Callahan residence, leaping the gate like a professional vaulter.

A few minutes later, she reached the Callahan house and began pounding on the door. To her dismay, no one answered. "It's Kit!" she called. "Please, help me!"

"Kit?"

She turned around. Martin Callahan was coming up the walk, his keys in his hand.

"Help me," she said frantically. "I need the police!"

"Of course," he said frowning. "We'll get into the house. Eli will be back shortly. He's a cop. He'll help."

He opened the door and ushered her in, looking anxiously around the house as he closed and locked the door. He propelled her toward the dining room and pulled out a chair for her. "I'll get you a brandy. Then you can tell me what's happened."

He came back a second later, offering her a snifter. "I don't need a drink," she murmured.

"A good jolt will help you. Swallow it, now."

What the hell? she thought. It couldn't hurt. She swallowed the brandy down, and was glad of the warming tingle that touched her throat. She squared her shoulders and took a deep breath. "My mother was definitely murdered. And Mary knows a great deal that everyone ignores, assuming that she's senile."

"Ah!" Martin said. "Well, it was always a sad, confused lot over there. Seamus was, in his younger years, quite a ladies' man. And then your mother came into the picture, and seduced everyone. You know, I believe she was actually evil."

Kit frowned. She started to protest, but felt strange when she opened her mouth. "No, she wasn't evil. Just wild and immature," Kit managed to say at last. It felt as if she was slurring her words. "She saw someone that night."

"Yes, well, she was always *seeing* someone."

Kit licked her lips, feeling incredibly odd. "Um…where did Eli go?"

"He'll be back."

Martin was just staring at her. She blinked, trying to keep her eyes open.

Martin smiled suddenly. "You wanted to know," he said softly. "Well…now you do."

"Know…what?"

"How your mother died."

At first, his words didn't register, didn't really make sense. Then she knew. She had been drugged.

"You!" she whispered. And then, incredulous and confused, "Why?"

He didn't answer right away. He rose, coming over to her. He gripped her face, trying to study her eyes.

"No!" she screamed with the energy and fury she could muster. "No!"

"Yep, it's time."

He pulled back the chair. She nearly fell but then he bent over, sweeping her into his arms.

She tried desperately to push away from him.

But he was strong, far stronger than she might have imagined. His left arm came around her. She still had some strength in her limbs. She scratched and clawed and fought desperately, her hands flailing ridiculously.

Martin Callahan! It was impossible. Why?

"I could have left you alone, except…you were so determined. I'm so sorry. Quit struggling. It will be easier."

She couldn't quit struggling. He meant to kill her. But the sickly sweet sensation filling her limbs until they were all but useless caused her head to spin as well.

"Why?" she tried to gasp out.

"Why?" he said curtly. "The bitch was sleeping with my son. Seducing a seventeen-year-old boy. She deserved to die, not run off and have a happy life with Mark."

"I…I would have never found out," she whispered.

"Yes, eventually, Mary would have given you names. I'm afraid I can't take any more chances with Mary, either."

"Eli…Shelley…will be back."

"Oh, no, they won't. Your husband called in a panic. They're all searching for you."

She was about to lose consciousness. Kit held her breath, and pretended to go entirely limp.

He carried her from the house.

She continued to fight inwardly, a truly desperate battle to remain conscious.

* * *

David would never know exactly why such a deep sense of panic had filled him.

Well, hell, why not? Far too much was out in the open.

Once he had ascertained she wasn't at the main house with Jen, he ran to Mary's cabin. Lenore called over to the Callahan house while Jen and Eli headed out together, ready to search the estate with flashlights while he went to Mary's. But when he reached the old woman's cottage, Alicia told him that Kit had already left.

David headed back to the cottage for a flashlight. Thor started barking, trying to follow him when he was stepping out. He hesitated. Thor cocked his head expectantly at David, wagged his tail, and whined.

"Oh, all right. Come on!"

With Thor on his heels, he raced out, heading first toward the pet cemetery, thinking that might be a place she would go to find solitude and nurse her wounds. There, by Whitney's grave. He heard a rustling in the brush, even before he got the light on.

"Kit? Who the hell is there?" he demanded.

He heard a moaning. Thor rushed on through the foliage and started barking. David followed the sound and came upon Josh, trying to sit up in the bushes.

"What happened?" David demanded tersely, hunkering down beside him.

"She creamed me!"

"Kit?"

"She's scared, really scared. I was just trying to talk to her, and she walloped me with the shovel."

"Are you all right?"

"Yeah."

"Where's Jen?"

"Running around lost somewhere."

David set a hand on his shoulder. "I've got to keep looking for Kit, Josh. Can you make it to the house?"

"Hell, yes. Go!" Josh looked at David, shaking his head. "It's happening again—go!"

David did. He ran through the bushes, thinking she might have headed for the Callahan property. Except that Lenore had called over there.

He leaped the gate and was amazed to realize that Thor did so behind him. He saw the house ahead of him. It was dark. He ran up the steps and banged at the door. No answer.

But he noted the porch. There were strange marks on the wood floor. It looked as if something—someone—had been dragged across it.

David followed the marks, frowning. Then continued through the high grass, and back toward Delaney property. He started to run again, Thor at his heels.

Kit heard water lapping against the boat. Despite her best efforts, she had blacked out.

But she wasn't dead.

Not yet.

She swallowed hard, trying to ascertain exactly where she was. A dinghy, she thought. She was in one of the little boats kept down at the dock. She'd been thrown to the bottom of it. The rhythmic sound she was hearing, along with the slap of the water, was Martin rowing.

Somehow, he knew that she had come to. "Just like your mother, Kit. You wanted to know so much. Well, now you do. You'll know every single second. You shouldn't have been so nosy, huh?"

Her mouth felt as if it weighed a million pounds. She couldn't quite work it.

"Your son is a cop," she managed to say at last. She doubted if he could hear her. She could barely gasp.

"Thanks to me. She would have destroyed him."

"They'll know the truth now."

"How? I'll return the dinghy. They can all accuse one

another. After that display this afternoon, it would be easy to convince almost anyone that you killed yourself—I mean, you have one major fucked-up family, don't you think? This is far enough," he said, interrupting his own enjoyment of his subtle humor.

She felt him moving toward her, trying to grapple her up in his arms. She managed to claw her fingernails hard against his arm.

She could swim. Like her mother, she could swim.

Except that she couldn't move her limbs. She had to stay aboard the dinghy, somehow. Once she went over, she was dead.

Like her mother, she would drown.

He had her. Had a good grip on her. He was swearing about the scratches she had caused, but still, he had his grip.

Then, the boat began to sway. At first, it appeared that the creature from the black lagoon was rising from the darkness of the sea. Then she heard a voice.

David.

"Martin! Let her go, now, this instant!"

Martin dropped her. She hit the bottom of the boat hard because Martin had turned, swearing, grabbing up one of the oars to slam against David's rising head.

She heard a sickening thudding sound and her heart sank, and she couldn't help but wonder if her mother had thought about the man who had really loved her, her husband, right before she had died.

"And now…!"

Arms gripped her again around the waist. She kept trying to struggle. She was dragged over the edge of the dinghy this time. But before her weight could pull her over, a counter pull from the other side of the dinghy righted it.

Martin didn't have time to reach for an oar. David was aboard and the two of them were caught in a power struggle. The little dinghy began to rock.

With all her strength, Kit fought to kick out. Her right heel caught Martin hard, in the ankle.

He turned. David swung.

She was aware of another shift of weight, and a sickening, smacking sound, before the dinghy tipped over completely and she was cast into the murky depths.

She began to sink, lower and lower. Seaweed trailed over her face. Her lungs hurt, blackness and stars alternated in her vision.

Marina! she thought, vaguely wondering if her mother could come to her somehow, take her hand as she perished within the sea.

Then something reached out. A hand. For a moment, delusional, she thought that her mother had come.

She was pulled hard. She found some strength in her limbs again, and managed a feeble kick.

Moments later, she burst through the surface, gasping, choking, coughing, gasping some more. She was being towed in the water with a firm grip at her nape, and she heard David shouting, "Here, over here!"

A motor roared, then died, and a boat was next to them again. Someone pulled her aboard. Kaitlin stared down at her anxiously. "Get her up quickly, quickly!" It was Michael speaking. "Jesus, is she breathing?"

She was. David pushed her, Michael lifted her. Lenore wrapped her in a blanket. She was held then, in the blanket, warmed. "Forgive me!" she heard, and she was aware of Seamus there, as well.

Her eyes closed.

"Brandy. Get some of the brandy into her!" Lenore cried.

"No!"

She coughed, breathed in a deep breath, and found some of her own strength.

"Coffee, give her the coffee," David said, and then, dripping wet, he was taking her from Seamus's hold, bringing a plastic thermal coffee cup to her lips and forcing her to drink. She stared into his eyes, dark and intent, and realized that it was her turn, that they all had their fears and their doubts, and definitely their sins.

"Forgive me!" she said softly to David. "I was afraid...of you. Afraid to trust that you really loved me. Afraid to believe that I wasn't a fool to be so much in love with you."

"Just live!" he told her. And the slow, rueful smile that had first won her heart curled into his lips. "Just live. With me. Forever."

His arms wrapped around her.

And no matter what lay ahead now, she could brave it.

Epilogue _____

As it turned out, Bougainvillea was Paradise.

Kit and David had gone away at first. For a long and extended vacation in Aspen, Colorado.

But then, they had come home.

And to Kit's amazement, everything had changed.

She had a family again. A family she wanted.

Lenore and Michael were going to leave shortly for the long voyage he had always wanted to take, sailing romantically through the Caribbean.

Kaitlin had been planning on leaving after that awful day on the beach, but Kit had managed to change her mind. It had helped that Kaitlin had burst into tears the night of her rescue, swearing that she had never believed that Marina had been murdered, or that anything could happen to Kit. The next day, she, Josh, and Kaitlin, all half siblings, had finally talked about their situation.

They were definitely on the raw edge of dysfunctional. But then, Kit figured, such was life for many people those days.

Kaitlin needed to plunge into the business more. She knew it as well or better than either David, Josh, and maybe even Seamus.

Mary was never going to believe that Kit was anyone but Marina. That was okay. As long as she could be assured that Marina was right there, she was fine.

Eli and Shelley had been in shock as well. It was Martin's body that washed up on the beach that time.

Shelley had thought that they could never be friends again. Kit had assured her that they could.

And Eli, well, Kit knew he was going to have to learn to live with it all. Plus, Jen was crazy about him and was ready to stand by him, and in time...

It came down to Bougainvillea.

Their first day back, David had reminded her that they could move. He'd be more than willing to quit Sea Life altogether and move to another state.

But Kit didn't want to leave. She wanted to know Kaitlin and Josh better.

And even Seamus.

She had point-blank told him that she would never consider him to be her father. But he could remain an uncle, and as such, she enjoyed him, and even loved him.

They could make it.

She could make it.

Mostly because of David, of course. It didn't matter if they did move, or didn't move. As long as they were together.

And there was Thor, of course. David told her that he'd never had realized that Martin was dragging her out on one of the boats if the puppy hadn't followed the trail so certainly.

And so...

Bougainvillea.

It was her home.

On her first morning home, she knew it for certain.

She woke up in her husband's arms, seeing the sun rise through the windows that looked out on the lagoon. She felt his eyes on her, and knew that look in them, and smiled, rolling into his arms. He reached out and his fingers moved against her flesh lazily, evocatively. His whisper was warm against her cheek.

"Welcome home, again," he said softly.

"Umm." She snuggled against him, then moved her toes against his inner legs, higher, higher. "Home, huh?"

A little shudder escaped him.

But then, suddenly, their bedroom burst open and Thor came loping across the room and leaped onto the bed.

In just a few months, he had grown huge.

"Out!" David ordered.

The dog howled. Kit laughed. She leaped up, and ran downstairs with the dog in pursuit, found a chew toy, tossed it to him, and raced back up, closing the door behind her.

She grinned at David.

"Welcome home to you!" she said softly, and somewhat like Thor, she raced across the room, and pounced upon David.

Home.

Bougainvillea.

David.

She was exactly where she wanted to be.

SHELTER ISLAND

Carla Neggers

To Sherryl Woods—
a wonderful writer and friend

1

"Antonia..."

Antonia Winter stopped abruptly in the middle of the mostly empty hospital parking garage, certain she'd heard someone whisper her name. She glanced at the parked cars and the exits, but saw no one else. She took a cautious step forward, her dress shoes echoing on the concrete. She'd changed from the more casual clothes she wore in the E.R.—she had a dinner date in Back Bay.

It was tension, she decided. Simple tension had her turning ordinary garage sounds into someone whispering her name.

"Antonia Winter...Dr. Winter..."

She gasped and ran the last five steps to her car, clicking the button on her key that automatically unlocked the door. Her hands shaking, she ripped open the door and threw herself in behind the wheel. She hit the button that locked all four doors.

This couldn't be happening to her. She *had* to be imagining it.

This wasn't the first incident.

Wasting no time, Antonia stuck the key into the ignition and started the engine. It was just after seven o'clock on Saturday evening. She'd been on duty a full twelve hours. She was a trauma physician in the busy emergency room of a downtown Boston hospital. None of her cases today had been easy ones. But that was her job, and she was good at it—she was accustomed to dealing with its demands. She wasn't one to go off the deep end and imagine things that hadn't happened, draw the most dramatic conclusion to innocent events.

At least she'd never been that sort. Maybe the demands of the rest of her life had finally gotten to her. Demands like Hank Callahan, she thought. He was her dinner date that night. She'd been half in love with him for months, but their relationship had complications. Her work, his work. Her family. His past. Her past.

Hank...

No. She couldn't blame him—she wouldn't.

She wasn't hearing things or making up things that hadn't happened. That was the problem. They were *real*.

Someone had just whispered her name in the parking garage.

She edged out of her space, glancing in the rearview mirror and side mirror every few yards as she made her way to the exit. She almost asked the parking attendant if he'd heard anything, but she knew he wouldn't have. Once out on the street, she forced herself to take several deep breaths.

Yesterday, it had been an anonymous instant message. The third in a row. *Your patients trust you, Dr. Winter. What if you betrayed their trust?*

All were on the same theme. A doctor's trust. A doctor's betrayal of that trust. Without going into detail, she'd asked a friend more familiar with computers than she was about instant messages, and he'd said that tracking down an instant messenger who wanted to remain anonymous was very difficult, if not impossible.

There was nothing overtly threatening in the messages. And certainly no mention of Hank Callahan, a candidate for an open U.S. Senate seat from the Commonwealth of Massachusetts. The election was the first Tuesday in November, less than two months away. If the messages had mentioned him, Antonia would have to report them, tell Hank. She didn't want to cause an unnecessary stir—she wanted a sensible explanation for what was going on. If something *was* going on. She still didn't want to believe someone was trying to get under her skin. Creep her out.

But who would want to?

Why?

Was someone stalking her?

No. It couldn't be. Tension, fatigue and her imagination must have turned the whir of a car engine or an exhaust fan into someone whispering her name. Maybe the instant messages were from someone whose screen name she just didn't remember. A friend or colleague working on a paper or struggling with an ethical question, idly instant messaging her. Maybe they weren't meant to be anonymous or creepy.

But when she reached the restaurant, Antonia paid extra to have her car valet parked and avoided another parking garage. She stood in the warm evening air and took several deep breaths to calm herself. *There. It'll be all right. I can do this.*

She had on a simple black dress, black stockings, black heels. Gold earrings. Her dark auburn hair, chin-length and straight, was tucked neatly behind her ears. No lipstick— she didn't have time for it now.

As promised, Hank was waiting for her at their table. He was, she thought as she smiled at him and waved, the most drop-dead handsome man she'd ever met. Forty-one and tall, with graying dark hair, a square jaw and eyes so blue they took her breath away. She'd met him last November in Cold Ridge, her small hometown in the White Mountains of New Hampshire. Almost a year ago, she realized. He'd just thrown his hat into the senate campaign in bordering Massachusetts. His weekend in New Hampshire was to have been a break. Hiking with his air force pals, Tyler North and Manny Carrera. Instead they'd come upon

Antonia's younger sister, Carine, a nature photographer, being shot at in the woods. Later that same weekend, Hank, Ty and Manny had rescued a wealthy Boston couple stranded on the ridge for which her hometown was named.

Complications, Antonia thought. So many complications.

Hank smiled, getting to his feet. Other diners watched. He was a man in the spotlight. There didn't seem to be any reporters around, but she couldn't know for certain, another reminder that it wasn't just her reputation as a respected physician that would suffer if she rushed to judgment or cried wolf about a possible stalker. His would, too, as a man who was asking Massachusetts voters to trust him. With just weeks left in the campaign, she had to be sure before she said anything, although she had to admit, her own nature made her reluctant to speak up. She was thirty-five and accustomed to handling her own problems.

But it wasn't just Hank's campaign or her own reserve that made her cautious—it was Hank himself. He was a Massachusetts Callahan, the current most visible member of a visible family of dedicated men and women who were expected to do their share in the military, in public service and in business. Hank had left the air force two years ago as a major, a helicopter pilot who'd flown countless search-and-rescue missions: on his last mission, he and a team of pararescuers had performed the dangerous high seas recovery of five fishermen whose boat had capsized. It had put his picture on the front pages of newspapers across the country. While emergency operations conducted in conjunction with civilian agencies sometimes hit the press, his many combat search-and-rescues hadn't received such coverage—Antonia had learned that the military didn't necessarily publicize when and how it went after aircrews downed behind enemy lines.

Hank would come to her rescue in a heartbeat.

And not just because he was trained to rescue people.

He lost his family ten years ago when his wife and young daughter were killed in a car accident while he was serving overseas. It still haunted him—everyone knew it, could see it. He wasn't even on the continent when the accident happened, a head-on collision with a car driving on the wrong side of the interstate. The other driver was a woman in her mid-fifties who'd had a stroke. Brittany Callahan, three, was killed instantly. Her mother, Lisa, thirty, never regained consciousness and died in the hospital three hours later. Hank wasn't with them—it wasn't possible for him to have been with them. But he didn't look at it that way, at least not emotionally, and probably never would, no matter how much he'd come to accept that his wife and daughter were gone.

No, Antonia thought, making her way to their table. She couldn't just *think* she might have a stalker or some weirdo trying to get under her skin. She had to be certain before she breathed a word of her fears to anyone—even Hank. Maybe even especially Hank.

Robert Prancer peered through the restaurant window. The bitch doctor was sitting across a small, candlelit table, drinking wine and having dinner with the wannabe senator.

Didn't she know?

Robert had to struggle to keep from screaming into the window and drawing attention to himself. Damn it, didn't she *know* what she was doing to him? Seeing her with another man. Knowing she didn't care about him. That all his fantasies were just that. Fantasies. Delusions.

He didn't know what to do. He'd been lashing out, acting on impulse for the past couple of days. But there was no satisfaction in instant messages—he couldn't see her getting them, could only imagine the look on her face. Her curiosity about who it was, whether the messages meant anything. Was she in danger? Was someone trying to scare her? She wouldn't know for sure. He'd designed the messages so she wouldn't.

And she wouldn't overreact. Not Antonia Winter, M.D.

Robert had watched her work for almost three years. She wasn't one to panic. Her coolness under stress was just all the more reason to build to a crescendo and see her quivering with fear, incoherent with it, begging for her life.

He thought a moment, watching the two in the restaurant laughing with the waiter. Was that really what he wanted? Dr. Bitch begging for her life? Was he willing to go that far?

Farther?

Tonight in the parking garage—brilliant. He'd heard her stop and gasp. But, still, he couldn't see her.

And he wanted to, he realized. He really, really wanted to.

He'd taken the subway from the hospital. He could still smell oil from where he'd sat on the concrete floor in the parking garage. How had he missed a damn oil slick the size of the Exxon Valdez spill? Fucking thing was huge. But he hadn't dared to move. He'd spotted Antonia Winter, M.D., Dr. Winter, the bitch doctor—he'd spotted her walking to her car, her heels *click-clicking* on the concrete. She was in a rush to see the wannabe senator. She didn't rush with her patients. Then she was all calm and empathetic and dedicated.

What crap.

Robert thought back to a few weeks ago when he had shot himself in the foot and had gotten a good dose of her idea of dedication to her patients. She'd turned him in. He'd had to explain the gun to the cops and the shooting himself in the foot to them and the shrinks. Took him days and days to get *that* all straightened out. His damn foot still hurt. He'd meant only to get her attention, try to bridge the gap between them. Her a doctor, him a fucking floor-mopper in the same hospital. He figured he needed to do something dramatic to test her, as a doctor, as a woman. As *the* woman. He had never loved anyone else. Never. He'd been completely true to her.

He should have shot someone else. Another of the floor-moppers, maybe. Get her attention that way. He could have delivered the victim to her. She liked heroes, right? Look at the hero wannabe senator, saving pilots and fishermen.

Live and learn.

After his foot healed, it was back to pushing his broom and wringing out his mop in the E.R. Putting up with the assholes and losers who thought it was a good job, patronizing doctors and nurses and administrators who told him what a contribution the cleaning crews made. Listening to them all talk about a hard day's work for a hard day's pay and how the hospital couldn't run without it being clean. His co-workers bought lottery tickets and followed the Red Sox and took their kids to school, exchanged recipes and fifty-cents-off coupons and thought they had a life.

Robert had a goddamn 156 IQ. He knew he should be running the place. His nitwit co-workers didn't see that. They teased him about his name. *Dancer and Prancer, Comet and Vixen...*

He didn't tell them his zero of a mother had made it up. He'd never known his father. She probably hadn't, either. But leave it to her to name her one and only son after a reindeer. She'd died when he was eleven. Good riddance. Stupid people annoyed him.

He'd thought Antonia Winter had recognized his brilliance, his potential. He'd seen in her a kindred soul. A soul mate. A woman who understood him.

Fat chance.

He walked up the street, trying to control his breathing. No! He couldn't talk like that. Maybe he still did have a chance.

"Maybe."

She was so damn beautiful, with her auburn hair and blue eyes, that straight nose and small, slim body. Brainy-looking but also physical.

His type.

"No." He shook his head, aware of people passing him on the street, looking at him like he was some loser who talked to himself. But he had important issues on his mind. "No, she's not my type."

His type wouldn't have betrayed him.

The bitch doctor had. As a physician, as the woman he loved. On every level. Broke his damn heart. He was smart—he wasn't bad looking. Sandy-haired. Fit. He'd taken up running on her account, before the foot thing.

The balmy late summer temperatures had brought out the crowds. Robert figured the bitch doctor and the wannabe senator would be at dinner for a couple hours, anyway.

Well, what the hell. He knew where she lived.

And he had a key.

2

Hank Callahan had exactly one hour between the lunch at the Cambridge homeless shelter he'd just left and his upcoming three o'clock meeting with local small business owners—enough time, surely, to drag information out of Antonia Winter's little sister.

If not, he'd just have to come back.

Antonia had gone missing on him, and he intended to find out what was going on.

He parked in front of the tenement building off Inman Square where Carine Winter had rented an apartment in late spring, a move that had caught her family and friends by surprise. She didn't belong in Cambridge. She belonged up in Cold Ridge, New Hampshire. She should be taking pictures of birds and mountain scenes, living in her little log cabin in the shadows of the ridge that gave her hometown its name. She was a nature photographer, a good one. But she'd had her life turned upside down in February when her fiancé walked out on her, and she'd made up her mind that she needed to live in the city.

Once a Winter made up her mind, that was usually it.

Tyler North—her ex-fiancé and one of Hank's closest friends—had tried to warn him about the Winter siblings, not that Ty had heeded his own advice. He'd fallen for Carine after some smugglers had shot at her last November, and then he'd asked her to marry him. They'd known each other all their lives, but the prospect of Tyler North and

Carine Winter actually marrying had taken everyone by surprise.

No one need to have worried. Ty pulled the plug a week before the wedding. He still insisted it wasn't cold feet— he said he'd come to his senses in the nick of time. He couldn't marry Carine. She'd lost her parents when she was three and wanted to lead a peaceful life, and Tyler North wasn't a peaceful man.

But now Hank had to suffer for his friend's bad behavior, too. It had put Antonia at arm's length from him for months. Only recently had Hank managed to get her not to think about her broken-hearted sister when she looked at him. It didn't matter that Antonia had known Tyler even longer than he had—they'd shared a military career. They'd performed missions together.

"The Winters are thick as thieves," Ty had once tried to explain. "Don't let their bickering fool you. Hurt one, you've hurt them all. They're about as hard-bitten and stubborn as anyone you'll ever meet."

It was true. When it came to being hard-bitten and stubborn, the only one who rivaled the Winter sisters, their brother, Nate, and Gus, the uncle who'd raised them, was Tyler North. He'd grown up in Cold Ridge and still called it home, although he was a master sergeant in the air force, a nearly twenty-year pararescue veteran. Ty had seen it all, and he'd done it all.

Except marry Carine Winter.

Which complicated Hank's life, but he wasn't just going to stop being Ty's friend. The mutual respect they'd developed for each other in the military had solidified into friendship now that Hank was out of the military and fraternization rules were no longer an issue. Ty was the one who'd invited him to Cold Ridge in the first place. Otherwise, Hank thought, he wouldn't have been there last November to meet the Winter sisters.

But he knew he had to be patient. Although Antonia

didn't say so in as many words—she didn't have to—she felt she was being disloyal to her sister by falling for one of Carine's ex-fiancé's military pals.

Hank gritted his teeth. He'd trust Tyler North with his life, but there were days he wouldn't mind tracking his friend down wherever he was—on a training mission, deployed to some remote battlefield—and knocking the shit out of him. Had he *ever* intended to marry Carine?

Five minutes, Hank thought. Five minutes he'd wasted dithering over his situation. He couldn't change reality. Carine Winter was living in Cambridge. She insisted she hated Tyler North. And Antonia was on her sister's side. Unconditionally.

And Hank now had less than fifty-five minutes to get her younger sister to give him the information he wanted.

He kicked open his car door and climbed out onto the busy, narrow street of multifamily houses. He'd been in combat. He'd ditched helicopters. He'd endured the media onslaught that came with being a candidate for the senate. Damn it, he could handle the Winter sisters.

Carine almost didn't let him in.

Hank frowned at her through the grimy front door window. "Carine—I'm worried about Antonia. I just want to talk to you."

It wasn't true—he wanted to pump her for information. But with obvious misgiving, Carine pulled the door open about a foot. She was two inches taller than her sister, her auburn hair a couple of tones darker, but she and Antonia had the same blue eyes. "She's not here."

"I know that. May I come in?"

"I'm kind of busy—"

"Carine. Please."

She sighed, and he could see that her heart wasn't into being rude to him. It wouldn't be nearly as satisfying as pitching Tyler off a cliff, which, last Hank had heard, was what she'd threatened to do the next time she saw him. But

Ty hadn't surfaced in Cold Ridge in months, and Carine, too, had stayed away. Hank could see it worried Antonia, but Carine's state of mind was, by unspoken agreement, a forbidden topic.

She opened the door the rest of the way and pretended to peer out onto the street. "What, no entourage?"

"I came alone."

"Really? They let you do that?" She didn't bother to curb her sarcasm, as if she lumped him in with Ty and he deserved for her to give him a hard time was the best she could get. "Do you have a limo waiting? I'll bet your people keep a tight leash on you—"

Hank unclenched his jaw and tried to smile. "I'm just a guy doing his best."

"Yeah, right. That's what all the ex-rescue pilots turned senate candidates say." But her sarcasm let up, her tone lightening slightly as she sighed, then motioned at him. "Okay, okay. You might as well come in."

He followed her down a poorly lit hall to her first-floor apartment. The place was the polar opposite of her little log cabin in New Hampshire, just down the road from the sprawling center-chimney house Tyler North had inherited from his wacky mother.

"I see you've been painting," Hank said, noting the bright colors of all the walls and furnishings in the apartment's adjoining three rooms. He couldn't see the bathroom, but expected it, too, was bright. The kitchen cabinets were a citrus-green, the walls mango-colored.

"My landlord said I could."

"You don't think he meant white?"

She gave him a quick, unexpected smile and sat at her kitchen table, painted a cheerful lavender-blue. Somehow, all the colors worked together. "I didn't ask."

A photograph of a red-tailed hawk hung above the flea-market table. It gave Hank a start, as most of Carine's photographs did. She had a gift, one she couldn't be using to its fullest in Boston. He'd avoided asking Antonia too many questions about her younger sister, but the last he'd heard, Carine had taken a commercial assignment with a Newbury Street shop.

But he stayed focused on his mission. "I'm wondering if you've talked to Antonia recently."

"Why?"

Hank didn't respond to her reflexive suspicion. "We had dinner together on Saturday." That was three days ago, he thought. Three days and not a word from her. "She'd just come off shift and was tired, maybe a little on edge. She seemed to have a lot on her mind. She said she planned to go out of town for a few days to work on a journal article she'd been putting off. I assume that's where she is?"

Carine was the youngest of the three Winter siblings, orphaned when they were three, five and seven, and she wasn't one to easily give up what she knew—even on a good day. "She didn't tell you?"

He shook his head. "I might not have been clear on the dates, or just missed it when she said where she was going. I left several messages on her cell phone. She hasn't returned my calls."

Carine lifted her blue eyes to him. "Maybe you should take the hint."

"Carine, for God's sake—"

She kicked out her legs and folded her hands on her lap in a gesture of pure unrepentance. "How's the campaign going?"

"Fine. It has nothing to do with why I'm here."

She ignored him. "A retired air force major. A hero. A Massachusetts Callahan. A candidate for the United States Senate. I guess you wouldn't be used to people giving you the brush-off, huh?"

"Antonia wouldn't sneak off if she wanted to get rid of me." He knew he couldn't back down, show even a hint of weakness—otherwise he wouldn't get a thing out of Carine. "She'd tell me. She's a straightforward woman—"

"A clean, quick death instead of a slow one," Carine said, her tone suddenly quiet. "Either way, in the end, it still hurts, and you're still dead."

"I'm not Ty North, Carine."

Her moment of melancholy vanished as quickly as it had appeared. "That's true. If you were, I'd have stink-bombed you out on the porch." She dropped her hands to her sides and sat up straight. "Hank, honestly, I can't help you. I'm sorry."

She wasn't sorry. He saw it now. She was stonewalling him—on purpose. It wasn't just her close-mouthed nature at work, or the tight bond between the two sisters. Carine knew something, and she didn't want to tell him. Or wasn't supposed to tell him. Or both.

"Carine, normally I wouldn't be here." Hank tried to keep his tone reasonable. "I'd wait for Antonia to get back and talk with her then. But she wasn't herself the other night at dinner. She blamed her work, but I'm worried it might be something else."

"You, maybe?"

Ty had warned him that Carine could worm her way right down to a person's last, raw nerve. Hank controlled himself, refusing to react defensively and let her see she was getting to him. "Maybe. I'm serious about her, Carine. If my campaign's made her nervous—"

"That's not what you think," Carine said confidently. "Am I right?"

"You're right. It's not the campaign."

"On the other hand, maybe whatever's going on with Antonia is her problem, not yours, and what you should do is mind your own business."

Her tone was matter of fact, as if he should have thought of this point on his own. Independent, Hank remembered, was another word Ty had used to describe the Winters, right after hard-bitten and stubborn. Hank figured his only defense was to stay the course—get Carine on his side, get her to trust him. But her emotions were still raw after what Ty had done, and she had good reason not to trust anyone, especially one of her ex-fiancé's friends, so easily again.

"What if it's something she can't or shouldn't handle on her own?" Hank asked, trying to appeal to her common sense. "What if she's in over her head?"

Carine averted her eyes, and Hank knew he had her—she was on the defensive. He wasn't crazy. Something was up with Antonia. But he made sure he didn't let any victory, any smugness, show. Too much was at stake. Every instinct he had said so.

But ten seconds stretched into thirty, thirty into a minute, and she didn't say a word.

Hank let a hiss of impatience escape. "If you don't want to tell me what's going on, Carine, okay, I can't make you." He paused, debating, then said, "I'll just call Gus."

She didn't like that. Gus Winter had raised them since he'd carted the bodies of his brother and sister-in-law off Cold Ridge thirty years ago, when he was just twenty years old himself and in no position to take on three little kids.

Carine jumped to her feet, her long hair whipping around as she flounced across the small, dingy linoleum floor to the scarred stainless steel sink. "What do you mean, you'll call Gus? Like Antonia and I are twelve years old or something?"

Hank leaned back against the ancient counter cabinets. This was working. He couldn't back off—he had to go for the jugular. "All right. Forget Gus. I'll get Tyler here. He can hang you out your window by your toes until you talk."

She stopped dead, one hand on the sink faucet, color rising high in her cheeks. "Go ahead. See if I care."

"I just want you to understand that I'm serious. Something's going on with Antonia. I think you know it, or at least sense it, but you want to make this hard because you promised her you'd keep your mouth shut.'' Hank let his tone soften slightly and attempted a smile. "I figure Antonia will forgive you for talking if you tell her I stooped low enough to threaten to sic Ty North on you."

"Meaning you're bluffing?"

"Meaning I wouldn't underestimate my determination."

She let out an exasperated sigh but said nothing.

"Is Antonia in some kind of trouble, Carine?" Hank asked. "Are you?"

"Not me." Her eyes spit fire at him. "I'm in good shape now that I have all you military types out of my life."

"I'm just a senate candidate these days."

She scowled. "Don't think I'll vote for you."

He grinned at her. "You will, and you know it. You liked me before Ty bailed on you. You have a soft spot for us military types." He took a step toward her. Tyler North was one of the bravest men Hank had ever known—except when it came to Carine Winter. She was without a doubt the one woman Ty would ever love, and the dope had skipped out on her. Hank knew it still hurt. "Give Ty a little time—"

"I'm not giving him anything. He's out of my life. I don't even think about him anymore, unless people like you insist on bringing up his name."

She was such a liar, but Hank decided not to tell her so.

"Anyway," she said, "he's got nothing to do with what's going on with Antonia."

That was his confirmation. He was right. There was something.

Carine turned on the faucet and filled a mason jar with water. Her cheeks were red, but her underlying color was pale, the strain of the last months evident. Despite the bright colors she'd used on the walls and furnishings, the place was still old and rundown, a testament to her hand-to-mouth existence. Hank didn't know if she lived the way she did because of the temporary nature of her life here or because she didn't have any money—or because she was just too tight-fisted to part with it. She could always sell her log cabin in New Hampshire, but Hank knew she hadn't even rented it out.

And she thought of herself as an artistic type, a sensitive soul, not a typical risk-taking Winter. Something about her tended to bring out people's protective urges. But as Hank watched her gulp down her water, he knew he had to keep up the pressure. "Tell me what you know, Carine."

She turned on the tiny television on a shelf above the table. Hank had no idea what she was up to. The TV was tuned to the Weather Channel, which was giving the latest coordinates on Hurricane Hope, a menacing Category 3 storm working its way up the east coast. Its maximum sustained winds were 120 mph, with even higher gusts. No watches or warnings had yet gone up in New England— Hope was expected to turn out to sea before it got that far north.

Carine glanced back at him with a studied nonchalance. "What do you think of naming a hurricane Hope?"

"I hadn't thought about it at all."

"We Winters are mountain types ourselves. We've been in the White Mountains since Madison was president. One of the high peaks is named after him, did you know that? Mount Madison."

"Carine—"

He might not have spoken. "Put me on top of a five-thousand-foot peak in the White Mountains when the weather gets bad, and I'd know what to do." She shifted back to the weather report. "I can't say I'd know what to do in a hurricane."

Hank wasn't following her, but checked his impatience. "Are you worried about Hope?"

"Not for my sake. I'm not as exposed here as you all

are on the Cape and the islands. Your family's on the Cape, right?''

"Brewster. We've done lots of storms." His family owned a popular marina on Cape Cod Bay. He spoke warily, uncertain of the ground he was on now—he didn't want to miss any signals, veer off in the wrong direction and lose her completely. "People have learned to pay attention to watches and warnings. They heed evacuation orders. They don't fool around.''

"That's because they know their coastal storms, and they have access to the warnings, weather reports, evacuation orders. If someone didn't—" Carine licked her lips, staring up at the small screen. "Let's say you don't know storms, plus you've got other things on your mind. You're alone on an isolated island, and Hurricane Hope doesn't turn out to sea—you could be in a mess real fast, couldn't you?"

"You could. But that's theoretical. I don't know how you could be alone on an island off the Cape—"

"It could happen. Even these days."

Hank narrowed his eyes on her, aware of her intensity of emotion—her ambivalence about what she was doing. "Carine, are you saying Antonia is alone on an island, without access to storm reports and evacuation orders?"

"I'm not saying anything."

But her breathing was more shallow and rapid as she shifted back to him, as if she was waiting for him to figure out what she was saying and do what she already knew he would do.

He fished out his cell phone and dialed Tyler North's cell number. Ty was stationed at Hurlburt Field Air Force Base in the Florida panhandle, where he was assigned to the 16th Special Operations Wing as the Team Leader of a Special Tactics Team. God only knew where he'd be. Hank expected to have to leave a message, but Ty picked up on the second ring. "North."

"Where are you?''

"Florida. Drinking a beer. You?"

"Cambridge. I'm with Carine."

Ty was silent.

"Something's up with Antonia. She must have sworn Carine to secrecy, so I can't get any straight answers."

"Good luck, pal. She's not talking unless she wants to talk."

"She's given me a hint. Apparently Antonia is on an island somewhere off Cape Cod, and Carine's worried she'll be stuck there if Hurricane Hope doesn't turn out to sea—or she'll ride it out, because she doesn't have access to weather reports or doesn't know any better."

Ty grunted. "She'd know better, but she'd ride out the fires of hell if she thought she had to. Both of them would."

"Yeah. Carine did almost marry you."

"We're not going there, Major."

Tyler only called him major nowadays when he wanted to distance himself. Hank had put him on the spot. "She knew I'd call you."

"Carine did?" His tone changed, becoming more serious. "Then you damn well know there's something wrong. I'm the last person Carine would let you turn to for help. Hank? What the hell's going on?"

"That's why I'm here—to find out."

"Carine's okay? She's safe?"

Hank's pulse pounded in his temple. He couldn't figure out what had happened to Ty. One day, Hank was making plans to attend his friend's wedding in Cold Ridge. The next day, the wedding was off, and Tyler had taken off into the White Mountains with not much more than a jackknife and a pair of crampons.

"She's fine," Hank said. "She's standing here watching the Weather Channel and pretending she doesn't realize I'm talking to you. I'm guessing she thinks you know where Antonia is."

Tyler sighed. He'd known these women all his life—in

many ways, they were the only family he'd ever had. "Shelter Island. You're a Cape Codder. You must know it."

Hank was confused. "Of course I know it—it's a tiny barrier island off Chatham. But it's a national wildlife refuge. I thought there weren't any cottages on it anymore, and it's illegal to camp there."

"You wouldn't get Antonia in a tent, anyway," Ty said. "There's one cottage left on the island. Antonia has this friend in Boston—she's like a hundred or something. She has a life-lease to the last cottage on Shelter Island. When she dies, it goes to the birds, literally. Antonia used to go there to study for exams when she was in med school."

She had never mentioned her friend or her cottage, another reminder, Hank thought, of just how much he still had to learn about her.

"You're going down there?" Tyler asked.

"Yes. As soon as possible. I have a feeling there's more going on than just a hurricane that might or might not hit. Antonia was on edge when I saw her last on Saturday."

"Carine knows more?"

"Almost certainly."

"Want me to drag it out of her?"

He'd do it, too, Hank thought. "I'm not having you go AWOL on my account. I'll handle it. If Carine knows anything that would help me help her sister," he added pointedly, for Carine's benefit, "she'd tell me."

Carine didn't respond, still pretending not to be listening.

"The Winters don't think like normal people," Ty said. "How many women do you know who would stay by themselves in the only cottage on a barrier island with a hurricane churning up the coast? If Antonia doesn't think she needs to leave, she's not going to."

"Any advice?"

"Bring her a toe tag. Then the rescue workers can identify her body."

"North, for God's sake—"

"It'll get her attention. She's an E.R. doctor. She knows what happens to people who don't heed safety warnings made in their best interest."

He hung up.

Hank stared a moment at his dead phone. The surprise wasn't that Tyler North had canceled his wedding to Carine Winter at the last minute. The surprise was that it had ever been on in the first place.

He sighed at her. "You were really going to marry him?"

She managed a halfhearted smile. "It seems crazy now, doesn't it? Are you—Hank, Antonia specifically asked me not to tell you—"

"I suspected as much. And yes, I'm going."

"She's very independent. She's not used to—" Carine broke off, then resumed. "She won't like the idea of anyone thinking she might need to be rescued. Me, you. It doesn't matter. It means we think she's in a situation she can't handle on her own."

"It's not a fun place to be. But if you're there, you're there."

Carine nodded, saying nothing.

"Carine, is it just the hurricane?"

"No." Her voice was barely audible, but she cleared her throat and went on in a normal tone. "There's something else. But she wouldn't tell me."

She left it at that, and for the first time, Hank saw the sadness that still clung to her. Usually it was buried under anger and stubbornness—the resolve not to let Tyler North be the ruin of her. But not this time. "Do you know anything?" Hank asked softly. "Do you have any ideas?"

"I think she's scared. That's not like her." She pushed a hand through her hair and seemed to force her mood to shift from its palpable uneasiness. "Are you taking a posse with you or going alone?"

By posse, Hank knew she meant not just the people who surrounded him as a candidate, but his air force buddies, led by pararescuers Tyler North. But he shook his head. "I'm going alone."

She forced a smile. "I guess there are some things you can still do alone."

3

Follow the wannabe senator.

Robert didn't know how he'd manage it without being caught, but he figured with the 156 IQ, he'd find a way.

How had he let the bitch doctor slip through his fingers?

Actually he knew. It was the sister's fault. She'd loaned Dr. Bitch her car so she could sneak out of town.

Carine Winter, the jilted nature photographer. Robert had slipped into her apartment one afternoon a week ago and borrowed the set of keys she had to Antonia's apartment, had them copied and returned them. Then he'd checked out her laptop and read some of her sent e-mails. Pitiful. Really pitiful. Except she had a tough streak—man, he wouldn't want to be the guy who'd given her the boot.

He'd sent the bitch sister one of the instant messages from the laptop. A stroke of genius, he'd thought.

He'd debated fire-bombing Miss Carine's dump of an apartment, but he had to keep his eyes on the prize.

Antonia Winter, M.D.

Scared. Sweating. At his mercy, the way he'd been at her mercy with his foot.

Begging for her life.

It was the image he came back to over and over as he considered his next move. He knew he should probably have a master plan, but he loved the spontaneity—hell, he didn't know what he'd do next, never mind Dr. Bitch Winter.

He honestly didn't know if he'd kill her. He might, he might not.

Probably he would.

He sat cross-legged on Dr. Winter's soft, pretty bed in her Back Bay apartment. It was kind of a girly room. Elegant, expensive, but Robert hadn't expected the framed photographs of flowers—the little sister's work—and the scented candles, the lace-edged sheets. He'd gone through her lingerie drawer. Nice stuff. Silky. But he got to thinking about how she'd treated him in the E.R., how she was so sweet and caring at first, making him think he might have a real chance with her. That he was right about her, and she just needed him to injure himself to give her an excuse to make a move on him, put out the vibes for him to make a move on her.

Then she turned him in to the cops. She said it was the law, that she had to report any suspected gunshot wound. Bullshit! It wasn't like he'd committed a crime. He'd shot *himself* in the foot! Big deal! She could have let it go. It wasn't as if he'd shot someone *else* in the foot.

They'd left him alone for about a half-second in the X-ray room, and he'd pulled out his IV and made a run for it, shot up foot and everything. The cops caught him in the parking lot. Chased him down like he was a runaway dog. If he hadn't had the limp, he'd have made it to safety. He knew the hospital terrain better than the damn cops did.

Yeah, thinking about his little trip to the E.R. had pissed him off.

He'd found scissors and shredded the bitch doctor's underwear. Bras, panties, slips, camisoles. All of it. In pieces.

That'd scare the shit out of her if he didn't catch up with her first and she made it back here. If he decided not to kill her after all.

It was only his second time in her apartment. He resisted overdoing it. Miss Carine, another loser, didn't realize the keys had even been missing, never mind that he'd scared the crap out of her sister using her very own laptop.

Robert grinned to himself. See? That high IQ at work.

His granny, who'd raised him after his loser of a mother croaked from a drug overdose, said he could do anything he put his mind to, he was just that smart. She'd dropped dead of a stroke when he was sixteen. He'd found her facedown in her rice plate. Poor old thing.

But Robert didn't want to think about his grandmother. He stood in the middle of Antonia's soft, thick rug. Somehow he had to pick up Superman Hank's trail again. How hard could it be? Figure out where he was making his appearance and follow him from there—Robert had done it before. As a strategy, it made sense. If the major knew where the bitch doctor was, he'd go to her. If he didn't know, he'd find her.

Robert snatched up her telephone and hit the redial button. See who the good doctor had talked to last. Why not?

"Good afternoon, Winslow residence."

What was this? Robert cleared his throat and adopted his most polite, kiss-ass voice. "Sorry to bother you. Mrs. Winslow, right?"

"Yes."

He loved old people. Who told shit to strangers over the phone anymore? He kept up with the polite voice. "I was wondering if Dr. Winter is there."

"Dr. Winter? No, no." It was a woman's voice, but she sounded like she was a million years old. "She was here several days ago. She's spending a few days at my cottage on Shelter Island. Excuse me, I didn't catch your name?"

"I'm a friend from the hospital. It's okay, Mrs. Winslow, I understand my mistake now. Thanks for your help. Have a good day."

He hung up before the old lady could say anything else. Shelter Island.

Robert had never heard of it, but he was a goddamn genius. He could find it.

4

Antonia stood on a mound of sand, beach grass and bear-berry down a narrow path from her borrowed cottage and, once again, concentrated on trying to relax. A white-crested wave pushed onto shore. The tide was up. The air was warm, decidedly not hot, the wind nearly constant. A lone bird—some kind of raptor, she thought—rode the breeze overhead.

She exhaled, feeling the tension release in her muscles. She was safe. It'd been a good idea to come down here. She'd bought herself a few days to work, think, rest.

"It'll be okay," she said aloud. "It really will."

How could it be otherwise on such an incredibly beautiful day? It was late afternoon, but she'd removed her watch once she'd arrived at the cottage and didn't know the exact time. Still, there was no mistaking that it was September—the sun was setting earlier and earlier. She'd never been out here in winter.

She was alone on a beautiful, peaceful island refuge, exactly, she thought, where she needed to be right now.

Shelter Island was a stopover for migrating birds, and home to shore birds, seabirds, waterfowl. Dozens of different species rested, fed and nested on the small island. Sand-pipers, plovers, terns, ducks, gulls, owls, falcons, eagles. Antonia had learned to recognize some of their calls and signs, but she was still a beginner at birdwatching—she didn't have her sister's skill or patience when it came to birds. But she recognized that she was the intruder here, and she did what she could to keep her impact at a minimum.

Only Carine knew where she was. Antonia had sworn her sister to secrecy, probably a bit of unnecessary drama on her part, but it had seemed to make sense at the time. She'd wanted someone to know where to find her in case of emergency, but she didn't want Carine involved in whatever was—or, more likely, wasn't—going on with her possible stalker.

She hadn't given Hank any specifics. The less he knew, the better. He couldn't worry about, act on or say anything about something he didn't know. A few days off on her own—it was all the specifics he needed.

The wind hinted of the tropics, tasted of higher humidity. It was a reminder that Hurricane Hope remained a danger. Antonia's crackly National Weather Service radio indicated a hurricane watch could go up for Cape Cod and the islands by morning—meaning hurricane conditions were *possible* within thirty-six hours. Evacuation orders would no doubt follow for exposed areas like Shelter Island.

Antonia wasn't sure she wanted to leave. The storm still could turn out to sea before it reached New England. It was tempting to take her chances, bet on Hope instead of her stalker.

Three days at her laptop, she thought. Three days going through patient records and thinking, thinking, thinking, and she still didn't have any answers. Who would want to get under her skin? Who would be so sneaky and relentless about it? She wasn't even sure herself that anything was going on, never mind had enough to convince anyone else. Strange instant messages. Whispers in a parking garage. What did that prove? Did she really want the police involved at this point, digging into her life on every level? What could they do? There was *nothing* to go on.

And that didn't even take Hank into consideration.

After dinner on Saturday, they'd almost ended up at her apartment together, but she was aware of how distracted she was, still preoccupied with the whispers she thought she'd heard in the garage. She knew Hank didn't understand. But she'd rationalized to herself that she was doing him a favor by not telling him. Figure out what, if anything, was going on. Then talk to him.

She'd trudged upstairs to her Back Bay apartment and fought back tears as she'd walked into her bedroom.

There, to her immediate disbelief, she found her bedroom curtains billowing in the evening breeze.

She was positive she hadn't left the window open—but there was no sign of a break-in, nothing in her apartment missing, nothing disturbed. Her window was cracked, and she knew she hadn't touched it. She *never* left her windows open when she wasn't home.

She'd grabbed her phone and dialed the 9 for 9-1-1, but stopped. She was on her way out of town. She could add billowing curtains to the instant messages and whispers in the garage and try to figure out who, if anyone, might be obsessed with her. Do her own investigation from the safety and isolation of Shelter Island. Away from her possible stalker. Away from her sister. Away from her work. And, perhaps most of all, away from Hank.

If given half a chance, the media would dig their teeth into her stalker story and not let go.

With any luck, while she was away, whoever was trying to scare her would pull himself together and give up his campaign against her.

But breaking into her apartment—if it was her stalker, it was crossing the line. It couldn't be explained away. It was black and white. A crime.

She referred to her stalker as "he" to herself and believed it was a man, but she supposed it could be a woman.

Or no one.

When she got back to Boston, she'd change her locks.

The wind was at her back as she followed the sandy path back among the pitch pine and juniper to the cottage. She had on a lightweight sweatshirt, shorts and water sandals, her leg muscles getting a good workout in the soft, shifting sand. The cottage was tiny and rustic, classic Cape Cod with its weathered cedar shingles, white trim and blue-painted doors. It sat on what passed for high ground on Shelter Island, its front porch overlooking Nantucket Sound.

Antonia had met Babs Winslow when she was in medical school and Babs was volunteering at the hospital. Despite their age difference, they became friends. Babs was a true blueblood eccentric. Wealthy, but not one for anything flashy. She hadn't made improvements to her cottage in years—she hadn't even been down here in years—but Antonia liked its simplicity and lack of modern amenities. A small generator provided limited power for the pump, a pint-sized refrigerator and a lightbulb that hung from a beam in the middle of the cottage's single room and was turned on with a string. Two ancient kerosene lamps provided supplemental lighting. There was no hot water—she had to heat water in a lobster pot for dishes and her sponge baths.

At least Babs had gotten rid of the outhouse. Antonia didn't think the cottage would be nearly as romantic without its modest bathroom facilities. Carine wouldn't have minded an outhouse, she thought. Tyler, either.

When she reached her front porch, Antonia checked to see if the beach towel she'd hung over the rail was dry, then went still.

She'd heard something. Not a bird, she thought. Not the wind, not the ocean.

She didn't breathe, forcing herself not to panic as she concentrated and tried to block out the sounds of the ocean and birds and listen.

Whistling.

Someone was whistling!

"It must be a bird," she said aloud, hearing her own tension.

But there it was again—and no way was it a bird.

She recognized the tune. It was "Heigh Ho," the dwarves' working song from Disney's *Snow White and the Seven Dwarves*.

Her first impulse was to smile at such a cheerful tune, but then she thought—*no. You don't know who it is.*

She couldn't let herself be lulled into a false sense of security.

She slipped into the cottage, careful not to let the door slam, and automatically, without thinking, grabbed a carving knife from the utensils drawer in the kitchen area. Just in case. Most likey, a passing boat had spotted her brightly colored beach towel hanging on the porch and reported the possibility of an inhabitant, and a local official was checking on her, making sure she knew a hurricane was approaching and she had a way off the island.

Surely a stalker wouldn't announce his presence by whistling a Disney tune.

But she wasn't taking any chances. Taking her knife with her, she darted out the back door, making no noise as she tiptoed quickly down the rickety steps, thinking only that she needed to get to a place where she could see but not be seen.

She ducked behind a sprawling beach rosebush that grew close to the back steps and, mindful of its thorns, crouched down. She held her knife as if it was a surgical instrument, not something she might use to defend herself against attack.

The whistling had stopped.

Maybe it was Gus. If Carine had even hinted about Cape Cod and a hurricane, Antonia obviously unnerved, their uncle would get in his truck and head south, without stopping to consider that she was thirty-five, an experienced physician capable of making her own decisions.

And who's hiding behind a rosebush with a carving knife?

She groaned to herself. Sometimes Gus did have a point.

It wasn't Carine, that was for sure. Carine couldn't whistle worth a damn.

Heavy footsteps sounded on the front porch on the other side of the cottage. "Antonia? It's me, Hank. Hank Callahan."

As if there were other Hanks in her life. She almost collapsed to her knees in relief. How had he found her? Carine? It had to be, but not voluntarily—Hank must have tripped her up. Charmed her. Used Ty North to throw her off balance. He and Hank were unyielding when they thought they were in the right and someone was trying to thwart them, keep them from getting done what they meant to get done.

What did Hank mean to do?

Belatedly, Antonia realized that her own behavior must have aroused his suspicions. She supposed she hadn't done a good job of concealing how upset she was at dinner, and then she'd taken off without telling him where she was going. Even if he hadn't seen her agitation, Hank would wonder what was going on with her. She'd hoped he'd be too busy to act on it. Then there was Carine—she'd recognized Antonia's jumpiness for what it was and had asked what was wrong. Antonia hadn't told her, which probably only fueled her sister's concern.

And now, for whatever reason, Hank had tracked her down.

He wouldn't regard crouching behind a rosebush with a knife as the ordinary precaution of a woman alone on an island. Innocent. Unsuspicious. If he wasn't already on alert, finding her right now would do it.

She stabbed the knife into the sand and stood up, easing

out from behind the bush. Her sleeve caught on a thorny sprig. As she freed herself, she pricked her index finger, drawing blood.

"I'm out back," she called, thinking she sounded reasonably composed. "How on earth did you find me?"

She heard him inside the cottage. He hadn't bothered knocking or waiting for her to let him in, which made her wonder just what Carine had told him. But, Hank wasn't one to stand on ceremony when he set out to do something.

The screen door creaked open, and he walked down the back steps to the small yard that was mostly overgrown with bearberry and beach roses, with a few patches of juniper, foot-tall doomed pine and oak saplings. Lilacs, long out of bloom, grew along one side of the cottage. An invasive, nasty patch of poison ivy swarmed up a stand of pitch pine that marked the yard's far border.

Antonia noticed she'd pushed through a cobweb on her way out from behind the rosebush. She brushed it off her arm and picked it out of her hair. "Hank, what a surprise."

His blue eyes raked over her, and he didn't smile. "You're looking a little pale there, Doc."

"Am I?"

"Did I startle you?"

"A little." It wasn't an outright lie. "I'm supposed to be alone out here. Don't you have campaign appearances?"

"I canceled them."

His tone was difficult to read. Was he angry? Worried? She'd piqued his curiosity—that much she could see. "I haven't heard the latest report on the hurricane. Anything new?"

"It's not looking good." He sounded calmer, his tone less abrupt. The sun hit his eyes, which seemed as blue as the sky and sea. "It's picking up speed. It could hit the Cape after all before it makes its turn east. That would put you in the bull's-eye."

The bull's-eye. She'd hoped being out here would take her *out* of the bull's-eye, at least her stalker's bull's-eye.

What was the saying? Out of the frying pan, into the fire. Out of the way of a stalker who might not be real, into the path of a hurricane that was very much real.

"I've got plenty of time to evacuate if a watch goes up," she said.

"How did you get out here?"

"Kayak—a new one. I bought it just for this trip. I know I shouldn't kayak alone, but there were enough boats out in the inlet when I paddled over here that I wasn't worried. I had a water taxi bring my supplies."

"Quite the adventure."

She ignored the bite—the hurt—in his tone. She hadn't told him she was coming down here. It was that simple. She shrugged, giving up on any attempt to smile. "It's been fun."

His eyes stayed on her. "Seas could get rough fast for a kayak."

"It's not that far to the mainland, and I'm a pretty good kayaker. I'd wave down help if I needed it."

"Would you?"

He didn't seem to expect her to answer. He stepped down onto the grass, browned from the long summer, and it struck her that he looked taller than she remembered. He had on khakis, a dark polo shirt and running shoes, but there was nothing casual about him. He had that straight spine of a military man and the power demeanor of a U.S. senator, even if he wasn't one yet. He wasn't a man who took a lot of b.s. From anyone. Ever. And he had to know, she thought, that that was exactly what he was getting from her. She was skirting the truth, hedging, dodging, lying. And she didn't much like herself for it, no matter her excuses and rationalizations.

His vivid blue eyes could be so kind and tender—she'd seen them that way. But they weren't that way now. They were calculating, questioning, alert, making her wonder again what all Carine had told him.

"My sister said I was here?"

"Not in as many words. I had to get Ty to fill in the gaps."

Antonia almost choked. "He's not in Cambridge with her—"

"He's in Florida. He says Gus'll kill him the minute he sets foot back in New England."

It was only a slight exaggeration. Antonia sighed. "I don't get it. Gus wanted to kill him for asking Carine to marry him—now he wants to kill him for *not* marrying her."

Hank managed a half smile, without letting up on his intensity. "Don't try to make sense of it."

She waved a hand and picked the last of the cobweb off her arm. "I stopped trying to make sense of anything to do with Tyler North a long time ago. Why were you whistling 'Heigh Ho'?"

"I didn't want to sneak up on a woman alone on an island."

"Good thinking." She resisted an urge to glance back at her knife stabbed into the sand behind the rosebush. "I suppose a bad guy could whistle a cheerful tune to put me off guard—"

"I'm not a bad guy."

His words were so direct, so unexpected, Antonia had to catch her breath. Despite her efforts not to, she thought of the instant messages, the whispers in the garage, the curtains billowing in the breeze. Maybe no one was stalking her. Maybe she was overreacting to a few odd coincidences because of Hank. Because she was falling for a retired air force officer, a national hero, a Massachusetts Callahan, a likely United States senator—a man who'd lost a wife and a child, who'd lived a lifetime before she'd even met him.

Hank Callahan could easily overwhelm the life she'd carefully built for herself day by day, year by year.

And none of that even took into account his longstanding friendship with the man who'd broken her sister's heart.

How could she let herself fall in love with him? It made no sense, and Antonia prided herself on being sensible when it came to matters of her own heart.

Maybe there was no "let" about it. She remembered the moment she'd walked into Carine's cabin last November and saw him standing there, felt the instant attraction, the sparks flying—all of it, every cliché there was.

Hank moved closer to her, until they were almost touching. He'd grown up on Cape Cod and had been around the ocean all his life—yet he'd chosen to become a pilot. A rescue helicopter pilot.

He eyed her again, studying her. She'd always suspected he had a keen ability to read people. He touched a finger to her hair and caught the last of the cobweb. "Tyler said I should bring you a toe tag in case you refuse to leave."

"He thinks he's funny, doesn't he?"

"He was serious. He said if you dug in your heels—"

"Why would he think I'd dig in my heels?"

"I wonder."

She didn't pursue that one. "Well, I don't intend to stay out here if a hurricane watch goes up, never mind a warning."

"But you're tempted, aren't you?" His expression lost all its humor and gentleness. "What's in Boston that would tempt you to ride out a hurricane on a barrier island instead of going back?"

It was a close call, she realized. Crazy, because a barrier island was no place to be during a hurricane. "We're not under a watch yet. I still have time."

As if to disprove her point, a strong gust of wind rolled over the top of the cottage and rattled the windows. "You don't do brinksmanship with a hurricane," he said.

"Hank, I trust myself to make good decisions. You should trust me, too." But Antonia curbed her sudden feeling of defensiveness. "Did Carine tell you I don't know anything about hurricanes?"

"More or less."

"More than less, I'll bet. Look, Hank, I can see you're concerned about me, but don't be. I've been a little preoccupied lately—I just wanted to come down and clear some things off my deck."

"You don't have a phone, do you?"

He wasn't backing off. She could see now that she'd miscalculated when she hadn't told him what she was up to. She shook her head. "No phone. There's no cellular service, either." She smiled suddenly. "I have emergency flares."

"Flares." He smiled back at her, his grim mood easing somewhat. "You're something, Dr. Winter. Most people would stay at an inn to clear their decks, not sit in an old cottage out here all alone."

"I love it out here." But she didn't belabor the point, because if he'd dragged her whereabouts out of Carine, she didn't stand a chance herself if he decided to press her about what all she wasn't telling him. "Did you come alone?"

"Yes, ma'am. All by myself."

His comment struck Antonia as deliberately intimate, and she felt a rush of heat and awareness so fierce she had to turn away. "At least you didn't come by helicopter. You're not getting me up in one of those things."

But he was good with both helicopters and boats—and she was good with neither. In many respects, she had more in common with Tyler North than she did with Hank Callahan. She and Tyler had grown up together in northern New Hampshire, and as a pararescueman, he was a highly skilled paramedic. But he was impossible. If Gus didn't skewer him for what he'd done to Carine, Antonia thought, she might.

But if she wasn't careful herself with the air force type she had in her own life, she'd end up like her younger sister, nursing a broken heart. Maybe there'd been something in the air that night in Carine's cabin, and they'd both been gripped by forces beyond their control, doomed to fall in love with the wrong men.

Antonia gave herself a mental shake. She was getting *way* ahead of herself. She and Hank had been out to dinner together, the theater, a couple of movies, a pathetic baseball game—and they'd landed up in bed once, memorably, a few weeks ago.

But no one was tinkling wedding bells in the background. Hank had lost a family once. Antonia could see it wasn't easy for him to get beyond just having a nice time with a woman, moving to something deeper.

Which was just as well, because "deeper" meant "more complicated," and right now, Antonia thought, her life was complicated enough. Was that why she'd lied to him, withheld from him? To put him at arm's length?

"I have a boat anchored on the other side of the island." His tone was matter of fact, but he wasn't relaxed. "It's out of the worst of the wind. We can leave in the morning."

The morning. It was, she thought, a very small cottage. One bed, a lumpy couch. Antonia pushed a flood of unbidden images to the back of her mind. "It'll get into the papers," she said. *"Senate candidate Hank Callahan rescues doctor from island ahead of hurricane."*

"Hate being rescued, don't you?"

"I hate having put myself in the position of needing to be rescued. I don't mind that you're here. It's nice you came after me."

But his eyes narrowed on her, his hard gaze lingering on her face until she had to turn away. "You're on edge,

Antonia." His tone was soft, but there was no mistaking his intensity. "Why?"

"A Category 3 hurricane bearing down on me, maybe?"

"That's not it," he said with certainty.

She stepped past him, her arm brushing against his arm, adding to her sense of agitation. How could she think? A stalker, a hurricane, Hank Callahan. She glanced back at him as she headed up the steps to the back door, a warm gust of wind rolling over the top of the small cottage. "What would you do if I change my mind and refuse to leave in the morning, even if a watch goes up?"

He mounted the step behind her and smiled. "Do likewise."

"You mean you'd stay?"

He grinned at her, with no warning. "Gives you a little shiver of excitement, doesn't it? You, me, a storm, a one-room cottage—"

"Don't you have staff and security people who'd worry?"

"So? You have people who worry. It hasn't stopped you."

"I'm not going to win this argument, am I? Luckily I don't have to." She returned his grin and faked a half-swoon. "I'm willing to be rescued."

5

Robert set up camp behind the tallest dune on the Nantucket Sound side of Shelter Island. He felt intrepid. He dropped his pack in the sand and tufts of grass—he didn't know his beach vegetation—and crouched down, pulling up his pants leg.

"Shit!"

Ticks. A million of them on his legs and ankles.

The bitch doctor's fault.

He was maybe fifty yards from her cottage, but she had no idea he was there. He was sure of it. He'd arrived about an hour before Superman Hank showed up on the island. Pissed Robert off, totally. He'd known Callahan would find her but thought, given his good fortune with Babs, that he'd get a better jump on him. Maybe work it out so the wannabe senator could find his new girlfriend dead.

Breathing hard, Robert used his fingernails to pick tiny deer ticks off his lower legs. He didn't have tweezers. Dr. Bitch probably had a medical kit in the cottage with her, but she wouldn't help him. She was such a phony.

One of the ticks had a good hold on him. He drew blood digging it out.

These weren't the big wood ticks, he thought—dog ticks some people called them. These were the tiny deer ticks that carried Lyme disease. It could be treated with antibiotics, but damned if he wanted to get it. Some of the little bastards were barely the size of ground pepper. He'd picked them up tramping through the poison ivy and brush, chasing the wannabe senator across the island. Being brighter than most people, Robert knew if he'd stuck to the path, Callahan would nail him. No point in that. A left hook from Mr. Air Force, and he'd be toast.

He had to think. Be proactive. He could put up with a few ticks, take his chances with Lyme disease.

"Keep your eyes on the prize," he said aloud, still panting and wheezing from exertion.

He supposed he could have shot Callahan and been done with him. Robert wasn't surprised the would-be senator had found his way to his bitch's island refuge. It was getting there so fast that bugged the hell out of him. Now he had to scramble, deal with two people instead of one.

He sniffled, digging at another tick. "You're making adjustments, asshole. You're not scrambling."

Right.

The guy, Callahan, was a stud. Robert had followed him once, seen him in the papers and on TV a lot, plus with the bitch doctor. The two of them. What a pair. The handsome hero senate candidate, the beautiful blue-eyed doctor. Robert was nothing to them. Like one of these ticks that had to be removed, squeezed dead and tossed. But not ignored—nobody ignored deer ticks anymore now that they carried Lyme disease.

A light rain that seemed to come out of nowhere washed some of the sand and blood off his legs, but when he moved, more sand stuck. He was covered in it. He felt like one of those little hermit crabs digging its way out of the wet sand at low tide. He didn't know whether it was low tide or high tide now, just that the ocean was out there, rolling, getting scary on the other side of his dune. He wondered if Hurricane Hope was kicking up the surf or if this was normal.

If Hope hit, he'd be swept away out here behind his dune. Drown in the storm surge. Get hit by flying debris.

Callahan's boat was anchored in shallow water on the other side of the island. Robert had come over by water taxi, telling the guy this big lie about meeting a friend and kayaking out before the hurricane had a chance to move in. It hadn't occurred to him until the taxi boat bounced back over the waves that now he was stranded out here, too. The only way off the fucking island was Callahan's boat and the bitch doctor's kayak, which Robert had spotted in the brush. Something to consider in his future planning.

He'd swiped the kayak paddle. That was thinking ahead. Antonia Winter wasn't going anywhere unless Robert wanted her to.

Granny used to tell him that even as smart as he was, she was afraid he didn't think like regular people. He used to think she was just a sweet old stick in the mud with no imagination, no sense of adventure, but nowadays, sometimes, he wondered if she'd been on to something after all. Here he was, stranded, on an island—a goddamn wildlife refuge—a hurricane on the way, deticking himself, risking his life—and for what? *A little payback. A little justice in this world. That's what.*

It made him sick, thinking about himself in pain, with the bloody foot, hoping Antonia—Sweet Antonia, he used to call her—would give him some kind of hint that she was interested in him. He'd fantasized that she'd seize the opportunity he'd provided for her and let down her guard, open up to him, show her feelings. Instead, she'd made him feel like a goddamn loser. A twelve-year-old with a crush. Some jerk-off who didn't have a clue, thinking he had a chance with a woman like her.

After she'd called the cops on him, she'd probably gone out with Hank Callahan.

Robert sank back against the dune, getting more sand on him. Justice. Revenge. She couldn't get away with what she'd done to him. It wasn't right. She'd betrayed him, humiliated him, and she had to suffer. She wasn't the woman he'd thought she was. He'd believed in her, and where had it gotten him? Out here behind a goddamn dune.

Whatever he ended up doing to her, he wanted her to know it was him. No more anonymity. He wanted to hear her beg, see her fear, and know he'd caused it.

"Amen." He opened his eyes against the rain, letting it wash onto his upturned face. "Amen!"

He smelled like salt and sweat and dead fish. He dug his camouflage rain poncho out of his wet pack and wrestled himself into it. It had one of those floppy hoods that wasn't worth a damn. It blew right off his head. He tried tying it on, but the stretchy tie snapped and the end hit him on the finger—it hurt like hell, made him want to kill someone.

It wasn't much of a campsite. No tent. No little stove or firewood. He hadn't even packed a sleeping bag. He'd brought food, but not that much. Some crackers, apples, cheese, all bagged up in plastic. A twelve-pack of water.

He wasn't riding out a hurricane behind a goddamn dune, not with a cottage just up the path. It must have survived dozens of similar storms, decades of crappy weather. If Hurricane Hope chugged north and reached Shelter Island before Robert could take care of business, he'd be in the last structure on this little island. No question about it. He did, after all, have a gun.

A spider crawled up his leg, as if the bitch doctor herself had sent it out to torment him. He yanked it off and tossed it into a puddle forming in the sand behind his dune. He crawled to his feet and looked over the dune, out at the churning water. He'd never understood the appeal of the beach, the ocean, Cape Cod. It was just sand and water to him. This place was supposed to be a bird refuge, but he hadn't seen that many birds. Maybe they were all clearing out for the hurricane. Maybe they knew it would hit. Never mind the meteorologists and the storm-tracking planes— just follow the birds.

He checked his gun. It was a .38 Smith & Wesson. Basic.

But he wondered if he could get by without it. If he played his cards right, Hope would keep Mr. Callahan and Dr. Winter on the island with him, and he could blame their deaths on the storm.

Kill two birds with one stone.

Have his cake and eat it, too.

Robert smiled. "Yeah. I like it."

6

He and Carine were right, Hank thought. Something was up with Antonia. And whatever it was, it wasn't good. He checked out her cottage, similar to countless old-fashioned cottages he'd been in since he was a kid. It was tiny, cozy, with inexpensive furnishings that were functional and at least as old as he was. A lumpy old couch. A heap of musty-smelling quilts, mismatched chairs and dishes, mason jars filled with matchbooks, tacks and rubber bands, soggy decks of cards and the ubiquitous Scrabble game. The bathroom was prosaic, to say the least. He noticed the stack of threadbare towels.

The bed was behind a curtain, the sheets clean and white. Hank didn't let himself linger gazing at the damn bed.

Antonia said that Babs Winslow was ninety-seven, and when she was gone, this place would be, too. That was the deal. She had a life-lease on the cottage, but the land under it was a National Wildlife Refuge. As, they all believed, it should be. Shelter Island and nearby Monomoy Island were uniquely located as stopovers for migrating birds, their spits of sand at the elbow of Cape Cod well-suited as home to dozens of species of rare and endangered birds. And time and time again, storms had rearranged what passed for land along this exposed stretch of the Cape—they would again. It wasn't the best spot for the trophy houses that surely would have doomed Babs Winslow's cottage long before now. Development pressures, the skyrocketing prices of beachfront land, were tough to resist.

But he could see why Antonia liked to come here to think, relax. It was about the perfect escape from a busy urban emergency room, not that getting away from work, hiding out to write this journal article she was supposedly writing, explained why she was here now. They certainly didn't explain her mood. She was a dedicated physician and hadn't taken a break in months, but she'd been on the island for several days—why still the drawn look? Why still the edginess that he'd noticed at dinner in Boston?

He motioned to the laptop computer on the rickety table. "How's the article coming?"

"What?"

She seemed to focus on him, then went pale and suddenly swooped in front of him and hit the power button, not bothering to shut the computer down properly. But this way, Hank thought, he couldn't see what was on the screen. Which made him wonder what was on the screen. He doubted she'd have jumped like that if it'd been medical jibberish about some aspect of trauma medicine.

"The article's coming along, but it's slow work." She snatched up a spiral notebook, closing it before Hank could read her scribblings there, too. She shoved it into a backpack on the floor and smiled unconvincingly at him. "I think I brought my laptop more so I could play FreeCell than anything else. Nights here can be pretty lonely."

"Tonight won't be."

Her cheeks turned a healthier pink, but even that didn't last as she grabbed the laptop and it followed the notebook into her backpack. "The battery's about run out."

"Antonia—Antonia, what's wrong?"

"Nothing."

Hank didn't respond this time, hoping to let the silence work for him. He heard birds outside—common seagulls—and the rhythm of the ocean, the whoosh of the wind, and all at once his own life seemed very far away. The pace of the campaign, the constant questions and careful consideration of every word he said, the burning desire to commit himself to doing what he could as a legislator. It wasn't that he could be himself here—he was himself on the campaign trail, too. He saw no point in pretending to be someone he wasn't. But out here, with Antonia, the "doing" part of his life didn't seem to matter so much. He remembered walking the long stretches of Cape Cod beaches as a kid, unaware of the hours ticking by.

But Antonia was obviously caught up in his intrusion into her escape here, into making sure he didn't stumble on whatever it was she was hiding from him. She zipped up her backpack and shoved it under the table, as if she'd marked her territory.

She sat on a chair that looked as if it'd been smuggled out of a sixth-grade classroom from the 1940s and twisted her hands together. "You meant it, didn't you? If I refuse to leave, you'd stay here with me."

"I make it a point to mean most things I say." He shrugged, trying to take any pompous note out of his words. "It's just easier that way. I never was any good at bluffing."

"It's what you leave unsaid—never mind. I'm in a profession where I have to watch my tongue, too. Mean what you say, say what you mean. But you never know what the other person's hearing, do you?"

"Do you have a problem with someone, Antonia?"

But she seemed preoccupied, staring at her hands as if he hadn't spoken, then jumped to her feet and walked out onto the small front porch. Hank didn't follow her. He remained standing in the middle of a thin rug and watched her through the window as she whipped her beach towel off the rail, tossed it over one shoulder and came back inside. "It's raining. I wonder if it's because of the hurricane."

Hank had seen enough fear in his military career to recognize it in someone else, especially someone as unaccustomed to experiencing fear as Antonia was. She was used to being the calm one in the room, the physician who had to concentrate on treating the patient in front of her—who saw fear in others but who couldn't let it affect her. She had a job to do, and her patients counted on her to do it.

Now she was the one who was frightened and fighting for control. He could feel it, see it in her stiff movements, in the way her dark auburn hair hung in her face and her eyes tried to avoid focusing on him for too long. But he'd had years of training and experience, too, that had taught him to push back his own fears and focus on the job at hand, to stay calm when it was necessary. Then later, when he was alone and safe and the job was done, he could fall apart.

He wondered if that was why Antonia hadn't told him about Shelter Island. She'd held herself together because she knew she had these days here coming up, and she could be alone and safe and let herself fall apart now that the job was done.

Had she screwed up with a patient?

No—she was *afraid*. It wasn't regret he was sensing, or self-doubt, or second-guessing. It was fear.

She nodded curtly at him, her tension palpable. "You'll want to check yourself for ticks. You don't want to get Lyme disease."

"Thanks, Doc. I'm from the Cape. I know about ticks and Lyme Disease."

"And mosquitoes. Did you get bit on the way over here? West Nile virus can be a nasty business."

He pointed at her and smiled, trying to break through her tension. "A good role model would be in long pants, not a little pair of shorts. At least you're wearing a long-sleeved sweatshirt."

"I know the symptoms of Lyme disease. And West

Nile." She seemed to try to go lofty on him, just to tweak him, but couldn't quite pull it off. "Most people who get bit by a mosquito don't get West Nile, and most people who get West Nile don't get its severest form—"

"I'm not worried about getting bit while I'm here," he said. "By a tick or a mosquito."

She gave him a halfhearted scowl. "Do you know how many times I hear something just like that every day? *I didn't think I'd get hit, bit, knifed, shot—*"

"And you didn't think I'd come after you." He stepped toward her, not in any kind of menacing way, just to be closer to her—to get into her space, maybe, and get her to relax with him. "Did you, Antonia?"

Her eyes lifted to him. "Why did you?"

"Because something's wrong, and I want to help."

She nodded. "Fair enough. Thanks for coming." All at once her tone was formal, even awkward, as if he were a fellow doctor on a consultation. She added, in a near mumble, "It really is good to see you."

Bullshit, he thought. But she seemed to sense he was about to pounce and shot over to the cottage's ancient sink, tossing her beach towel over the back of a chair.

Hank sat on the old couch, watching her, decided he'd give her a chance to dig a deeper hole for herself.

Then he'd pounce.

He wasn't sure of much when it came to the lovely Dr. Winter, but he knew whatever was wrong, it wasn't just him, it wasn't just his friendship with the man who'd pulled the rug out from under her sister. They were a part of why she hadn't confided in him, perhaps, but he doubted they were much more than that. Still, he knew he had to proceed cautiously. Antonia was a woman used to dealing with her problems on her own. He was aware of the baggage he carried. There had been days, many days, when he'd thought he'd break under the weight of it, but he hadn't. And he wouldn't.

He'd been attracted to Antonia the minute he'd met her in Cold Ridge last fall, but Tyler's subsequent behavior toward Carine had put a damper on their own budding romance. When they started seeing each other again a few months ago, he'd never meant to go beyond having a drink and raking Ty over the coals with her—he'd had a family once. A wife, a daughter. He'd loved them with all his soul and didn't think he wanted to make that kind of commitment again. Have fun with Antonia. Enjoy her company. Keep his emotions on the surface. Don't go deep, he'd told himself a thousand times.

But here he was, with her because she was in trouble—because, he thought, he was already in deep with her.

"You've left out a few details of this island vacation of yours, haven't you?" he asked.

"I'm working on a difficult article. I needed solitude."

"Medical journal articles make you jumpy and pale? It's not me, is it?"

She shook her head, rinsing off a plate. "No."

He knew it wasn't but thought it was a way to get her talking. But she didn't go any further, and after a moment, Hank gave up. "Carine thinks you're more like Gus and Nate." Their uncle was an outfitter and guide in the White Mountains, their brother a U.S. Marshal in New York. "You like the thrill of adventure."

"My life's much more ordinary than Carine thinks it is."

"Everyone's life is more ordinary than Carine thinks."

Antonia wiped her hands on a ragged dish towel. "That's because she only has a theoretical idea of what an ordinary life is, never having lived one herself. She'll survive Tyler North—she *is* surviving him. She was so in love with him, though."

"She'll never admit it. She thinks she was possessed by demons."

"Maybe she was." Antonia walked over to the couch

and, without warning, sat on his lap, draping her arms over his shoulders. "She doesn't like you."

"She'll get over it. And she used to like me just fine, before Ty drop-kicked her into oblivion. Gus likes me."

"That's saying something. He doesn't like many flat-landers."

Hank laughed. "I impressed him with my mountain-climbing skills last fall."

"It's that you know how to fly a helicopter—he hates them as much as I do. But a rescue helicopter saved his life in Vietnam. He doesn't talk about it. I think it was a marine helicopter." She let her fingers ease up his neck, into his hair. "Which is the real Hank Callahan? The Pave Hawk pilot or the man who would be senator?"

"Different chapters in the same life."

"I like having you here with me. I feel safer with you here. But if you hadn't figured out where I was, I'd have managed on my own. If I didn't—if I capsized kayaking or fell off the porch—it wouldn't be your fault."

He could feel his eyes darkening, but she kept hers on him and didn't turn away. "Antonia—"

"You're not responsible for what happens to me."

"Guilt isn't always rational."

She nodded. "For years, I thought I bore some respon-sibility for my parents' deaths. If I'd been better, they might not have gone mountain climbing that day. If I'd asked them not to go—if I'd realized the weather was getting colder and they'd be caught up there—"

"You were five years old."

"I know."

"It's not the same—"

"No, it's not the same. You were an air force pilot doing his duty overseas when your wife and daughter were killed. But there was nothing you could do to save them, and there was nothing I could do at five to save my parents." He could see her swallow. "I'm sorry. I have no right—"

"You have every right."

His mouth found hers, and she smiled into the kiss, pulling him down onto the lumpy, quilt-covered couch. He'd thought of this moment for hours. During the drive from Boston to the Cape, during the short boat ride from the mainland. He'd even imagined the pitterpat of raindrops on the roof. But her urgency took him by surprise. Not, he thought, that he was complaining. She slipped her hands under his shirt and smoothed her palms up his sides, even as their kiss deepened.

"I hoped you'd come," she whispered into his mouth. "Not consciously, but—" He eased his hand up her thigh, over her hip, and she inhaled. "Hank…"

He smiled. "We can talk later." Her skin was warm under his hands, but she had on one of those sports bra things that would take a war plan to get into. "Antonia…hell…"

"Allow me."

She stretched out under him on the couch and lifted off her shirt and the armored sports bra in a couple of swift, efficient moves. Hank caught his breath at the sight of her. "You're the most beautiful—"

"What was it you just said? We can talk later."

A gust of wind rattled the windows and doors. The old cottage creaked and seemed almost to move with the wind, not fighting it. Hank felt the isolation of the place. It was as if he and Antonia were the only two people on the planet. He couldn't even hear the birds over the sounds of the wind and ocean.

He tasted salt on her skin, savored the taste of her, the small moans of pleasure she gave as he took her nipple into his mouth. He didn't rush. It was late afternoon and raining, and they had no other distractions. He pulled her shorts down over her hips and heard her sharp intake of breath when her silky underpants came with them. In a moment, she was naked under him.

She managed to clear her throat. "No—no fair."

But when she touched him, he pulled back, knowing that he'd lose all patience the second he felt her hand on him. "Let's take our time."

She didn't protest, just took a small breath when he slipped one hand between her legs. She was warm, moist, and he doubted either of them would last much longer. When he touched her, there was none of the tentativeness of the first time they'd made love. Her natural reserve fell away, which only emboldened him. He wanted to touch, lick, nibble on every inch of her—and she urged him on, until he couldn't stand it anymore and finally ripped off his own clothes. He had to feel her hand on him. Her mouth. Her tongue. Feel himself inside her.

When he entered her, she stopped breathing. He wondered if he'd hurt her, if he'd thrust too hard, too deep. "I'm okay," she whispered, moving under him. "Don't stop...don't stop."

She matched his rhythm, lost herself in it. He could see it, feel it happen. They rolled onto the floor, where they had more room, and she tried to pause, tried to keep herself from coming first—but it didn't work. He felt her quaking under him. She grabbed his hips and pulled him harder into her, again and again. There was nothing he could do. She filled up all his senses, and he exploded with her, crying out with his release.

A long time later, he managed to pull a thick quilt onto the floor and lay with her on it. He kissed her forehead, realized she was still sweating from him. She looked at him, her blue eyes serious, but not, he thought, because of what they'd just done.

Her voice was a hoarse whisper.

"I think I have a stalker."

7

Before she explained, Antonia felt the need to get dressed. She slipped behind the curtain that separated the sleeping alcove from the rest of the cottage and pulled on fresh clothes. Lightweight sweatpants, sweatshirt, athletic socks and sneakers. It was cool in the cottage now that the sun had gone down. She'd never gotten spooked out here by herself—until she'd heard Hank whistling his Disney tune.

She sat on the bed and tried to collect her wits, staring at the pillows and blankets. She'd never spent an entire night with Hank. But he wasn't going anywhere tonight, especially now that she'd told him she might have a stalker.

He'd want to know everything.

Well, she thought, there wasn't all that much to tell.

She rejoined him in the outer room. He was fully dressed and making tea, pouring boiling water from a dented pan into two mismatched mugs. The wind and rain had died down, and Antonia wondered if they were a leading edge of the hurricane or an entirely separate weather system. Hank had the National Weather Service radio on. A static-filled report indicated that Hope had picked up speed but lost a bit of its strength as it hit colder northern waters. It probably would be downgraded to a Category 2 storm by morning, but was still a powerful, dangerous hurricane. A tropical storm watch was up for the Cape and the islands— it would undoubtedly be upgraded to a hurricane watch before morning.

So much for her island refuge, Antonia thought as she sank onto a rickety chair at the table. Hank glanced at her expectantly, and she took in a breath and began. "I've tried hard not to jump to conclusions."

And she told him, as if she were reciting a patient's vital signs to a colleague, about the instant messages, the whispers in the garage, the billowing curtains. Hank didn't interrupt. He just went on making tea.

Finally, she sat back in her chair and sighed. "It's probably just a series of unrelated coincidences."

Hank glanced at her. "Have you ever had strange instant messages?"

"No. I normally don't have instant messages at all. I don't even know how I ended up with that feature on my computer."

He brought her a mug of tea, the tea bag still dangling over the rim. "Have you ever had someone whisper your name in a parking garage?"

She shook her head. "But I could have imagined it—"

"Did whoever it was whisper Antonia or Dr. Winter?"

"*Antonia…Antonia Winter…Dr. Winter.* At least, that's what I heard." She winced, touching the end of the tea bag with one finger—it was one of her tea bags, not one of the ones left in the cottage. "Or think I heard."

"And the curtains—you don't have a cleaning service?"

"No."

He smiled. "Gus's influence. You Winters are all too damned cheap."

"Frugal," she corrected, "not cheap."

"Hair-splitting."

She laughed in spite of her tension and lifted the tea bag out of the mug, setting it on the folded up paper towel Hank had also brought. "I'm not home often enough to make a big mess. And I don't mind cleaning. It makes me feel as if I've accomplished something."

"Unlike sewing an accident victim back together?"

"It's different."

He sat at the end of the table with his own mug of tea. "Did you clean that morning?"

"No."

"The window didn't open itself, Antonia."

"Carine has a key. She might have done it."

"Did you ask her?"

"No." She sipped some of the tea. It was stronger than she normally would make it. "She'd have worried."

"She worried, anyway."

Antonia felt a pang of guilt. "I know. I wish I'd never involved her."

"But you haven't mentioned any of these events to anyone?" Before she could answer, he added seriously, "Not that I'm your stalker, Antonia, and trying to see if you've said anything—"

"Hank! Of course I know you're not this guy, if there even *is* a guy. Anyone. It never occurred to me you could be the one—" She groaned in amazement at the thought of Hank Callahan hiding in a parking garage, whispering her name. "I didn't tell you what was going on because I thought you were responsible, but because—"

"You didn't want to worry me. You were trying to protect me." He leaned toward her, his eyes piercing even in the dimming light. "I don't need protecting, not that kind. I don't care if I'm in a tight campaign race for the senate. I don't care if I become a senator. If something's going on with you, I want to know about it. Period."

"It's not that simple."

"It *is* that simple."

Most people, she thought, would back down under that kind of certainty and conviction, but Antonia stood her ground. "What if our positions were reversed, and I had a lot of important commitments at work and didn't need any distractions, if you thought you might hurt my reputation—''

He shook his head. "I'm not buying it. You're just not used to telling people anything. You play it close to the vest, Antonia. It's not just me and my reputation, my guilt over what happened to my family—it's you. The way you are."

She paused. "You're probably right," she admitted finally.

His eyes flashed with sudden humor. "Probably?"

She waved a hand at him. "You cocky military types. Honestly. Okay, I didn't know what to do. I'm not sure I realized how rattled I was until you got here and I—"

"Ran for your life?"

"Damn close. Maybe I've been in denial, I don't know. I had this time on the island planned—I hoped it'd all go away by the time I got back to Boston. It still might, you know."

"Or it might not." His outward calm deteriorated, and she could see his jaw tighten. "Damn it, Antonia, what if someone attacked you because you didn't go to the police to save me the embarrassment in case you'd imagined the whole thing? Tell me that."

She drank more of her tea, which was still very hot, and looked at him over the rim of her mug. "You're not responsible for the choices I make."

"That's not what I'm saying, and you know it."

"Frankly, I think I've behaved very sensibly." But her bravado didn't last, and she set her mug down. "I've been so immersed in my education and career for years—I never thought—" She broke off, at a loss for the right words. "Carine wears her heart on her sleeve, but I don't."

"I'm not Gus. I'm not your brother. I'm not Carine. God knows I'm not Tyler North. I don't fit into your life that

way. I'm not family, I'm not a friend you've known all
your life—"

"Tyler's not a friend anymore."

"He is. You all can't help it. First sign of trouble with
one of you, and who did I think to call?"

"Big help he was. *Toe tag.*"

"He gave me the name of the island." Hank drank more
of his tea, then leaned back in his chair, eyeing her with a
seriousness she found unnerving. "All right. You know
what I'm saying. I won't belabor the point. You have any
ideas who this stalker might be?"

"If he's real—"

"He's real."

She fought a shiver of fear, uneasiness. "I brought a disk
with recent patient records on it. I get my fair share of
difficult cases. Crime victims, crime perpetrators, psychi-
atric patients—I thought something might jog my memory,
make sense to me."

"No luck?"

"Not yet. I don't think whoever it is wants to hurt me.
If he did, he's had plenty of opportunities."

Hank shook his head. "Just because he hasn't hurt you
yct docsn't mean he won't. He could be toying with
you—"

"The cat with the mouse."

Hank didn't answer, and she got to her feet, feeling the
darkness all around her, just the one naked 80-watt bulb
penetrating the pitch black. Antonia debated lighting the
kerosene lamps. She didn't even know what time it was.
Past dinnertime, for sure. She was faintly hungry but knew
she couldn't eat.

"I thought coming here would at least help me clarify
my options." She didn't look at Hank as she tried to put
words to the conflicting thoughts and emotions she'd ex-

perienced the past week. "Call hospital security, don't call hospital security. Call the police, don't call the police."

"Tell me, don't tell me."

There was no hurt in his voice—he was under tight control. She didn't flinch, made herself turn and look at him. "That's right."

He was on his feet, and before she knew what was happening, he had her in his arms. He held her shoulders. "Antonia, listen to me. When you look at me, I don't want you to see a senator or an air force officer, or a man who's lost his family and can't bear to be hurt again—I want you to see me. Just me. Do you understand that?"

"I do, Hank, but you're all of those things. You can't separate—"

"What I can't do is let someone I care about put herself in danger because of me. I can't have a woman I'm in love with hold back on me because she's trying to protect me."

She was too stricken to speak.

"I *am* in love with you. I know it's awkward as hell. My timing couldn't be worse with your sister's botched wedding, my campaign, this mess you're in, but—" He stopped, letting his hands slide down her back, his mouth find hers in a kiss that was brief, fierce and impossibly tender, leaving her breathless, even more out of control. When he pulled away, he smacked her on the butt and smiled. "Talk to me next time, okay?"

"I was trying to do the right thing. You know that, don't you?"

"You're a Winter, Antonia. You're a natural risk-taker. Take a risk with me. *Talk* to me."

"I will, but tell me something first, Hank. You say you're in love with me. I don't mind, because I've been in love with you since I saw you in front of Carine's woodstove. But are you fighting it?"

He stared at her a moment, then didn't answer. "What do you have in here for supper?"

"Hank—"

"The only thing I'm fighting is whether I'd rather eat dinner now or make love to you now."

He'd wormed his way under her defenses, until she could only laugh. "First things first. Always."

8

A hurricane watch went up overnight for Cape Cod and the islands. Mandatory and voluntary evacuation orders had been posted for vulnerable areas. Hope remained a Category 2 hurricane and looked as if it would hit the Cape before it made its expected turn east.

No one, Hank thought, would be concerned about the one cottage left on Shelter Island, even if they thought of it. The spits of sand along the elbow of Cape Cod had been rearranging themselves for millennia and would again with this storm. Shelter Island could take an entirely different shape by the time Hope blew over. North Monomoy and South Monomoy Island were formed in the notorious blizzard of 1978, when the single main island split into two islands. Both were part of the Eastern Massachusetts National Wildlife Refuge Complex, eight ecologically diverse refuges that provided habitat, resting and feeding grounds for a wide variety of plants and animals, in addition to birds.

Hank hoisted his backpack onto one shoulder, Antonia's onto the other as they set off across the narrow island. If the powerful winds and surf and torrential rains of Hurricane Hope rearranged these stretches of sand again, at least he and Antonia wouldn't be around while it happened.

They took a twisting path through stunted pitch pine and patches of juniper, low-growing wild blueberry bushes, the ever-present bearberry and beach grasses. It was just spitting rain, but the wind had kicked up, and he could hear the waves pounding the shoreline. Antonia would never have made it across the narrow inlet to the mainland in her kayak. The inlet wasn't as choppy as the Sound, but, as they walked out onto the beach, which was just down from a fertile salt marsh, he noticed the whitecaps. Even with the stiff, steady wind at her back, she'd be lucky to keep herself afloat, never mind on course.

She'd put on jeans, a polo shirt and a windbreaker for their ride back to the mainland and seemed less strained and preoccupied. Hank liked to think it was his presence. She'd finally told someone about her unsettling incidents—he thought their lovemaking might have helped a little, too. He smiled to himself, but noticed her frown as she paused at the water's edge. "Where's your boat?" she asked.

Hank hadn't even thought about his boat, just assumed it'd be where he left it. But it wasn't. He squinted out at the water, seeing only whitecaps and seagulls against the graying sky. Where the island's myriad of birds were, he didn't know—it was as if they'd all vanished ahead of the hurricane. "It should be right here," he said. "I dropped anchor just off shore."

"Maybe it pulled loose."

"It should have held, even in this weather. Damn it, I grew up in a marina. I know how to secure a boat."

"But you spent all those years in the air force tinkering with helicopters."

"Tinkering?"

"It's not like you were in the Navy or the Coast Guard." But Antonia's halfhearted attempt at humor didn't seem to work even with her, and she abandoned it. "I don't know what to say. Now what? I still have my flares. We can always try to alert a passing boat."

Hank continued to gaze out at the water, not liking this development, then glanced at her. "Where's your kayak?"

"We can't both take it. It's just a one-person kayak—"

"Antonia, I didn't make a mistake. My boat should be here, and it's not." He studied her, her skin quickly going pale again, ghostly, her eyes taking on the strain he'd seen in her yesterday when he'd first arrived. Her muscles were visibly tight, and he guessed she was thinking along the same lines as he was—that his boat wasn't missing by accident. "You know I didn't screw up, don't you?"

"My kayak's over here off the beach."

She hoisted her backpack high onto her shoulder and, with a nod of pure determination, set off across the wet sand, back along a sloping dune. Hank followed her with the two other packs, and she led him into a stand of pitch pine.

"Mind the poison ivy," she said, pointing to a vine of it streaming up one of the pines.

Her kayak was tucked among the trees. It was a sleek red touring kayak, obviously expensive, obviously new. Fat drops of rain splattered on its unscratched finish. Hank noticed rain shining on Antonia's hair, felt it splatting on his shoulder, the top of his head. Except for the occasional lull as the storm moved north, the weather conditions would get worse—far worse—before they got better.

"The paddle." She almost couldn't get the words out and had to pause to clear her throat. "Hank, the paddle's not here."

"You left it with the boat?"

She nodded.

"When?"

"When I arrived. I haven't been back here."

He turned over the long, narrow kayak, but the paddle wasn't under it. Antonia checked the brush and the surrounding area without success. Hank absorbed what had transpired so far—his boat gone, her kayak paddle gone.

"Maybe the wind blew the paddle away," she said lamely, then sighed, some of her physician's calm and decisiveness restoring itself. "If someone finds your boat adrift, there might be enough time for them to launch a search before the hurricane gets here.''

''It won't be that easy to put the pieces together. The boat belongs to friends of mine in Chatham. They said I could borrow it anytime, and I did. They're in Prague right now. It'll take a while for authorities to sort all that out.''

Antonia digested his explanation without any evidence of increased anxiety. ''Given the conditions, it wouldn't be unreasonable for them to think the boat pulled loose prematurely and no one was in it. I hope that's the case. Better you messed up than—''

''I didn't mess up. Someone scuttled my boat and took your paddle.''

She swallowed, nodding. ''I know.''

''It means we're not alone.''

Robert swore viciously. He was in agony. His skin was burning, itching, covered in lumps and bumps and oozing crusts. Now thorns were pricking his arms and back from the rosebush behind the bitch doctor's cottage.

Just what he needed, more shit gnawing on him.

He was covered in bites and red welts. The humidity was building in ahead of the storm, and he couldn't stand it in his poncho—it was like a damn steam bath, and sweating made him itch and burn even more. He couldn't think. He couldn't plan. But he didn't see what choice he had, and he put his poncho back on, just for protection from the thorns and the bugs. He'd given up on the deer ticks. One ankle was damn near black with them. He'd just have to get some antibiotics when he returned to the mainland. Maybe he could get Dr. Antonia to write him a prescription before he killed her.

Meanwhile, bring on the Lyme disease.

At least he was well-armed against the bitch doctor and the stud boyfriend. It had nearly killed him last night, knowing the two of them were in the cottage. But now he had no illusions whatsoever. He had no doubts. He didn't have to second-guess himself. He'd done the right thing, stalking her, sneaking out here with his Smith & Wesson. Deep down, he knew it would come to killing her. And killing the wannabe senator, too. It was why he'd kept picturing her begging for her life. Because it was the right thing to do. It was necessary.

The bitch doctor would never let him into her orbit.

He was a nonentity to her. He didn't have the nuisance value of even one of the ticks stuck to his leg, sucking his blood, spreading disease. He was just the floor-mopper who showed up for work every day and once, for reasons that she must have thought didn't concern her, had arrived in the E.R. for treatment.

Well, the instant messages, the spooky way he'd whispered to her in the garage and left her bedroom window open, cutting up her underwear—that all had more than deer-tick-level nuisance value. But she didn't know it was him. She didn't even know he'd slashed up her silky underthings. She didn't know he was the one who'd set Superman Callahan's boat adrift, who'd stolen her paddle, who was out here now, plotting his next move.

That was paramount, he thought. She *had* to know it was him. He couldn't just sneak up on her and gun her down. There was no satisfaction in that, no real justice. Damn it, he wanted credit.

''What's this?''

It looked like a knife handle. He pulled on it, and realized it was a five-inch carving knife. A signal from God! The green light!

Here's another weapon, Mr. Prancer. Do what must be done.

Amen!

Robert wiped the blade clean on his wet pants. Another length of thorn-studded rosebush backhanded him in the face and ripped a trail of scratches across his cheek. It was all he could do not to start hacking at the goddamn bush with his new knife.

Patience, he reminded himself. He had to remember what he was here to do—it wasn't getting all pissed off at a rosebush.

Crouching down, he undid the paddle so that it was in two parts. Too easy to end up smacking himself in the head when it was one long paddle, but one of the halves he could maneuver easily. He pictured himself jumping up out of nowhere and whacking Callahan on the side of the head with it—Robert didn't mind if the wannabe senator never knew what hit him.

A paddle, a gun, a knife. Not bad.

It was his own damn fault he was under the rosebush and not in the cottage. He'd decided to follow his two hostages—even if they didn't know it yet, they were his hostages as far as he was concerned. He wanted to see the looks on their faces when they discovered they were stuck on the island for the duration—when they realized they weren't alone.

Keeping them from hearing him wasn't a problem with the wind, the rain, the ocean. It was keeping them from seeing him that almost tripped him up. Not a lot of tall trees to hide behind out here. Once, he'd had to burrow down in the bird shit.

He sank the boat last night just after dark. It wasn't easy, either. He'd had to wade out into the water and beat a hole in the bottom with the anchor. He'd cut his hand. He'd been tempted to shoot the damn thing, but he didn't dare risk alerting his hostages to his presence prematurely. Mr. Military Man would recognize gunfire when he heard it.

And Robert didn't just want to set the boat adrift—for all he knew, it could float back to shore. He wanted it at the bottom of the ocean.

Even when the damn thing filled up with water, it didn't go down fast. He'd sat out there in the dark, mosquitoes chewing on him as he watched the boat float out into the inlet and slowly sink.

By the time he reached his campsite, he was covered with at least a hundred mosquito bites. He wondered if Dr. Antonia would treat him if he broke out in a fever or got West Nile or malaria or something. She *had* to. It would be unethical not to. Illegal, even. She was the one who'd told him she had to report his gunshot wound to the police.

The looks on their faces when they discovered the boat was gone—it had been worth it. They were back in the cottage by the time he'd slipped back across the island, but that was okay. He still had time, and he liked the idea that they had a few minutes to fret, try to put the pieces together, come to terms with the gravity of their situation.

It did suck. He wondered if they had any idea just how much it did, in fact, suck.

The cottage broke some of the wind coming off the Sound, but it was raining again, not a soft, gentle rain, either. Robert was already tired of it, but knew it'd only get worse.

He had to get his final plan together, but he couldn't think with all the distractions of his pain, his itching, his delight in imagining the two of them scared shitless just a few yards away.

The back door creaked open.

Robert sank low, not breathing, as Hank Callahan walked out onto the back steps.

Superman Hank. He didn't look as if he'd been fretting. He looked like some kind of sniper on the lookout. He had an alert, military feel about him that Robert didn't like at all.

Bastard. The arrogant *bastard*.

He should be quivering! Scared out of his mind!

Robert felt his nostrils flare, like he was a pissed off bull in a rodeo or something. "Screw it." He didn't know if he spoke out loud, didn't care. He wasn't taking any more chances with this puke—time to put the major out of commission. "Yeah. Screw it."

Without further angsting, Robert raised one half of the kayak paddle in one hand and the knife in the other and leaped out from the sprawling rosebush, thorns ripping harmlessly across his poncho. He slipped in the wet grass, but didn't fully lose his footing as he lunged for the back steps.

Callahan was looking in the opposite direction. The wind and the ocean were making so much noise, Robert was able to get a split second jump on him.

Flawlessly, in one effective motion, he hit the major in the kidneys with the paddle.

It was like hitting a tree trunk.

Robert was stunned. "Fuck!"

He'd planned to follow up with a knife in the heart, but Superman Callahan didn't even go down on his knees. He absorbed the blow and swung around fast and hard, his entire body poised for the fight. Major Stud knew how to handle himself in battle. That was clear. Robert did not. He was a floor-mopper—he used to get the shit kicked out of him at school. He could feel the old panic welling up in his throat.

He slashed the knife wildly, catching Callahan in the upper arm.

Next thing, the major had the kayak paddle. Robert had no idea how the bastard had gotten it. He could feel himself breaking out in a sweat under his flapping poncho. Now what?

His gun—damn, it wasn't in his waistband under his poncho. He must have dropped it behind the goddamn rosebush!

He pointed the knife at the major. Stand off. Robert knew if he went after Callahan, he'd get the kayak paddle up the side of his head. On the other hand, if the wannabe senator went after him, he'd get the knife up whatever Robert could reach first.

"You don't want me to kill you now," Robert said, like he had the definite upper hand and didn't realize it was a standoff. "Then the bitch doctor will be at my mercy."

They were both drenched, fighting the wind. Puddles formed at their feet. The grass was so slippery, it made it almost impossible to get any decent traction. If he fell, Robert figured he'd end up stabbing himself. Then he'd bleed to death. The doctor wouldn't help him now that he'd stabbed her stud boyfriend and nailed him in the kidneys. Forget the Hippocratic Oath. Forget the law. She'd let him bleed to death in the sand. Pretend Hope had done the damage.

That would be it for him. The end of the story. There'd be no revenge, no justice, no satisfaction.

"The storm's hitting," Callahan said, ignoring his bleeding arm as he kept a tight, menacing grip on the paddle. "You don't want to be out here. Put down the knife—"

"So you can kill me and tell the police it was self-defense? Hell, no."

The major didn't react. It was amazing. Talk about control. "What's your name?" he asked, all tight-lipped.

"Fuck you."

"Come on. Put down the knife. You haven't hurt anyone yet."

"You."

"Not that much. I'll let it go if you put down the knife and come inside with me. The hurricane—"

"I'm not worried about the hurricane."

But Robert glanced up at the cottage. The bitch doctor was there in the screen door. *So beautiful.* Damn, it wasn't easy to be strong and go through with what he knew he had to do.

He wasn't going to beat Callahan in a fair fight.

That left him two choices, Robert thought. Surrender, or get the hell out of there.

He wasn't surrendering.

He turned abruptly and ran away from the cottage, leaping through the brush and sand and bird shit, hoping he didn't slip and stab himself in the heart. Another bad ending to the story. No ending at all, accidentally stabbing himself to death.

But he didn't slip, and he hung onto the knife, so at least he could defend himself if Callahan followed him.

He didn't look upon himself as retreating. In a way, he'd accomplished his original mission. Callahan wasn't dead, maybe not even entirely out of commission, but he was hurting. He knew Robert meant business.

They'd both be scared now.

Robert pushed through pine trees and junipers and splashed through ankle-deep puddles, then rolled down his big dune on the other side of his campsite.

Christ Almighty. The ocean was there.

A monstrous wave caught him and knocked him backward on his ass. He choked on saltwater and rain, the wind tearing at his clothes, kicking up sand that ate away his skin. He screamed in agony and frustration, letting it all out, knowing no one could hear him, and scrambled up the dune, back down to his campsite on the other side. He didn't have long before the water would reach it.

The red welts on his hands and forearms were on fire. He thought he'd go out of his mind.

Fuck. They weren't bug bites. He had poison ivy. It bubbled and oozed and burned and itched and swelled. No wonder he hadn't managed to give Callahan a knockdown blow! He was a goddamn mess!

Robert managed to stand upright, but he could see that the sky and the sea and the landscape were all a greenish-gray now, the wind gusting hard enough to lift him off his feet. He could taste the tropics in the air, feel the cloying humidity sucking at him.

And this wasn't even the full brunt of the hurricane.

Jesus.

He had to get back to the rosebush and find his gun. He dug in his pack and checked his ammo. Twelve bullets. That was it. He wished he had a machine gun, but his .38 and a dozen bullets would have to do. He still hoped he wouldn't need to shoot them, not with a perfectly good hurricane on its way.

Snorting, trying not to scratch, or scream again, he made his way back to the cottage and took up position in the scrub pine, never mind the water dripping off the tangle of poison ivy. Why worry about poison ivy now?

The good doctor would be tending the major's wounds. Robert knew he had to act now, while they were distracted.

He gulped in a breath and dove for the rosebush.

His gun was still there, in the sopping grass. Leave it to the two losers inside not to know he'd left it behind. He cocked it, so that all he had to do was pull the trigger and a bullet would zip out. He knew just enough about guns and shooting to be dangerous, he decided. Not that he'd ever had any instruction in firearms. He figured any idiot could handle a gun, and since he was smarter than most people, he wouldn't have any trouble. He had no patience with learning things, practicing—he liked just to know them.

He retreated back to his position in the pines. He was drenched. Mad with itching. He used his thumbs to get the rain out of his eyes, figured he was spreading poison ivy into his eyes and pretty soon they'd be swollen and itching, too. But he could see okay now and peered at the cottage. It had two windows on this side, a bunch of lilac bushes— he could see the front porch and the back steps from his vantage point. He didn't worry about the one side he couldn't see, because it had no windows.

But if he could see them make a move, they could see him. It wasn't another standoff since he was the only one with a gun.

Presumably, he thought. He wasn't about to stick his head up and get it blown off. Not the best way to find out for sure they were unarmed. But a doctor? A guy running for the senate, out here after the doctor, no idea she was in trouble? Nah. They didn't have a gun.

"I've got you covered." Even to himself, he sounded like a maniacal John Wayne. "You have no way out. Stick your foot out a door or a window, I'll blow it off. Your head? Same thing."

No response. He wondered if they'd heard him. If they were in there, cowering. He could do it, he thought. He could shoot Antonia's foot off. He was a good enough shot—why wouldn't he be?—and he'd waited long enough to see her bleeding and in pain.

"Scared?" He waited, but still no answer. "Good. I hope you are. I was scared when I came to the bitch doctor for help. How about it, Dr. Winter? Suppose I give you the same treatment you gave me? How'd you like that?"

He remembered her slender hands on him as she'd examined him. Her soft, kind words. He'd trusted her, believed in her. He thought she'd finally open up to him. He assumed she'd recognized him.

But she didn't. She'd asked him his name, as if she'd never seen him before, and even before she turned him in to the cops, he knew he'd misplaced his trust and affection.

He was a nobody to her. A zero.

Then he thought—hell, she and the boyfriend didn't know he had a gun. They didn't know they had to take him seriously.

"In case you doubt me, here's a little taste of your future!"

Robert fired a bullet into the side window, the gun kicking back the way it had when he'd shot himself in the foot. The loud bang startled him. The wind was howling so much, he didn't hear the old glass in the window shatter. But he saw it, and smiled.

He didn't know what he'd do next, but right now, he had the big important doctor and her hero boyfriend under his total control.

9

The wind blew water and bits of leaves and twigs in through the shot-out window above the sink. The bullet had lodged in the bathroom door. It hadn't hit anyone, no thanks, Hank thought, to the son of a bitch outside. Why the hell take a potshot at them? Just to scare them? Why not burst into the cottage and shoot them both, before they realized he had a gun?

Whoever the guy was outside, he had his own agenda, his own way of thinking—but now that they knew he had a gun, Hank realized, they had a chance. Staying low, out of the bastard's line of sight, his arm bleeding from the knife wound, his back aching from the hit with the kayak paddle, he and Antonia had quickly barricaded the front door with an overstuffed chair and the back door with a couple of extra folding chairs. Their handiwork wouldn't stop an intruder with a gun, but it'd give them warning, trip him up so Hank could act. He had a knife of his own now, as well as the kayak paddle and the determination not to be taken by surprise a second time.

But he didn't think Antonia was up to any kind of combat, and he hoped it wouldn't come to going after the man outside—killing him—in front of her.

Despite her obvious fear, she stayed calm and, once they'd secured themselves as best they could inside the cottage, insisted on bandaging his arm. "Fine," Hank said, "provided I can keep an eye out for our friend."

She nodded. "If I were him, I'd hide in the trees along the edge of the side yard. That way I could see both entrances and the windows. Since he shot the window above the sink—"

"It makes sense."

They moved the table down along the wall so that Hank could sit at one end and still have a view of most of the side yard, without exposing himself in the window.

Antonia set an ancient first-aid kit she'd pulled out from under the bed on the table and rummaged in it. He could see her tension, but knew she had the training and experience to focus on what she was doing. "You should have stitches."

Hank grunted. His arm throbbed, but he'd endured worse injuries. "I should have fed the bastard that goddamn knife."

"Ty would have."

"North's trained to feed people knives." Hank smiled, because he knew she'd deliberately made that comment to get him to smile. The doctor easing her patient's mind. "I'm just a mild-mannered helicopter pilot."

"Ah." She found a tube of antibiotic ointment and squeezed a bit onto a supposedly sterile gauze pad—the stuff had to be long past its "use by" date. "That's *just* what I thought when I saw you take the kayak paddle from our friend outside. Mild-mannered helicopter pilot."

"Scared the hell out of you, didn't he?"

"Yes. He has a gun—"

"I know, but first he has to get to us."

She glanced at him. "You're not saying we have the upper hand, are you?"

"I'm saying right now we're okay. First things first, Antonia. We're doing everything we can."

If possible, she was even more pale, but she wasn't one to panic. "Let's see this arm of yours."

She helped him get his shirt off, and he'd been touched

when she blanched at his injury—not because she didn't see worse every day, Hank assumed, but because this time it was him. She worked quickly and efficiently. He watched her, noticed that her hands were steady as she swabbed and dabbed and bandaged.

"You won't have to amputate if I don't get stitches, will you?" he asked lightly.

"Only if you get a nasty infection and we can't get to proper help."

"Thanks, Doc. I appreciate a straight answer. You're supposed to say no, you'll be fine."

She managed a smile. "No, you'll be fine."

He moved his arm the wrong way and caused himself a stab of pain. "Now I feel a lot better," he said with good-natured sarcasm. He wasn't worried about his arm. He'd done worse working on boats as a kid. What he worried about was the bastard outside with the gun. He peered through the rain and wind, but saw no sign of their guy. "I can't believe I let that s.o.b. nail me."

Antonia taped a gauze bandage over the ointment-covered wound with a few deft moves. "You're lucky. The cut's not deep, which is a good thing. I'm not set up here for major wounds and fractures."

It didn't look to Hank as if she was set up for three-inch superficial knife wounds, either, but he liked the feel of her fingers on his skin. "I should at least have followed him," he said. "I don't think he had his gun on him when he came after me. I could have kept him from getting it—"

"What if you were wrong and he did have the gun? What if you'd passed out?"

"I wouldn't have passed out."

She added one last piece of tape, then waited, appraising her handiwork, he assumed. "Ty not only could take on this guy outside, but he could bandage your wound. He jumps out of helicopters with a fifty-pound med ruck strapped to him—"

"I know. He jumped out of my helicopter enough times."

She nodded absently, and he could tell her mind wasn't on Tyler North or helicopters, or even Hank's wound now that it was bandaged. She wasn't trying to distract him anymore. She was trying to distract herself. She peeked out the window. "Tell me what he looked like to you," she said quietly.

"You saw him—"

"I didn't get a close look—I was more worried about you. And you're objective. I'm not. Not if it's who I think it is."

Hank didn't push her for more information. "White male in his mid-twenties. Five-eight. Blond. Clean-shaven. His hair was medium-blond, curly, long enough to put in a ponytail if he wanted to. He was quick—quicker than you'd expect at first glance."

"Physically, you mean?"

"Yes. Mentally, I'd say he's a survivor. He wanted me to think about what would happen if I went after him and didn't succeed—I fell for it. It distracted me long enough for him to clear out."

"If not for the hurricane—"

"I'd have his ass."

Antonia smiled faintly, but was still clearly distracted. She nodded at his bandaged arm. "I can't vouch for the ointment, but the bandage is just about perfect. How's the pain?"

"I hurt more where he smacked me with your kayak paddle."

She didn't smile. "There's not much I can do about that with anything Babs has left behind. Just let me know if you pee blood."

"Sure, Doc, I'll do that." He rolled his eyes, but he couldn't make her smile again. "I can take on bad guys if I have to?"

"I have plenty of bandages."

He winked at her. "That's the spirit."

"Hank—"

"We'll get out of this mess, Antonia." He got to his feet, avoiding standing near a window, and slipped his shirt back on. It was damp and bloody, but he was running out of dry clothes. "You recognize this guy, don't you?"

She sighed, nodding reluctantly. "It's Robert Prancer."

Hank had never heard her mention the name before. He was sure he'd have remembered if she had. "Is it a guess, or are you positive?"

"I'm positive. The knife—" She lifted her eyes to him. They were doctor-serious. "I should tell you that it was my knife. I grabbed it when I heard you whistling. It made sense at the time."

"You thought I might be this Prancer character."

"I didn't have him in mind as a suspect at the time. He's one of perhaps a dozen names that I jotted down to look into—patients I'd treated in the past few weeks."

"Who is he?"

But he doubted she'd even heard him. "I thought I'd covered my tracks, so that no one could follow me from Boston. I didn't tell anyone where I was going. I even borrowed Carine's car."

"That all makes sense now that I know—"

"But I—I had no idea. I hid behind the rosebush out back. It seems ridiculous now."

"Imagine if it'd been Prancer instead of me," Hank said. "Not so ridiculous after all."

"You're probably right, but when I look at your arm—" She didn't finish the thought. "I didn't want to look silly when I realized it was you whistling, so I stuck the knife in the sand and forgot about it."

Hank shrugged. "Prancer could just have easily got it out of the sink while we were on the other side of the island. Hell, we're lucky we didn't find him hiding under the bed when we got back. He's probably kicking himself for not thinking of it now that he's outside and we're in here.''

Her eyes settled on him. ''I'm sorry.''

He stood to one side of the back door and looked outside, but saw no sign of Prancer. ''If he hadn't had the knife and the kayak paddle, he might have used his gun on me instead of the window. Maybe the knife's what saved my life. Antonia—this guy—''

''I treated him for a gunshot wound to his left foot. I had to report him to the police.''

Hank nodded. ''It's the law.''

''I don't think he realized that. It's surprising how many people don't. He wouldn't tell me what happened—the wound was almost certainly self-inflicted. I sent him for X-rays, and he took off from the X-ray room. I don't know how he managed it. He was in a johnny, he was on an IV, he had a bullet wound in his foot—he must have pulled out the IV himself.''

Hank pictured the lunatic who'd come after him and could see him pulling out his own IV, running off with a bullet wound in his foot. ''How long ago was this?''

''Three weeks? Maybe less. The police caught up with him out in the parking garage. I don't know what made him think he'd get away, not with that injured foot.'' Antonia groaned, tense, frustrated. And scared, Hank thought. More scared than she wanted to admit, possibly because she knew the guy outside. ''He works at the hospital. He's on the cleaning crew. Hank, I have the greatest respect for the people who clean—''

''That's not what this is about, Antonia. It's about some sick ideas he has about you, not any ideas you have about him.''

''I understand he's very intelligent, but he can't get along with people. I didn't recognize him at first when I was treating him—I was focused on what I was doing. Then I played it cool. I wasn't sure what was going on. I didn't want to embarrass him or make his situation worse. It was an awkward moment, to say the least.''

"Think he has a crush on you?"

Color rose in her cheeks, which Hank took as a good sign. "It's possible. I'm usually oblivious to that sort of thing."

"Then not only did you betray him by turning him in to the police, you betrayed him by going out with me. And now if he can't have you—"

She shuddered. "I know. That's what I've been thinking. I just wish it didn't have to involve you. You're getting swept up in something that has nothing to do with you."

"If it involves you, it has everything to do with me."

She said nothing.

He grinned at her. "At a loss for words, Dr. Winter?"

"You amaze me," she said. "I have a feeling you always will."

Hank buttoned his shirt, feeling the throb in his upper arm where Prancer had nicked him. It could have been worse. He didn't want to think about what would have happened if Prancer had managed to incapacitate him. If he'd done the sensible thing and shot him on the back steps. "It doesn't help to try to figure this guy out at this point, does it? He's operating according to his own logic. Did you save his life?"

"I cleaned his wound, which probably kept him from getting a nasty infection, but that's unpredictable. Otherwise—no, I can't say I saved his life."

"He came in on his own?"

"He called for an ambulance himself."

"He wanted you to treat him. It could have been a ploy for attention and sympathy."

A strong gust of wind shook the cottage and rattled the windows, and more debris and water blew in through the shot up window. They'd have to do something about it or they'd end up with the whole Sound in on them. The National Weather Service radio was just static now, but Hank thought it was a fair bet the Cape and the islands were under a hurricane warning at this point—Hope was moving fast.

"We should concentrate on getting through this hurricane," Antonia said. "At least Prancer won't have a chance to surprise us again."

Hank grabbed her beach towel and, staying low, stuffed it in the blow-out window above the sink. "Damn straight."

"If we can't get off this island, neither can Robert." Her voice was less strained, and he knew she was focused on what they had to do now—not what she'd done, or should have done, weeks ago. "He's not going to want to stay outside in a hurricane, not when he's the one with the gun."

"Then we have to get to him first."

10

Robert was up to his ankles in water. High tide, torrential rains, storm surge. Fierce wind that never stopped. He didn't know if it was Hope or the leading edge of Hope or what, but he had no intention of staying outside one minute longer than was necessary. Babs Winslow's little cottage awaited him, he thought, wrapping himself in his camouflage-style poncho. He'd also managed to grab a bright blue tarp that'd blown off the cottage porch and wrapped up in it, too.

He felt like he was in a body bag, but a part of him also savored his misery. His suffering would make killing the two in the cottage that much more satisfying.

Killing someone should have its costs. Granny had told him that the best things came with sacrifice and commitment, even suffering.

The rain and humidity were intolerable. He was clammy, sweating inside the poncho and tarp. He might as well have been breathing water. He coughed, tasting salt, and looked around for any dry ground where he could think straight and put together his plan of attack.

"Robert! Robert Prancer!"

He went still, crouching down low under the tree. It was Antonia Winter, calling his name as if in a dream. He stopped breathing and listened over the sounds of the rain and wind. She knew him now. She realized he was the one out here with the gun. The one who'd attacked her stud boyfriend.

Yes, Robert thought, he was in her thoughts now. He wasn't just some mindless, nameless attacker on the loose. He was Robert Prancer. She could picture him, even if it was with his goddamn mop.

Perfect.

He couldn't see her through the blinding rain. Was she calling him from the back door? A window? He doubted she was at the front door, not with the porch in the way— he'd never hear her over the howling wind, the crashing surf, the lashing rain. What a mess.

"Robert, you can't stay out there."

Although she had to yell to be heard over the oncoming hurricane, she managed to sound concerned, reasonable. But she was an E.R. doctor. She was good at faking concern and reason.

He didn't answer her. The hell with her. This wasn't a dream. This was a ploy on her part. She was trying to play to his weakness for her.

"Hurricane Hope is hitting us," she continued. "It'll only get worse. Robert, you'll be killed if you don't take cover."

"What do you care?" he yelled, despite his resolve to keep his mouth shut.

He knew he was giving away his position. Didn't matter. She and Callahan weren't going to do anything. He was the one out in the goddamn hurricane, and he was the one with the gun. They weren't going to seize the lead from him. What happened next was *his* choice.

"I'm a doctor, but I'm also your colleague at the hospital. I know how hard you work—"

"Fuck you! You don't know anything about me! You'll celebrate if I'm dead!"

He sounded like a head case. He winced, pulling the tarp

more tightly around him, the rain pelting on it, bouncing off. He had to *think*. If he stormed the cottage—gun or no gun—they'd see him coming and set up a defense. Ambush him some way. He needed to create a distraction, then move in when they weren't looking. A Molotov cocktail. Homemade napalm. Something like that. Firebomb the cottage. His hostages would have to deal with the fire, and he could move in with the gun.

He'd just have to be careful not to burn down the place. Talk about cutting off your nose to spite your face.

Where could he get the fixings for a Molotov cocktail? A bottle. Some gasoline. Dry fabric for a wick.

But the bitch doctor hadn't given up. "Robert, please. Let's talk before we get in any deeper. I know you're here because of me." He thought he could hear her hesitation. Her regret. "Because of a mistake I made. Come inside. We'll ride out the hurricane together."

Was she serious? Had his actions helped her to see the light? Robert edged out of his cover of pines, the blue tarp trailing after him like a bridal train or a king's robe. The poncho hood wouldn't stay on his head. He was soaked, rain pouring down his face and neck, and the poison ivy and bug bites were driving him insane. He could feel his .38 tucked in his waistband and realized he didn't much like toting a gun.

Visibility sucked with all the rain and wind. Dr. Winter and Superman Callahan couldn't possibly see him.

"If I come in," Robert yelled, "you and Callahan are my hostages!"

"We are, anyway. Robert, you can't stay out there. You can't!"

That last sounded like she was desperate to save him. Like she didn't want his death on her conscience.

Did she care, now that she knew it was him out here, drowning, in danger of being swept into the ocean? Maybe

Callahan didn't look so good to her, now that Robert had taken him on, drawn a little of his blood.

But he fought back any sympathy for her. Who did she think she was, inviting him to join her inside? Offering up herself and her boyfriend as hostages? Like she had the upper hand. *He* had the fucking upper hand.

He paused, fighting the poncho and the tarp so he could get to his gun, get it and his hand out in the open where he could start shooting. Did she really think he was so stupid he wouldn't use the advantage he had? Stay out here when he could shoot them both dead and make himself a nice cup of tea and ride out the hurricane in the cottage?

He could kill her and Superman Callahan without reloading. Just do it. Get it over with.

No more fooling around.

Robert had no intention of waiting out a hurricane with two hostages who'd be looking for any advantage, any opening to slit his throat. No way. Forget letting the storm kill them. Forget prolonging the pleasure of their misery. They had to die now. *He* had to do it.

Then he'd have the cottage to himself. After Hope, he'd find a way out of there before anyone found the two bodies he left behind.

He used the lack of visibility to his advantage and headed toward the cottage, gun drawn, ready to fire.

The wind grabbed the front door and almost ripped it off its hinges, but Hank was prepared and managed to latch it before it gave him away. He stayed low, out of Robert Prancer's line of fire. He seemed to be in the line of trees off to the side of the cottage. A good position, one that he could hold indefinitely if not for the oncoming hurricane.

Inside the cottage, Antonia knew what to do. Hank didn't like it, but they'd agreed that Prancer would go on the attack—he wouldn't remain outside in the hurricane. He'd risk everything, and he'd kill them this time. His little cat-and-mouse game was over. All he needed was the right opening.

Hank had the half a kayak paddle he'd appropriated in one hand and a kitchen knife, not as good as the one Prancer still had, in the other. If he got close enough to Prancer, it'd be a fight, at least.

He heard a shot out back.

It didn't startle him or concern him, because he was confident Antonia had done her part and poked open the back door with a broom handle. Prancer, as they'd predicted, had responded to the provocation by firing, instead of waiting until he saw an actual person. If nothing else, it meant he wasn't worried about running out of ammunition.

As backup, Antonia also had a pan of water boiling on the tiny cottage stove. If Hank failed in doing his part and Prancer got into the cottage, she'd throw it on him. She was a doctor. She'd know how and where she could do the most damage, should she be required to act in self-defense. But she wouldn't unless she had no other choice. She treated the results of violence. She didn't cause violence.

Pushing aside his misgivings, Hank focused on the task at hand, letting his years of training and combat missions kick in, take over. He stepped into the swirling water and sand at the bottom of the porch steps. Rain lashed at him, and the roar of the ocean and wind surrounded him—he meant to use all of it to his advantage. The noise, the lack of visibility, the sense of urgency. Robert Prancer couldn't be in a good place right now, mentally or physically.

Hank edged around to the back of the cottage, using the lilacs and the weather for concealment.

"Antonia! Bitch doctor!" Prancer had definitely moved down from the trees toward the cottage, but Hank couldn't see him. "Come outside. I want my gun at your head. I want the wannabe senator to see you cower and hear you beg for your life.''

Hank gritted his teeth and kept a tight hold on the kayak paddle and the knife.

"I'm afraid," Antonia said. "Not of you—of the storm.''

That's it, keep him talking. Hank peered through the dripping lilac leaves and the gray rain and spotted a bright blue tarp about five yards behind the cottage. It moved, and he realized it was Prancer, the tarp half off him, more hindrance than help.

"Come out where I can see you," he screamed. "Now. I have lots of bullets. You can't win.''

"All right—"

"Wait." The blue tarp stopped moving. "Where's Callahan? Your stud ex-major. Have him talk to me.''

Antonia ignored him. "Robert, I'm coming out—"

"I said wait! Shit. He's not in there, is he? You fucking bitch.''

He dropped the tarp, kicked his way out of it as he ran toward the cottage, splashing through the water-soaked grass and sand. Hank could clearly make out the gun in Prancer's right hand.

Moving fast, Hank jumped out from the lilacs. Prancer spotted him and fired—but not at Hank. At the back door.

Antonia was supposed to be inside with her pan of boiling water.

Hank dove for Prancer, hitting him in the solar plexus with the paddle. Prancer staggered backward, and Hank followed up with another hit, dislodging the gun. But the s.o.b. was still on his feet. And he had his knife.

Antonia swooped down from the back steps and, without the slightest hesitation, stomped on Prancer's left foot—the same one she'd treated a few weeks ago. He screamed out in agony, dropping the knife as he fell onto his hands and knees.

Hank grabbed the gun out of a puddle and pointed it at Prancer. "Up on your feet. Hands in the air where I can see them."

His hands went up, but he sneered as he got to his feet. He was white-faced but seemed oblivious to any pain he was in. "You won't kill me. It'd do in your chances to be elected."

Hank paid no attention to him. "Antonia?"

"I'm okay. He didn't hurt me."

She was lying. There was blood on her upper right arm. Hank could see it out of the corner of his eye. "Can you make it back inside on your own?"

"Of course."

He almost smiled. His lovely Dr. Winter was nothing if not independent. "We'll need something to use to tie him up."

"Gus says duct tape works best."

Leave it to Gus to explain such things to his doctor niece. Hank waited until she was back in the cottage, then compelled Prancer inside at gunpoint. He'd lost some of his cockiness, moaning in pain, limping. His shirt was torn, his skin ravaged, his long hair matted down from rain. Blood trickled down one side of his mouth—he'd probably bit his lip. Hank knew he hadn't hit him hard enough to cause internal bleeding. He hadn't got good footing in the wet grass.

Hank ordered him to sit on a chair at the kitchen table.

"Go to hell," Prancer said.

But he sat down, and Antonia rummaged around under the sink and produced the roll of duct tape. Hank saw the blood on her arm but didn't say anything until they finished tying up their prisoner. She had a surgical approach to the duct tape, and he saw her examining Prancer for injuries.

She would treat the patient in front of her, even if it was someone who had just tried to kill her.

Finally, she sank shakily onto a chair at the end of the table. "A bullet grazed my arm. I think—" She made a face, obviously not relishing what she had to say. "I might need your help patching it up."

Hank smiled at her. "Don't pass out, Doc. You'll need to tell me what to do."

11

Hank didn't need as much help treating her wound as Antonia had anticipated. He'd flown scores of search-and-rescue missions in his military career and knew medical basics, never mind that he was a pilot, not a pararescue-man like Tyler North. But none of them could prescribe medications, she thought, feeling a little woozy and defensive—she was a doctor, so she could write prescriptions. She wished she had something for the pain.

The bullet hadn't lodged, but it was a nastier gash than what Prancer had done to Hank with the knife.

"Why were you in the doorway?"

"I wasn't. The bullet—I don't know how it hit me."

"The police can figure it out."

The police. It had come to that, after all.

Robert, tied securely to his chair with duct tape, looked on silently. He was wide-eyed, fuming, soaked and in pain himself, although there wasn't a lot Antonia could do for him. She sat on the couch and focused on what Hank was doing as he cleaned and bandaged her wound.

"You're going to watch?" he asked.

"Of course."

He worked quickly, efficiently, no visible tremble to his hands. She admired his ability to concentrate. "You need stitches," he pronounced, applying the last bit of the ancient first-aid tape to hold her bandage in place.

It was true. The bullet had torn a gash in her upper arm,

but at least it had gone right out again—she hadn't relished the idea of walking Hank through digging a bullet out of her. But her wound did need stitches, if not surgery. She sighed. "I don't think we'll be off the island in time. But it'll be okay. You've done a nice job."

He looked troubled. "Antonia—"

"There's nothing more we can do. How's our prisoner?"

There was a lull in the weather, but the storm was still approaching, relentlessly, from the south. Antonia had no idea how long before it arrived. But Robert Prancer was no longer a threat. He was obviously in some discomfort from his bites and poison ivy and the kayak paddle to the solar plexus. His foot was bruised but Antonia hadn't done any serious damage—she'd checked.

Her arm bandaged and throbbing, she applied ointment to his bites and offered him Benadryl, but he refused. She wasn't surprised. As they'd tied him up, he'd spat out his lengthy list of grievances. He was convinced she'd betrayed him as a patient, as a co-worker at the hospital, as a man who had fallen in love with her from afar. He'd adored her, fantasized about her—or at least an idealized version of her. Supposedly not remembering his name, telling the police about his gunshot wound, taking up with Hank Callahan. It was one betrayal after another. Antonia was responsible for everything he'd done since that day she'd treated him in the E.R.

Hank discouraged her from trying to talk to him. At this point, Robert Prancer was a problem for the authorities.

But first, she thought, they all had to deal with Hurricane Hope.

Babs Winslow's cottage had endured countless storms, but there were no guarantees it would survive this one. Antonia and Hank collected towels to tuck under the doors and windows in case water started seeping in, and they filled every jug, pitcher and bowl available with fresh water. She tried not to envision the roof blowing off, the cottage splintering with them inside.

"You betrayed me." Robert's voice was calm, almost matter of fact. "You're a traitor to your profession. Bitch doctor. That's what everyone's going to call you. I'll say it loud and clear at my trial. I won't be convicted. You know that, don't you?"

Hank picked up the roll of duct tape. "One more word, and you're getting gagged."

"Fuck you. Fuck the bitch doctor."

That was all Hank needed. He ripped off a six-inch length of duct tape, but Prancer promised to keep quiet. Hank winked at Antonia. "He'll be convicted." But he went still, then grinned suddenly. "I hear a helicopter."

"What? I don't hear anything." But she stopped, because now she heard it, a steady whir that she'd thought was the wind or the surf. "Do you think—I should get my flares."

But she didn't need them. When they ran out onto the front porch, the helicopter was already low over the island. Hank grinned. "Feels weird to be on this end of a rescue."

"Carine. She must have sounded the alarm."

"Tyler, too. He'd raise hell."

"He's in Florida—"

"Not if he found a way up here." Hank opened the front door and shouted back to Prancer. "I'm looking forward to introducing you to my friend Master Sergeant Tyler North."

Antonia felt a tightness in her chest. Her arm ached, but she didn't mind that so much. "Hank, I've put you in a terrible position."

"I put myself here. You didn't. I did what I had to do. No regrets. No second-guessing." He slung an arm over her shoulder, careful to avoid her injury. "Well, Doc, looks as if you're going to have to ride in a helicopter after all."

She managed a laugh. "For once, I don't mind. It beats

staying out here in a hurricane.'' But that was bravado—she didn't like helicopters. ''The police aren't going to like it that a senate candidate was knifed.''

''Hell, I don't like it. They won't like having an E.R. doctor shot, either.''

The helicopter landed on a relatively dry spot near the cottage, and within minutes, Hank was proved right. Compact, green-eyed, tawny-haired Tyler North, a lion of a man, jumped out. He had somehow wormed his way onto the rescue flight. Now he was their link between disaster and the helicopter.

Hank swore under his breath. ''Damn. I'm never going to hear the end of this, am I?''

Tyler grinned at him. ''Never. Dr. Winter? You need a litter?''

''I can walk.''

But, actually, she couldn't. He saw that before she did. So did Hank. They strapped her into a litter and got her on board the helicopter, another crewman waiting with Robert Prancer. Then they got him on board.

Mercifully, Antonia, who didn't like helicopters, passed out for the short ride back to the mainland.

Tyler disappeared before Hope hit.

''Marry Antonia, will you?'' he told Hank. ''It'll take Gus's mind off killing me.''

''Carine—''

''She'll be fine. She won't want to get in the way of her sister's happiness. Trust her.''

''Is she here?''

''She's here. Gus, too.''

Hank had known his friend wouldn't stick around. He knew, too, that Ty hadn't found his way to Cape Cod to earn Hank's undying gratitude—he'd done it because that was what he did, because it was Antonia, and it was Carine.

Ty was gone before she made her way to Antonia. Gus was at her side, fifty years old, rangy, totally pissed off.

Antonia ignored all of them and got access to a proper medical bag so she could sew up her own arm, informing everyone who tried to dissuade her that she did this sort of thing for a living.

Stubborn. Hard-bitten. Independent. Hank grinned. For all his faults, Tyler North did know the Winter family of Cold Ridge, New Hampshire.

There were police to talk to. Antonia muttered something about pulling another faint to get out of it, but she handled all the questions with a calm and directness Hank had come to expect of her, and knew he would always admire.

Carine, it turned out, had let herself into her sister's apartment in Boston and found shredded lingerie hanging out of Antonia's dresser drawer, and that was it. She called the police. The evidence led them to Robert Prancer. They got a warrant to search his apartment and found it wall-papered with pictures of Antonia. There were some of Hank, too. Most were smeared with red paint.

A missing E.R. doctor. A missing senate candidate.

"That's when the shit really hit the fan," Carine said with a faltering smile as they finally gathered in a local tavern to ride out the storm. It was too late to make it over the bridge to Boston, or farther inland to higher ground.

"Gus was already on his way?" Antonia asked.

"He was already *there*. Ty called him. The bastard."

Hank suspected no one had told her that Ty had participated in the rescue—the media hadn't got hold of that one.

Gus shifted in his chair. He was drinking hot chocolate—no alcohol, he said, until the storm was over. No one else paid any attention. He glowered at the older of his two nieces. "You should have come to the mountains. What do you know about the ocean? We could have pitched this Prancer asshole right off a cliff."

She smiled. "I love you, Gus. And Hank and I handled him."

"Yeah. You and Hank."

Carine raised her pink drink—a cosmopolitan. "I think you and Hank make a great couple. An E.R. doctor and a U.S. senator. Has a nice ring to it, doesn't it?" She sipped some of her drink, of which she'd already had too much. "To an autumn wedding for a Winter!"

"Carine!" Antonia blanched, sinking low in her chair. She'd popped a pill—pain medication, Hank suspected—and was avoiding alcohol. "We've all had too much excitement, I think."

The wind howled and whistled outside, but the inn they'd picked had been around since the late eighteenth century. It was filled with various rescue and work crews ready to go out after the storm had passed, and they all were making no pretenses about listening in.

Carine was unapologetic. "Oh, come on, Antonia. No time to be repressed. Hank's so in love with you. What's the word I'm looking for, Gus? Besotted?"

"Sloshed," her uncle said. "Time to keep your mouth shut, Carine."

Hank, sitting next to Antonia, leaned in close to her. "Your sister's right. I am in love with you. Besotted."

"I'm feeling light-headed." Antonia sipped her water. "I think it must be the medication. I forget what I took—"

"You didn't forget," Hank said.

She smiled. "No, I didn't." She couldn't seem to stop herself from giggling, something Hank doubted Antonia Winter, M.D., did often enough. "Oh, God. I love you so much. I have from the second I laid eyes on you. You remember? You were standing in front of the woodstove in Carine's cabin."

"I remember. I knew you were stricken." He grinned at her. "I could tell."

Carine sniffled. "I love happy endings."

The two auburn-haired, blue-eyed sisters started giggling, and Gus rolled his eyes and motioned to the bartender. "No more of those pink drinks." He looked darkly over at Hank. "You set the date, you're sticking to it. You got that? I'm not mending another broken heart."

Hank nodded but said nothing. Antonia touched his thigh under the table. "We'll make it a simple wedding."

"Not account of me, you won't," Carine said, shaking her head adamantly. "Hank, if you want Tyler to be in your wedding—"

"Carine!" Antonia sat up straight, more alert now. "We wouldn't do that to you! You're going to be my maid of honor."

"Do what to me?" She set her jaw in that stubborn Winter way that Hank had come to know. "I've known Ty since we were tots. I have the scars to prove it. It's no big deal. He can be in your wedding."

"He'll be out of the country," Hank said quietly.

Carine scoffed. "What, on a secret mission?"

"Maybe."

But someone at the bar pointed to the television, and a meteorologist was saying what they could all feel—hurricane force winds were hitting Cape Cod.

Hope weakened rapidly and didn't do its worst to Cape Cod. Damage would be limited mostly to flooding, torn shingles, trees down, flying debris, lost boats. Everyone in the tavern agreed they were lucky. They'd dodged disaster.

A Coast Guard helicopter flew over Shelter Island after Hope had moved on out to sea, and the pilot reported that Babs Winslow's cottage had survived with just a few shingles torn off and a window blown out.

Antonia felt a pain in her gut, remembering that Robert Prancer had shot out the window. The damage wasn't from Hope.

Her quiet refuge was now a crime scene.

The rescue and work crews had dispersed, but she and her sister and uncle—and Hank—remained in the tavern. The bartender passed out free sandwiches and reported media swarming in the lobby.

Gus grinned. "Must be because of me."

Carine, who'd fallen asleep on their uncle's shoulder as if she were a little girl again, elbowed him in the stomach. "Gus, you're not that funny."

Antonia realized they were just trying to distract her. They'd rehashed the events on the island all through the storm, tried to make sense of Robert Prancer and his motives, his reasoning, but he clearly operated according to his own logic, reacting to events according to whatever he was feeling at the time. He'd never had a clear, specific, calculated plan, which, in a way, made him even more frightening. There was no way to predict what he'd do. Taunt her. Scare her. Hurt her. Kill her.

But she and Gus and Carine, and Nate, were a family who'd seen their share of crises, and they knew how to deal with them.

Hank tucked stray locks of her hair behind her ear. "Looks like I need to conduct an impromptu press conference."

She nodded. "They'll want to know everything."

"I plan to tell them everything. I'm a man who was worried about the woman I love, and I went to her." He kissed her on the forehead. "Do you want to be there?"

"At your side?" She smiled, kissing him softly. "Always."

CAPSIZED

Sharon Sala

For my auntie, Lorraine Stone,
who shares my love of writing, and who waves the
flag of my success as fervently as my mother does.
Thank you, Auntie, for talking my talk.

Even though there was a gentle breeze teasing the palm fronds hanging over the second floor balcony of Dominic Ortega's Mexican mansion, for DEA agent Kelly Sloan, the pseudo-Eden was in fact a true hell. At twenty-seven, she was one of the best undercover agents the Drug Enforcement Agency had, which was why she was so far away from her home state of Maryland. It was her dark hair and eyes, as well as her fluency in Spanish, that helped her blend easily into assignments such as this, as did her Masters in chemistry. As an undercover agent, she was used to dangerous situations, but something about this case was different.

Tomorrow would be the fourteenth day since Ortega had invited her into his home. Before, she'd been staying in the sleeping quarters near the lab where the other chemists worked, but since her move into the mansion, she had used every tactic she knew to keep Ortega pacified without having to sleep with him.

Only now time was running out. She had enough information to put him away for life, but she had a problem. For the past two days, she had been unable to reach her contact in Tijuana. She didn't want to think about what that meant.

But tomorrow, Dominic was going to Mexico City, and she'd talked him into taking her with him. She'd made plans to ditch him there and get back to the States. She'd already accumulated the evidence to qualify him for the death penalty. Right before she'd moved into the mansion, she'd mailed everything she had back to herself in the States. Everything would still work out. She would get back to D.C. with time to spare before testifying at Ponce Gruber's trial, then wait for Ortega to be arrested, then extradited.

Coming here had been chancy, but necessary. Three months ago, Ortega's brother-in-law, Ponce Gruber, had been arrested for arson and murder. They had enough on him to warrant the death penalty, and Gruber knew it, but he'd offered to deal. Giving up his brother-in-law would have been a death sentence of another sort, so the deal had to be something different. That was when the DEA had offered him the option of giving them enough information to get someone inside Ortega's organization. Tell them what to look for and where, then they would do the rest. Gruber had been more than willing to trade information for a life sentence. There would be no way Ortega could link the mole to him, so he would stay alive.

It had taken Kelly a month to make the first connection Gruber gave them, then another month to work her way into Dominic Ortega's immediate surroundings. Using her knowledge and skills in the manufacturing of designer drugs, and posing as a chemist named Paloma Santiago, she quickly became invaluable at the research laboratory on Ortega's estate.

After that, it was only a matter of time before Ortega noticed her. Assuming she would be impressed by his power and good looks, Ortega had invited her to stay in the mansion. She'd accepted his invitation, but with reservations. She had announced no mixing business with pleasure. Ortega had been interested enough to let her get by with it, but Kelly knew his patience was running thin.

Today, she had lingered in the house, reluctant to go to the lab. She would wonder later how her life might have been different if she had done what she was supposed to do.

Instead, she turned to face the breeze, enjoying the momentary break in the heat while holding a Tropical Suicide in one hand and a pair of sunglasses in the other. It was a bit early in the day to be drinking, but she felt a restlessness—almost a wariness—that she couldn't explain. Thinking the alcohol punch in the fruit-flavored drink might be just what she needed, she'd readily accepted it. But now an hour had passed, and except for a couple of sips, she'd barely tasted it.

"*Señorita...* do you wish another drink?"

Kelly shook her head, then smiled down at the houseboy who had called up to her from the patio below. One Tropical Suicide was dangerous. Two could make her lose her edge, and that she couldn't afford. Not when she was this close to bringing Dominic Ortega down.

She looked up, then turned her gaze to the north. Home was somewhere beyond the horizon, and she wished she was there. The Mexican side of the border could be beautiful, but she was not here on vacation.

She took a small, careful sip of her drink, wincing at the potency of the rum and tequila mix, then went back into her room to get ready to go to the lab. In doing so, she missed seeing the arrival of Dominic's latest guest.

Jose Garza was a third-rate pusher working in the stateside faction of Ortega's organization. He'd seen the woman up on the balcony as he'd driven up, but she'd turned away before he'd gotten a good look at her face. Dominic was a man who liked beautiful women, and Jose thought nothing more of her as Ortega himself came out to greet him.

"Jose! It is good to see you again!" Dominic enfolded Garza in a manly hug.

Jose smiled as he returned the affectionate greeting. It was good to be back where he belonged.

"It is good to be home," Jose said, then stepped back, eyeing Dominic's elegant white shirt and pants, as well as the diamonds he was wearing.

"Nice ice," Jose said, eyeing the two-carat stud in Dominic's left ear.

Dominic's thank you was a smile as he slid a hand across Jose's shoulder and guided him into the house. As he did, sunlight caught and fired through the ring he wore on his right hand. It was an emerald-cut diamond set in a chunk of pure silver, and yet another diamond glittered as it dangled from a silver chain around his neck.

Ortega coveted the precious gems as a greedy woman might have done, and while he was movie star handsome, his looks were not enough to hide his ruthlessness and greed. Jose Garza wished, on a daily basis, that he could be this man.

Dominic turned, calling out to a passing servant to bring them some food and drink, then led the way into a large, open room with doors flung wide onto an adjoining, flower-lined, terrace.

"Sit. Eat," he said, as a servant brought a large tray of food; then he stepped out into the foyer and called up the staircase. "Paloma…I need you."

Moments later, Kelly appeared at the head of the stairs, wearing a backless red and white ankle-length dress. Dominic smiled wolfishly at the dark-haired beauty, then waved her down. Although he had plenty of other willing women to fulfill his sexual needs, he had yet to bed this one.

As soon as Kelly stepped off the last step, she shifted mental gears. Dominic Ortega knew her as Paloma Santiago, and Paloma not only worked for Ortega, she was supposed to be attracted to him, despite her insistence on keeping her distance. She hid her revulsion as he threaded his fingers through her hair.

"I was just on my way to the lab," she said.

He fingered the front of her dress just above her breasts.

"In this dress?"

"I like to look nice for you," she said softly.

Dominic's heartbeat accelerated as he considered telling Jose to entertain himself and taking Paloma back upstairs to his bed, then he discarded the thought. Instead, he slipped a hand beneath the weight of her hair.

"Paloma, my love, there is someone I want you to meet."

Kelly nodded as he led her into the salon. It wasn't until the man on the sofa looked up that she realized today she would die. The last time she'd seen this man, he'd been on his way to prison.

"Madre di Dios!" Jose said, and jumped to his feet.

Kelly tensed, then sighed. There was nowhere to run, and even if there had been, there was no time to do it. Besides, she knew not to let them see her fear.

"Well, well," she drawled. "Jose! Long time no see."

Dominic frowned. "What is going on here? You two know each other?"

"We should," Kelly said. "I helped put him in prison."

Dominic's lips went slack. "What are you saying?"

Jose started to smile. "So…*chica*…now the shoe is on the other foot, no?"

"You still stink," Kelly said, bracing herself for the blow. The fist to her gut doubled her over.

Dominic cursed with dismay and grabbed Jose's arm.

"Talk to me now, or I swear to God I will kill you myself," he said.

"Somebody played you for a fool. She's DEA."

Dominic flinched, his eyes widening and his nostrils flaring as he stared at her in disbelief.

"No," he muttered. "I do not believe this."

Kelly pulled herself upright, then lifted her chin, unwilling to let them see her fear.

"As much as I hate to admit it," she said. "Old Joe is right."

Using the American version of his name made Jose flush with anger. He grabbed her hair and yanked, pulling her head backward and exposing the tender vulnerability of her neck.

"Let me kill her," he begged. "She cost me three years of my life. Please, Dom…give her to me."

"No," Dominic said, and slapped Jose's hand away, then curled his fingers around Kelly's neck. "Why?" Dominic asked. "Why are you here?"

"Had to use some vacation time or lose it," Kelly said.

Dominic slapped her, as if brushing a fly from his sleeve, then turned and shouted. The sound reverberated throughout the entire downstairs.

"Miguel! Come here now!"

Seconds later, a stocky Latino with a pockmarked face and a ponytail hanging halfway down his back came running into the room. It wasn't often that Dominic behaved in such a manner, but when he did, they all knew someone had made a mistake.

"*Sí, Patron,* how can I help you?"

Dominic pointed at Kelly. "You brought this woman into my organization."

Miguel started to sweat. "But no, *Patron*…you are the one who hired her to come to this lab."

Dominic pulled out his gun and shot him where he stood. At the sound, a half-dozen men came running with guns drawn.

"Get him out of here," Dominic snarled.

Fearing they might be next, they did as he asked without question.

Then Dominic turned to Kelly. "So, *puta,* you think you can take me down?"

Kelly smiled.

It wasn't the reaction Dominic expected. Suddenly realization dawned. His stupid brother-in-law. He should have killed him years ago.

"It was Ponce, wasn't it?"

"Who's Ponce?" Kelly asked.

Dominic slapped her again.

"Please, Dom...let me kill her," Jose begged.

Dominic stared at her for a moment, then nodded.

"Yes, I will let you kill her...but not until I know what information she's already told...and to who." He pointed toward the back of the house. "Go find Esteban. Tell him to get the chopper ready. It's such a fine day, I think we'll fly to the coast and take the boat out on the water. I have a hunger to see Galveston...maybe do some fishing in the beautiful waters of the bay."

Jose started to smile. Now he understood. Torture was a noisy business, and screams were easily lost in the vastness of the ocean.

Kelly stifled a shudder as she held herself erect.

"Better bring along some Dramamine. I have a tendency toward motion sickness."

Dominic smirked at her. "You should not worry about getting seasick. Before I am through with you, you will wish you were dead."

Kelly made herself smile. "Don't any of you assholes have new material? That's what all the bad guys say."

Dominic doubled up his fist and hit her on the chin. She went down without a sound.

"Now, miss smart-mouth, what do you have to say about that?"

Kelly woke up with the sun in her face again. She thought it was the second, or maybe the third, day on Ortega's boat. As she had predicted, she'd been seasick—so seasick that the beatings he had administered had been ineffectual. She'd thrown up on his pants and his shoes, and once on the front of his shirt. Ironically, it was Kelly's misery that was keeping her alive.

Now she was awake again. She lay without moving or

opening her eyes, wanting them to think she was still unconscious, even though her stomach had finally settled. It took a few moments for her to realize the boat was at anchor and the sea was relatively calm. Fear spiked. If she couldn't get sick, she would probably get dead.

God help me out of this…please!

Footsteps sounded aft. She wanted to turn around and look but was unwilling to face her devil. A seagull squawked from somewhere overhead; then she heard another, then another, as the sound of flapping wings broke the stillness of the air. As she listened, another familiar sound penetrated her consciousness, but one more distant than the birds. It was the sound of waves upon the shore. But what shore—and how far away was it? If only she knew where Ortega had anchored the boat.

"She's awake."

That was Jose Garza. Kelly recognized his voice and moaned, wishing for that familiar lurch in her stomach that would signal another outpouring of bile, but nothing stirred.

"If she pukes on me again, I will kill her where she lies."

That voice belonged to Dominic Ortega. Silently, Kelly started to pray.

Pain shattered her concentration as the toe of a boot connected with her ribs. She moaned and tried to roll over, only to find one of her wrists had been tied to the deck.

"Sit up, bitch."

Kelly opened her eyes. Dominic was leaning over her with the blade of a knife held to her throat.

"Then untie me," she mumbled.

Dominic frowned, then motioned to Jose, who quickly released her.

Kelly sat up slowly, testing her equilibrium against the gentle rocking of the boat. She looked up just in time to see Ortega's fist coming at her. She turned, trying to miss the blow, and in doing so, caused it to land at the back of her head, rather than the side of her jaw. The blow was teeth-jarring, as was the pain that shot through her head as his ring cut through her flesh.

She fell backward from the impact, then rolled onto her side. As she did, the image of her mother's face flashed through her mind. Her mother had been dead for almost nine years. Maybe this was God's way of preparing her for her own "crossing" into another life. Then Ortega's fingers fisted in her hair.

"Who is your contact?" he growled. "What have you told him?"

Kelly rolled over onto her back, her eyes blazing with anger and hate.

"You're crazier than you look if you think I'm going to tell you anything," Kelly muttered. "For once, be a man and just get this over with."

Ortega sneered. "I'll show you a man." He began to unbuckle his belt.

"If you've seen one, you've seen them all," Kelly said, then stifled a groan when Jose ran the blade of his knife along the bottoms of both her feet.

Her dismissal of his manhood fueled Ortega's hate even more. He moved closer, ready to take her there on the deck, when someone shouted from below.

It was the first time Kelly had ever felt relief on hearing someone shout "Fire!"

Dominic spun abruptly, telling Jose to guard her, and bolted toward the door leading below deck.

Jose grinned as he straddled her legs, then ran a hand down the front of his fly, as if promising Kelly that he was next.

But that didn't scare her. In fact, his presence was almost a gift, because for the moment they were alone. As if on cue, he leaned down, reaching for the bodice of her dress. He grabbed it and pulled, ripping it away. Now, except for a pair of panties, she was completely nude. His mouth went slack as his gaze slid to the lushness of her breasts.

In that moment Kelly pulled her legs up against her belly, then kicked, driving the bones of his nose into his brain with the heel of her right foot. Jose Garza was dead before he hit the deck.

Kelly rolled to her feet and grabbed the knife from his hand just as a gun-toting guard came running up the steps. She kicked again, taking satisfaction in the sound of breaking bone as his head suddenly lolled on a broken neck.

With only moments to spare, she checked the horizon, then stared in disbelief. Unless she was dreaming, what she was seeing was the skyline of Galveston.

Before she could react, she heard someone coming back up the steps. Whatever had been on fire down below had obviously been dealt with. When she saw Dominic appear, she tensed. He saw the bodies of the two men on the deck and reached for his gun. Kelly threw the knife before his gun cleared his belt. It hit with a solid, sickening thud, piercing Ortega's chest and burying itself up to the hilt. The last thing she saw before going over the side was the disbelief on his face.

The water enfolded her, wrapping her in the cold wet arms of freedom. Even if Ortega was dead, it didn't mean she was safe. There were still men on the boat, and they had the guns, not her.

Then she thought of the anchor chain and dived under the hull. If it hadn't been for the buoyancy of the water, she would never have been able to tangle the anchor chain through the blades of the propeller. Almost out of breath, and afraid of what was waiting up above, she kicked off from beneath the boat and began to swim, surfacing only after she'd put some distance between herself and her captors.

She looked back only once when she broke the surface of the water. Men were running about the deck with cell phones at their ears, while others were leaning over the side, looking for her. Just then a shout went up as someone saw her. She took a deep breath and was going back under when she heard the captain trying to start up the engine. The propellers sheared instantly, leaving them dead in the water.

It was the only break Kelly was going to get. She surfaced again a few moments later, took one last look toward the west to get her bearings and began to swim.

There wasn't enough electricity to make Texas comfortable in July. And for that reason Texas Ranger Quinn McCord had opted to use up some mandatory leave by fishing at the Galveston beach. It wasn't any cooler there, but it was wet, and the cove where he was fishing was, for the moment, unusually quiet.

He kept thinking of his partner, Frank Hardy, and how much he would have enjoyed being here. Frank liked to fish. Quinn didn't. But today Quinn was fishing for Frank, because last week Frank had been murdered. Four months from retirement, Frank Hardy had walked into a bar to meet Quinn, then died at his feet. Of course the bullet in his back had helped matters along. Quinn's reaction had been to put a third eye on the forehead of the scum-sucking backshooter and ask questions later. Thus the reason for his mandatory leave and the still-brewing anger in his gut.

He picked up a chunk of fish from the bucket near his feet and worked it onto the hook, then cast into the surf. The odor emanating from the bucket, as well as from his hands, set his teeth on edge. It was only Tuesday, with six days remaining in his week of R and R. He wasn't sure, but he might just go mad from the lassitude.

A stiff and unexpected breeze suddenly lifted the Texas Rangers baseball cap from his head and sent it rolling across the sand. He dropped the fishing rod and gave chase, retrieving it moments later. It wasn't until after he'd knocked off the sand and was turning around that he realized someone was coming out of the surf.

He settled the cap back on his head and readjusted his sunglasses as he continued to watch. He didn't know when he became aware that it was a woman, but he knew to the second when he realized she wasn't wearing any clothes. It was right before the breath in his lungs somehow sank into his belly, then did a one-eighty flop. He tried to tell himself the reaction was from lack of breakfast and not his self-imposed moratorium on sex, but it was a hard sell. Except for a pair of thin, filmy panties that had gone transparent when wet, she was as naked as the day she'd been born. And, like the flesh and blood man that he was, he stood in silent appreciation of the sight, thinking how Frank would have loved to be standing beside him right now.

He tossed around the thought of a polite retreat and then ignored it. If she wanted to skinny-dip on a public beach, then she couldn't be the bashful type, so he watched, admiring the length of bare leg emerging from the receding water, and unconsciously took a step forward.

Quinn saw her freeze as she caught the movement of his body. Swiftly, she turned to face him. It was then that he saw her panic, at the same time that he saw the blood trickling down from her hairline. The cop in him took over as he realized she hadn't gone skinny-dipping after all. He started toward her, and as he did, she took a tentative step backward.

At that point, Quinn stopped.

Uncertain how to proceed without frightening her more than she already was, he lifted his hand then called out.

"Lady…are you all right?"

She staggered on her feet, then squinted, as if trying to adjust her vision to the man before her.

"Mel? Mel Gibson?"

Quinn frowned. "No, ma'am. I'm sure no Mel Gibson."

"Could have fooled me," she said, then looked over her

shoulder and then back at him, as if debating with herself as to whether to face the devil she knew or the one she did not. Something seemed to settle her decision as she turned her back to the water and began coming toward him. Before she'd gone a yard, she began to stumble.

Quinn cursed beneath his breath and bolted toward her, catching her as she went to her knees. Her long dark hair was plastered to her shoulders in ribbons, and her skin was as cold as ice. It seemed strange, considering the heat of the day, and he feared she was going into shock. He kept reminding himself that he'd sworn to uphold the law, not break it, and wondered if there was a catch and release rule for mermaids on this beach.

"I think I need help," she mumbled, and started to shake.

It was then that he saw the scratches and cuts on her arms and belly, and a large and fading bruise on the right side of her face. Whatever had been happening to her hadn't happened all at once. It looked as if someone had been beating the hell out of her for the better part of a week.

Waves broke against Quinn's legs as he scooped her into his arms and started wading out of the surf toward shore. He headed toward his truck, her head lolling limply against his shoulder as he went. Moments later, he slid her into the passenger side of the seat and then reached across her, retrieving his cell phone from the console.

At that point the woman opened her eyes, saw the phone in his hand and grabbed his wrist with surprising force. Her teeth were chattering and her lips were blue, but her voice was surprisingly firm.

"Hey, Mel...what are you doing?"

"Calling an ambulance and then the police."

She shuddered, then took a deep breath, not knowing how far Ortega's power might reach, she opted for staying out of public. Maybe they'd think she drowned.

"If you do, they'll find me. If they find me, I'm dead."

"Who?" Quinn asked. "Who's after you?"

She pointed back toward the ocean, then slumped forward.

Quinn grabbed her again, just in time to keep her from banging her head on the dash of his truck. With a heartfelt sigh of frustration, he settled her into the seat, then took off his T-shirt and covered her nudity as best he could.

Now what? he wondered. Don't let *who* find her? Was she one of the good guys or one of the bad ones? Just because she was beautiful and naked didn't mean she was innocent. He wasn't sure what to do.

"Goddamn it," he muttered, then looked out at the horizon, wondering what—or who—she'd been looking for.

She moaned, and it was enough to drag him out of indecision. He glanced at her one last time, then went to retrieve his things. Leaving the bait bucket on the shore, he folded up his lawn chair and grabbed his gear, then loaded everything into the truck.

The woman was still lying motionless inside the cab. Her stillness was beginning to concern him even more than what she'd said. Making sure she was safely inside, he shut the door. By the time he slid beneath the wheel and started the engine, he'd made up his mind to trust her. Every instinct he had told him he was probably making a mistake by not notifying the authorities, but he kept remembering the fear in her eyes when she'd looked back at the sea.

Then he reminded himself that he was a Texas Ranger, so technically, the authorities *had* been notified. He just needed to get her warm and dry, and her wounds tended. After that, he might get the answers to his questions.

Satisfied that he'd worked out the immediate details, he began to back away from the beach toward the access road. When the tires hit firm ground, he turned the vehicle around and headed toward his motel.

He was so busy watching the woman and the traffic that

he almost didn't see the sleek cigarette boat paralleling the shore. But when he glanced up in the rearview mirror and saw sunlight catch on the windshield of the boat, his heart skipped a beat. It didn't have to mean anything. There were plenty of boaters, but this one was going slow—too slow— as if searching for something or someone. He looked again and saw a trio of men standing on the deck with binoculars, searching the coastline. When the skin on the back of his neck suddenly crawled, he laid a protective hand on her shoulder and stomped on the gas.

About five minutes into the trip to Quinn's motel, a horn honked loudly behind them. Kelly gasped, then sat up with a jerk. As she did, the T-shirt that Quinn had laid over her body fell into her lap.

"Christ almighty," she muttered, and grabbed the shirt with both hands as she looked wildly around.

The look in her eyes made Quinn withdraw as far away from her as possible.

"Easy, lady, it's only a—"

"Who the hell are you?" Kelly asked, and then clutched her head, as if the sound of her own voice caused her pain. But when she raised her arms, the T-shirt fell back into her lap.

Quinn didn't know whether to answer her question or hit the brakes and get out of the truck. Something told him that putting distance between himself and his reluctant mermaid was a really good idea. However, traffic precluded the notion, so he kept his hands on the wheel and pretended he didn't see the lush sway of her breasts as she picked up the T-shirt and pulled it over her head.

Kelly Sloan felt as if her face was going to implode. The pain between her eyebrows was wrapping around her head with increasing tension. But the pain was nothing compared to the fact that she was nearly naked and riding with a stranger. She had a vague memory of calling him Mel, then decided she'd imagined it. Desperate to put something between them besides panic, she managed to pull the T-shirt over her head. Having done that, she dropped her head between her knees for fear she would faint.

"Lady?"

The man's voice was gentle, as was the touch of his hand on her back.

"I'm all right." Then she took a deep breath. The intake of oxygen was too much. "On second thought, no I'm not," she mumbled, and slid off the seat onto the floor.

"Son of a—" Quinn didn't finish what he'd been going to say as he floored the gas and shot through the intersection. The motel was closer, or he would have headed for the hospital right then.

Only a couple of minutes later, he pulled off the highway into the motel parking lot and slammed on the brakes. Once the motor stopped, the silence in the cab was almost frightening. Quinn glanced around the area, then at his watch. It was obviously still early for tourists. From all appearances, the guests of the Sea Gull Inn were still sleeping.

He jumped out of the truck, palming his room key as he circled the cab. When he opened the passenger side door, the woman's legs slid out. He caught them—and her—before she hit the pavement. Then, lifting her into his arms, he headed for his room, thankful it was on the ground floor.

A tousle-headed man wearing nothing but a pair of gym shorts and a hangover came around the corner with a bucket of ice. He eyed Quinn, then the woman he was carrying, and lifted the ice bucket as if in a toast.

"Way to go, buddy," he said, then lurched into his room.

Quinn played along by grinning and nodding, but he kept on walking. Seconds later, he had the key in the lock. When the door swung inward, he strode through quickly, careful not to bang her head on the frame. Only after he'd kicked the door shut and laid her on the bed to check her vital signs did he begin to relax. Her pulse was strong and steady. He checked her hairline for the source of the blood flow and found a small break in the skin near the crown of her head. It didn't look serious, but he couldn't be sure.

She needed a doctor. The possibility of a concussion was too strong to ignore, although instinct told him that the worst things wrong with her were exhaustion and hypothermia. Her skin was cold as ice.

He slid his hands beneath the hem of the T-shirt and ran his fingers along her rib cage, checking for broken bones. Almost immediately, she flinched, then moaned.

"Ooh...sorry, honey," he said softly, then rocked back on his heels. He had nothing resembling first aid supplies. At the least, she needed to be examined by a physician, not a beached cop.

But he couldn't forget the urgency in her voice, begging him not to call the cops. Until he knew the reasons why, he would have to err on the side of caution. The best he could do was clean up her cuts and douse them with alcohol. Ice packs would have to do for the bruising, and a few quick prayers for the stupidity of what he was about to do would suffice for the rest, but not until he got her warmer. He cleaned up the scratches, used a washcloth for a bandage on her head, and then piled all the bedcovers in the room on top of her.

Somewhere in the back of Kelly's mind, she sensed she was safe. At least for the time being. Even though her eyes were closed, she knew she was lying on a bed. The sheets were soft against her skin, as was the pillow cradling her head. She could hear the man moving about the room and remembered the strength of his arms. Twice she tried to open her eyes, but each time the gentleness of his touch as he urged her to lie still reinforced her need to let go and just sleep. Only once did he cause her pain. When he did, she heard the tenderness and regret in his voice.

She was trying not to go under. Fearing, if she did, the memories that would come. But exhaustion and the relief of knowing she'd cheated death—and Dominic Ortega— were too great. When she felt the warmth of the covers he was pulling over her body, she gave up the fight and let go. Just for a while. Just until she was warm.

It was her last cognizant thought until she woke up in the water.

2

The woman was still shivering, despite the pile of covers Quinn had put over her. He knew he needed to get her warm, and the quickest way he knew how to do that was a hot bath. He ran the tub full of water, keeping it as hot as he dared. Hesitating only briefly, he slipped the T-shirt over her head, then carried her into the bathroom. Gently, he began lowering her into the tub, unprepared for any kind of protest. But when the water reached her knees, it obviously triggered a memory she would rather forget. She bucked in his arms, then began to thrash and moan. Before he knew it, she'd swung a fist in his direction. He ducked as she cursed and then swung again. At that point, he realized the wiser thing would have been to wake her first.

"Lady…lady…it's okay. I'm trying to help you, remember? You're freezing cold. You need to get warm."

She swung at him again and slung a long, shapely leg over the side of the tub, still trying to get out.

"Christ almighty!" Quinn said and, in disgust, just let her go.

Unprepared for the sudden freedom, Kelly slipped and then sank beneath the water before coming up sputtering, still ready to fight. Only there was no one trying to push her head beneath the water or stick a knife to her throat—just a wet and rather disgusted looking man watching her from the doorway.

"I'm sorry I've misunderstood your quest," Quinn said. "If I had realized earlier you were trying to drown, I would have left you at the damned beach."

And then Kelly remembered—everything from the knife sinking into Ortega's chest to the stranger on the shore. He'd probably saved her life.

"I'm sorry," she spluttered, wiping hair and water from her face. "I thought you were...I mean...I didn't know where I was."

Quinn's frustration faded. "You were trying to get away from someone, weren't you? Who is it? Who are you afraid of?"

Kelly grabbed a washcloth from the edge of the tub and held it over her breasts.

"Do you think we could continue this conversation after I've finished my bath?"

Quinn eyed the minuscule bit of terry cloth she was using as a shield. He wanted to tell her he'd already seen all there was to see and then some, but he figured it wasn't the prudent thing to do.

"Yeah, sure," he said. "I'll lay some dry clothes on the bed for you to put on. Yell at me when you're ready to come out and I'll close my eyes."

With that, he turned around, closing the door behind him as he left. Kelly didn't know whether to be relieved or more nervous than ever.

Close his eyes?

That was rich. It was clear that he'd already seen everything. However, she appreciated the fact that he had failed to mention it. She sat without moving, staring at the door, ready at any time to bolt if the need arose. But the doorknob didn't turn, and except for the sound of a television being turned on in the next room, she might have thought she was alone. Satisfied that he meant her no harm, she slowly sank into the warm, steamy depths and closed her eyes.

* * *

More than thirty minutes passed before Quinn heard water running out of the tub. He tried not to think of what was going on behind the door and concentrated on the television program instead. It was a rerun of *Walker, Texas Ranger,* and he frowned as he watched, doubting that Chuck Norris ever had this much trouble helping a damsel in distress. Before he knew it, the door was open. He glanced up, swallowing past the knot in his throat, and pointed toward the T-shirt and boxer shorts on the back of a chair.

"Dry clothes," he muttered. "Doubt they'll fit as good as what you're wearing, but they're clean."

Kelly's eyes narrowed. He had just alluded to the fact that, except for a rather skimpy towel, she was still naked. But beggars couldn't be choosers, so she grabbed the clothing and slipped back into the bathroom. Minutes later, she was back, this time girded for battle.

But when she came out, the television was off, and the man was sitting on the side of the bed with his elbows resting on his knees, staring at the toes of his tennis shoes. When she opened the door, he looked up.

"My name is Quinn McCord."

Kelly flinched. He certainly wasn't a man to waste words.

"I'm…uh…Kelly Sloan."

"Are you sure?"

"What do you mean?" she asked.

He stood, and as he did, Kelly took a protective step back.

"Well, you didn't sound so sure. Is that a made-up name, or are you just forgetful?"

She frowned; then, remembering what she'd endured the past few days, she lifted her chin and pushed past him.

"It's mine," she said, and sat down on the side of the bed, then reached for the phone. She started to dial a number, then remembered she didn't know how much she could trust this stranger who called himself Quinn McCord. "I need to make a phone call. Do you mind?"

Her high-handed attitude rubbed him the wrong way. Instead of exiting the room, as she expected him to do, he took the phone out of her hand, replaced it on the cradle, then stood in her space.

"Actually, yes, I do mind," he said. "This is my room, which makes this my business. This goes no further until you tell me what the hell is going on."

"Look," Kelly said. "My name *is* Kelly Sloan. I'm a cop. Actually, DEA, okay? And the call I need to make is private."

A cop? All Quinn could think was halla-freakin'-lujah. He started to grin. "I don't suppose you have any ID to back that up?"

She glared. "Did you *see* any ID when you carried me out of the bay?"

His grin widened. "I guess I saw everything *but* ID."

Kelly's glare intensified. "You're certainly no gentleman."

"You're right about that," Quinn said, then sat down beside her. "So you're DEA?"

She nodded. "Yes. Now back off, smart-ass. I don't have time to play your little games."

Quinn's grin disappeared as he got up and walked to the table and opened his duffel bag. A few seconds later, he turned around and tossed something onto the bed beside her.

Kelly stared at the silver star in disbelief.

"You're a Ranger?"

"Yes, ma'am, that I am."

"What are you doing in Galveston?"

"I *was* fishing. Caught a mermaid instead."

She fingered the badge. "Is this for real?"

"At least you can see mine. I'm taking your story on faith."

Her shoulders slumped with relief; then she winced as the motion caused her some pain.

"You need to see a doctor," Quinn said.

"Can't take the chance," Kelly said. "They've got to think I'm dead."

"Who's they?"

"Ever hear of Dominic Ortega?"

Quinn's eyes widened. "That's who you're running from?"

"Not him specifically...at least, not anymore. Before I got off the boat, I left a ten-inch knife in the middle of his chest."

Quinn stared at her, judging the wounds that she had against the strength of mind it must have taken to get away from someone that powerful and that bad.

"What happened?"

"My cover was blown. He spent a few days trying to find out what I knew and who I'd told it to."

Without thinking, Quinn touched the bruise on her face, then the cuts on her legs.

"How did you manage to stay alive?"

Kelly shrugged. "For the first three days, I kept throwing up on him. It was only today, when the seas calmed, that I knew he was through playing around. Never thought I'd be happy to say I suffer from motion sickness, but it's for certain that I won't complain about it again."

Quinn laughed, and the sound curled Kelly's toes.

"They need to think I drowned," Kelly said. "But I also need to contact my boss at the DEA. He's helping coordinate a federal case against Ortega's brother-in-law, Ponce Gruber. The Feds made a deal with Gruber in exchange for the information it took to get me inside Ortega's organization. Only I think Gruber double-crossed both of us, and it almost cost me my life."

"How so?"

"A man showed up at Ortega's place down in Mexico.

I arrested him three years ago and watched him go to prison. I knew he and Gruber were in the same prison, but what I didn't know was that Garza was going to get early release. I'm guessing Gruber told him to reconnect with Ortega and hope that he would recognize whoever the DEA had sent undercover. That way Gruber was off the hook both ways. He'd made his deal with the Feds. It wouldn't be his fault if it didn't work out. And he'd pointed Jose Garza in my direction, knowing if the undercover agent was someone Garza knew, then Ortega would have him or her killed. Either way, Gruber was going to be a winner. And if I don't show up to tell them what he did, then Gruber misses the death penalty he deserves.''

"What about Ortega? Are you sure he's dead?"

Kelly sighed. "No. Only that I hurt him bad. If he *is* alive, I have enough evidence linking the two to put both of them beneath six feet of Mother Earth. And if Ortega *is* alive and he finds out that I didn't drown, he will do everything in his power to make sure I don't get to Washington, D.C., alive.''

"What are you going to do?"

"May I use your phone?"

Quinn sighed. "Be my guest.''

Kelly picked up the receiver and made the call. Her fingers were shaking as she punched in the numbers. She hated being weak. Then Quinn McCord moved into her line of vision as he sat down in the chair across from the bed. He'd seen her weak *and naked*. How much worse could this get?

"Michael Forest speaking.''

The male voice in her ear made her jump. She'd been so busy thinking about the Ranger that she'd almost forgotten she'd made the call.

"Captain Forest, it's Kelly.''

There was a soft gasp on the other end of the line; then Kelly heard the delight in her boss's voice.

"Kelly! Thank God! We had intelligence leading us to believe you were dead."

Kelly sighed. "You weren't so far off the truth."

"Are you all right? Where are you?"

"I'm fine. As for where I am, let's just say I'm no longer in deep water. I called to let you know that I'll be in D.C. on July 15 as planned."

"Fantastic. What about Ortega?"

"I might have killed him."

There was a moment of silence; then Michael Forest spoke, but this time the elation was gone from his voice.

"What did he do to you?"

"I'm in one piece. Leave it at that."

Reluctance was heavy in his voice. "Okay, but—"

"There's something else you need to know," Kelly said. "I think Gruber double-crossed us."

"What do you mean?"

"Was he incarcerated in the same prison as a man named Jose Garza?"

"I don't know. I can find out. Why?"

"I helped put a man named Jose Garza in prison about three years ago. He had a five-year sentence, but apparently they turned him out after three. He was one of Ortega's men. The first place he went when he got out was back to the fold, so to speak."

"Son of a—"

"Yeah, that was pretty much my reaction," Kelly said.

"How did you find out?"

"Garza showed up at Ortega's, recognized me, of course, and that was pretty much it."

"Damn. I'm sorry, Kelly. We didn't know."

"Just make sure that Gruber knows his deal is screwed. I want him to think about how many ways there are to die while he's waiting for his trial."

Forest sighed. "If I tell him that, then he's going to know

that you're alive…and that you're going to testify against him.''

"I know."

"I'm not going to do it, so get over the notion. Please, Kelly. Let me send some men to bring you in. We'll put you in a safe house until the trial."

Kelly looked up, eyeing the long-legged Texan with the stubborn jut to his chin, and stifled a smile.

"I'm in a safe house already. Just look for me at the trial."

She hung up as Michael Forest continued to argue.

Quinn leaned forward without taking his gaze from her face.

Kelly stared back, judging the man without finding him wanting.

Quinn was silently pleased that Kelly considered herself safe with him. He didn't stop to think about why that mattered, only that it satisfied something inside him to know there was, at the least, trust between them now.

"Your head is still bleeding," Quinn said.

Kelly lifted a hand to her forehead, frowning as her fingers came away sticky with blood.

"You also need your cuts tended, but all I have is some antibiotic cream and a bottle of alcohol."

Kelly hesitated. If she was going to trust him, then that meant all the way.

"So do what you can," she said, and pulled the T-shirt over her head, then held it in front of her like a shield.

Quinn tried to hide his surprise, but without success. The knot in his belly tightened. Didn't she have any idea what the sight of a beautiful, naked woman did to a man?

She sat, watching him without moving.

He sighed. Obviously not.

"I'll just get the stuff," he muttered.

"I'm not going anywhere."

Yeah, well...lucky for you, lady. Personally, I'm going out of my mind.

Wisely, Quinn kept his thoughts to himself as he began to clean her wounds.

"Are you in Galveston on a case?"

Quinn frowned and thrust a dry washcloth into her hands. "Sit still," he said. "You'll make me get alcohol in your eyes."

She held the washcloth near her hairline, trying not to squeal as he poured the antiseptic liquid onto the cut in her scalp. Damn, but it burned.

"Well...are you?" she persisted.

"I told you, I was fishing," Quinn said.

She waited, sensing there was more.

Quinn surprised himself by telling her the rest, from the moment of his partner's death to his boss telling him to take a vacation or he would fire his ass.

She sighed. That was the hell of working with someone day in and day out for years.

"Survivor's guilt," she said.

Quinn paused in the act of dabbing antibiotic ointment on some cuts on her back.

"What?"

"You're alive and he's not. Survivor's guilt."

"I don't feel guilty," Quinn snapped.

"You said you'd called him to meet you at the bar, right?"

The hair on the back of Quinn's arms suddenly crawled. He put the cap back on the ointment, then sat down on the side of the bed—too stunned to speak.

Kelly laid a hand on Quinn's knee.

"If you hadn't called him, he wouldn't have been shot, right?"

Quinn started to shake. He couldn't look at her. Wouldn't look at her. Damn the woman. How had she known something this personal...something he had yet to face?

"It's what you think. It's what you believe, isn't it, Quinn?"

He looked down at the floor. There was a thin spot in the carpet near the foot of the bed. It reminded him of the bald spot on the back of Frank's head. Frank had been using some of that hair regeneration stuff, trying to grow it back.

"You don't know what you're talking about," he muttered.

Kelly sighed. "Yes, I do. May I remind you that you're not the only cop who's ever lost a partner?"

He looked up at her then, unaware there were tears in his eyes.

"You too?"

"My fifth year on the job. I still dream about it sometimes. It doesn't go away, but I know now it wasn't my fault. It's part of the job, McCord. Your partner knew it, and you know it, too." Then she stood, a little shaky, but determined. "I don't suppose you've got anything in this place to eat? I haven't eaten in almost three days."

Quinn's eyes widened. "Holy hell, woman. Why didn't you say so sooner?"

She almost smiled. "I guess I was too busy defending my naked self from your lecherous gaze."

Indignation shifted within Quinn, driving the grief into a darker part of his mind.

"I did not lech at you."

"Then turn around while I put this back on," Kelly said. As soon as he turned around, she pulled the T-shirt back over her head.

His anger felt good. At least now his focus was on her and not the brutality of his partner's passing.

"So, is there anything to eat or not?" she asked.

Quinn turned, and as he did, the anger he was feeling suddenly faded. She'd done that on purpose. Without thinking, he reached out and cupped the side of her face.

"Thank you," he said softly.

Kelly allowed herself the luxury of his hand against her face long enough to nod; then she moved away. There was no sense in going all gooey on a man like McCord.

"You're welcome. Now, about that food?"

"I've got a friend in town. His name is Daryl Connelly. He's a retired Texas Ranger and I'd trust him with my life. If you'll let me give him a call, we can have food within the hour."

Kelly's stomach growled as her knees went weak. She sank back onto the bed, too shaky to stand.

"Make the call," she said. "And tell him to hurry."

Dominic Ortega was alive.

It had taken less than thirty minutes for his men to get another boat, then get him to a waiting chopper. They'd transported him to a private clinic run by a man who'd done business with them before.

The doctor had removed the knife from his chest in the operating room, repaired the damage, then dosed Ortega with enough painkillers to drop a horse to its knees. Ortega was breathing on his own and feeling no pain. The men standing guard outside his room made no attempt to hide their weapons. It was to the doctor's advantage that Ortega did not die in his facility.

And so the wait began. Just before midnight, a nurse noticed movement beneath his eyelids and called for the doctor, who came on the run. Moments later, Dominic Ortega came to, muttering the same name over and over again.

"Kelly... Kelly Sloan... Kelly Sloan."

The doctor looked to one of Ortega's men for an explanation.

"Is she family? Is she someone we should call?" he asked.

Ortega inhaled. "No. She is someone we should kill."
Then he moaned as pain shattered his concentration.

Daryl Connelly watched the leggy brunette tip the cup
of soup sideways, trying to spoon out the last bit of liquid,
then grinned when she gave up in disgust and drank it
instead.

"Quinn didn't tell me how much you enjoyed your food
or I would have brought more."

Kelly eyed the pile of empty throwaway containers from
the Hungry Wok as she seriously considered his offer, then
shook her head.

"Better not," she said. "I don't want to overdo."

"Uh...yeah...right," Daryl said, and looked to Quinn
for reassurance that he'd done the right thing.

Quinn grinned at the rangy, gray-haired ex-Ranger. It
was time to explain.

"She hasn't eaten for three days," he said.

Daryl frowned. "You hadn't oughta go on any diet,
missy. You look just fine the way you are."

"Thanks," Kelly said, as she cracked open a fortune
cookie. "Hmm...says here I'll meet the man of my
dreams." She waved the tiny slip of paper in the air and
grinned at Daryl. "I always did favor an older man."

Daryl turned red.

Quinn laughed.

Kelly ate the fortune cookie in one bite.

"She's not dieting, Daryl. She's DEA. Let's just say that
a case she was working went sour, okay?"

Daryl eyed her with new respect. "Is that true?"

Kelly frowned. The fewer people who knew the truth
about her, the better she would feel.

"Yes, but keep it to yourself, okay? I would really like
them to think I drowned."

This time it was Quinn who caught the brunt of
Daryl's gaze.

"You gonna get mixed up in this, too?" he asked.

Quinn shrugged. "I already am."

"No, you're not," Kelly said. "And trust me when I say neither one of you wants to be a part of this."

Quinn's expression hardened. "I'm gonna excuse you for the insult on the grounds that you don't know me, but I'm telling you now—and for the last time—you're wrong. I am a part of this already. I became part of it when I pulled you out of the water, then took you away from the scene before the guys in that boat had a chance to see you."

Kelly flinched as if she'd just been struck.

"What guys? What boat?"

Quinn silently cursed his big mouth. He hadn't intended to mention that, simply because it was probably nothing; then he reminded himself that it was her life that was at stake. She had a right to know all the facts.

"When I was driving away from the beach, I saw one of those speed boats…the kind they call cigarette boats. It was cruising pretty close to the shore."

"Was it going fast or slow?" she asked.

"Slow."

"Damn it."

"Do you think it was some of Ortega's men?" Quinn asked.

"You talking about Dominic Ortega?" Daryl asked.

Kelly sighed. "Just forget I said that, will you?"

Daryl frowned. "I'm thinkin' you two need a keeper. He's bad business."

"He's *my* business," Kelly said. "Both of you back off." Then she added, "But thank you for the food."

Daryl eyed her cautiously, then looked at Quinn. "I don't think you should have fed her. She's turning real mean."

"She's going to get even meaner if we don't get her some stuff to wear," Quinn said.

Daryl looked nervous. "What do you mean *we?* I don't know how to shop for no girl."

Kelly turned on Quinn. "Damn it, McCord. You need to quit running my life. I can shop for myself."

"See…she wants to shop for herself," Daryl said.

"And what if one of Ortega's men sees you? What if they're already in Galveston asking around? What then, Ms. DEA? If you get yourself killed, you're going to screw up your friend's trial big time."

Kelly frowned. Damn the man for being right.

"Okay, fine. Just find a Wal-Mart and do your best, Daryl. I'll write down my sizes. At least everything I need will be under one roof."

"What do you mean…everything?" Daryl asked.

"I'll make the list. If you can't find some of the stuff, ask an employee. They'll help you find it."

Daryl blanched. "Just don't tell me it's your time of the month, cause I swear to God, friend or no friend, I'm not buyin' anything that comes under the heading of feminine hygiene."

Kelly grinned, then surprised both men by giving Daryl a quick hug.

"Daryl, my man, this is your lucky day. I am in no need of anything quite so personal."

"Thank the Lord," Daryl muttered, then glared at Quinn. "Why don't you go buy the stuff and I'll stay here with her?"

"Because…if anyone did see my truck and put two and two together, they'll be looking for me. And if they see me, then follow me back to Kelly, we're both dead. Right?"

Daryl's shoulders slumped. "Right. I'll just sit right here and wait for the list."

He flopped down on the side of the bed as Kelly began writing. A few moments later, she handed him the piece of paper.

"I really appreciate this, and I'll pay you back as soon as I can get my hands on some money."

Daryl stood, read the list slowly to himself, then shook his head.

"No need paying me back. I'm happy to help you, honey. Really I am. I'll be back in a while with your things."

"Take your time, Daryl. We've got some plans of our own to make," Quinn said.

Kelly refrained from arguing until the old man was gone. Then she turned on Quinn.

"You have no jurisdiction in this," she said.

"I'm not going with you as a cop."

She frowned. "You just lost your partner, remember? You're supposed to be getting some R and R."

"I'm not likely to forget Frank is dead," Quinn said. "As for R and R, I don't believe in it. All it is, is more time to dwell on things you can't change. I'd rather be doing something productive, like keeping your hard little head in one piece. Okay?"

Kelly hesitated. She hated to admit it, but having someone at her back was becoming more of a necessity than she would have preferred.

"Okay. But I'm still the one in charge."

"Honey, I've never met a woman who wasn't."

She glared. "If we're going to do this without coming to blows, you're going to have to stop calling me, honey."

Quinn's eyebrows rose. "Really?"

"Really."

"Well, all right, then, but I didn't think we'd known each other quite long enough for *darlin'*. However, I'm man enough to admit I was wrong."

"Damn it, McCord. I'm serious."

Quinn flipped a loose strand of hair away from her face and then winked.

"I know, darlin'. So am I."

3

After giving up the only bed in the room to Kelly, Quinn was sleeping on the floor. Or, it would be fairer to say, he was lying on the floor. He had yet to fall asleep. Every time he closed his eyes, he kept seeing that boat in his rearview mirror and the trio of men with binoculars standing at the rail. They had probably gotten the tag number and make of his truck, but it still didn't link her to him. They could have been tourists. Galveston was a place for tourists, and tourists came seaward as well as landward, but his first impression had been that they were searching for something—or someone. And given Kelly's story, it was most likely her.

It had also occurred to him that if Ortega was dead, his men would most likely have headed back to Mexico to regroup. A new leader would have to be named within the organization, and new plans would have to be made. But if they were searching for her, someone had given the order to do so, which could mean that Ortega wasn't dead. Muscle didn't make decisions or seek retribution. The men behind the brawn took orders and meted them out. It took brains and organization for that to happen, which meant someone was still in charge.

The fact that they'd seen his truck made him nervous. But he was almost positive they hadn't seen her with him, which was the only way they could link him to the missing DEA agent. He wanted to believe he'd been seen as nothing but a fisherman, but, in law enforcement, assuming could get you killed.

But Quinn was a careful man, so he lay near the door, listening to the comings and goings of vehicles out in the parking lot and making sure that the footsteps he heard on the walkway outside the door did not linger too long in his vicinity.

Kelly went to sleep, unaware of Quinn's concerns. Knowing he was an officer of the law might have given her a false sense of security, but for tonight she didn't care. Tomorrow she would begin to make plans to get to D.C. Tonight, she was willing to let Quinn McCord be her eyes and ears to the world.

It was just after midnight when Quinn heard her moan. He remembered closing his eyes just to give them a rest, but he must have drifted off to sleep. The terror in her voice was enough to bring him to a rude awakening. He came to in a heartbeat, with his pistol in his hand, only to realize that they were still alone and she was having a bad dream.

With his heart still thumping from the adrenaline rush, he laid the gun on the floor and hurried to the bed where she was sleeping. She was moaning and shaking, muttering words he couldn't understand. He thought of her head wound. Although it hadn't seemed all that serious, he worried that she had suffered a concussion after all. Regretting his decision not to take her to a doctor, he gently laid the back of his hand against her cheek to test for fever, then smoothed back the hair from her face. Instead of comfort, his touch set off her panic.

She moaned. "Not the knife… God, please…not the knife." Then she began pushing at his hands.

Quinn cursed beneath his breath. Sorry that he'd frightened her, he had no option now but to awaken her and let her know she was safe. He cupped her shoulders and gave her a slight shake.

"Kelly... Kelly...wake up. You're okay. You're safe. You're just having a bad dream."

She gasped long and loud, as if surfacing from watery depths for a life-giving gulp of air, then sat up in bed.

"Where...?"

"It's me. Quinn. You're safe, remember?"

Kelly stared, as if memorizing every facet of his features, then covered her face.

"Crap," she said.

He chuckled as he slipped a finger beneath a stray lock of hair and lifted it from her eyes.

"Know something, Sloan?"

Kelly looked up, defiance back in her voice. "I know a lot of somethings."

His smile widened. "You are my kind of woman."

"What kind of woman is that?"

"A woman of few words."

Kelly resisted the urge to snort. "You are so full of it," she muttered, then swung her legs off the bed as she stood.

Quinn got a better than average look at her shapely little butt before she strode past him and into the bathroom, shutting the door firmly between them. He would have asked her to explain herself, but he was pretty sure he wouldn't like her answer. A few seconds later he heard the shower come on and then the hard spray of water hitting the back of the stall.

He frowned. She'd already had two baths. He was at the point of thinking she had some kind of cleanliness phobia. He sat for a few moments, wondering how long this would take. Then the softness of the mattress enticed him. He would lie down only until she came back. After that, it would be back to the floor.

He didn't know it, but it had been the dream that had sent Kelly back to the shower. Just the memory of Jose Garza's leer and Dominic Ortega's hands on her body had been enough to make her want to puke—never mind what they'd done to her in the name of revenge. As she stood beneath the spray, letting the water cool her heated flesh, she wondered if she would ever feel clean again.

A short while later she emerged to find the Ranger sprawled across two-thirds of the bed.

"Great," she muttered, then winced as the motion of her body sent pain rocketing through her bones.

Obviously sleeping on the floor was impossible. Not until whatever Ortega had broken in her could heal. She walked to the side of the bed, staring down in the darkness. Quinn McCord was good-looking, if you liked the dark-haired, dark-eyed, smart-ass type, which she told herself she did not. And he *was* trim and leggy, with strong bones and well-defined muscles. Then she rolled her eyes and resisted the urge to snort.

Lord. I sound as if I'm describing a good horse.

Determined to get some rest, she pulled the covers back on what was left of the bed and gave him a slight shove.

"Move over, Lone Ranger. You're taking your half out of the middle, and I don't like to share."

"Hmm?"

"Scoot," she said softly, and gave him an easy push.

He rolled without waking, taking her pillow with him.

"Well, crap all over again," Kelly said, then picked up his pillow from the floor, carried it back to the bed and crawled in.

Moments later, they were both sound asleep.

Just before daylight, Kelly started to cry in her sleep. She didn't know it and would have kicked herself all over the room before doing it in front of her bed partner. But Quinn heard it, and the sound shattered what was left of his rest.

He rolled over to find himself face-to-face with a very bruised angel, saw the tears on her face and took her in his arms.

"It's just me," he kept whispering, as he wrapped his arms around her and held her close against his chest. "Rest easy, honey. They won't hurt you again."

This time his voice soothed, rather than panicked, and his touch gave her comfort, not fear. Instead of waking completely, she began to relax. Moments later the nightmare had shifted to a dark, unplayed corner of her mind. And so she slept with her ear against his chest, lulled by the steady, unrelenting beat of his heart.

Kelly dug through the sack of clothes that Daryl had brought for her yesterday. She'd gone through the toilet articles last night in getting ready for bed, but she'd ignored the clothes. Now she was faced with a wardrobe that looked more fitted to a waitress at Hooters instead of a Federal Agent.

There were two pair of shorts, two pair of jeans, five T-shirts, some underwear, a pair of red cowboy boots and a nightgown that was so sheer it was a joke.

Quinn fingered the nightgown, eyeing the red lace on the black nylon, and then sighed.

"Sorry about this," he said. "Daryl's never been married. I guess we should have been more specific."

Kelly picked up a pair of panties with two fingers, as if touching them might contaminate her.

"How the hell does one put these on?" she muttered.

Quinn eyed the minithong warily, fearing she might use it to throttle him in the next breath.

"Real carefully?"

She looked at him and then tossed them aside. "At least we know what kind of woman appeals to him. I think I need to talk to your buddy. What's his number?"

Quinn sighed. Poor Daryl. He was going to catch hell for this—he just knew it.

He dialed, then handed her the receiver. The old man answered on the first ring.

"Hello."

"Mr. Connelly, this is Kelly. I wanted to thank you for the clothes."

Daryl shoved his plate of bacon and eggs to one side and patted the part in what was left of his hair.

"Well, now, missy…it was my pleasure."

"Yes. I'll bet it was," Kelly drawled. "However, we have a slight problem."

"Uh… I'm real sorry about that. Wrong size?"

"No. Wrong style."

"Huh?"

"Let's put it like this, Daryl. Did anyone ever give you a wedgie?"

She heard him choke, then cough, and figured he'd gotten the point.

"Well now, I don't know as—"

"It's the underwear, Daryl. I'm sorry to be so blunt, but I can't wear underwear that goes up the crack in my ass. Do you think we can rectify that?"

There was a moment of silence, then a swift intake of breath before Daryl answered.

"I was an officer of the law for thirty-one years. I can rectify anything. You talkin' granny panties or what?"

Kelly rolled her eyes. "Just somewhere in between."

"Yeah, I got the picture. Give me thirty minutes."

"Gladly, and thank you," she added, then hung up the phone.

Quinn had made himself scarce, but she could hear him laughing through the bathroom door. She slapped her hand on the flat of the door to get his attention.

"Hey, in there, it's not funny."

"Hell yes, it's funny," Quinn said, then turned on the shower, drowning out her answer before she had a chance to reply.

She stared at the odd assortment of clothing and told herself it shouldn't matter what she wore. She was alive, which was more than she had expected this time yesterday morning. And as soon as she had some underwear that didn't disappear in her nether regions, she would brave the rest of the lot.

She spread the T-shirts out on the bed, trying to decide between the slogans, then opted for the pink one with a smoking gun and the letters PMS in purple below it. She held it up to herself in the mirror and then sighed. Between the scratches and bruises on her face and the mess her hair was in, the message on the shirt should be the least of her worries. God, how had her life gotten in such a mess?

She tossed the shirt aside while she waited for Daryl to arrive, then sat down on the side of the bed, contemplating her options. She was twenty-seven years old. She'd been with the DEA for the past five years, three of which had been in undercover, and this was the first time she'd come so close to dying. She was mad at the situation she'd gotten herself into and worried about getting to D.C. to testify. If only she knew for certain that Ortega was dead.

A faucet squeaked.

She turned toward the bathroom door. Quinn had turned off the shower. Within minutes, he would be back in her space, needling her with those chocolate-dark eyes and that smirk of a grin. He made her uncomfortable in a way no man had done before. It wasn't as if he was any kind of a physical threat. And she was assuming that, since he was an officer of the law, he could be trusted not to betray her in any way. But she couldn't relax around him.

Then the door opened, and he came out wearing nothing but a towel.

"Forgot my clean shorts," he said, then opened the dresser and pulled out a pair of white cotton briefs.

It was fortunate that a response was unnecessary, because for the life of her, Kelly would have been unable to make one. Dressed, he'd been interesting, even attractive, but she'd already acknowledged that to herself. However, butt naked, he was downright devastating. One thing that had been bothering her was suddenly clear. Now she knew why Quinn McCord made her nervous. He was boyfriend material, even serious relationship material—never mind possible husband material. Kelly didn't have time for any of the above—hadn't even considered the latter since her last serious relationship, which had been over for almost three years.

"Go put some clothes on," she snapped.

He eyed her long bare legs and the feminine curves of her body beneath his T-shirt and frowned.

"The same could be said for you."

Before she could get past the hiss in her throat, he yanked the towel from around his hips and tossed it in her lap as he disappeared into the bathroom.

Kelly closed her eyes, but it was way too late. She'd seen all there was to see of Quinn McCord and then some. She wadded up the towel and threw it at the door, where it fell to the floor with a soggy thump.

"Put on some clothes, indeed," she muttered, as she grabbed a pair of shorts and yanked them over her own panties, ignoring the rips and the shredded elastic. "I'm not the one parading around naked by choice," she yelled.

He punctuated her statement by flushing the toilet, which only ticked her off more.

She picked up the pink PMS T-shirt and yanked it over her head, only afterward realizing she'd forgotten to put on a bra. "To hell with it and with all men in general," she muttered, as she crammed everything back into the sack but a pair of white socks.

Eyeing the red cowboy boots with disgust, she pulled on the socks, then the boots, stomping her feet as she stood in order to jam her feet the rest of the way inside. Then she strode to the full-length mirror on the back of the closet door and rolled her eyes.

There was a two-inch gap of skin between the tail of her

T-shirt and the waistband of the shorts. With the long length of legs between the shorts hem and the top of the boots, she looked like a bad version of the token female on that old television show *The Dukes of Hazard.*

"Eat your heart out, Daisy Duke," Kelly muttered, then sat down in the only chair to await Daryl Connelly's return.

Quinn was still smarting from sexual frustration when he came out of the bathroom. And what he saw didn't help matters any. She was a teenage boy's vision of heaven on earth, and he felt himself regressing. The only way he knew to make sure he stayed safe was to keep her ticked off.

"Nice outfit," he said.

"Go to hell," Kelly countered.

The knock on the door saved both of them from making a miserable situation worse.

Kelly flinched, then stood, her posture betraying her nervousness.

"It's probably Daryl," Quinn said.

"I wish I had my gun."

"You'd shoot a man over a tight pair of panties?"

Kelly glared. "Shut up. Just shut the hell up and see who's at the door. And if it's not your friend Daryl, you'd be wise to duck. Ortega's men don't give second chances."

The teasing in his voice ended. "I'm sorry," he said softly. "Just trying to make a bad situation a little better."

Kelly sighed. There was no reason to take her clothing limitations and sexual frustrations out on someone who had saved her life—and who was still trying to help her.

"I'm sorry, too," she said. "I don't know what's come over me. I guess we could chalk it up to a big case of nerves."

"Or PMS?" Quinn pointedly eyed her shirt as he turned toward the door. "Who's there?"

"It's me, Daryl."

Kelly was struggling with the urge to just shove Quinn out the door when Daryl came striding into the room. He was carrying the sack of underwear as if it contained something foul. When he saw Quinn, he shoved it in his hands, then stared pointedly at Kelly.

"Missy, these here better fit, cause I ain't gonna go back into the store for a third round of shoppin'. Those lady salesclerks are startin' to look at me funny."

Kelly took the sack from Quinn, then kissed the old man on the cheek.

"Thank you, Daryl, more than I can say. I promise I'll repay you."

"Oh hell, honey. It's not about the money. I'm just not in the habit of buying this kind of stuff," Daryl said, as he blushed. Then he realized what she was wearing and started to grin. "I knew you'd fit into that stuff just fine."

Kelly resisted the urge to roll her eyes. "Yes… well…thank you again for being so thoughtful."

"You're welcome," he said.

"Uh…I'll just be a minute," Kelly said, and headed for the bathroom to put on the clean underwear. She was in the act of closing the door when she stopped and turned around. "Hey, Daryl?"

"Yeah?"

"I'm guessing that you're a big *Dukes of Hazard* fan. Am I right?"

His eyes widened. "Why…yes, I am. How did you know?"

Kelly wouldn't look at Quinn. She couldn't. Not and maintain her composure.

"Oh…I don't know. Women's intuition, I guess."

She could hear Daryl talking as she closed the door behind her. He was saying something to the effect of she might be a little bit psychic and for Quinn to watch out. She didn't hear Quinn's answer, which was just as well.

* * *

Ortega hurt, and he wasn't used to feeling pain, only administering it. Even though he was being given enough morphine to fell an ox, he continued to demand more. In doing so, he also managed to alienate most of the staff. God knew he would rather have been drugged out of his mind than have to deal with this misery. But revenge was a strong taskmaster, and he wanted Kelly Sloan to die—at his hands.

"So...Mr. Ortega...how are we feeling today?"

Dominic glared at the doctor who'd just entered his room. His name was Fry. In Ortega's opinion, it was not a name that demanded respect.

"*We* don't feel anything," he snarled. "However, I hurt like hell."

The nurse handed Ortega's chart to Dr. Fry.

"We'll see what we can do about that," Fry said, and wrote some new orders on the chart.

As soon as the nurse left the room, Ortega grabbed the doctor's arm.

"When can I be moved?"

Fry frowned, then removed Ortega's hand from his wrist. "I'm not sure. Why?"

"I am not safe here."

Dr. Fry smiled. "Of course you are. You were admitted under the name of Howard Jones. No one knows who you are."

"You know it," Ortega said.

Sam Fry took a step back while fixing Ortega with an angry stare.

"That sounded like a threat. I am assuming that when you leave you're aren't planning on 'eliminating' the man who saved your life. Because if you are, I can promise that doing that will raise far more questions than you would want to answer. I cross all kinds of legal lines when I treat men like you. But I'm not stupid. I have my own set of notes. Call them insurance, if you will. Should I die unexpectedly, the contents of my safety deposit box will be of great interest to the authorities.''

Ortega shifted restlessly in the bed, suddenly realizing it wasn't smart to threaten the man responsible for his welfare.

"I am not a monster. I did not mean that the way it sounded," Ortega said. "Of course you are in no danger."

Fry arched an eyebrow and then nodded.

"That's good to know…. However, just so we understand each other, this only works if both sides keep their word."

"Yes, certainly," Ortega muttered.

"The nurse should be here shortly with your injection. I've increased the dosage a bit, but not much. Truthfully, you need to start weaning yourself from the painkillers, not demanding more."

"You never did tell me when I could leave," Ortega asked.

Dr. Fry patted him on the leg. "We'll know more tomorrow, okay?"

Ortega wanted to slit his throat. Instead he smiled and nodded. "Yes. Okay." But as soon as the doctor left, Ortega picked up the phone and made a call. There was only one way to find out for sure if Kelly Sloan was alive. He would put a bounty on her head that would bring her out of hiding and force her to run.

Quinn and Kelly were circling each other like snarling dogs. A day and a half of being shut up together with nothing but the television and a worn-out pack of cards to keep them occupied was wearing thin. Added to the discomfort of the situation were Kelly's healing cuts and bruises. She was stiff and sore and had yet to be completely rid of the headache from the cut in her scalp. They'd been eating takeout food and sleeping in the same bed with a pillow between them. It was by no means a perfect situation, and with each passing hour, their fragile détente was coming undone.

Quinn leaned over Kelly's shoulder and pointed. "Red four on a black five."

"There's a reason this is called Solitaire," Kelly muttered, even as she slapped the four onto the five.

"Just trying to help," Quinn said.

"I don't need any help," she countered.

Quinn flopped backward onto the bed and reached for the remote, aiming it at the television as he muttered beneath his breath.

Kelly frowned. "I'm sorry. I didn't hear what you said."

"I said...obviously you do need help, or you wouldn't be losing to yourself."

It was the last straw. In a fit of frustration, Kelly swiped the cards into a pile, then flung them onto the bed, showering Quinn with the entire deck.

There were several long moments of silence; then Quinn moved a card from his mouth.

"Was it something I said?"

Before Kelly could answer, the telephone rang.

"Saved by the bell," she muttered, and shoved her hands through her hair in frustration as Quinn rolled toward the phone and picked up the receiver.

"Hello?"

"Quinn, it's me."

"Hey, Daryl, what's up?"

"I heard something at the bar today that you need to know."

Suddenly Quinn was all business. He sat up on the side of the bed, ignoring the cards that fell to the floor.

"Tell me," he said.

"Heard a couple of wanna-be badasses talking about a million-dollar contract that's gone out for whoever can find and kill a certain DEA agent."

Quinn's stomach turned as he looked at Kelly. A million dollars? This wasn't good. Their days of "playing house" were over.

Kelly could tell by the look on his face that something was seriously wrong.

"What is it?" she asked.

Quinn held up his hand, indicating that she should wait as he finished the call.

"I'm thinking you two need to find some new scenery," Daryl said.

"Yes, I'm thinking you're right," Quinn said. "And, Daryl…thank you."

"You're welcome. Just take care of yourselves."

"The best that we can," he said, and hung up the phone.

"Damn it, McCord. Talk to me," Kelly said.

"We've got to get out of here."

"What are you talking about?"

"There's a million-dollar contract out on you."

Kelly flinched. "Then Ortega is alive."

"You don't know that for sure," Quinn said.

"Sure I do," she said. "He's the only one who has a vested interest in seeing me dead."

Quinn reached for her, but Kelly pulled away and strode toward the closet.

"What are you doing?" Quinn asked.

"Packing."

"You can use my suitcase. It's big enough to hold all our things."

Kelly stopped, then slowly turned around.

"What do you mean *our?*"

"I'm going with you."

"Like hell," Kelly said.

"Probably will be, but I'm going just the same," Quinn said.

Kelly's shoulders slumped. "You've already helped me

more than I had reason to expect. I can't ask you to do this. It could get you killed.''

"You didn't ask. I volunteered, remember?''

Kelly wanted to hug him. Instead, she only smiled.

"Who do you think you are? The cavalry?''

Quinn grinned back at her. "One Texas Ranger. One cavalry troop. Same firepower. Less noise. So is it a deal?''

He was holding out his hand. Kelly took a deep breath, then held out her hand.

"It's a deal.''

4

Quinn carried the suitcase to the truck as Kelly went to call her boss. She knew he was going to tell her to wait, to let him send guards to help bring her in, but she had a gut feeling that the more people who knew what she was doing, the less likely it would be that she'd make it in alive.

She sat down on the side of the bed and made the call.

When Michael Forest finally came on the line, Kelly was waiting to make her case.

"This is Forest."

"Captain Forest…this is Agent Sloan."

The tone of his voice lifted.

"Kelly, it's good to hear from you again. I trust you're healing?"

"Yes, sir. Almost good as new."

"Good…good. Let me know when you're up to traveling and I'll send someone for you. The trial is coming up, and Marsh, the Federal prosecutor, is getting antsy."

"Yes, sir, that's part of why I'm calling. There's a problem that's developed since we last spoke."

"What kind of problem?"

"There's a million-dollar bounty out on me."

Forest made no attempt to hide his shock. "A million dollars! Damn it. That has to mean Ortega is alive."

"It could have come from someone else within the organization, but I don't think so. Dominic Ortega and his brother-in-law, Ponce Gruber, have a lot to lose if I testify.''

''I don't like this. I don't like this a bit. It changes everything. Give me a pickup location. We'll bring you in under guard.''

''Sir…if I may, I'd rather come in on my own.''

''That's out of the question. Not with a million-dollar incentive to bury you. It'll bring out every scumbag in the country.''

''But if you come after me, word will get out. And we both know that much money can turn even a righteous man if the need is great enough.''

''Are you saying you don't trust your fellow agents?''

Kelly sighed. ''Not in so many words.''

''But you need help,'' Forest argued.

At that point, Quinn walked back into the room. Kelly looked up.

''I have help…good help,'' she said, her gaze locking with Quinn's as he waited for her to finish the call.

''Can you trust this *help?*''

''He saved my life once already. I think I can trust him to do it again if the need arises.''

''I'd rather we did this my way,'' Forest argued.

''Sir, it's my life that's on the line. I know what I'm doing, okay?''

There was a brief moment of silence; then Kelly heard her boss give a slow, weary-sounding sigh.

''Okay. But stay in touch.''

''Yes, sir.''

''And be careful.''

''Always,'' Kelly said, and hung up.

''Well, now,'' Quinn said.

The grin on his face made Kelly's blood pressure rise.

''I trust you're not about to make me sorry I complimented you to my boss?''

''Who? Me? Never,'' Quinn said, then put his hands on

Kelly's shoulders. Before she knew it, he'd leaned down and brushed his mouth across her lips. "Just call that a thank you for the vote of confidence," he said softly. "Are you ready to go?"

Kelly's mouth was burning. She wanted to put her fingers on her lips to see if they were as blistered as they felt, but she wouldn't give him the satisfaction.

"No thanks are necessary. I was simply stating a fact, and yes, I'm ready to go."

"Then put this on," Quinn said, and tossed a white wide-brimmed straw Stetson in her lap.

"What on earth for?" she asked.

"Disguise. The less people who see me leaving with you, the less chance we have of blowing our cover."

"Oh. Right," Kelly said. She was already wearing the red boots, a pair of blue jeans and a white T-shirt with a logo that read Cowgirls Do It In The Mud. The hat would be the crowning glory to the white trash look to which Daryl seemed to be drawn. She bunched her hair up beneath the crown as she settled the hat on her head. The brim shadowed most of her face, which was exactly what she needed.

"How do I look?" she asked.

Quinn eyed the tight denim and even tighter T-shirt and opted for pleading the Fifth.

"I refuse to answer on the grounds that it may incriminate me," he drawled.

Kelly laughed. "That bad, huh?"

"Oh no. To the contrary, Agent Sloan. That good. You'll pass just fine as a real cheap date."

Kelly felt herself blushing. She couldn't remember the last time she'd blushed and began to worry what other responses Quinn McCord might bring out in her before this trip was over.

"Just shut up and let's go," she said.

Quinn slid an arm around her shoulder as they started out the door.

"McCord...what the—"

"Hey, don't fight this. It's part of your cover, remember?"

Kelly stifled her dismay. He was right. Besides, what did it matter? They'd shared the same bed. Putting his arm around her was nothing.

They started toward his truck with their hips bumping as they walked, and the farther they walked, the tighter his grip became. Finally Kelly's right breast was mashed flat against Quinn's side.

"Come on, McCord. Ease up, will you? I appreciate your help, but not at the expense of my right boob."

Quinn looked startled, then loosened his grip.

"Sorry, I didn't mean to—"

Kelly grinned. "It's okay, the damage isn't permanent."

"Thank God," Quinn said. "I'd hate to mess up something that perfect."

Kelly stifled a sigh. There was no need to respond, because she knew he wouldn't stop until he'd gotten the last word. It was only after Quinn had settled her safely inside the truck and then paused and looked around that she realized he'd been teasing her to keep her mind off the danger to her life. She started to remind him that he wasn't the only cop here, and that she was perfectly capable of taking care of herself. But that was no longer true. If it hadn't been for Quinn, she would never have made it to safety before passing out. And if that had happened, either she would have drowned, or Ortega's men would have found her and turned her into fish food. Now, with the million-dollar bounty on her head, Ortega had once again turned her into bait. This was going to bring all the worms out of the underbelly of society. She needed to be gone when they started turning Galveston upside down.

She rode leaning forward, with an eye to the mirror on

the outside of the cab. It wasn't until they had passed the city limits and begun heading north that she started to relax.

It was eleven minutes after 10:00 p.m. when two men walked into the office of the Sea Gull Inn. The desk clerk, Charlie Warden, looked up.

"Evening, gentlemen. How can I help you?"

A tall Latino man wearing a blue silk shirt and dark slacks leaned over the counter.

"I'm looking for my brother, Quinn McCord. I thought he was staying here, but I don't see his truck in the parking lot. He drives a black Dodge pickup. Can you tell me if he's still registered here?"

Charlie shrugged. "Sorry. We can't give out that kind of information."

"You don't understand. It's a family emergency. If I don't find my brother, he might never get a chance to tell our mother goodbye."

Charlie frowned. He'd heard all kinds of stories, and as stories went, this one was pretty lame. He remembered the man who'd driven the Dodge truck, and he didn't look anything like this guy. This man was Latino. The Dodge guy was not.

"You two don't look anything alike," Charlie said.

"That means he was here!"

Charlie's frown deepened. "You already said he'd been staying here. So what's the deal? What's going on?"

Suddenly the man pulled a gun and pointed it in Charlie's face.

"Talk to me, damn it. Where is he?"

"No. No. Don't shoot me, man! I got a wife and four kids."

"Then tell me what I need to know," the man growled.

"He's gone. He checked out this morning, and that's all I know."

"Just shoot him and let's get out of here," the other man said.

Luis de Jesus was set on claiming that million-dollar bounty. His cousin Franco worked for Ortega, and it had been Franco who'd given him the heads-up on the tag number of a black Dodge truck that had been sighted on the beach the morning Kelly Sloan had escaped. He hadn't come this far to take no for an answer.

"Shut up, Armenio. You talk too much. Let me think."

Even though the air-conditioning was blasting a thirty-four degree wind down his neck, Charlie was sweating. He had to think of something—and fast—or he was a dead man.

Luis turned back to Charlie. "This man...the man in the truck...did he have anyone with him?"

"He registered alone. He was supposed to stay a week, but he left early. That's all I know."

"That's not what I asked," Luis said. "Was he alone when he left?"

"I didn't see anyone with him."

"Think harder," Luis said, and shoved the gun up the desk clerk's nose.

"I don't pay any attention to who comes and goes. If you'll look out the window, the only view I have of this place is the front entrance."

"So who came and went that wasn't a client?"

"God almighty! How would I know that?"

"Then I'll rephrase the question, and you better by God have an answer I like. Did you recognize anyone coming in here that wasn't registered?"

Charlie frowned, trying desperately to remember anything that would get them out of his face. And then it hit him.

"Yeah! Yeah! Actually, I did."

"So who?"

"There's this old guy who lives just off the strip. I saw him come and go a couple of times in the past few days."

"What's his name?" Luis asked.

Charlie rubbed at his chest. "I'm not sure.... Don, David, Daryl...maybe it's Daryl. But I don't know his last name."

Luis twisted the gun a little tighter against Charlie's nose. "Then how do you know him?" he asked.

"Seen him down at the Baytown Bar. He's always talking about the good old days."

"What do you mean?" Luis asked.

"He was a Ranger...a Texas Ranger, and that's all I know."

Luis started to smile. It was the lead they'd been looking for, because according to his information, the Dodge truck belonged to a man named Quinn McCord. Current employment—a Ranger for the state of Texas. Now all they had to do was find the old man and see what he knew about Quinn McCord's hasty exit.

"You've been very helpful," Luis said, and flipped off the safety on his gun.

Charlie's eyes widened, and then he started to gasp. He grabbed at his chest, wadding the fabric of his shirt into his hand as he stumbled backward.

"My heart...my heart...I got a bad heart."

Luis eased up on the trigger.

"Aren't you going to shoot him?" Armenio asked.

Luis hesitated, then put the safety back on and slipped the gun in his jacket.

"Why? It would only alert the police...and any one else who might have information similar to ours."

"But he'll tell," Armenio said.

Luis smiled. "Not if he's dead of natural causes, he won't."

Armenio stared at the desk clerk, who was turning paler

by the second. When he doubled over and then dropped to his knees, Armenio elbowed Luis.

"Ten dollars says he won't last another thirty seconds."

Luis looked at the desk clerk, then nodded. "You're on."

Charlie rolled over onto his side and started to moan as Armenio began timing what he thought were the throes of Charlie's death.

Fifteen seconds, then twenty, then thirty seconds passed. A minute and fifteen seconds after he fell to the floor, Charlie Warden rolled over onto his back, exhaled loudly, then stopped breathing.

"Pay up," Luis said, as he held out his hand.

"What if he's not—"

Before Armenio could finish what he was going to say, the headlights of a car flashed across the wall behind the desk. Both men looked toward the window, then headed through the door behind the desk, exiting the motel through the room reserved for the clerk on duty. They were in their car and driving away by the time Charlie Warden sat up and crawled to the phone.

As he dialed 911, he knew he had his wife to thank for being alive. If it hadn't been for all those murder mystery shows she insisted on watching, it would never have occurred to him to fake his own death.

Meanwhile, Luis and Armenio were heading toward the Baytown Bar. If they were lucky, someone would know where the old Ranger lived.

The next morning and half a country away, Dominic Ortega walked out onto the veranda of his Florida home with the aid of a nurse, then took a seat in the shade as a waiter handed him a glass of cold juice.

"Thank you," he said, as the nurse pushed a foot stool up to the chair and helped him lift his feet.

"You're welcome," she said softly, then shook two of

his pain pills out into her hand and gave them to him. "Are you comfortable, sir?"

Ortega swallowed the pillows, then nodded. "Yes. You may go. If I need you, I will ring."

He leaned back in the chair as the nurse disappeared, then took a small sip of the chilled juice. It felt good to be out of that hospital, although the helicopter ride from Houston to the west coast of Florida had been extremely uncomfortable. But once they'd arrived, he'd settled in just fine. Here, he had peace and quiet when he needed it, and guards that he trusted. And here, he was, once again, in control. Satisfied that, for now, all was right with his world, he closed his eyes and relaxed.

Overhead, a flock of seagulls squawked noisily. An easy breeze was coming in off the water, cooling the heat of mid-day. The scent of jacaranda and oleander overpowered the smell of salt air just enough that Ortega could almost believe he was back in Mexico, and he would be, as soon as his wounds had healed.

His thoughts drifted as the pain medicine took effect. But when he slept, his dreams turned to nightmares, and once again, he felt the pain of the knife plunging deep into his chest.

Somewhere in another part of the house a phone began to ring. It filtered through his sleep until he began to wake. He was struggling to sit up when his house man came hurrying outside with the phone.

"*Señor! Señor!* The call…it is an emergency."

Dominic frowned as he took the phone.

"Hello?"

"Dominic…this is Ponce."

Dominic sat up too quickly, then grabbed at the front of his shirt, grunting in agony as he shifted the phone to a better position.

"Damn you, Ponce. You should not be calling me here. They can trace your call."

"No, no, it's safe. I'm using my lawyer's cell phone. There's something you need to know."

"What is it?"

"Kelly Sloan is alive."

Ortega cursed. "How do you know?"

"I have someone on the inside who's feeding me information. They said she's not only alive, but on the move. My lawyer said the deal we made is off the table. If she testifies at my trial, she'll crucify me."

Ortega frowned. "What deal?"

"I'm sorry? What did you say?" Ponce asked.

"I asked you…what deal? You said you had made a deal with the Feds. What deal could you possibly have made that did not involve me?"

Suddenly Ponce realized that he'd given himself away. Desperate to get back in his brother-in-law's good graces, he began whispering, as if he were about to hang up.

"I can't talk anymore now," he said. "The guards are coming to take me back to my cell."

"Damn you, Ponce…what did you tell them?"

"Nothing! I told them nothing!" Ponce cried. "I've got to go. Just make sure you stop Kelly Sloan or we're both dead."

He hung up before Dominic could say anything more.

"Damn it," Dominic muttered, then staggered to his feet. He walked to the edge of the terrace overlooking the ocean and stared out across the water.

It didn't matter now what Ponce had said or what he had done. He would deal with him later. For now, what he needed was to make sure that Kelly Sloan didn't make it to D.C.

He hurried back to the table, picked up the phone and made a call. It rang once. Twice. It was answered on the third ring.

"It's me," Dominic said. "Spread the word. The bounty

is up to two million, but only if they do her before the week is out.''

He hung up without waiting for an answer, then rang for the nurse. She appeared within seconds.

''I need something for pain.''

The nurse glanced at her watch. ''It hasn't been three hours yet, sir.''

Dominic repeated his request. ''I said…I need something for pain.''

The glitter in his eyes was more frightening than if he'd shouted at her.

''Yes, sir. I'll bring it right now.''

''Thank you,'' he said, then returned to his chair. He made himself focus on the undulating water, rather than the pain and frustrations of his life, and reached for his juice. Despite the fact that the ice had melted and the drink was no longer cold, he drank it all. The tart-sweet taste of the freshly squeezed juice washed the bitterness from his mouth.

It would be all right. It had to be.

It was evening when Quinn crossed the state line into Louisiana. They could have gone farther and made better time if they'd stayed on the interstate highways, but Kelly was afraid that if someone was looking for them, they would be too easily spotted that way. Quinn had agreed, so they'd stayed on the old two-lane highways, often being forced to detour due to road construction—once even getting lost. He found it hard to believe that only three days ago he hadn't known she existed, because now she had become a very important part of his life—so much so that he was playing bodyguard to make sure she stayed alive.

Kelly had fallen asleep over an hour ago and was now slumped against Quinn's shoulder, her hands lying loosely in her lap. Quinn could smell his shampoo in her hair. He'd never thought the odor was sexy before, but on her, it was gold-plated.

Somewhere back in Oklahoma, he'd offered to buy her some more sedate clothing, but Kelly had refused, saying she needed a disguise and the "trashy" look was as good as any. Quinn wasn't going to tell her, but that "trashy" look, as she called it, looked damn good on her. One of Frank's favorite country songs had been about a man liking his women a little on the trashy side. He remembered how much he'd teased Frank about the song, but now he got it. Tight blouses and even tighter blue jeans left nothing to the imagination except what Kelly would look like without them. He'd thought of little else all day, and it was driving him crazy.

An SUV sped past him with the stereo blasting. Even though the windows were up on his truck and the air conditioner was going, it still woke Kelly.

She sat up with a jerk, instinctively reaching for her gun, only the last time she'd had her gun had been at Ortega's Mexican *hacienda*. She saw Quinn, remembered where she was, and sat back with a sigh.

"Where are we?"

"Welcome to Tuskeegee, Louisiana," he said softly.

Her eyes widened. "Louisiana...as in...beignets and café au lait Louisiana?"

Quinn smiled. "That makes you happy?"

"Oh, yeah...so now you know my secret."

"What's that?" Quinn asked.

"That I can be had for coffee and doughnuts...in any form."

Quinn threw back his head and laughed. "Ah, God...I don't believe it. How stereotypical—a coffee and doughnut cop."

"What time is it?" she asked, refusing to rise to his taunts.

"Almost seven. I think it's time to stop for the night.

We need to regroup. I'm going to call Daryl, see if I can find out what's going on, and then we'll get something to eat. I'll even spring for dessert.''

Kelly nodded, watching as he maneuvered through the small town traffic. She'd never let herself be this dependent before and wasn't quite sure how to take his help.

Sensing her discomfort, Quinn asked, ''What's wrong?''

She shrugged. ''Nothing, I guess.''

''Come on, Sloan…it's me you're talking to.''

Kelly sighed. ''It sounds petty.''

''So?''

''So, it took me twice as long to become an undercover agent with the DEA as it would have taken a man. No matter what I do, I have to do it better and faster to be accepted. It's not fair, but it's just the way things are. I guess what's bothering me is, the first time I run into really rough water, I wind up letting some man help me.''

Quinn paused at a stoplight, then turned to her.

''Honey…by the time I came along, you'd endured what…? Three days of torture, rescued yourself from a boat load of drug runners, killed two of them and mortally wounded the boss. You swam God knows how far toward shore to save yourself before I even came on the scene. Who the hell do you have to be? Superwoman?''

''Pretty much.''

''Then screw the whole lot of them,'' Quinn said. ''All you have to know is that they won't find anything different out from me. I offered to get you to D.C. The rest is your story, okay?''

There was a knot in the back of Kelly's throat as she managed to nod.

''Then we don't need to hear any more about who's got the bigger set of—''

''Stuff it, McCord,'' Kelly said. ''We both know the answer to that.''

He was still grinning as the light turned green.

"There's a motel up ahead and a little café across the street. Looks like a good place to stop," Kelly said.

"See," Quinn said. "You're back in charge already."

This time Kelly was the one laughing as she punched him lightly on the shoulder.

A short while later they had a room at the back with two double beds. It wasn't the Hilton, but for Quinn, who'd been driving all day, the chance to stretch out on that bed made it look like heaven.

"Are you hungry?" he asked.

Kelly nodded. "How about you?"

"I could eat a horse. I'll settle for a plate of fried catfish and hush puppies."

"I promise I'll pay you back for all this," Kelly said.

"I'll total up the bill when this is all over. For now, just forget about the small stuff, okay?"

The sincerity on Quinn's face shamed her. He kept giving and giving without ever asking for anything back. She didn't know whether it was a skillful ploy on his part or not, but it made a woman thankful—in a very big way.

"Then let's go eat. After that, I'll call in and find out what's going on."

Without giving Kelly time to think, Quinn took her by the hand, and together they crossed the street toward the small town café.

It wasn't until they'd come back from supper that their fragile peace was shattered.

"Are you calling Daryl?" Kelly asked, as Quinn took out his cell phone.

"Yes. If I call anyone else, then that's one more person who knows I'm with you, and if they know what you're traveling in, then that makes you even easier to find."

Kelly nodded, then kicked off her red boots and sat cross-legged on the bed as Quinn made the call.

But the call didn't go as planned. The phone rang and rang, and Daryl's answering machine never came on.

"What's wrong?" Kelly asked, as Quinn disconnected.

"Maybe nothing," Quinn said. "But he didn't answer, and his machine didn't kick on. That's not like Daryl."

"He could be at the bar."

"Not this early."

"Maybe he went out to dinner with some friends."

"This is Friday, right?"

Kelly nodded.

Quinn glanced at his watch. "And it's just after seven. *Unsolved Mysteries* is on television. Daryl never misses it. It's his favorite show."

Kelly leaned forward. "Should we be worried?"

For a few moments Quinn was silent; then he nodded. "Yeah, I think so."

"Who can we call to check on him?"

"There's this lady who lives across the hall from him. She should know what's going on."

"Do you know her number?"

"No, but I know her name."

He dialed information, got the number and dialed it. When the old woman answered, Quinn quickly introduced himself.

"Mrs. Weatherly, this is Quinn McCord…Daryl's friend from Fort Worth. We met last fall, do you remember?"

"Oh, yes! Of course I do," the old woman said. "It's just so awful what happened to Daryl, you know."

For a moment, it felt as if Quinn's heart just stopped.

"What happened to Daryl, Mrs. Weatherly."

"He was beaten badly. He's in Houston Medical Center. They airlifted him right from the scene."

"Where was he when this happened, Mrs. Weatherly?"

"Oh, at that awful bar he goes to. I've told him and told him that he needs to stay away from lowlifes like the people there. Now see what's happened? I'm just sick about it, you know. I don't drive anymore, and I can't even go see him."

"Okay, Mrs. Weatherly. Thank you for the information."

"You find out who did this to him, won't you? You are a Ranger like Daryl, right?"

"Yes, ma'am, that I am. And I can assure you this won't go unpunished."

Quinn hung up, then threw his phone across the room. It hit the back of a chair, then dropped into the cushioned seat. Within seconds, Kelly was off the bed and grabbing his arm.

"What? For God's sake, talk to me! What happened?"

"Daryl was life-flighted to Houston Medical. His neighbor said he was badly beaten."

Kelly felt sick. "It's because of me, isn't it?"

"We don't know that," Quinn said. "And even if it is, it's not your fault. It's that son of a bitch drug runner."

"You need to leave. Go be with Daryl. I can rent a car and get myself to D.C. or call my captain. Either way, you're off the hook."

Quinn gripped her shoulders with both hands, his voice shaking with anger.

"I'm not going anywhere but with you," he said.

Kelly retrieved Quinn's phone, checked to see if it was still in one piece, then handed it to him.

"Fine, but call Houston first and check on Daryl."

Quinn's hand was shaking as he took the phone. Instead of making the call, he sat down on the side of the bed and dropped his head.

Kelly slid onto the bed beside him, then laid her hand on his thigh.

"What's wrong?"

When Quinn looked up, there were tears in his eyes.

"I guess I'm scared he won't be able to answer."

Kelly sighed. "One thing at a time, McCord. Just make the call."

5

"Houston Medical. How may I direct your call?"

"Daryl Connelly's room, please."

"I'm sorry, sir. He's in ICU. I'll connect you with the nurses' station."

ICU? Quinn's stomach knotted. "Yes, thank you," he said, and waited to be connected.

"Fourth floor…ICU nurses' station."

"Ma'am, my name is Quinn McCord. I'm with the Texas Rangers and inquiring about the status of retired Ranger Daryl Connelly."

"He's critical, but stable."

"Is there anyone who can tell me what happened to him? Was he robbed? Did he—"

"I'm sorry, sir. We don't have that kind of information. There was a police officer who gave his name to be contacted as next of kin."

Quinn frowned. "Mr. Connelly doesn't have any next of kin."

"But I'm sure that—"

"No, ma'am. I've known him most of my life, and he's never married. He has no living relatives…anywhere. Do you have the officer's name?"

"You need to talk to the doctor. I can't give out that kind of information."

"All I'm asking for is the name of the police officer on

record. That's not privileged information, and you and I both know it.''

There was a long moment of silence. Then Quinn could hear some whispered conversation in the background, but the nurse wasn't talking. Just when he thought she'd disconnected, she came back on the line.

''Yes, well, all right. His name is Travis. Will Travis.''

Suddenly all the panic Quinn had been feeling dissipated. He knew Will Travis. The hospital must have taken the information down wrong. Whatever was going on, Will would have Daryl's best interests at heart.

''May I please have his contact number?''

Quinn wrote quickly as she rattled off the number, then disconnected. The moment he was off the phone, Kelly grabbed his arm.

''Quinn…talk to me.''

''Daryl is in ICU. He's critical but stable.''

''Do we know what happened? And please tell me it has nothing to do with me.''

''I wish I could, but right now I can't, because I don't know. However, I've got another call to make. There's a cop who came in with him. Maybe I'll know something more after I talk to him.''

''I shouldn't have stayed. I should have let my captain come get me that first day,'' Kelly said, then looked away.

Her eyes were wide and swimming with tears, but there was a jut to her jaw that told him she would be a fierce enemy if crossed.

''Yeah, good thinking,'' Quinn said. ''And if you had, there's a good chance someone would already be planning your funeral.''

''Better mine than Daryl's.''

Quinn laid down the phone and then cupped her face with his hands. Kelly twisted away, but he caught her again.

''Look at me, damn it!''

Kelly turned, meeting his gaze without flinching.

"You don't have to like this, but I'm going to say it. What you're doing matters to all of us. Illegal drugs are, in their own way, as dangerous as bombs. We're in a war, honey, and you're on the front line. If Daryl and I got involved, it was because we wanted to." Then he took a deep breath, his voice softening. "And I'm still in this with you, because, frankly, you're driving me crazy. I slept beside you for three nights and wanted to hold you in my arms instead of hugging my side of the bed. You're smart and you're funny, and I think about you far more than I should. Selfishly, that means I want to keep you alive and in one piece."

Kelly was speechless. It was the last thing she'd expected him to say, and yet it echoed something in her that she'd been trying to deny.

"I don't know if I can match those wonderful words, but I do know that I am profoundly grateful you were fishing the day I washed up on the beach." Then she laid her hand on the flat of his chest, feeling the steady, rhythmic beat of his heart. "Having only these few days on which to base my feelings for you, you come across as hardheaded, single-minded and something of a wiseass. However, I was always partial to macho-type Texans with dark eyes and nice buns."

Quinn grinned as he took her in his arms.

"So…we finally agree on something," he said softly, as he traced the arch of her eyebrows with the tip of his finger.

Kelly shivered as his mouth brushed her lips. Then his hand slid beneath her hair. He cupped the back of her head, pulling her closer until there was nothing between them but heat. The kiss went on and on, until Kelly felt as if this time she was truly drowning and she was ready to let it happen.

But it was Quinn who was the first to pull back.

"Hold that thought," he said. "I've got to call Will Travis. He might know something *we* need to know, and the last thing we can let ourselves do is lose focus. It could get you killed.''

"Right,'' Kelly said, then handed him his phone.

But she was shaking as she waited for him to call the other number. If Quinn hadn't stopped, they would have been rolling naked on the bed. If someone had told her she would so easily fall into bed with a man she'd just met, she would have called them a liar. Yet it was happening. She didn't know whether to attribute it to a real and growing attraction between them, or chalk it up to being in such close quarters with a very sexy man. Either way, it would be only a matter of time before they made love.

Quinn dialed the number the nurse had given him, then leaned over and kissed Kelly one more time as he waited for the call to be answered. He was admiring Kelly's Cowgirls Do It in the Mud T-shirt when he heard a man's voice in his ear.

"This is Travis.''

Quinn quickly shifted focus.

"Travis…this is Ranger Quinn McCord. Daryl Connelly introduced us a couple of years ago at his barbeque, remember?''

"Yeah, yeah, McCord. I've been expecting your call.''

"What?''

"I'm assuming you know about Daryl or you wouldn't have this number. Daryl couldn't do much talking when they found him. He was beat all to hell. But as soon as he recognized me, he started saying the same thing over and over. 'Tell Quinn that it's up to two mil and I didn't tell.'' Does that mean anything to you?''

"Jesus,'' Quinn muttered. "Yeah, it means something. Put round the clock guards on the old man and don't let anyone in that room except authorized personnel.''

"What the hell's going on?'' Travis asked.

"Does the name Dominic Ortega mean anything to you?''

There was a brief silence, then a heavy exhaled sigh.

"Oh, yeah. How did Daryl get mixed up with him?"

"He knows something that could get him killed. Just keep him alive, okay?"

"I'll do my best. Is there anything else I can do from this end?"

Quinn glanced at Kelly, then said, "Can you hang on a minute?"

"Sure," Travis said.

Quinn covered the receiver, then looked at Kelly.

"It was Ortega. He found out about Daryl, which has to mean he knows about me, too. I don't know how, but—"

"The motel," Kelly said. "Ask your friend if there've been any disturbances at the motel where you were staying."

Quinn eyed her curiously. "Did anyone ever tell you that you're real good at what you do?"

"Yes."

Quinn returned to the phone. "Travis, can you check and see if there've been any disturbances at the Sea Gull Inn?"

"What does that have to do with—"

"Just do it. I'll hold, okay?"

"It may take a few minutes. Why don't I call you back?"

"I'll hold," Quinn said.

"It's your nickel," Travis said, and put the call on hold.

"What's happening?" Kelly said.

"He's checking out your theory, and for what it's worth, it's a damn good one." Then he began to pace. "You know…the only way Ortega's people would be looking for me is if the men on that boat had gotten my tag number. They had no reason to assume you were with me, and yet they took the number…just in case. I'm thinking they're just eliminating the suspects, so to speak, in their search to find you. More thorough than I would have guessed."

"Ortega isn't a man who likes failure." Then she got up

from the bed and began to pace. "I can't believe Ortega isn't dead. I buried that knife in his chest up to the hilt." She spun, her face twisted with anger. "How come the bad guys are the hardest to kill? Tell me that, Quinn. How come?"

Before Quinn could answer, Will Travis came back on the line.

"Okay, you were right, and there's a connection to Daryl in here. Yesterday evening the manager, a guy named Charlie Warden, was accosted by two Latino men who were looking for a man named McCord, who was driving a black Dodge truck. One man was claiming to be your brother. Said there was a family emergency with your mother and he needed to contact you. The manager wouldn't give out any information and kept telling them that you had checked out and he had no idea where you went. Then it got ugly. They threatened to kill him. Wanted to know if you'd had any visitors or if you left alone when you checked out."

"What did he tell them?" Quinn asked.

"Said he didn't see anyone with you, but that he'd seen a guy come in a couple of times who wasn't registered. As bad luck would have it, he recognized Daryl and told them they could talk to him down at the Baytown Bar. That's where Daryl was found, so I'm guessing the men found him and tried to beat information out of him."

"Goddamn it," Quinn muttered.

"What is it?" Travis asked. "What are these men looking for?"

"Let's just say a witness and leave it at that."

"Okay. It's your call. This has put a new slant on the incident for us. We'll be questioning Charlie Warden to get a description of those men. Maybe we can find them before they find you."

"That would be good, but I doubt they're the only ones on my trail."

"What do you mean?" Travis asked.

"That two mil? It's million, as in money, and it's what Ortega will pay to get what I have."

Travis whistled softly beneath his breath.

"Man, I would not want to be in your shoes."

Quinn looked across the bed at Kelly and then slowly smiled.

"Oh, I don't know about that. Things are looking real good from where I'm at."

There was a moment of silence; then Travis chuckled.

"A woman. It's got to be a woman. Am I right?"

"I've got to go, Travis. Just make sure to keep guards on Daryl until you hear different from me, and when he comes to, tell him he did good."

"You got it," Travis said. "Let me know if I can be of any further help."

"I will, and thanks," Quinn said, then hung up.

"We're in trouble, aren't we?" Kelly said.

"You were right," Quinn said. "They saw my truck at the beach, but so far, I don't think they have any real proof that we're together. However, upping the bounty on you to two million is serious. Are you sure you don't want the DEA or the Federal prosecutor's office to bring you in?"

"Hell no," she said. "They obviously know I'm alive, and since they didn't find it out from the desk clerk or from Daryl, then someone else tipped them off. That means there's either a mole in my office or in the Federal prosecutor's office. You think I'm going to trust them to keep me safe when someone from inside is feeding Ortega information?"

"Okay, I see your point," Quinn said. "So where do we go from here?"

"I need to stay out of sight until the day of the trial. If I show up beforehand and try to barricade myself in some hotel or safe house, I'm dead. But if I make my appearance at the courthouse on the day of the trial, they won't have time to make the hit. If you're still set on staying with me through this, then we've got to ditch your truck, and I've got to change my appearance.''

"I can handle the truck business," Quinn said.

"I need some money," Kelly said. "Damn it, if only I dared access my checking account."

"Look, I'm good for whatever you need," Quinn said. "I have a pocket full of cash and traveler's checks."

Kelly frowned as he pulled out a wad of bills. "Didn't anyone ever tell you it's not safe to travel with a lot of money?"

"Don't like ATMs," Quinn said.

"Lucky me," Kelly said. "Can you part with a couple hundred dollars?"

"Here," he said, handing her a wad of bills. "Knock yourself out."

"Are you always this generous with your money?" Kelly asked.

"No," Quinn said, then picked up his car keys and grinned. "But you forget, I've seen you naked."

Kelly eyed the smirk on his face, then looked him up and down.

"And the favor was returned, remember?"

Quinn pointed at her. "We'll continue this conversation as soon as I get back with a new ride. Then we'll go shopping for a new look."

"I can do that while you're getting a different car."

Quinn frowned. "Please, Kelly, wait for me to get back, okay?"

"Look, Quinn, be reasonable. The sooner this all takes place, the better. Go. I'll be here when you get back."

"I don't like this," Quinn said.

"I've been taking care of myself for a long time," Kelly said. "Trust me when I tell you I can handle Wal-Mart alone a lot better than going into the Ortega organization by myself."

"Yeah, okay, I get your point," Quinn said. "But don't

forget to pay attention to who's around you. I don't think we were followed, but there's no way to know for sure."

"Go," Kelly said. "I'll see you soon."

Quinn hesitated, then took her in his arms. "How about one for the road?"

"One what, McCord?" Kelly asked, then wrapped her arms around his neck and let nature take its course.

The feel of his mouth on her lips was staggering. The kiss was hard—demanding—then urgent. The tension of trying to stay alive was being translated into a powerful lust.

Quinn groaned as he tore himself away from her.

"Why do I feel like I just got offered a bite of the apple?"

"I've been called a lot of things, but never a temptress," Kelly said. "Trust me, I'm no Eve, and this is certainly not the Garden of Eden."

Quinn sighed. "I'm going to get rid of my truck."

"And I'm going to get rid of Kelly Sloan," Kelly said.

"Don't lose too much of her," Quinn said. "I'm pretty partial to her the way she is."

Kelly touched Quinn's cheek with the back of her hand in a gentle, stroking motion.

"I won't lose her, I promise. I just want to hide her for a while."

Tuskeegee had no rental cars, which had put a dent in Quinn's plan to change rides. But then he'd seen an advertisement for a paint and body shop on a sign in a vacant lot and made an adjustment to the plan. His truck was now in Little Ed's Paint and Body Shop on a rush job, and Little Ed, who weighed somewhere near three hundred pounds, was putting red and orange flames from front to back on both sides and had talked Quinn into a three-foot decal of the Confederate flag on the hood. Added to that was a six-inch lift kit to accommodate the forty-four-inch Gumbo

Monster Mudder tires Little Ed had talked him into adding to the package. The tires, which would normally cost several hundred dollars apiece, were so cheap Quinn figured they were hot, but at this point, who was he to argue? He needed to disguise his truck, and if a paint job and some stolen tires did the job, then so be it. Kelly was worth it. And for an extra hundred dollars, Little Ed was trading the license tag on Quinn's truck for one off a car that had been totaled. Quinn admired Little Ed's initiative and thanked him for the rush job on the truck. By this time tomorrow, they would be on their way out of town and virtually untraceable.

He started back toward the motel where he and Kelly were staying, and the farther he walked the faster he went.

Kelly watched Quinn leave the motel, then headed for the pay phone outside the manager's office. She was so angry with the situation that she was shaking. Someone pretending to be on the side of the good guys was a traitor. She didn't know who to blame, but there had to be a starting point, and Michael Forest was it.

She dropped some coins into the slot and dialed his direct number. He answered on the first ring.

"This is Forest."

"Someone with the DEA or the prosecutor's office sold me out," Kelly said, without introducing herself.

"Kelly?"

"Who else do you know who's got a price on her head?"

"What do you mean, you were sold out?"

"The bounty on my head is up to two million. The only reason that would have happened is if Ortega knows for sure I'm alive. And for that to happen, someone had to tell him. Was it you, Captain? Did you sell me out?"

Forest was stunned. "You can't believe that!"

"I don't know what to believe," Kelly said. "But if it's not you, then you need to clean house. And if it's not someone in the DEA, then it's coming out of the Federal prosecutor's office. I hate to speak in clichés, but someone better find that leak and fix it, or we're sunk."

"Kelly! Wait! Tell me what's going on! Let me—"

She hung up in his ear then started up the street toward the Wal-Mart, her step lighter than it had been in weeks.

Forty minutes later, she was back in the motel. She dumped her purchases on the bed, then picked up a pair of scissors and a can of colored hair spray, and headed for the bathroom.

The closer Quinn got to the motel, the more he felt like running. He shouldn't have left her alone. He just knew it.

He slipped the key into the door without knocking and then rushed inside. Then he saw her clothes in a pile on the floor outside the bathroom door and went weak with relief.

"Kelly, it's me. I'm back."

"Be right out," she said.

He sat down in the chair, needing to let the panic subside. He combed his hands through his hair, then leaned forward, resting his elbows on his knees. His heart was hammering. His hands were shaking. And all because he'd let fear get the best of him. This wasn't like him. He was a better cop than this, or at least he had been—before Kelly.

"God," he muttered, and closed his eyes. How had she become so important to him in such a short time?

"Okay…how do I look?" Kelly asked.

He opened his eyes, then grunted as if he'd just been punched in the belly.

"Kelly?"

She put her hands on her hips and lifted her chin in a defiant tilt.

"Never heard of her. Call me Candy."

Quinn got up and moved closer, touching the sharp pointy spikes where her hair used to be.

"Nice touch," he said, eyeing the red hair spray she'd added to the spikes. Then his gaze moved to her clothes. "You bought those at Wal-Mart?"

"No, there's a secondhand shop a couple of blocks up." She ran her hands down the front of the black leather mini-vest. "I always wondered what it would be like to be a biker babe."

Quinn started to grin. "Wait till you see our ride."

"What have you done?"

"You'll see tomorrow."

"Okay, fine. I can wait."

Quinn eyed the tight black leather pants she was wearing, as well as the wealth of skin showing beneath that skimpy black vest. If it wasn't for a white tube top, she would be naked beneath.

"I'd take you out to eat, but I might have to fight my way back home later," he said.

Kelly grabbed his elbow and pulled him toward the door.

"I'll save you," she said. "Now let's go. I'm starving."

Quinn followed her out the door, his gaze so focused on the sway of her backside that he stumbled on the steps.

Kelly heard him curse and turned around just as he grabbed the railing.

"You okay?"

He eyed the swell of her breasts pushing against the vest and sighed.

"No, ma'am, I am not. I may never be all right again."

Kelly grinned. "It's just black leather."

"You give new meaning to the term 'hot.'"

Kelly started to tease him, then saw something in his eyes that stopped her. He wanted her. The thought of making love with this man turned her appetite for food into a different kind of hunger.

"Quinn?"

"Yeah?"

"How hungry are you…really?"

"I'm starving."

"Oh, well, then I—"

"For you," he added.

Kelly's stomach tightened with a longing she hadn't felt in years. She started toward him, her hips swaying with a slow, rhythmic gait.

Quinn took her by the hand and pulled her back into the room, then shut and locked the door. For a few moments they stood in the shadows of the room and stared into each other's eyes.

Then Kelly exhaled slowly. When she did, Quinn sighed. "Honey...it's time."

She nodded.

Quinn put his finger in the vee of her vest and gently tugged. The first snap came undone.

Kelly lifted her chin, watching the flare of his nostrils and knowing he was remembering his first sight of her.

She reached for his hand and pushed it away, then undid the rest of the snaps herself. When she shrugged out of the vest and let it fall to the floor, she thought she heard him groan.

"Kelly... Kelly...you are so beautiful."

"It's Candy...remember?"

"And just as sweet," Quinn whispered, then stripped the rest of the clothes from her body and carried her to the bed.

6

"Now yours," Kelly said, pointing to his clothes. "Take them off."

Quinn stripped in record time and stretched out on the bed beside her. He started to kiss her, then held back when he saw the look in her eyes.

"This is crazy, isn't it?"

"About the craziest thing I've ever done," she said.

"Please don't regret this."

"Only if you stop," she whispered, and wrapped her arms around his neck.

He brushed his mouth across her lips, lingering tenderly on the sensual curve of her lower lip until Kelly started to moan. Then he moved down the length of her neck, dipping into the valley between her breasts with his tongue, then encircling the sweet brown areolas surrounding her nipples.

Kelly fisted her fingers in his hair. When his teeth tightened gently on the peak of one nipple, the sensual pain traveled the length of her body, building shockwaves of pulsing need.

Quinn heard her gasp, then felt her body arch up from the bed. It was exalting to know he was giving her pleasure. And so the loving began.

Night came to the small Louisiana town, cloaking the motel in what seemed a temporary refuge. The air was close—almost sultry. No breeze stirred other than what was generated by a couple of outdoor ceiling fans hanging from the portico off the office. But the heat building inside their room was of a different kind. One that threatened to consume them both.

The air conditioner rattled noisily near the foot of their bed, but the sound was lost in the act of making love as their bodies joined in a dance as old as time. Sweat-slicked, with hearts pounding, they clutched at each other in mute desperation and raced toward a finish that couldn't be denied.

One moment Kelly was riding a ripple of pleasure, and then she slammed into the wall. Shattered by the climax that ran through her, she could do nothing but cling to Quinn and let it engulf her.

Quinn heard Kelly gasp. He looked down just as her eyes rolled back in her head. Her neck arched first, and then her body, as a low, gut-wrenching groan came out of her throat. It was the most sensual thing he'd ever experienced, and the knowledge that he'd given her such pleasure was the sign that his wait was now over. The muscles in his forearms were shaking as he slammed once more into the valley between her thighs. Once, then again, and the climax came upon him in a mind-shattering blast, emptying his mind as he spilled himself into her.

Too exhausted to move or speak, they turned to each other and slept, while across the South, the search for Kelly Sloan continued to escalate.

Michael Forest was livid. Being accused of selling out a fellow agent was not only humiliating but infuriating, but it wasn't Kelly Sloan that he was mad at. It was the situation.

He'd started an investigation inside the ranks of the DEA that would put a Federal Grand Jury to shame. And he'd set a fire under the Federal prosecutor, Robert Marsh, that was echoing his own investigation. Forest wanted to be confident that the mole was not within their ranks, and yet how could he be sure? Kelly Sloan was well within her rights to be mad as hell. She'd put her life on the line by going undercover in the first place. Escaping three days of torture should have, at the least, garnered her a letter of commendation. Instead, she was still on the run, with a two-million-dollar bounty on her head and no one she felt she could trust.

Suddenly his phone rang. He reached across his desk to answer it, frustration still strong in his voice.

"This is Forest."

"Michael, it's me, Robert."

The Federal prosecutor sounded far too chipper to suit Michael's case.

"Do you have any news?" he asked.

"Yes, actually, I do," he said. "You were right. We had a guy selling information to Gruber. He's been arrested, although, as you said earlier, the damage has already been done. All I can say is how sorry I am that this is affecting your agent. Have you heard from her again? Do you know if she's all right?"

"I don't know anything except what I told you before. So if you want answers, I suggest you pray."

Michael Forest hung up, relieved that the traitor had been identified and arrested, but that didn't fix what was already broken.

Kelly woke to the sound of rain, then felt the heat of another body behind her back and remembered what she'd done.

God. Making love to Quinn had been a revelation. He'd brought out a sexuality in her that she hadn't known existed and, at the same time, had given her a renewed faith in herself. Not until she'd felt the surge of life power from the climax of making love had she realized that she'd been going through the motions of living. During the three days of torture at Dominic Ortega's hands, she'd been subconsciously preparing herself to die. When she escaped instead, she had liberated her body but not her soul. It had been tangled up with old fear and pain until the touch from a dark-eyed Texan had set it free.

She turned, still locked within the safety of Quinn's arms, and found him watching her.

"Hi," she said softly.

He leaned forward and kissed her forehead, then her lips. "It's raining," he said.

She nodded. "Yeah, I heard it."

"You know what my favorite thing to do is?" he asked. "No."

"Make love when it rains. What about you?"

She traced the shape of his eyebrows, then his mouth, with the tip of her finger and frowned.

"I think I have a new favorite thing."

"What?" Quinn asked.

"You."

Emotion stifled what Quinn had been going to say. Instead, he cupped the side of her face and pulled her close.

Rain peppered against the roof as Kelly crawled on top of Quinn. Her eyes were bright with unshed tears as he lifted her up, then slowly lowered her down onto his erection. She sighed as his body filled her, then cried out from the pleasure as he started to move.

Luis de Jesus and his partner, Armenio, were coming out of a Texaco truck stop outside Oklahoma City when the first highway patrol car appeared. They thought nothing of it until two more topped the hill right behind the first.

Armenio looked at Luis, then threw down the bag of chips and bottle of pop he'd been carrying and ran toward the car. Luis was right behind him. By the time Luis had the key in the ignition, the first patrol car had slammed to a stop, blocking the only exit. The patrolman was out of his car and kneeling behind the open door of his cruiser, yelling for them to get out. The other two patrol cars added to the melee by stopping on either side of the first, creating a phalanx of black and white.

Luis was reaching for his gun when Armenio grabbed his arm.

"No, Luis. They will kill us."

"And Ortega will kill us if we fail."

Armenio cursed and then threw himself out of the door onto the ground, screaming at the police not to shoot.

Luis chose the other way out and opened fire.

It was over in a matter of seconds. The third shot entered Luis de Jesus's head near his ear and exited—with a large portion of his brains—into the back seat.

Armenio started talking before they could get him off the ground. By the time he was handcuffed and situated in the back of a patrol car, the patrolman knew they had more than they'd bargained for.

The patrolman got on the radio, eyed the man in the back of his car, then keyed the mike.

"This is Whaley. Someone tell the captain to notify the Oklahoma State Bureau of Investigation. We've got someone I think they need to see."

As the car pulled away, Armenio looked back, saw the body of his friend lying on the ground in a spreading pool of blood and breathed a sigh of relief. He was alive. That was all that mattered.

There was a party going on in the Dead Pig, outside of Jackson, Mississippi. As bars went, it was on the lower rung of society, as were the patrons who frequented it. The theme of the party was something new—sort of a scavenger hunt for ex-cons and lowlife. They called it Hunt the Fed, and with a two million dollar prize for the winner, the crowd was growing by the hour. Sometime during the last forty-eight hours, a picture of Kelly Sloan, along with a description and the tag number of Quinn McCord's truck, had begun to circulate within the underbelly of society. A stack of photocopies of her picture were sitting at the end of the bar beside a half-empty bowl of pretzels and an unopened bottle of beer.

Suddenly someone let out a rebel yell and then shot off a gun. For a heartbeat the sudden silence after the roar was startling. Then the shooter, a long-haired biker with a death's-head tattoo on his forehead, yelled, "Let's get it on!"

The bar emptied within seconds, as men and women alike grabbed a copy of her picture, then raced for their vehicles. Nearly one hundred cars, vans and trucks, as well as a half-dozen Harleys, took to the highway. The race was on to find a woman named Kelly and claim the prize for her life.

Kelly was finishing the last bite of a sausage biscuit when Quinn came back to the Tuskeegee motel. He'd been gone for almost an hour, and Kelly had been starting to worry. But now he was back, and the grin on his face was contagious. Kelly found herself returning the smile even before she knew why.

"What?" she asked.

"You ready to ride?"

"Yes. I saved you a sausage biscuit," she said.

"Hold it for me until we get on the road. Is everything in the bag?"

"Yes, but I still want to know what's so funny."

"You'll see," Quinn said, and picked up the suitcase with their joint collection of clothes. Then he eyed her black leather and new hairdo, and his grin widened. "We were definitely on the same wavelength yesterday. You're gonna fit the new ride just fine."

"I don't get it," she said.

"You will."

Quinn exited first, casually sweeping the parking lot with a careful gaze before moving aside for her to follow.

Kelly came out the door, then stood on the stoop, waiting to see where Quinn went. When he headed to the monster truck parked near the office, her mouth dropped. She couldn't decide which was worse, the black and orange flames down the sides or the Confederate flag on the hood. As for the new tires, they'd elevated the clearance of the truck by several feet. She wasn't sure she would be able to get in without help.

"That's your truck?"

"Yep. This is it," he said. "Hop in."

Kelly walked toward the passenger side, then looked up at the door handle.

"Got a ladder?"

Quinn opened the door, then grabbed her around the waist and lifted her into the cab. While Kelly was settling in, he tossed their suitcase in the truck bed then slid behind the wheel. When he fired up the engine, it rumbled lightly. The sound was similar to jet wash before takeoff as he put it in gear.

"Who did this?"

"A guy named Little Ed."

"Is anything on here legal?"

"I doubt it."

Kelly laughed. "This just might work after all."

"That was the plan," Quinn said, and drove out of the parking lot and back onto the street. A few minutes later they were back on the main highway, still heading north.

Twenty-seven hours later, a green Ford 4 x 4 pulled up in front of Little Ed's Paint and Body Shop. Little Ed looked up and then started to grin.

"Françoise, you old son of a bitch! Long time no see!"

Françoise Marin was a man who'd lived hard and large

and paid often for the price by chalking up a sizable rap sheet. He'd been on the road for the better part of the week in search of his own pot of gold. The picture in his pocket was his ticket to the easy life. All he had to do was find a woman named Kelly Sloan, then make a call.

"Hot damn, Little Ed. You got to cut back on those pork ribs or you're gonna pop."

"We all die," Little Ed said. "What brings you to Tuskeegee?"

"A leaking radiator hose," Françoise said. "Figured you might be able to help me out."

"Sure, sure," Little Ed said. "Business has been pretty slow. Except for a fancy paint job yesterday morning, I ain't had a customer all month."

"What? Don't people around here ever wreck their cars?"

Little Ed grinned. "That ain't the trouble. Just not too many people around here can afford a car to drive."

"Yeah, well, then they need to get on the same trail I'm on and their luck might turn," Françoise said, as he kicked back in an old iron chair and took the cold soda that Little Ed handed him. "Thanks," he said, and took a long drink.

"You're welcome," Little Ed said, as he settled his bulk onto a long iron bench. "Now tell me about this lucky trail you're following."

Françoise took a piece of paper out of his pocket and handed it to Little Ed.

"Look at this," he said.

Little Ed unfolded the paper. He wasn't a good reader, but the number, two million, quickly jumped out at him. The woman's face was unfamiliar. He laid the paper aside as he reached for a bag of peanuts. He tore it open and popped a handful into his mouth before looking at Françoise.

"So what's the deal with this woman? What has she done?"

"Who knows?" Francoise said, then added. "Who cares? She's worth two million to someone. I intend to find her."

"Who hired you?" Little Ed asked.

"Oh hell, no one hired me," Françoise said. "I picked up this paper in Missouri, but I seen others around. There was a bunch of them floating around the Mississippi delta country."

"You sayin' that everybody and their hound dog is on the hunt for this woman?"

"I reckon."

"Damn, Françoise. You ain't got a snowball's chance in hell of being the lucky one, and you know it."

Françoise shrugged. "Someone's gotta find her. Why can't it be me?"

"I guess," Little Ed said, and dumped the rest of the package of peanuts into his mouth.

Françoise picked up the paper and, as he had countless times in the past few days, stared at the image of Kelly Sloan's face.

"Reckon she knows about this hunt?" Little Ed asked.

"Probably."

"If she's smart, she'll change her looks."

"Yeah, I thought of that," Françoise said. "They say she's with this guy drivin' a black Dodge truck. Probably changed that, too, but I'm not ready to quit."

Little Ed gasped, then choked on the half-eaten nuts in his mouth. Françoise thumped him on the back several times until he caught his breath. When he could talk without coughing, Little Ed grabbed the paper out of Françoise's hands.

"Let me see that again," he said.

Suddenly it dawned on Françoise that Little Ed had choked on more than peanuts. He grabbed his old friend by the arm and yanked him around.

"What? What do you know? Tell me, damn it!"

Little Ed looked past Kelly's picture to the small print beneath it.

Black Dodge truck, then the tag number. At that point he started to grin. He twisted out of Françoise's grasp and lumbered over to the trash bin, then dumped it onto the floor. Empty beer bottles and pop cans fell out, along with a pile of used grease rags and a handful of disposable face masks that Little Ed used when painting. He kicked the refuse aside and then, with great effort, bent over and picked up the license plate that he'd taken from Quinn's truck.

He turned around and waved it at Françoise.

"I get a cut of the take."

Françoise bolted to his feet, his heart thumping. "Where in hell did you get this?"

"Took it off the paint job yesterday. The man wanted a new look to his ride. I gave it to him…for a price."

Françoise stared, unable to believe what he'd stumbled onto. If it hadn't been for a worn-out radiator hose, he never would have sidetracked to Tuskeegee.

"Half a million," Françoise said. "Just tell me what he's driving."

"That sounds fair," Little Ed said, and gave him a description of what he'd done to the truck.

"Help me fix that radiator hose," Françoise said.

Little Ed grinned. "I'll do it. You go get yourself something to eat. You gotta keep up your strength. He's got a whole day's jump on you."

An hour later, Françoise was back. Little Ed slammed the hood down on his car and handed him the keys.

"He headed north out of town," Little Ed said. "Now don't forget to stay in touch."

"You got it," Françoise said, and took off, heading north.

* * *

Will Travis's pager went off just as he was finishing the paperwork on Daryl Connelly's assault. It did him good to know they'd nailed the perps responsible. He glanced down at the pager, then frowned. It was Houston Medical. He reached for the phone.

A few minutes later he disconnected, then turned around and walked to the window. It was a hot, muggy day in Houston, with the ever-present thunderheads hovering off the coast, promising a chance of rain later in the day.

Daryl Connelly was dead. The news staggered him. He'd thrown a blood clot and died. That suddenly.

He swiped his hands across his face and then cursed. The paperwork he'd just filed on the Latino who called himself Armenio would have to be amended to murder.

"God damn the scum of this earth," he muttered, and reached for his phone.

Quinn pulled into a truck stop just outside of Mobile, Alabama, then killed the engine before he looked at Kelly.

"Hungry?" he asked.

She nodded, then stretched wearily.

"I think so," she said. "Either that or I'm faint from the sight of your beautiful face."

Quinn leaned across the seat and planted a hard, hungry kiss on her lips, then unbuckled her seat belt.

"Get out before I lay you down in the seat of the Fire Monster and have my way with you."

"Fire Monster?"

"Yeah. I like the sound of it. What do you think?"

"I think you enjoy being a chain-wearing, card-carrying redneck."

"Honey, I'm from Texas. Except for the chains, society already considers me a redneck. Let's eat."

Just as they started to get out, it began to rain.

"Shoot," Kelly said. "This is going to mess up my hair."

Quinn eyed the short red and black spikes and grinned. "It's already messed up," he said.

"Just for that, you pay for dinner," she said.

"Don't I always? Besides, I'll take it out in loving later."

They made it inside, laughing as they ran, and quickly took one of the last empty booths. Their rain-soaked entrance into the smokey truck stop café warranted little more than a few curious glances before the other diners went back to their meals.

The waitress appeared, took their orders for burgers and fries, and promised to return with their drinks. Quinn was watching a lingering raindrop rolling down the side of Kelly's face when he saw a red sports car wheel into the parking lot.

"Somebody's sure in a hurry," he said.

Kelly turned around, catching a glimpse of the car as it cruised through the lot. Something about the way the car was moving up and down the rows made her nervous.

"No. I think they're looking for someone," she said, and the moment she said it, she turned and looked at Quinn.

"Do you think—"

"Get up," he said. "Walk out the back door and wait for me. If I don't show, hitch a ride with one of the truckers and keep moving."

"No. We do this together or—"

"I'm the one with the gun," Quinn muttered. "Now do what I said."

As she was getting up, the car suddenly slid to a stop behind Quinn's truck.

"It's too late," she said, pointing out the window.

"Son of a bitch," Quinn said. "How did they find us?"

"Little Ed?"

"Get out, Kelly. Do it now!"

"No one is going to recognize me. I'm going out first. I'll get behind them, then you come out and head for the truck. There's only one guy in the car. Surely a DEA agent and a Texas Ranger can handle one bounty hunter.''

Then she headed for the door before he could argue.

"Damn it," he muttered, tossed some bills down on the table and followed her out the door.

Kelly shifted into a tough-girl stride as she came out of the café. Her head was up, her eyes shifting nervously as she gazed across the parking lot. Then she swiped her hand beneath her nose and combed her hands nervously through her hair, giving whoever might be looking the notion that she was nothing more than a junkie in need of a fix.

From the corner of her eye she saw the driver of the red car look at her and then look away. It was all she needed to know. She began to walk, moving parallel to Quinn's truck, then ducking behind an eighteen-wheeler. She squatted down and moved under it, then started working her way back toward the sports car.

Quinn came outside and headed toward his truck. The fact that his gun was under the front seat made him nervous. Two million dollars was enough to make a fool out of anyone. There was always the chance that the driver would shoot first and ask questions later. He palmed the car keys and hit the button on the remote to unlock it. As he did, the driver got out of his car.

"Hey, buddy," Quinn said. "You're gonna have to move your car so I can back out."

Françoise Marin was so high on excitement that he hadn't even noticed the man was alone. He stepped out from behind his car.

As he did, Quinn saw the gun. He held up his hands and started to talk.

"Come on now, buddy, let's take it easy here. I'll give you my money and we'll call it even. You go your way, I'll go mine."

"I don't want your money," Françoise said, almost dancing with glee. "I want your woman. Where is she?"

Quinn frowned. "Woman? I don't have any woman."

"You're lying," Francoise said, and waved the gun toward Quinn's head. "Talk to me now, or I'll shoot you where you stand."

"Look, man, I'm not married. Never have been, and I don't have any woman with me. Look around you, damn it. There's nothing around here but a bunch of trucks. I went in alone. I came out alone. How much plainer can I get?"

Françoise started to frown. This didn't make sense. The paper said the woman was with this man.

"What's your name?" Françoise asked.

"Henry Shepler. What's yours…Jesse James?"

Françoise shifted sideways. The man didn't seem rattled. Maybe Little Ed had been wrong. Maybe—

Kelly swung the crowbar she'd snagged from the underbelly of a truck, hitting Françoise Marin in the back of the head just above his neck. He grunted, then dropped.

Quinn grabbed the gun, then dragged the man between two parked semis.

"There's some nylon rope in the back of my truck. Get it for me," he said.

"I can't get in your damn truck. I'll hold the gun on him. You get the rope," Kelly said.

Quinn grinned, handed her the gun he'd confiscated from the man and ran to his truck. Moments later he was back. Quickly he tied the man up, gagged him with a handkerchief, then slapped a piece of duct tape over his mouth and dumped him in the back of an empty bull hauler.

"He's probably gonna stink some by the time he's found," Kelly said.

"Yeah, and judging by the tags on this truck, he's gonna be a long way from home."

"So they know your truck," Kelly said. "How do you think that happened?"

"I guess Little Ed isn't a man who can be trusted," Quinn said.

"I'd say you were right."

"Then what do you say we trade vehicles with our friend here?" he asked.

Kelly nodded. "At least I won't need a ladder to get inside."

"I'll get our things. Pop the trunk, okay?"

"That I can do," Kelly said, and hurried toward their new ride.

They were leaving without food and a little more anxious than they'd been when they'd arrived, but they were still alive—and they were still together.

About an hour later, Quinn handed Kelly his cell phone.

"Let's call Will Travis. I want to check on Daryl and see if anything else has come up that we should know about."

"Right," Kelly said, and dialed the number Quinn gave her.

When the phone started ringing, she handed it back to him.

Travis answered on the second ring.

"This is Travis."

"Travis, it's me. Quinn. How's Daryl doing?"

"He's dead, Quinn. Threw a clot and died. They're having a memorial service for him tomorrow, but no funeral. He wanted to be cremated. It's a hell of a thing to burn. Don't know if I'd have the guts to schedule it, even knowing I'd be dead."

Quinn couldn't think. He kept driving while struggling with the urge to cry. Travis kept talking, filling in the silence without knowing why.

"We caught the two bastards who did it. The desk clerk gave us a real good description of the two men, then identified their mug shots. We put out the call. They were spotted in Texas, then again in Oklahoma, where they were

arrested. Or I should say, where one was arrested. The other
one chose to shoot it out. He's dead. As for the one we've
got, he's still talking. But we do know for sure that they
were working for Ortega, at least indirectly. We're looking
for him now. Turns out he was treated at a Houston clinic,
but we got there too late. We have a pretty good guess at
where he's gone, though.''

"Is he still in the States?''

"We think so,'' Travis said. "At any rate, is there anything you need? Anything I can do?''

"Send flowers in my name.''

"Yeah. Sure. I'll do that.''

Quinn hung up, then laid the phone down before pulling
to the side of the road. He turned to Kelly. She was staring
out the window.

"He's dead, isn't he?'' she said.

"Yes.''

"God. Oh, God.'' Then she started to cry.

Quinn took her in his arms and cried with her.

7

About seven hours after Françoise Marin left Tuskeegee, Little Ed had a revelation. He'd thought of nothing else but the half million dollars he would get should Françoise find the woman. But he knew that was far from a sure thing, even with Françoise's inside information, and Little Ed was not a man to waste a good thing. So he began making calls—hedging his bets, so to speak—and sold his information to a few other men he knew would be interested. If Françoise came up empty, that didn't mean Little Ed had to lose, too.

And while he was hatching new plans, Quinn and Kelly continued their flight north. After learning about Daryl, their demeanor had taken on a somber tone. They had just under four days before the trial, and in normal circumstances could have made the drive from Alabama to D.C. in less than twenty-four hours. But that would have left them with three days to twiddle their thumbs and dodge bounty hunters around D.C. until the trial.

Once again Quinn took to the woods, so to speak, using old two-lane highways. Knowing that Little Ed had probably been the one to finger them made him nervous. Uncertain as to how far the tentacles of his involvement might reach, it was still evident that he'd put a huge dent in their plans.

They drove all night, stopping twice for gas and once for food and a rest stop. The last time they'd stopped, Kelly had taken the wheel, and she was now driving as Quinn slept. He was still sleeping when they crossed the line into West Virginia. The old highway on which they were driving threaded deep through the heart of Appalachia, winding up the mountains like an errant string that had come undone from a discarded ball of yarn. Ancient and towering trees bordered both sides of the thin ribbon of concrete, shading the pavement from the early morning sun.

Just as Kelly started up another steep incline, the red sports car started to sputter. Quinn sat up with a jerk.

"What's happening?" he asked, looking around in sleepy confusion.

"The car...I think it's about to give up the ghost."

"Damn it," Quinn said. "Maybe it's just out of gas."

Kelly glared. "I'm a woman, but I'm not stupid. It's not out of gas. The tank is over half full."

No sooner had she said that than the car clattered and died.

"Well, hell," Quinn said, and reached for his cell phone. He turned it on, only to find he had no signal.

"It's the mountains," Kelly said.

"Great. Now what?" he said, as she guided the car over toward the side of the road as it rolled back down the slope.

"I don't know about you, but since there are no rest rooms in sight, I'm going to find a bush. After that, we'll talk, okay?"

Quinn sighed with frustration. "Yeah, sure. I might walk up the hill a ways and see if I can't get a signal."

Kelly nodded, then got out of the car and quickly disappeared into the brush at the side of the road. Quinn watched until he was sure she was safely out of sight, then started hiking up the hill.

Françoise Marin came to in a pile of half-dried cow dung. He rolled over on his back, realizing he was tied and gagged, and then closed his eyes against the glare of early morning sunshine. He inhaled sharply, then flinched as the smell of cow dung hit him full force. He froze, then forced himself to think of something else instead of the overwhelming urge to puke. He would be damned before he'd die in his own vomit.

Finally his stomach settled and the urge passed. He tried to stand up, but the empty cattle trailer in which he was riding kept bouncing like a Nerf ball against a net. Every time the tires rolled over a bump in the road, he fell back to his knees. His head hurt like hell, and his clothes were matted with something dark, wet and green. As he stumbled and bounced, he mentally vowed that if he ever got his hands on Kelly Sloan, he would kill her for free.

After several false starts, he managed to pull himself upright, and as he did, he realized his troubles were about to be over. There was a van tailgating the truck, and the driver had just spotted him. He could see the man gesturing wildly to the woman beside him. Françoise leaned against the trailer, hoping they could see that he was bound and gagged, then hung on for dear life as the trucker took a turn too fast.

The driver of the van saw Françoise fall. Believing that the trucker was a kidnapper, he grabbed his cell phone and called the highway patrol.

When the highway patrol finally arrived and stopped the truck, no one was more surprised than the trucker himself. Not wanting to be questioned too closely by the police, Françoise explained away the incident by concocting a wild story about drinking with friends, then passing out, only to come to in the truck. He said it was just like his buddies to play a joke on him like this, and that when he got home, he was going to get them good.

Finally convinced that no real crime had been committed, the highway patrolman let everyone go except for Françoise, who was now forced to ride with the trooper to the nearest town. Only he had to undress before the trooper would let him in the car. Françoise pulled off everything except his boxer shorts and T-shirt, then crawled into the back. It was the first time he'd ever been in a cop car and not been under arrest.

The trooper had little to say except to suggest that he take a bath and get some new clothes before buying a bus ticket home. They stopped at a small town on the outskirts of Phoenix, Arizona, told the local police chief what had happened, and asked for permission for Françoise to clean up at the local jail. Since the man could hardly walk down main street in his underwear, the chief quickly agreed.

Françoise washed out his clothes and then washed himself, before asking directions to the nearest bus stop. Dressed in dripping clothes and limping from the bruises from falling in the truck, he made a hasty exit.

Once at the bus station, he made a frantic call to Little Ed, told him of the latest development, then bought a ticket home.

Little Ed quickly put out the word that Quinn and Kelly were now driving Françoise's red sports car, and the race to Hunt the Fed took a new and dangerous turn.

Quinn was almost at the top of the hill when he heard the sound of a car coming up the grade behind him. While there was every reason to assume it was just normal traffic, he still wasn't willing to take the chance. So he glanced down at the phone, saw that there was still no signal and darted off the road into the trees. He stood for a few moments, debating with himself as to what he should do next, then started running toward the last place he'd seen Kelly.

Kelly was on her way back to the car when she, too, heard the engine. She stopped suddenly; then, remembering the sports car from the truck stop, she darted behind a large pine tree and settled down to make sure the car went past. From where she was standing, she couldn't see Quinn, but she told herself he was fine. As she waited, it occurred to

her to go out and flag the car down. It would definitely be
a way out of their current predicament. But there was also
the chance that it was someone who was after her. Frustrated by the mess she was in, she decided to wait it out.

The car's engine was pulling hard, as if the grade of the
hill was too steep for it to climb. Quinn ran without stopping, dodging low-hanging branches, and jumping dead
logs and brush. He saw the back of Kelly's head just as the
new arrival pulled to a stop beside their stalled car.

Oh hell. Either a Good Samaritan had arrived or it was
someone looking to boost what was left of an abandoned
vehicle—or worse. He stopped moving immediately and
took cover behind some trees. He picked up a small rock
and tossed it at Kelly. It hit her on the back of her shoulder.
When she turned, he motioned for her to take cover.

She nodded, then slowly moved backward until she
reached a clump of oak trees with some heavy undergrowth
beneath. Without hesitation, she dropped to the ground,
then belly-crawled into the thicket.

At that point Quinn took his handgun from the back
waistband of his jeans and flipped off the safety—just in
case.

Harley and Pointer Green were brothers. They did everything together, including steal. But theft wasn't what
they had on their minds as they came to a halt beside what
was left of Françoise Marin's red car. They'd gotten a call
a couple of days ago from a cousin twice removed who
lived in Oklahoma. He had told them about the woman and
the two million dollar bounty, and had even faxed them a
copy of the paper with her picture. They'd had to go to the
tag agency in Burn County to pick it up and then been
forced to endure the curious stare from the clerk who'd
obviously read it before finally handing it over. Yesterday
they'd learned about the change in vehicles and had been
driving aimlessly ever since. Truth was, Harley Green had

been more than a little stunned when they'd come around the bend and seen the very car in question parked at the side of the road.

"That's it, Harley! I swear to God, that's the car. Ooowee, we're gonna be rich!" Pointer yelled.

Harley Green lifted the rifle from the back seat of their extend-a-cab truck and frowned.

"Why don't you yell a little louder and let them know we're comin'?"

Pointer frowned. "Hell, Harley, I didn't mean nothin'. I was just excited, is all."

"Yeah, well, remember what Momma always said? 'Don't count your chickens a'fore they's hatched'? You don't see no man or woman around here, do you? Chances are this car broke down and they took off on foot. Or even worse, they hitched a ride out. If they did, we ain't gonna find them nowhere around."

Pointer frowned. "I hadn't thought about that."

"That's why you got me," Harley said, then thumped his brother lightly on the shoulder. "Now come on. Let's see what we can see."

They exited their truck and headed for the car. When they realized it was unlocked, they started going through everything in sight.

Quinn cursed himself and the situation in general as he watched them tearing through their things. Then he heard the taller of the two men say something that made his skin crawl.

"They didn't take nothin'," Harley said, as he dumped the contents of their suitcase out on the road. "Right here's their clothes and even some money. I lay odds they're off in them trees."

"Maybe they's gettin' themselves some," Pointer said.

Harley frowned. "It ain't ever'one who feels the need to fuck at ever' turn in the road. They's probably hidin'." Get your gun. I'll take that side of the road. You take the other.''

Pointer Green ran back to the truck, pulled out a long-range hunting rifle with a telescopic sight and started walking toward Quinn and Kelly, while the other brother took the other side of the road.

Quinn glanced toward Kelly's place of concealment and held his breath, knowing that a confrontation was inevitable and the slack-jawed man coming toward them was packing a rifle with a gauge higher than his IQ.

Kelly had palmed the handgun she'd taken off Françoise Marin the moment she'd hit the ground, and she was now lying as flat and still as she could, with the gun aimed directly toward the highway. When she saw a rifle-bearing stranger approaching her place of concealment, she tensed. Her finger was steady on the trigger, waiting for him to make a move, when she heard him start to shout.

Pointer was beside himself when he saw the tracks. They were small. It was the woman—the two-million-dollar woman—he just knew it. He turned toward the highway.

"Harley! Hey, Harley! I done found her tracks!"

Quinn groaned. It was all over now. He had to take this one out of commission before they double-teamed him. He stepped out from behind the trees with his gun aimed directly at Pointer Green's chest.

"Drop your weapon," he said softly. "Do it, and do it now."

Harley might have done it, but Pointer wasn't as smart. Panicked that he'd been caught off guard, he started shooting as he turned, pumping one shell after another into the chamber of the deer rifle and pulling the trigger.

Quinn dove to one side as he fired, knowing that his shots were probably going to miss. So when the man suddenly staggered and dropped with a bullet hole in his head, he didn't know what to think. Then, before he could react, Harley Green came bursting through the trees, shouting his brother's name.

"Pointer! Pointer! Answer me, damn it!"

"Drop your weapon!" Quinn shouted. "Now!"

Harley spun toward the sound of Quinn's voice and fired off a round.

The bullet dug a hunk out of the tree behind which Quinn was hiding. He flinched and ducked as he ran toward a new hiding place. Another round of rifle shots followed him; then there was one single shot, then silence.

He turned. Kelly was coming out of the brush. He saw the gun in her hand and realized that she'd just saved his life. For a moment neither of them moved as they looked at each other, then at the two bodies on the ground.

"What are we going to do with them?" Kelly asked.

"Leave them," Quinn said. "We can tell the authorities later."

Kelly nodded and walked past them without looking down.

Quinn removed the hunting rifles from the men's hands, then followed Kelly out of the woods. When he got to the highway, she had gathered up the clothes the brothers had scattered and was unloading the things from the red car and tossing them in the back of the Green brothers' truck.

"Your turn to drive," she said, and got into the cab without further comment.

Quinn sighed. He knew what she was feeling. He got in, shoved a can of Skoal off the seat and tossed some empty beer cans out of the car onto the road.

"You're littering," Kelly said.

"Arrest me," Quinn said, then started the engine and drove away.

They'd been driving for nearly fifteen minutes, and Kelly had yet to speak. Quinn kept glancing at her from time to time, trying to read her expression, but it was hopeless. He reminded himself never to play poker with her. She would probably win. Finally he reached across the seat and took her hand.

"Thanks for saving my life," he said softly.

She shuddered, then looked at him. "This has got to stop. If I don't do something now, it's only going to get worse."

"What do you suggest?" he asked.

"Find a place where your cell phone will work. I need to make a call."

Quinn frowned. "Are you going to call your boss? Now? After all that's happened?"

"Just do it.... Please," she added.

Quinn shrugged, handed her his phone and then kept driving.

"Tell me when you get a signal," he said.

She took the phone. A few minutes later she grabbed at his arm.

"Stop! Right here. There's a good clear signal."

Quinn hit the brakes and pulled off onto the shoulder.

Kelly was looking around the area for a landmark on which to base their location when she realized there was a mile marker only a few yards ahead. She got out of the truck. Quinn followed, watching as she punched in a series of numbers.

Then she suddenly sat down on the side of the road, as if her legs would no longer hold her upright. Quinn hurried to her side just in time to hear what she was saying.

"Jen, it's me. Kelly. Yes, I know. It *has* been a long time. I miss you, too, but that's not the reason I called. I need you to do me a favor. Call your daddy. I need help, Jen, and I need it now, or I'm dead."

Quinn frowned. He couldn't figure out why the hell she was calling a girlfriend instead of her boss at the DEA.

"Tell him it's regarding a case for the Federal prosecutor," Kelly added. "Give him this number, and please, *please,* tell him to call me right back. I'll be waiting."

She rattled off the phone number, then disconnected.

Quinn laid a hand on the back of her neck. She was trembling so hard that he could feel the muscle spasms beneath his fingers.

"Kelly…honey…talk to me. Tell me what you're doing."

She looked up at him, weariness etched in every facet of her expression.

"I should never have involved anyone in this. It was my case. My business. It got Daryl killed, and if something doesn't change, you'll be next."

Quinn sighed. "We've already been through this. I knew what I was doing from the start, and so did Daryl. But I don't understand what you're doing now. Who's Jen, and why would you ask her father for help?"

Before she could answer, Quinn's phone rang. She looked down at the caller ID and then answered.

"Hello, Mr. President. Yes, sir, thank you for taking my call."

Charles Barrett leaned back in his chair in the Oval Office.

"It's been a while since the college days, hasn't it, dear? I trust you're well?"

Kelly sighed. "Only for the moment. That's why I'm calling. I have a problem."

President Barrett frowned. "Yes, you do, don't you, girl? We know about the bounty. I've spoken to Michael Forest, as well as Marsh, who's the prosecutor on the Gruber case. We know what's happening. How can I help you?"

Kelly bit her lower lip to keep the tremble out of her voice. Back in college, she wouldn't have thought twice about letting her best friend's father see her cry. But that was before Charles Allen Barrett had become President of the United States. Now the least she could do was maintain the decorum of an agent of the Federal government.

"I need help. Could you send someone to come get me?"

"Consider it done," President Barrett said. "Tell me where you are."

She gave him the coordinates of the highway number and mile marker, as well as the style of vehicle they were in.

"Help will be there within the hour," Barrett said.

Kelly sighed with relief. "Thank you, Mr. President. I don't know how to thank you."

"I do," Barrett said. "I understand you have plans to testify at the Capitol within the next few days. You would make Helen and I very happy if you would be our house-guest until that time."

"Sir! In the White House?"

Charles Barrett smiled. "Can you think of a place that's safer?"

"No, sir."

"Neither can I," he said. "And I understand you've had a partner of sorts along the way. Please extend the invitation to him, as well."

"Yes, sir, and thank you, sir," Kelly said.

"No, Agent Sloan. It's we who should be thanking you. Now watch the skies. Help will come soon."

There was a click in Kelly's ear. She disconnected the call and handed Quinn his phone.

"It's going to be okay," she said.

But Quinn was too stunned to move. "Who was that on the phone?"

"You heard me," she said. "It was President Barrett."

"He just calls you…like that?"

Kelly shrugged. "His daughter, Jennifer, and I were roommates all through college. She's my best friend. I've stayed at their home many times in the past, but never since the election."

Quinn sat down beside her and then put his arm around

her. She resisted for a moment, then laid her head on his shoulder. Sometimes it felt good to have someone to lean on.

"Thank you," she said softly.

"For what?" Quinn said.

"For everything. Oh, and by the way, we're staying in the White House until the trial."

Quinn hugged her and grinned. "You know something, I would have taken a vacation years ago if I'd known it would be like this."

Kelly tried to laugh, then choked on a sob. She laid her head down on her knees and prayed for this day to be over.

Fifteen minutes passed, then twenty, then twenty-five. They were still sitting on the shoulder of the road when Kelly suddenly looked up.

"They're here," she said, and jumped to her feet.

Quinn followed her, trying not to gawk as two helicopters appeared over the trees.

"He sent Blackhawks?"

"Nothing but the best," Kelly said, and breathed a huge sigh of relief as the first chopper landed and a half-dozen of Uncle Sam's finest jumped out. Four of them took a defensive stance with rifles drawn, while two others came toward them.

"Agent Sloan?" the first marine asked.

"Yes, and this is Texas Ranger Quinn McCord," Kelly said.

"Ranger," the marine said, acknowledging Quinn's presence with a sharp nod. "If you and Agent Sloan would follow me...."

Quinn started back to the truck to get their bag when the second marine stopped him.

"Sir, we'll see to your things. They'll be delivered to your quarters. Just get in the chopper."

Quinn nodded, then added, "About a half hour's drive

west, you'll find a red sports car on the side of the road. There are two bodies on the north side, up in the trees.''

"Yes, sir. We'll take care of it.''

"Appreciated,'' Quinn said, and grabbed Kelly's hand. Moments later they were climbing into the Blackhawk, surrounded by six armed marines, who then got in behind them. But it wasn't until later, when Kelly saw the dome of the White House below her, that she let herself believe the worst might be over.

The houseman was in the act of serving the first course of Ortega's dinner when there was a knock on the door. Ortega flinched. The soup spoon he was holding clattered to the floor as he stood abruptly.

The houseman stepped back. "Sir?''

"I am not receiving visitors. Whoever it is, get rid of them,'' Ortega ordered.

"Yes, sir,'' the man said, and headed for the front door.

Ortega held his breath, listening to the sound of the butler's receding footsteps, and told himself it didn't mean anything. There was no way the authorities could know where he was. But then, neither did anyone else, so there should have been no one to come calling at his door.

He could hear voices, but not what was being said. He thought about slipping out the back way, but then where could he go? There was nothing back there but ocean, and even if he were whole and healthy, he could not swim to Mexico. So he waited. It was the wrong thing to do.

Suddenly there were too many footsteps coming back into the dining room to bode well. He glanced about the luxurious room, eyeing the elegant fixtures and the scent of perfectly prepared food, and knew that this lifestyle was over. What he had to consider now was if he would have a life left to live.

Four men in dark suits entered the dining room ahead of a frantic butler.

"Señor Ortega, I tried to—"

"It's all right, Emilio. This is none of your concern."

One of the suits stepped forward. "Dominic Ortega, I'm Agent David Harwell with the FBI. You are under arrest for the attempted murder of DEA agent Kelly Sloan, as well as the murders of Javier Sosa and Mitchell James. You are also being indicted on charges of the sale of illegal substances, racketeering and blackmail. You have the right to an attorney. Should you not be able to afford one, one will be made available to you."

The agent continued the Miranda Warning, but Ortega had heard it before and blanked it out. His thoughts were focused on Sosa and James, two men who'd made the mistake of getting in his way. It was ironic that he was being charged with those murders only, when there had been so many before and after. And if it hadn't been for his weak-kneed brother-in-law and the woman who'd put a knife in his chest, he would still be riding the wave. As it was, it was time to focus on what he could do to get out of this. There was still the bounty out on Kelly Sloan, and if his luck held, she would never make it to the courtroom.

8

Never in her wildest dreams would Kelly have imagined herself sleeping in the Lincoln bedroom, let alone with the man who'd stolen her heart. The past three days in the White House had been heaven compared to what she'd endured the month before. But never had she wanted anything to be over as much as she did this trial. Once her testimony went on record, her connection to Ortega and Gruber would be severed. They might hate her guts. They still might want her dead. But it was not going to change their fate. And that was what she was holding on to with all her might. She couldn't bear to think that she would be a target forever, or that Ortega would want revenge so badly that he would continue the bounty after he was convicted. And yet, because she couldn't ignore that possibility, she wouldn't let herself think of a future with Quinn.

President Barrett had been emotionally supportive, and to her knowledge, no one, not even her boss or the prosecutor in charge of Ponce Gruber's trial, knew where she was. That was something else for which she had the President to thank. She'd been sheltered behind the impenetrable wall of security that protected him on a daily basis, protected without anyone's knowledge but a special few.

But it would soon be over. She knew Dominic Ortega had been arrested. Today she would appear at his arraignment. She couldn't wait to see the expression on his face.

It would be all the justice she needed for what she'd endured at his hands.

Two days ago a team from the FBI had gone to her local post office in Maryland, where her mail was being held. They'd confiscated the lot, including a large, paper-wrapped package that she'd sent to herself while still in Mexico. Inside were documented invoices, taped phone calls, and copies of both personal and business correspondence pertaining to Dominic Ortega's illegal activities. Everything had been turned over to the Federal prosecutor without explanation, other than to say that when the time came, he was to call Kelly Sloan to the stand. The prosecutor had begged for more information. But the agents only knew what they'd been told and repeated their message one more time before leaving him to deal with a box of new evidence.

Within the hour she would be leaving for the Federal courthouse, and it was all she could do to face herself in the mirror. She'd taken on the persona of a biker babe to stay alive, but the need for a disguise was over. The only problem was, she still had a butchered haircut and a limited wardrobe. Why hadn't she thought of that earlier?

As she was bemoaning her appearance, Quinn knocked on the bathroom door.

"Kelly…honey…it's me. Can I come in?"

She ran a brush through her hair again, then groaned in dismay when it spiked back up into short, unruly tufts. The only saving grace was that she'd abandoned the red hair spray that had adorned it before.

"Only if you're carrying superhold hair spray," she mumbled.

The door opened. "I'll go you one better," Quinn said.

He handed her a half-dozen boxes from an exclusive D.C. boutique.

"For me?"

"Yes, unless you're hoping I'll bend my gender. Besides, they're not my size."

Kelly laid them all on the bed, then started digging through the boxes. Almond-colored lingerie edged with silky-soft lace spilled out onto the bed, followed by a turquoise pantsuit that was a perfect blend of business and beauty. When Kelly saw the pink and turquoise camisole he'd picked to go under it, she started to grin. The last box held a pair of backless silver sandals with a two-inch heel.

"Oh, Quinn, how did you know?" Kelly said.

"It's not that I wouldn't have loved to see you in that black leather again, but I figured the judge would appreciate this a little more."

Kelly threw her arms around his neck. "Thank you. Thank you a million times."

"Not two million?"

She made a face. "That's real funny, mister. Now stand back. I don't have much time to get ready, but thanks to you, I'll look as good as I feel."

He touched her hair, loving the feel of it beneath his fingers.

"You know…this is starting to grow on me. I'm liking the look."

Kelly frowned as she combed her fingers through her hair again.

"It looks like I've been rolling in the hay."

Quinn grinned. "Maybe that's why I like it so much. You've got the look of a woman who's spent the night having mind-blowing sex with the man of her dreams."

Kelly smirked. "And that would be you, I suppose?"

"I try," Quinn said. "Now hurry and get dressed. There's one more box you need to open, but not unless we have the time."

Kelly's eyes widened. She looked around for the box, then assumed he'd left it in the hall.

"I'm hurrying," she said, and started yanking off her robe and trading her Wal-Mart underwear for the delicate lingerie on the bed.

Within minutes she was dressed except for the shoes, which Quinn helped her put on. Then she stepped back and held out her arms.

"How do I look?"

The smile slid off Quinn's face as he looked at the woman who'd stolen his heart.

"Like an avenging angel," he said softly.

Kelly knew he was thinking about Daryl, and about everything that she'd gone through.

"I wish Daryl could be here to see this," she said.

"He's here in spirit. That will suffice," Quinn said, and then glanced at his watch. "With just enough time to spare."

"For what?" Kelly asked.

He pulled a small box out of his pocket, hesitated briefly, then handed it to her.

"This is for you, too, but only if you think it's right."

Kelly took a deep breath. There was only one thing that came in a small black velvet box like this. She looked up at Quinn, unaware that all the love she felt for him was there on her face. Her hands were shaking as she opened the box. The solitaire glittered as it caught the fire from the overhead lighting.

"Oh, Quinn," Kelly whispered.

"I love you," he said. "We've never said the words, and you don't have to say them back. And I'm not asking you to quit what you do, because part of what I love about you is the woman who saved herself and then saved me, too. But I *am* asking you to marry me. Whenever you can…whenever you're ready.''

Kelly handed him the box. ''Put this on me,'' she said. ''Then ask me again when this mess is over.''

Quinn's heart skipped a beat. ''Is this a sort-of yes?''

''No. It's a definite yes, with a rider as to when it will happen.''

Quinn slid the ring on her finger, then took her in his arms.

''You make me weak,'' he whispered, and held her close to his chest.

''And you make me crazy,'' Kelly said. ''Crazy in love.''

Before Quinn could answer, there was a knock on the door.

''It's time,'' she said, and then stepped out of his embrace. She held out her hand, and he took it. ''Let's get this over with,'' she said. ''I've got a life to live, and I'd like to finish it with you.''

Dominic Ortega looked like he'd stepped out of a men's magazine. His summer gray suit and pale yellow shirt were impeccably tailored to fit his short, stocky frame, giving it an air of elegance that he sorely needed to play the part of an innocent man. His dark hair had been cut close to his head, lying against his scalp like a thick black cap. He kept fiddling with the collar of his shirt, checking and then rechecking to make sure his tie was perfectly centered. His lawyer glanced at him, then frowned at the nervousness of his gestures. Ortega quickly dropped his hands into his lap. He didn't want to telegraph anxiety in any way.

''Just relax, Dominic. We've got it covered,'' his lawyer said.

Ortega nodded, then smoothed down his hair, making

sure it lay neatly, and leaned back in the chair. Moments later the court clerk came in, announced the arrival of the judge, and the proceedings began.

The give and take of legalities always left Dominic feeling as if he were out in left field. He heard the words but didn't always understand what they meant. He hated the Americans and their English-speaking courts. Everything was always so long and drawn out. It was his personal opinion that Americans should take a leaf out of Mexico's book of justice. If enough money was spent in the right place, a powerful man could always count on the judgment he desired. And right now, he desired these charges to be dismissed. And while he hadn't heard anything concrete about the hunt for Kelly Sloan, he felt certain that someone surely had her body and was waiting to claim the bounty. Once that happened, his troubles would be over.

And then the prosecutor said a name that made Ortega sit up. He stared at his lawyer, who was turning pale.

"What?" he whispered. "What did he just say?"

"They've called Kelly Sloan."

"She can't be here," Ortega muttered. "She's got to be dead."

The doors at the back of the room opened. Ortega turned in his seat, his gaze fixed on the opening. For a long quiet moment, no one appeared. Just when he thought it was all a hoax, she came through the doorway, then walked down the aisle.

She looked different. Still beautiful, but strong, almost defiant, and yet it was the same bitch who'd put a knife in his chest. Instinctively he leaned forward, fighting the urge to grab her and wring her neck before she could open her mouth.

She turned her head slightly—just enough that their gazes met—and then she smiled.

Ortega grunted as if he'd been punched, then leaned back in his chair. That was when he knew it was over. After that, everything happened in a blur. The words that came out of her mouth ended his hopes of freedom, and when the prosecutor introduced the evidence to corroborate her testimony, he knew he would be fortunate if they only gave him life. He heard the judge binding him over for trial and denying him bail. Then the judge made an announcement that sealed Ortega's fate.

"Given the severity of what Agent Sloan has endured, and the fact that there is still a two-million-dollar bounty on her head, it would be prudent for all concerned to note that her testimony today will be considered valid and binding, and that the transcript of it can be used as evidence in the upcoming trial without further need of Agent Sloan's physical presence."

Kelly hadn't known that was going to happen. She looked over Ortega's head to the back of the room, where Quinn was sitting, and saw him slump with relief. So he hadn't been the only one who'd feared further repercussions. But thanks to the judge, the pressure on Kelly was off for good.

The look the judge gave him made Ortega nervous. Without actual accusation, he'd laid down a warning to Dominic that he knew he should heed. Cursing the day he'd ever set eyes on the woman, he frantically whispered to his lawyer to pass the word along that the bounty had been withdrawn.

"Agent Sloan, you are excused," the judge said, and then added, "although it's not my place to do so, I feel that a public commendation of what you endured to make sure that justice has prevailed should be forthcoming. Having said that, I thank you on behalf of the citizens of the United States of America."

Kelly nodded, a little embarrassed by what he'd just said. "Thank you, sir, but I was just doing my job."

Then she got up from the witness stand, walked out of the courtroom and never looked back.

Epilogue _____

Two weeks had come and gone since the day of the arraignment. To make sure of her safety, the FBI had given out some of her story. The rest of it was conjecture, but they let the media run with it. A woman with a two-million-dollar bounty on her head was big news, but they'd done it with the media's assurance that they would stress the fact that the bounty had been withdrawn. The only thing waiting for someone who harmed Kelly Sloan was prison.

The news had accomplished what was necessary, which was making sure that every lowlife who'd been playing Hunt the Fed knew the sordid game was over. And while Kelly was profoundly grateful that her life was no longer in danger, the national coverage had destroyed a part of her career. Everyone knew her name and her face. There was no way she would ever be able to work undercover again.

Which brought her to Quinn. She hadn't seen him since the arraignment, and truth be told, she felt as if she were missing a piece of herself. The ring he'd put on her finger was a beautiful and vivid reminder of what they'd shared, but she wanted more—much more. She wanted Quinn every day, not the occasional long-distance phone call and empty bed existence since he'd been pulled back on the job. He'd told her that all she had to do was let him know she was ready and he would come to her. But somehow that felt wrong. Why should he be the one to drop his work when she was the one who was now free?

Ponce Gruber had waived his right to trial and pleaded out, thankful that he would not be facing the death penalty. Ortega was in a Federal prison up north, awaiting a trial that wouldn't take place for another six months, and Kelly was still on mandatory leave.

She had the time and she had the freedom to come and go as she chose. And the longer she thought about it, the more she realized where she needed to be.

She reached for the phone, made a reservation on the next flight to Fort Worth and went to pack a bag. She couldn't wait to see the look on Quinn's face.

Quinn was pulling into the parking lot of the headquarters of the Texas Rangers after a two-day investigation on the south side of Austin. He'd been driving for hours, had a headache the size of Dallas, and still had a good hour of paperwork before he could go home. Then he thought of how lonesome home had become since leaving Kelly in Maryland and decided the paperwork was better than another night alone.

The frown he was wearing deepened as he got out and started across the parking lot. On his way home from D.C., he'd called a towing company to retrieve his truck from the parking lot where they'd left it, then had it towed home. He'd managed to change the monster tires for normal ones and replace his license tag, but he still hadn't had time to get rid of the orange and red flames or the Confederate flag, a fact for which he caught hell on a daily basis from the other men.

He was halfway up the long flight of steps that led into the building when he heard a voice from above.

"Hey, McCord…long time no see, but what's the deal with that truck?"

He looked up. Kelly was standing at the top of the steps, dressed in black leather. His heart skipped a beat, and then another, as she started toward him.

"What's a girl to do when she goes to see her old man and he's a no show?"

Quinn dropped his briefcase, wrapped his arms around her and swung her off her feet.

"Kelly, sweetheart, you don't know how I've missed you."

She planted a kiss on his lips that sent him reeling. Someone whistled, while another man yelled at Quinn, "Hey, McCord, how'd you get a babe like that?"

Quinn looked up and saw another Ranger grinning at him from the top of the steps. Before he could answer, Kelly turned around, tilted her hip in a suggestive thrust and then put her hand in Quinn's back pocket.

"It's the truck," she said. "Can't get enough of it…or him."

The look on the Ranger's face was worth all the prior teasing.

"You're kidding, right?" the Ranger said.

Kelly leaned against Quinn, letting him feel the curve of her hip against his groin, and pushed. Not much, but just enough to remind him of what he'd been missing.

"I never kid about my man…or his truck," Kelly said, then turned around and whispered so only Quinn could hear, "Wipe that smile off your face or I'll blow your cover."

Quinn groaned, then kissed her again. "I love you, Kelly Sloan. Have you come to stay?"

"Yes, if you'll still have me," she said.

Quinn whooped aloud, then once again, then lifted her

off her feet and swung her around. By now quite a crowd had gathered to watch, most of whom Quinn worked with on a regular basis.

"Hey, Morris!" Quinn yelled, and then tossed his briefcase to the startled Ranger who was coming down the steps. "Put that on my desk, will you? And tell the captain that I'll be in tomorrow."

"You just got back, now you're leaving again?" Morris asked.

"Yeah, but I'm not going far," Quinn said. "I'm taking Candy here to meet my mother."

Morris's eyes widened as he looked from Quinn to Kelly and back again, trying to imagine what Quinn's homebody mother was going to say about the biker chick in black leather.

"I need to change first," Kelly said, as they started back down the steps.

"Hell no," Quinn said, as he guided her toward the now infamous truck. "They've been plaguing me for years about settling down. They're due for a good shock before they find out the truth."

Kelly grinned. "They may never forgive me for the deception."

"Naw, I promise you, honey. When they find out that you're not only on the up and up, but DEA, they're gonna kiss the ground you walk on."

"As long as you're the only one kissing me, it's a deal."

Quinn started the truck, then accelerated. Just for good measure, leaving rubber all the way to the street.

*Turn the page for a sneak peek
at the upcoming edge-of-your-seat stories
from these* New York Times
*bestselling authors
and MIRA Books*

*HAUNTED by Heather Graham
Available in paperback September 2003*

*COLD RIDGE by Carla Neggers
Available in paperback August 2003*

*OUT OF THE DARK by Sharon Sala
Available in paperback October 2003*

The dream came again.

Darcy had dreaded that it would, and she had been anxious as well, desperate to experience what had happened in this room, and *see*. See clearly, know exactly what had happened.

She entered into the mind of the man from the past. Saw what he saw.

The woman.

She was, the man knew—beneath the rage that had risen within him, a fury in his blood—always urgent, obsessive, beautiful. He had seen in her again everything that he had desired when she had appeared at the upper landing. He had seen the structure of her face, the shadow and light of the night, enhancing the curves of her body, granting moonlit magic to her hair. She could create a fire with a single glance, whisper words that could drive a man to a pure frenzy.

She could touch a man…and do so many things. Bring arousal to life in seconds, manipulate the senses, tear into the mind.

Ah, yes, and she could do so much more.

His head was spinning, torn with pain. And then she was running, but it appeared she did so in slow motion. He rose in much the same way, seeing the wall, the bed, the clock ticking away the seconds, minutes, hours.

Ticking away the night.

He staggered to his feet. She was running; he had to run too. She was so gorgeous in flight. Her appearance so fragile, so innocent. She ran....

As if she could escape.

She wasn't so fragile, and certainly not at all innocent.

Still he was far stronger.

And faster.

He followed her out the door.

Captured in the replay of the past, her own resource guiding her blindly, Darcy rose in her sleep, anxious to catch up with the specters of time gone by. She moved like a wraith in the night, sliding across the floor, opening the door—that through which the spirit images had so easily drifted.

She came to the landing, to the rail, and looked down the stairway.

But a sound behind her startled her back to life. She felt a fierce shove, slamming her hard against the upper landing rail, teetering precariously there for several seconds.

She came to full wakefulness in a split second, realized her position and instinctively fought to right it. She was strong enough herself, and quickly maintained her grasp and equilibrium, her mind working quickly and with out rage.

Someone real, alive and well, had been on the upstairs landing. She had heard a real noise. And real hands had attempted to push her over!

Righted, she spun around.

Matt's door was ajar.

Opening? Or closing?

She stood against the rail, her heart in her throat, staring. The door seemed to close another inch, and then opened.

In boxers and a robe, Matt emerged, striding out on the landing, eyes touching on Darcy, then looking up and down the second level.

"What are you doing out here?" The question sounded like a bark.

She swallowed hard. She knew him—didn't she? *Or did she think that she knew him because she had been so tempted to sleep with him?*

No. Whether or not they ever again spoke civil words to one another, she didn't believe that Matt Stone was the type of man who would push a woman over a railing to her death. *Was he?*

"Darcy! What's going on?"

Still, she hesitated. *She couldn't tell him.* She didn't believe that she had been accosted by a ghost, but then…it hadn't been until she had heard the noise, felt herself in extreme danger, that she had really snapped clearly from the force of the vision.

And if she told Matt that she believed she had been attacked—by either a ghost or a living being—he would start insisting again that she was somehow in danger. He would force her from the house. And her instincts were good—she could protect herself.

She hoped.

"I was just trying to…imagine what might have happened here," she lied.

"You should never stand leaning against a railing like that."

"No? I suppose not." She pushed away.

He was tense. His hands were knotted at his sides, his features drawn. She was certain he had no idea he looked so fierce.

"You shouldn't run around the house at night," he continued.

"Why not?" She was suddenly indignant.

"You know that I believe there's a person behind all this ghost crap."

"Oh? Who, Matt? You? Penny? Or do Carter and Clint slip into the main house at night? Or could it be the groundskeeper, Sam?"

"I don't know," he said flatly. "The point is, you, of all people, shouldn't be running around the house at night."

"Why me—of all people?"

"Because you've got an imagination that would put a child to shame."

"Really?" she inquired icily.

"Oh, come on, Darcy, that's the point. You believe everything that you say."

"Ah. Damn, I guess I really do need a psychiatrist," she said sarcastically.

"Maybe you do."

It seemed as if the words pained him. His fingers were still balled into fists. A pulse throbbed at his throat.

"Why are you so ridiculously angry with me?" she demanded.

"Because you've let this happen to you!" he exclaimed. "Darcy—"

He started to take a step toward her. She shook her head vehemently, backing away. "No, Matt, I haven't let anything happen to me. *You* should see the psychiatrist. You're so set in your ways it's amazing that you even agree to daylight saving time. Excuse me, will you? I'm going back to bed."

She walked by him, heading for the door to the Lee Room. As she passed him, it was almost as if he touched her. He didn't move. She could still feel the heat emitting from him in great waves. She could somehow feel his vitality, his tremendous strength, and his emotions.

She walked on by, breathing the scent of him. Not mean-to be. She didn't have an overactive imagination, and she wasn't acting. She *knew* ghosts existed.

Fuck him.

She could bend.

Matt Stone could not.

She wanted to cry. Spin around, beat against his chest. To what end? She had no power to change what lay within a man's mind. What she knew, what she did, had no tangible proof.

"Darcy?" Her name sounded somewhat strangled on his lips.

"Good night, Matt."

She walked into the Lee Room and closed the door.

The dream didn't come to her again that night. She slept easily, yet awoke with a strange sense of fear slipping into her thoughts.

The sense had nothing to do with ghosts.

She had slept on through the night; she had not been bothered again.

And yet, by day, her vision seemed clear, and her mind entirely rational. *Someone* had been out there on the landing with her last night.

Living, breathing.

And with deadly intent.

Cold Ridge

She walked slowly, in no hurry. Her hair was pulled back neatly, and she wore jeans, a black turtleneck, her barn coat and waterproof ankle boots, comfortable clothes that permitted her to go up and down ladders, trek over drop cloths and stacks of building supplies and tools, do whatever she had to do to get the picture she wanted. She was used to climbing mountains and edging across rock ledges to get the right light, the right color, the right composition. Negotiating house renovations didn't seem that daunting to her. It had been a quiet morning—she hadn't even taken her camera out of its bag. She was using her digital camera today, because Jodie Rancourt wanted to see it and get a better understanding of the technical differences between digital and film.

A shiny black sports car pulled alongside her, and Louis Sanborn, also newly employed by the Rancourts, rolled down his window and flashed his killer smile at her. "Hey, Ms. Photographer, need a ride over to the big house?"

Carine laughed. "Thanks for the offer, Mr. Security Man." He was tall and, despite his prematurely gray, scrub-brush hair, younger than he looked, probably just a year or two older than she was. He'd been hired two weeks ago as assistant to the chief of security for the Rancourts. "I don't mind walking. We won't get many more days like today. It's beautiful out."

"Only according to you granite-head types."

"It's in the fifties!"

"That's what I'm saying. Have a good lunch hour?"

"An excellent lunch hour."

"Me, too. See you over on Comm. Ave."

His car merged back into the Newbury Street traffic. Carine continued on up to Exeter Street, then cut down it to Commonwealth Avenue, the quintessential street of Boston's Back Bay with its center mall and stately Victorian buildings. All of Back Bay was on reclaimed land that used to be under water.

Still in no hurry, she sat on a bench on the mall, famous for its early springtime pink magnolias, now long gone by. A toddler ran after a flutter of pigeons, and Carine smiled, trying not to think about the babies she'd meant to have with Ty, instead feeling a momentary pang of regret. The toddler's mother scooped him up and swung him in the brisk November air, then set him back in his stroller. He was ticked off and started to kick and scream. He wanted to chase more pigeons. Two months ago—a month ago— the scene would have made Carine cry, but now she smiled. Progress, she thought.

She walked across the westbound lane to the brick-front historic mansion the Rancourts had snapped up when it came onto the market eighteen months ago. It was a rare find. The elderly owner had never carved it up into apartments—in fact, had done few renovations—and many of the original features were still intact. Hardwood floors, ornate moldings, marble fireplaces, chandeliers, wainscoting, fixtures. It had taken most of the past eighteen months for the team of architects, preservationists, designers and contractors just to come up with the right plans for what to do.

Carine's photography job could easily take her through the winter, while still leaving room for her to pursue other projects. She'd been at it for six weeks. Work would happen in a frenzy for a few days, the place crawling with people. Then everyone would vanish, and nothing would happen for a morning, an afternoon, even a week. That left her with spurts of time.

She noticed Louis Sanborn's car parked out front and smiled, shaking her head. Leave it to Louis to find a convenient parking space—she never could, and almost always took public transportation.

Since she'd left for lunch, someone had set out a pot of yellow mums on the front stoop, the wrought-iron rail cool to the touch as she mounted the steps to the massive dark wood door. It was open a crack, and she pushed it with her shoulder and went in, immediately tossing her latte cup into an ugly green plastic trash bin just inside the door. Sweeping, graceful stairs rose to the second floor of the five-story house. She'd never been in any place like it. It was the polar opposite of her little log cabin with its rustic ladder up to the loft.

"Hello?" she called. "Anyone here?"

Her footsteps echoed on the age-darkened cherry floor of the center hall. To her left was a formal drawing room with a marble fireplace and a crystal chandelier, then a smaller room and the library. There was even an elegant ballroom on the second floor—Sterling had promised to invite Carine the first time he and Jodie used it, just to see her in sequins.

She retrieved her camera from a cold, old-fashioned radiator in the hall. There had to be someone around. Nobody would leave the door open with the place empty.

"Louis? Are you here? It's me, Carine."

He could be upstairs, she thought, slinging her camera bag over her shoulder. She'd thought workers would be in this afternoon, but she didn't keep close track of everyone's comings and goings. She turned to head back up the hall to the front entry, but stopped, something catching her eye through the double doorway of the library. She wasn't sure what—something out of place. Wrong.

She took a shallow breath, and it was as if a force stronger than she compelled her to take a step forward and peer into the library, still untouched by any restoration work. Intense discussions were still under way about whether its yellowed wallpaper, possibly original to the house, was worth the expense to have copied.

Carine touched the wood molding, telling herself she must have simply seen a shadow or a stray drop cloth. But she jumped back, inhaling sharply, at the sight of a man facedown on the wood floor—Louis. She recognized his dark suit, his scrub-brush hair. She lunged forward, then stopped abruptly, almost instinctively.

A pool of something dark, a liquid, oozed toward her. Her mind couldn't take it in, couldn't absorb what she was seeing—refused to.

Blood.

It seeped into the cracks in the narrow-board floor. It covered the man's outstretched hand.

Help…

She couldn't speak. Her mouth opened, but she gulped in air, no sound coming out.

His hair…his hand…in the blood…

"Oh, God, oh, God—Louis!" Carine leaped forward, yelling back over her shoulder. "Help! Help, someone's hurt!"

She avoided stepping in the blood. It wasn't easy—there was so much of it. *Louis…he can't be dead. I just saw him!*

She had only rudimentary first-aid skills. She wasn't an E.R. doctor like her sister or a highly trained combat paramedic like North and Manny Carrera. But they weren't here, and she forced herself to kneel beside Louis Sanborn and control her horror and fear as she touched two fingers to his carotid artery. That was it, wasn't it? Arteries beat with the heart. Veins didn't. To see if he had a pulse, she had to find an artery.

There was no pulse, not with that much blood.

"Louis. Oh, God."

She looked around the empty room, her voice echoing as she yelled again for help. Had he fallen and landed on a sharp object—a stray chisel or a saw, something? The back of his suit was unmarred. No blood, no torn fabric. Whatever injury he had must have been in front. But she didn't dare turn him over, touch him further.

She rose shakily. No one had come in answer to her yells for help. Louis Sanborn was dead. She was alone. She absorbed the reality of her situation in short bursts of awareness, as if she couldn't take it all in at once.

Hey, Ms. Photographer, need a ride over to the big house?

What if she'd said yes? Could she have saved his life? Would she be dead, too, if she had?

How had he died?

What if it wasn't an accident?

She ran into the hall, her camera bag bouncing on her hip. Where was her cell phone? She needed to call the police, an ambulance. She dug in the pocket of her barn coat, finding her phone, but she couldn't hang on to it, and dropped it on the hardwood floor, startling herself. She scooped it up, hardly pausing as she came to the front hall.

The front door stood wide open. She thought she'd shut it when she came in from lunch. Was someone else here?

She could feel the cool November air.

"Help!"

She looked down at her cell phone, realized it wasn't on. She hit the power button and ran onto the front stoop, knocking over the pot of mums, hoping someone on the street would hear her. She charged down the steps to the wide sidewalk. She'd call the police, stop a passing car.

But Manny Carrera was there, as if she'd conjured him up herself. He'd danced with her at her sister's wedding to Hank Callahan a month ago and had cheerfully offered to cut off Ty's balls the next time he saw him.

"It's Louis…he…" She couldn't get out the words. "He's—oh, God—"

Manny swept her into his embrace. "I know," he said. "I know."

Out of the Dark

Jade had little to no memory of anything before her mother took her to join the People of Joy and adopted the name of Ivy. Only now and then did she dream about a tall, dark-haired man who had played with her in a wading pool and rocked her to sleep. But the facial features were always vague, and when she woke, the image was always gone.

Most of the time, the face in her nightmares belonged to Solomon. Solomon of the smiling face, who smelled of incense and smoke—who brushed her hair and stroked her face and, the day after Ivy had died, sold her tiny, six-year-old prepubescent body to a pedophile who preyed on little girls. He had been the first, but certainly not the last, man who'd paid money to ravage her body. And for the ensuing six years she, like Raphael, became a marketable product for the People of Joy.

She couldn't remember a time when Raphael had not been part of her life—the young, beautiful boy/child three years her senior who had never known a mother or a father and, to the best of his knowledge, didn't have a last name. He was a product of the same commune in which Ivy had died, and he had no existence outside Solomon's control.

Solomon had been his father figure. He had known nothing beyond obeying the wishes of the charismatic leader—doing anying to garner the rare moments of affection that Solomon bestowed upon him. He'd suffered the uncles Solomon had brought for him to play with, not knowing that there was any other kind of life.

Then, one day, something happened that shattered his perception. It was a small crack—hardly more than a weakness in the ties that bound him to the world into which he'd been born. But to a child who'd never had a say over one waking moment of his life, it was huge. Raphael hadn't known it was possible to say no until he'd witnessed Jade throw a screaming fit and refuse to obey Solomon's demand.

She'd been screaming for her mother, and Solomon had laughed and told her that her mother was gone, that she was never coming back. Raphael wanted to tell her it would be okay, that the uncles wouldn't keep her, that they always left after they were through playing, but he didn't get the chance.

Even though her tiny rebellion had been futile, it had planted a seed in his head that had slowly taken root. He hadn't known until he'd witnessed Jade's rebellion that it was okay to have an opinion of his own.

The bond that was forged between the two children grew stronger with each passing year, so that by the time Jade was twelve and Raphael fifteen, they had become inseparable.

Then the unthinkable happened. Jade began to mature. Her body was no longer that of a thin, hairless doll. She was becoming a woman, which made the uncle who'd paid Solomon five hundred dollars for an entire night with Jade very unhappy. He'd been with her before, numerous times, but not in the past six months. When he'd gotten her to his room and seen what nature had done to her body, it infuriated him. The sight of her budding breasts and shapely hips had stopped him in a way that nothing else could have done. Angry and embarrassed that he couldn't use her sexually, that his own body failed to respond, he began hitting her with his fists.

Raphael heard her screams and did the unthinkable. At fifteen, he was already six feet tall and strong beyond his years. He broke into the room, took one look at Jade's battered and bloody face, and broke the man's neck. There were footsteps on the stairs as Raphael scooped the unconscious Jade up out of the bed, and just as she had been at four years old, she was carried out into the night without her knowledge. Only this time it was to escape the hell to which her mother had taken her. Raphael laid Jade in the passenger seat of Solomon's Jeep and started the engine. Solomon came running out of the house, screaming Jade's name, as Raphael gunned the engine and took off down the driveway. He didn't know where he was going or how badly Jade had been injured, but he did know that their survival hinged upon escaping the old farmhouse and the People of Joy.

Twelve years later, they were still running, living by their wits and the occasional turn of good luck, but certain that if they were found, they would both go to prison for murder.

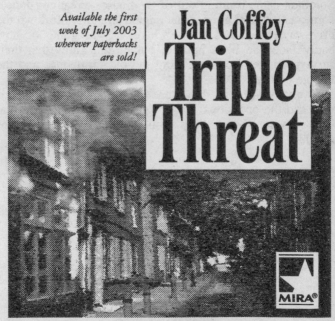

From the bestselling author
of *The Deepest Water*

KATE WILHELM

SKELETONS

Lee Donne is an appendix in a family of overachievers. Her mother has three doctorates, her father is an economics genius and her grandfather is a world-renowned Shakespearean scholar. After four years of college and three majors, Lee is nowhere closer to a degree. With little better to do, she agrees to house-sit for her grandfather.

But the quiet stay she envisioned ends abruptly when she begins to hear strange noises at night. Something is hidden in the house…and someone is determined to find it. Suddenly Lee finds herself caught in a game of cat and mouse, the reasons for which she doesn't understand. But when the FBI arrives on the doorstep, she realizes that the house may hold dark secrets that go beyond her own family. And that sometimes, long-buried skeletons rise up from the grave.

"The mystery at the heart of this novel is well-crafted."
—*Publishers Weekly*

*Available the first week of July 2003
wherever paperbacks are sold!*

MIRA®

Visit us at www.mirabooks.com

MKW749